PROLOGUE

Acre, Kingdom of Jerusalem
June 1272

W hen the hell was Prince Edward going to give up this absurd Crusade?
Richard de Claiborne, sole heir to the Earl of Dunsmore, gazed at the city of Acre spread out below. The hill upon which the English army encamped commanded a sweeping view of the sun-bleached buildings and dusty streets. Beyond lay the great expanse of sapphire that was the Mediterranean sea.

A breeze off the water, so rare this time of day, stirred across the camp. The hair on the back of his neck prickled inexplicably.

From air pregnant with silence, an explosion of sound erupted. The tent walls rippled. The crash of furniture and the muffled grunts of men hung in the oppressive stillness.

Richard's heart leapt in his throat as he bolted for the opening. He threw a prayer to the heavens, begging God to take him instead of Prince Edward, and darted inside.

A turbaned man struggled in a death embrace with the heir to the English throne. Blood spattered the two mens' clothes, a knife flashing between them as each tried to wrest it from the other. A parchment lay on the floor, the seal broken, forgotten in the fight. Cushions were scattered wildly, chairs upended, the table toppled.

The Saracen forced Edward backwards, the knife perilously close to the Prince's throat.

Richard lunged. Grabbing the assassin, he jerked him off Edward and wrapped an arm around the man's neck, yanking the Saracen's chin toward him with his free hand.

One clean jerk, and it would snap.

Edward seized the man's wrist, wrenching the dagger free with his remaining strength. The arm of Edward's tunic lay open, slashed. Blood spurted from a deep gash that ran from his elbow to his wrist. He sank to his knees.

"Who sent you?" Richard demanded, twisting the assassin's neck until his veins bulged. The man gave a strangled laugh, babbling in Arabic.

Richard tightened his grip.

"Sultan Baibars of Egypt!" the man spat in thickly accented French.

Edward swayed. "There is no honor in Crusading anymore. Saladin sent a horse to my great-uncle, Coeur de Lion, during the Battle of Jaffa, when his was cut from beneath him, so much did Saladin admire him for fighting a hopeless battle . . ." The Prince's eyes were glazed, his voice soft.

The assassin laughed. "He is a dead man . . . the blade is poisoned."

Jesú, no! Richard felt as if the earth were dropping from beneath his feet. Edward Plantagenet, the man who would be England's king, the greatest warrior-king since Richard the Lion Heart, *could not* die!

Edward looked up, his eyes focusing on the messenger. With a swift movement, he drove the dagger upward into the man's gut.

Startled, Richard let the infidel fall in a heap. The man jerked convulsively, blood gurgling in his throat and spilling from his mouth, before he was still.

Too late, men swarmed into the tent, voices raised in confusion. A woman screamed. Princess Eleanor rushed to her husband's side, sobbing in her native Spanish.

"Send for a doctor!" Richard cried, yanking a white linen cloth from beneath the table.

NATASHA WILD

The DARK KNIGHT'S CAPTIVE BRIDE

First Edition: August 2016
Library of Congress Cataloging-in-Publication Data

Wild, Natasha
The Dark Knight's Captive Bride / Natasha Wild – 1st ed
ISBN-13: 978-1540342904

1. The Dark Knight's Captive Bride—Fiction
2. Fiction—Romance
3. Fiction—Historical Romance

*For my wonderful husband who always believed,
and who took me to Europe.*

He wound it around Edward's arm while Eleanor held her husband's head, stroking his hair and crying. She did not seem to notice the crimson stain seeping into the rich silk fabric of her dress.

Edward struggled to get up.

"Rest, Highness," Richard said, pushing him back.

"You saved me, de Claiborne. I will not forget it, will make you the most powerful earl in the realm when I am king." His voice was a whisper as he grasped Richard's sleeve.

Richard nodded numbly, the assassin's words echoing in his ears.

The blade is poisoned . . .

Richard entered the Prince's tent quietly. 'Twas three days since the attack. The sight that greeted him made him want to recoil in horror.

Edward was no longer the glorious Plantagenet prince, shining brighter than any star in the heavens, but a frail man lying close to death. Fever burned on his brow, his eyes blackened pits in his gaunt face. His arm swelled grotesquely out of proportion to the rest of his body.

Eleanor held his hand, weeping softly. Physicians hovered at the end of the bed, their voices but a murmur in Richard's ears.

Several of Edward's intimates, men of rank and power, sat nearby, glaring at Richard.

His heart pounded in his breast. Dunsmore was but a petty earldom when compared with the might of Gloucester or Richmond.

"Come," Edward rasped.

Richard started forward slowly. "Highness," he said, kneeling at Edward's bedside.

"Even the Moor surgeon does not know the poison used," Edward said, motioning feebly to the knot of men. "I am to die in God's very bosom it seems."

A small sob escaped the Princess.

Richard could not move, could not speak. He stared at the bloated hand lying only inches from his face.

"You tried to save me, my friend. God will not forget that. Eleanor will that see my father rewards you when you return to England."

"Highness?" the Moor ventured, sliding into view next to Richard.

"Aye?"

"There is perhaps a chance. If I were to cut away the decaying flesh, it might stop the poison from spreading. 'Twill be painful—"

"I counsel against it, Your Highness." Another doctor, one of Edward's own, stepped forward. "'Tis heathen and cannot possibly work!"

"What say you, Richard?" Edward asked.

Richard turned to the Moor. "'Tis the only chance?"

"He will certainly die otherwise . . . and he may die anyway."

"'Tis your decision, Highness, but if there is no other option . . ."

"Do it then," Edward commanded. "Stay with me, Richard."

"Aye, Your Highness."

"Eleanor, love, you must go. I cannot bear your tears. And take these wet nurses with you," he added, casting a scathing look at the anxious lords.

"Nay, Edward, I want to stay with you," she sobbed.

He motioned to the two knights standing in the door. They came forward and tried to lead Eleanor from his bedside.

She screamed. The knights turned helpless faces on their future king. His jaw clenched, but he nodded. They picked up the screaming princess and dragged her, kicking and scratching, from the tent.

Richard could feel the enmity flowing from the barons as they filed out. Gilbert de Clare, Earl of Gloucester, was only six years older than Richard, and yet even at eight and twenty, Red Gilbert was the most powerful baron in all of England. His face was every bit as red as his hair as he aimed a look of fierce hatred at Richard before disappearing through the flap.

The doctor finished heating the knife, then gave the Prince a piece of wood to bite upon.

"If you value your lives, do not interfere," Edward said to the other physicians. He looked at Richard, his blue eyes suddenly grim. "Pray for me, my friend."

Richard nodded.

At the first touch of the hot blade, Edward passed out. The smell of charred flesh filled the tent. Richard swallowed the bile rising in his throat, prayers tumbling over one another in his mind as he sought to ignore what was happening before his eyes.

"It is done," the physician said at last.

"Will he live?" Richard asked.

The Moor shrugged his shoulders. "'Tis in Allah's hands now. We can only wait and see."

Richard squeezed his eyes shut. It was two years since Prince Edward and his army of gallant one-thousand had sailed from England.

The voyage had been leisurely. They'd made port in Aquitaine and Brittany, Lisbon and Tangier, Rome and Sicily. They'd traversed the Greek Isles; Corfu, Crete, Rhodes, where the sun was blistering and the sands bleached white, and where the water shone vibrant turquoise.

To pass the long days at sea, Richard worked beside the ship's men, honing his body to razor-sharpness. It did not matter that he was an earl's son and would one day be an earl himself. To simply breathe the tang of the salt-drenched air, to feel the sun's kiss on his skin, to know the sensation of back-breaking work were the things he needed to keep his energy focused.

His visions of glory had not dampened in the one and a half year journey to the hot and dusty land of Christ. He'd set foot upon the hallowed ground of Outremer determined to turn the infidels to God and to wrest the birthplace of Christ from their savage hands.

But, in the months he'd been here, his conviction had seeped away, leached from his body by the scorching Mediterranean sun. Infidels and Christians mingled freely in the streets of Acre and Jerusalem, and the Christians did not seem gladdened to see the English knights who would once again attempt to conquer the heathens. Indeed, the English army's victories at Nazareth and Haifa failed to bring any aid from the knights of Christendom.

Gallantly, Edward had struggled on, refusing to allow the dwindling numbers of his army and the lack of reinforcements to discourage him. King Henry sent paltry excuses where he had once sent vast sums of money.

And now it had all come down to this. Richard opened his eyes to gaze at the unconscious man in front of him. He didn't believe in anything anymore -- anything except this man.

"I swear upon my honor that if you live, I will never desert your cause, whatever it may be," he whispered fiercely.

Edward recovered quickly, although he remained weak for some time, spending the lengthening days of summer resting in his tent. Sultan Baibars, seeing he could not rid himself of the Prince so easily, agreed to a ten-year truce. The army worked diligently to prepare the ships for the return voyage to England.

The afternoon was sultry as usual, and Richard reclined on a cushion, sipping a cup of chilled wine. He was a constant companion of Edward's now. The Prince welcomed him into the royal circle enthusiastically, frequently eschewing the company of his other lords. Richard knew it did not endear him to the powerful barons to be so favored by the next King of England.

"When I am king, I intend to subjugate Wales and Scotland," Edward was saying. "One island, one kingdom. Prince Llywelyn will pay for tricking my father into giving him dominion in Wales whilst my father was Simon de Montfort's prisoner."

"Welsh savages have no honor," Richard repeated by rote. He stroked his short beard with a bronzed hand. The months spent beneath the sweltering eastern sun had burnished his skin to a copper so deep it would never come out.

"You grew up in the March. What do you think Llywelyn's weakness is?"

"His chieftains fight amongst themselves constantly. Not all of them support him. My father is friendly with Gruffydd ap Gwynwynwyn, lord of Powys. There is no love lost between Gruffydd and Llywelyn, and Gruffydd is his most powerful vassal."

Edward toyed with his cup. "I cannot declare open war on Prince Llywelyn, but if what you say is true, an opportunity is bound to arise that I can use to my advantage." His eyes took on a zealous light. "You must help me, Richard. I want you to lead the Marcher lords. Gilbert is a poor choice. He changed sides twice during the Barons' Revolt. I cannot entrust men such as that with the good of the realm."

Richard reeled. *Jesú, Gloucester!* "Red Gilbert holds more lands than my father. He owes the crown more rents than any other in the kingdom! How can you do it?"

Edward smiled a deadly smile. "When I am king, none will challenge my authority as they do my father's. By elevating you, the others will see their positions are not so permanent as they might think."

Richard's hand strayed to his sword hilt. "To think my father did not want me to come with you."

Edward laughed suddenly. "Aye, my friend, we have much in common. My father begged me not to leave England. But, we do what we must, eh?"

"Aye, we do what we must." Mayhap now, his father would admit he'd been right to go. Just because the old earl had never gotten over the death of Richard's mother was no reason to always try and keep his son by his side.

A messenger appeared in the open flap of the tent. He handed missives to Edward, bowing deeply before being dismissed with a nod.

"I will leave you now," Richard said, rising.

"Nay, nay. 'Twill only take a moment."

Richard sank onto the cushions. Edward broke the seal on the first document and poured over the contents. He paused, raising his eyes to Richard briefly, before continuing.

Edward cast the letter aside and passed a hand over his face. "'Tis from my mother."

"Is King Henry . . .?"

"Nay, he is ill, but the doctors think he will not die yet. I . . . I do not know how to tell you," Edward said, his blue eyes searching Richard's face.

Richard sat up. "What?" he asked, apprehension washing over him.

"Your father was killed in a border skirmish, the beginning of spring. I am sorry."

Richard closed his eyes. God's blood, almost three months! Guilt stabbed through him, sharp and cold. His father had feared for *his* life, and now he was the one dead. And Richard hadn't been there.

He swallowed the painful lump in his throat. Despite the victory he'd just gained, he'd failed his father miserably. William de Claiborne would never know what his son had achieved.

Hot tears pressed against his eyelids, begging to spill free. He would not let them. When he was only seven, and his father's mournful wails echoed through Claiborne castle after a night of drinking and drowning in memories of his dead wife, Richard had wiped away his own tears and sworn never to cry again. It was a vow he'd never broken.

"How did it happen?" he asked quietly. His father had ridden the border for years. It was hard to believe the Welsh had finally beaten him.

"Ambush, it seems. One survivor, and he swears it was Llywelyn."

Richard clenched his teeth so hard it made his jaw hurt. Goddamn Welsh savage! In that moment, a hatred so intense was born that his first thought was to shrink from it, to hide from its brilliant white-hot glare. But he embraced it instead, locking it into the depths of his heart and finding comfort in it.

Prince Llywelyn would pay dearly.

1

Snowdonia, Wales

"Father is home!" Gwen cried from her lookout. Riders were fast approaching and she could just make out her father's banner at their head. She turned and ran past Alys, then down the long winding stairs to the entryway. Father was home at last. Too long he'd been gone, fighting the English invaders.

Already, men and women rushed about in excitement, preparing for their lord's arrival. Gwen halted in the shadowed entryway of the keep, pushing impatiently at a lock of hair that had fallen across her nose.

The men rode into the bailey, snow flying from beneath their sturdy ponies' hooves as they skidded to a stop. Her father's face was grim. She clutched the edge of her mantle with trembling fingers, her welcoming smile ebbing away.

Prince Llywelyn dismounted and handed his reins to a waiting groom. Einion, his seneschal, hurried to follow suit, his wrinkled face twisting in a grimace as he slid his old bones from the saddle.

"Llywelyn, you cannot surrender!" he hissed when he had caught up with the prince.

Llywelyn darted his gaze around furtively, then answered in a grinding whisper, "I will not wait for starvation to set in! 'Tis better to do it now while we still have our dignity."

Gwen put a hand to her mouth to muffle her cry. The Prince of Wales surrendering to the English? 'Twas unthinkable!

The household continued about their frenzied tasks, heedless of the devastation they faced. Gwen ran headlong into her father's arms, desperately needing his reassurances.

"You are home and safe!" she cried, hugging him tight. He stiffened and she loosened her grip to gaze up at him. Heavy lines creased his face, dark circles smudging the skin beneath his amber eyes.

"Aye, I am safe," he said, patting her back briefly and clearing his throat.

Her heart ached, but she smiled and stepped back. He was a good man, never harsh. For the most part, his people loved him, although he had caused great upheaval many years ago when he first came to the throne of Wales. Defying tradition, he staked sole claim to the princedom, shutting his brothers out in a bloody civil war.

Some of the chieftains had never forgiven him. Neither had his brothers, only one of whom was still alive.

He was a great man. She knew it was because he always had so much to do, being the Prince of Wales, that he never seemed to have any time for her. He strode ahead, entering the ancient stronghold that had belonged to countless Welsh princes before him.

Einion winked, smiling weakly to cover his distress, and held out his arm. She took it and they followed Llywelyn's lead.

"Are we truly surrendering, Einion?"

The old man stumbled. "Aye."

"But we are Welsh, we cannot give up!"

He sighed. "I cannot talk him out of it. Your father has ruled Wales for thirty years and has gained more than any prince before him. He feels he must give in now to gain later."

"Why? Why must he give up?" Her voice caught and she bit her lip to stifle her tears. It was not fair! Her father had worked so hard, gained so much, and now--now it was being wrung from him piece by precious piece.

"King Edward captured the mouth of the Conwy. He is building a castle to hold it." Einion hesitated, then wet his lips before continuing, "Black Hawk de Claiborne blockaded Ynys Mon. Without the harvest, Gwynedd will starve."

Gwen sucked in her breath. *"Gwalchddu."*

Black Hawk. Northern Wales trembled at the name of the evil lord who controlled the borders with an iron fist. The court bards said he was ten feet tall and broad as an oak. His colors, like his legacy, were of blood and death, crimson and black.

She slammed a fist against her leg. "I hate the English! They are cruel and grasping. Unsatisfied with what they already have, they want Wales too!"

Einion patted her hand. "Aye, child, the Norman kings have been after us since William the Bastard conquered the Saxons. I am an old man now. I was but a youth when your great-grandfather was our leader, and I've watched Welsh princes struggle against an ever-tightening yoke. If only Llywelyn could have put aside his pride and sworn homage to Edward on his coronation!"

"But King Edward would not return Dafydd for punishment. Father could not swear fealty whilst the King harbored that traitor!"

"Aye. Your uncle's defection was certainly the catalyst Edward needed." He sighed heavily. "'Tis nearing the end, I am afraid. Edward is no hapless Henry or twisted John--he will succeed where they have failed, unless..."

"Unless what?"

Einion grasped her shoulders with sudden urgency. "'Tis prophesied that a Llywelyn will drive the Normans out of England and wear the crown of King Arthur and be ruler of all of Britain. Merlin made that prophecy. The bards say that your father *is* that Llywelyn." His faded brown eyes searched her face. "You have the Sight, girl! Tell me, do you not see it?"

She closed her eyes. She had dreams sometimes, dreams that came true, but she had no control over when they occurred. The first time was when she was a little girl and she dreamed of a horrible snowstorm that locked up the mountain passes until spring. It was nothing significant, but when it came true, people began to whisper of her mother and the fairy gift of Sight. How could she tell Einion it couldn't be forced?

"Nay... I... cannot... see... anything..." she said, her voice barely a whisper.

Einion gulped in air like a drowning man. "'Tis our last hope." His eyes misted over and he squeezed her fondly before turning to limp after Llywelyn.

Gwen stood in mute shock, oblivious to the commotion around her. Good, sturdy Einion had shown her a side of himself she'd never seen, a side that was afraid for his prince and his country. It shook her to the core.

Whenever it was attention she craved from Llywelyn, Einion had always been there to fill the gaps. He had bounced her on his knee when she was a little girl, kissed her skinned elbows, and brought her presents of gold and silk and jewels. His old face was always ready with a smile. Never had he asked anything of her. Until now.

Brushing at the tears streaking her face, she ran to find Alys.

Alys would know what to do. The rosy-cheeked maid was more like the mother Gwen barely recalled having than a servant.

When she reached her chamber, she found Alys sitting calmly, nimble fingers working their magic on one of Gwen's surcoats. The golden thread whipped in and out of the garment, a delicate bird beginning to take shape under her careful artistry.

Alys dropped the garment and got to her feet. "Whatever is the matter, Your Highness?"

"We are surrendering, Alys," Gwen said, spilling the details in a rush. "'Tis the witch's curse!"

Alys's breath hissed sharply. "Your mother was not a witch! What tales have you been listening to?"

Gwen sank onto the bed and rubbed the back of her hand across her face. "Did he not meet her on the banks of Llyn Eleri in the twilight? She appeared out of the mist like a fey creature. She had no home, no clan. And she disappeared without a trace when I was but a babe."

"Aye, but she was a fairy maiden, not a witch. Lady Eurwen was kind and beautiful. She loved your father! I do not believe she cursed him to a life of misfortune, no matter what tales the bards tell."

"Then why did she leave?" Gwen asked miserably.

Alys sighed and picked up her work, plucking at a stitch. "I do not know, child. I do not know."

An air of brooding hung over the great keep in the coming days. Warriors came and went, sometimes meeting with the Prince for many hours before the air erupted with angry shouts.

Nearly one by one, the chieftains who'd remained loyal to Llywelyn answered his summonses—and then stalked out.

When her father finally sent for her, Gwen ran all the way to his chamber. She was certain he would tell her it wasn't true, that he really wasn't surrendering to the King of England—and then life could be normal again.

The door was open and he stood with his back to her, his knuckles cracking softly.

"Father?"

He spun around. "Jesú, Gwenllian, you are as quiet as your mother was."

Gwen smiled. It was unusual for him to mention her mother. It was also unusual for him to pay her this much attention. "You sent for me?"

"Aye." His gaze darted away. "I am to surrender to the King at Rhuddlan castle. You will accompany me. We leave on the morrow."

"You are really surrendering?" Her heart pounded with excitement and fear. He had never before taken her anywhere with him.

"I have no choice, lass."

"Oh," Gwen replied. "I am sorry."

"I'm tired, lass. I do not wish to discuss this with you. Go and have Alys ready your trunk."

"Aye... trunk? But why—?"

"Don't ask questions, girl! Just do it," he snapped.

"Aye, Father. Forgive me," she mumbled, hastening from the room. Why did she always disappoint him?

Richard de Claiborne, third Earl of Dunsmore, and his company of knights thundered over the water-logged ground, galloping toward the king's headquarters. The rain had changed to sleet and it slapped against his armor, the sound an almost musical ping.

The strong odor of sweat and leather rose from the stallion laboring beneath him. Though the pace had been hard, the animal still gnashed his teeth with coiled energy, his black ears pinned against his head savagely.

They rounded a bend in the road and suddenly before them rose Rhuddlan Castle, its new walls and high towers jutting out of the Welsh mist that clung to it like a ghostly wraith.

The tang of salt mixed with the sleet and the faint white bodies of gulls circled in the distance, their piercing cries carrying on the wind. Storm clouds, black and ominous, hung low over the Irish Sea.

Three golden lions on a blood-red background rippled over the turrets of Rhuddlan, proclaiming to all of Wales that King Edward Plantagenet was here to stay.

The company slowed to a walk before they reached the massive gates. The road was a slosh of mud from the constant traffic of the laborers. Carpenters, carters, plumbers, masons, and diggers traversed this path daily as they worked to complete the fortress.

Richard let his gaze slide up the sheer walls. Jesú, but the king had chosen right when he picked Sir James of St. George to be his master builder. Even now, men perched on scaffolding high above the bailey. Occasionally, the ring of hammers sounded over the din in the courtyard.

Richard reined in the prancing stallion. He chuckled to himself when a groom came forward, eyes widening as the giant horse snorted great plumes of steaming breath into the frigid air.

"Do not eat the boy, Sirocco," Richard said, sliding from the horse's back and patting the arched neck. He handed the reins to the groom.

"Walk him 'til he's cool or I will have your hide," Richard threatened, sensing the boy's intention to put the horse in a stall and get away from him.

"Aye, milord," the boy replied, swallowing. His hand trembled as he closed it around hard leather. Sirocco pranced half a step and then settled, following like a puppy.

Richard strode up the wooden steps and into the Great Hall. The room was still rough, hewn from stone and wood and not yet whitewashed. The green smell of fresh timber hung heavy in the air.

Numerous knights were seated at the trestle tables, drinking ale and carousing with the serving wenches. Shrill laughter rose from female throats as girls passed from lap to lap.

One particularly lusty wench slapped the hand of the man who had just pinched her, and turned to watch Richard's progress across the room.

He smiled in answer. It had been weeks since he'd had a woman. She tipped her head before picking up her tray and hastening to the buttery for more ale. He would not sleep alone tonight.

He continued through the hall and up the steps to the third level, where he found King Edward closeted in his solar with Prince Llywelyn's brother, Dafydd ap Gruffydd.

"Ah, Richard. Thank heavens you are here at last," Edward said.

"I came as quickly as possible, Ned."

"Llywelyn signed the treaty yesterday. He will be here today to formally surrender."

"I look forward to it, Majesty." Llywelyn could not be humiliated enough as far as he was concerned. He sank into a chair opposite the King and stripped the gauntlets from his fists before unlacing the chain-mail coif and pushing it from his head.

Mud splattered his chausses, and his cloak dripped water onto the carved chair, trickling into a puddle at his feet. He took the mug of ale the servant held out for him, grimacing only slightly as the bitter liquid washed down his throat.

"'Twas a stroke of genius cutting off Ynys Mon like that, Lord de Claiborne," Dafydd said.

Richard leaned back and swept Dafydd with an appraising stare. When he spoke, his voice was a drawl. "'Tis funny you find it so, but could not manage to suggest it yourself. You are a Welshman after all, and you know the importance of that island."

Something glittered in the depths of Dafydd's green eyes before it was extinguished and replaced with a complacent look.

"If I had thought of it, I most certainly would have suggested it. Alas, I am not the great battle commander you are." He smiled and Edward nodded pleasantly.

"I should say not. I would not have failed if I had planned to kill Llywelyn."

Dafydd leapt to his feet, clenching his fists at his side. Richard offered him the ultimate insult by not bothering to rise to the mute challenge.

Dafydd spun on his heel to face the King. "If you will excuse me, Majesty, I must see to my men."

"Certes, Dafydd. You will join us at table?"

"'Twould be an honor, Sire," Dafydd replied, glaring at Richard before stalking from the room.

Edward sighed in exasperation. "Why do you antagonize him?"

"I do not like him. He speaks false, and he is shrewder than you think. He of all people would know how to bring Wales to its knees."

"Mmm, but if ever he were to make peace with his brother—two wolves are worse than one and they can hound a bear to death."

Richard laughed. "Llywelyn is no fool, Ned. How many times now has Dafydd betrayed him? Two? Three? He'll not work his way into the den so easily this time."

"Aye, but I still prefer to keep him close. You should be grateful to Dafydd. If not for his failed murder attempt, we would not have Llywelyn in this position now."

"And what happens when Dafydd finds out you don't intend to make him Prince of Wales? That you have allowed Llywelyn to keep the title?"

Edward's jaw tightened. "I am a king first, my friend. This victory has been more complete than either of us imagined. I no longer need to remove Llywelyn. Besides, you said yourself that you do not trust Dafydd. Should I trust *him* as Prince of Wales?"

"I was not suggesting you should. Llywelyn has behaved treasonably by refusing to acknowledge you as his overlord, despite all his claims you harbored his enemies." He leaned forward abruptly, his voice coming hard-edged and low, "Let me challenge him to single combat."

"Nay!" The word bounced off the walls, echoing in the bare chamber.

"'Tis my right to avenge my father!"

"Not at the expense of my kingdom!"

Richard clenched his teeth, his lungs filling to bursting as he sucked in air that was stale with the smell of ripening wood and newly chiseled stone. He let it out again in a great rush, savoring for an instant the light as a feather feeling that accompanied his escaping breath.

Edward raked a hand through dark blonde curls, then turned to stare out the oriel windows. Side by side, three floor-to-ceiling windows faced the sea, imparting a view that was somehow even grander than the gardens of Windsor.

"You know I cannot allow it. Is it not enough we have reduced him to this? He has less now than when he inherited his throne. Wales is *mine*. It is what we both wanted."

Richard drew in a ragged breath. "'Twill never be enough, Ned. He can never pay for what he has done. When he has nothing left, when he lies cold at my feet, it will not be enough."

Silence stretched between them. Richard accepted another mug of ale, the cool liquid doing little to soothe his dry throat.

Edward tapped a beringed finger on the arm of his chair. "Was the harvest brought in?"

Richard nodded. "I left the garrison on Ynys Mon—Anglesey—in charge of loading it on the ships. What are you going to do with it?"

Edward grinned suddenly, all else seemingly forgotten. "I plan to sell it back to Llywelyn."

Richard stared at his friend for a moment. Edward's face creased in a broad smile, his blue eyes twinkling. Richard threw back his head and laughed, and Edward joined him.

Both sides of the Great Hall were lined with English lords, some Marchers, some not. Dafydd stood next to the dais, his face split in a triumphant grin. Other Welsh chieftains who had joined the cause stood with him.

Edward settled onto his throne, and Richard stepped behind him.

The hum of the crowd rose sharply to a buzz, then cut off altogether when Prince Llywelyn appeared in the entryway. He strode into the great hall of Rhuddlan, his back stiff, his mouth set in a grim line.

He looked neither right nor left, his gaze focused only on the King as he refused to acknowledge the gloating lords around him. His boots clopped against the wooden floor, the dull thud echoing the beating of Richard's heart.

Llywelyn stopped before the dais and unsheathed his sword. His hands clenched over the hilt for the space of one moment. Two. Three. The tip wavered, pointing at the King.

Richard gripped his own sword until his knuckles were white.

Do it. Try to strike the King down.

Llywelyn's eyes shifted to his, icy contempt flaring in them, before he jerked his gaze back to Edward.

And then he kneeled and reversed the blade, handing it hilt first to Edward. His voice rang out over the gathering. "I submit unto the king's will and the king's justice."

"Rise, Prince Llywelyn," Edward said, turning the sword and handing it back to him. "By the terms of the Treaty of Conway, you may keep the cantref of Gwynedd and your title. You will cede the Isle of Anglesey, Ynys Mon as you call it, and all lands east of the Conwy River. Upper and Lower Powys will be returned to my vassal, Gruffydd ap Gwynwynwyn."

Llywelyn flushed at the reminder of all he had lost, but said nothing. Gruffydd ap Gwenwynwyn beamed. The look on Dafydd's face could only be termed mute shock. He shot Richard an accusing look, full of loathing.

"Name the ten highborn hostages you will give into my keeping to ensure your loyalty," Edward commanded.

Llywelyn sheathed his sword, then swallowed and stood silent for a long moment. His voice was cold and emotionless as he began to recite the names.

"My daughter, Princess Gwenllian. Goronwy ap Tudur, son of the chieftain of..."

2

Gwen shivered and pulled her cloak tighter, rubbing her face against the fur-lining of her hood. What was taking so long? And why were they still astride their horses in this freezing rain?

The smell of cooking food drifted to her nose with a slight shift of the wind. She realized she was hungry when her stomach responded with a low rumble. Had it really been that long ago since she had risen to break-fast and then clambered into the saddle to make the journey from Aberconwy Abbey to Rhuddlan?

She could take it no longer. She dismounted, her aching limbs protest-ing every movement. The others huddled atop their horses, their woolen cloaks wrapped around them. No one stirred as she led her palfrey toward the stables.

She pressed her reins into the hand of a boy coming from inside the structure. When he opened his mouth to protest, she froze him with a haughty glare. He licked his lips hastily, then snapped his mouth shut and began to tend her mare without another look in her direction.

Gwen walked into the stable, the smell of fresh hay and the unmistak-ably musty smell of horse mingling in her nostrils. Chargers lined the walls, packed into narrow stalls like discarded weapons, safely tucked away until needed. She strolled along, patting noses and whispering soft words, and the big horses marked her passing with low whickers.

At the end of the row, away from the rest of the animals, stood a big black brute of a stallion, neck arched, eyes rolling back in his head. One massive hoof beat the ground, cleaving the dirt like an ax.

"You are a beauty," Gwen said softly, holding out her hand. He sniffed it, then blew out like a great bellows, warming her with his breath.

She moved closer. He nickered and lowered his head. Gwen scratched behind his ears, laughing as he leaned toward her. "You are not as fierce as you pretend, you big bully."

The stallion nodded his head, trying to direct her scratching to the places he wanted it.

A deep male voice startled her. She spun around, her heart hammering. A knight strode toward her, speaking in English, but she didn't understand him.

She realized he must think her a stablehand, dressed as she was and standing beside this horse. The English nobility spoke French and Latin, while English was reserved for servants and commoners, though many lords spoke it as well. They had to if they wanted to direct their households.

Her father had made her learn court French and Latin. She drew herself up, prepared to put this knight in his place. "Pardon?"

He looked surprised at first, then switched into French. "I said get away from that horse." He walked very deliberately toward her. He was mail-clad, tall, moving with a feline stealth that belied his size.

Gwen steeled her spine. She'd had enough of these English bastards this day. Their cool arrogance sorely tried her patience.

But she did acknowledge that mayhap this one had a right to worry about a stranger standing beside his horse. Certes, 'twas no ordinary charger.

Cold fear washed over her when she realized the sheer size of the man. She cursed herself for straying into the stable alone. Englishmen always took whatever they wanted.

"I beg your pardon, Sir Knight," she said, her gaze darting to the opening at the other end of the stable. She gave the horse a final pat and stepped away, keeping her eyes downcast.

He stopped in front of her. Gwen focused on his black boots. Against her will, her gaze strayed up. And up. And up.

Her pulse skittered. He was a giant!

She peered at him from beneath her hood, unable to control her curiosity. His hair was black as a witch's soul, cropped short to fit under his helm.

Gwen frowned at the short beard and mustache. That was unusual, certainly. Only Welshmen wore beards these days. She couldn't stop herself from looking at him. He must surely be the most handsome man she had ever seen. His shoulders were so broad...

She nibbled her lip. Eyes of purest silver speared her in place, draining her will to escape, though at the same time she desired escape more than ever. The angry smell of steel and potent male sweat surrounded her senses. Danger emanated from this dark man's forbidding presence.

"You are Welsh," he said. He made it sound like the worst of afflictions.

"Aye," she gritted from between clenched teeth. Damn, why hadn't she learned to speak French with less of an accent?

"Take off that hood," he commanded.

Gwen thought her heart might leap from her chest. She backed away. Nay, she couldn't let him see her! He was so handsome, and she must look frightful after such a long ride. Why couldn't she have encountered this man at a feast, when she was richly garbed and more confident? "I-I must go now."

She tried to dart past him but he caught her and flipped the hood off all in one motion. Gwen jerked away and tilted her chin up. She was a princess for God's sake! She would not let a lowly knight intimidate her.

Gwen recognized the strange gleam that flared to life in his eye. She'd seen it before, in her father's hall, when a warrior fondled a slack-jawed wench. Soon after, the two of them would disappear into the dark recesses of the castle.

Fear danced along her nerve endings as he took a step closer. She forced herself to stand her ground. He was but a hair's breadth away and more than anything she desired to run.

Except he would catch her again.

"You should not get so close," he said, his finger wisping down her cheek in a silky caress. "These horses are trained for battle. You could get hurt."

Gwen trembled. This man was very dangerous, much more dangerous than warhorses. And she sensed he was speaking about much more than chargers. "B-but I was n-not," she stammered.

"Not this time," his rich voice intoned, "but will you be so lucky again?"

She jerked away and lowered her lashes. Damn the bastard! Typically arrogant, like all Englishmen. Still, she was relieved at the implication he wouldn't hurt her, although her instincts told her not to believe it for a second.

"How old are you?"

"I will be sixteen in two months," she replied with all the haughtiness of a princess.

He threw back his head and laughed, startling her with the deep timbre of his voice. "Too young for a leman, though I am sorely tempted. What is your name?"

"Pr—Gwen," she said, coloring. *Leman!* The thought was disturbing, not for the outrageousness of it, but because she actually tried to imagine being this man's lover, though she was uncertain just what it was lovers did. Whatever it was, it would likely be thrilling with him for a teacher. "And your name, Sir Knight?" she asked, her courage returning.

"Richard," he replied, amusement edging his voice.

Richard. She itched to say it out loud, to taste it on her tongue, but she kept her mouth shut and stared at her feet.

Finally, after what seemed an interminable length of time, he spoke. "So, you were admiring my Sirocco?"

"Sirocco? What sort of a name is that?"

"'Tis Arabic. I brought him back from the Crusade."

A knight of honor, she thought. "What does it mean?"

He paused for some moments, his gaze sweeping over her so slowly she felt as if she were naked. She looked away, trying to slow her thundering senses. She was nothing but a clumsy little girl next to this magnificent male animal.

"'Tis the name of a hot desert wind that blows over the Sahara, carrying dust storms across the Mediterranean to Italy and Spain."

She chanced a glance at him. "The Sa-ha-ra?"

He studied her for a moment, and she found she couldn't tear her gaze from his face. No man should be so beautiful.

"Aye, 'tis a place of flames and sand the color of gold. In the evening, when the setting sun turns blood-red and casts its shadow over the dunes —" He picked up her braid. "—'tis the exact same color as your hair."

Gwen blushed, damning herself for reacting so visibly. He would surely think her a little girl now, though why she even cared she couldn't say. He raised her hair to his nose, inhaling its scent. His eyes were like sparkling jewels and she found herself drawn to them, unable to move or speak.

"Roses," he murmured.

"Aye," Gwen whispered. She did not doubt he was a predator, possessed as he was of feline grace and a mesmerizing stare. She knew what the hunted bird must experience in the moment before the hawk struck it dead.

Mustering all her fading willpower, she turned toward the horse. "He is beautiful," she said, scratching the stallion's jaw.

"As are you." His voice was suddenly husky as he caught her outstretched hand and raised it to his lips. She stifled a gasp at the contact of flesh on flesh, the jarring whisper of his tongue across her knuckles.

"Are you a servant to one of the hostages?"

"Hostages?" she repeated blankly. His warm breath stirred over her hand, sending shivers down her spine.

"Aye, the hostages Prince Llywelyn has given to the king."

Gwen's legs buckled. The knight caught her. She clutched him, felt the mail under his surcoat, and knew beneath all that his body was every bit as hard as the steel encasing it.

Hostage. It all made sense now: her father's insistence she accompany him when she never had before. The trunk. Alys.

Her fists twisted in his surcoat. Without thinking, she pressed her face to the travel-stained fabric. "Oh God," she moaned against his broad chest. "Oh God, no. Please, no."

"You did not know there would be hostages?"

She didn't answer. Richard's hand came up to stroke her red-gold hair of its own volition. She was so small, so vulnerable. He held her close, a sudden urge to protect her overwhelming his baser thoughts.

"Do not worry, they will not be harmed," he said softly. Not unless Llywelyn broke the treaty. But Richard was not about to tell her that.

He couldn't believe the effect she had on him. She smelled of things Welsh—wind and water and mountain heather. And, over everything, roses. Sweet, wild roses. He was certain if he never saw her again, she would haunt him for the rest of his life.

She pushed away from him, swaying slightly. He reached for her, but she remained upright. Women had swooned just to get into his arms before, but she seemed too young to play such a trick. Besides, she was alluring enough without need of feminine wiles. If she were older—which she was *not*, he reminded himself—he would gladly spread her silken thighs and impale her without any seduction necessary on her part.

Richard swore silently. He desired skilled courtesans for his bed, not blushing girls barely old enough for marriage. Bloody hell, what was wrong with him?

But she was beautiful. Beautiful as the morning mist on a spring day, fresh as the wind against his face when he and Sirocco raced the River Dee past Claiborne castle, delicate as the wild roses that grew in his valley.

He was drawn to her against all reason. God, what *would* she be like in a couple of years when she bloomed into womanhood? His throat went dry at the thought. He had an urge to keep her just to find out.

"Highness! Highness!" a female voice shouted in Welsh.

Richard turned. He was born and raised in the March. Welsh was second nature to him, though he rarely liked to admit it.

A stout woman hurried toward them, her rosy face mirroring the anxiety in her voice. "Highness!"

Who—? He turned to Gwen.

Gwen. Something tickled the back of his mind.

Princess Gwenllian!

He stared at her in horror. Sirocco stuck his head in the center of Richard's back and pushed. Richard stumbled to the side to keep from coming in contact with her.

"You must come, Highness," the woman said, reaching for Gwen's hand as soon as she stopped. She puffed with the stress of her exertion and tears trickled down her cheeks. She gave Richard a tremulous smile.

"Alys. I am to be a hostage, Alys," Gwen said, her voice flat, emotionless.

Strangely, it tore at Richard's heart to hear her sound so dejected. He wanted to pull her in his arms and soothe her. Goddamn Llywelyn to lowest hell for this!

"Come, Highness," Alys urged, gently tugging her mistress's hand. The girl followed woodenly.

Richard was immobile for a long time afterward. He stared in the direction she had gone, stifling the urge to follow. Something pushed him. He turned to glare at his stallion. He would have sworn the horse was laughing at him.

"Dammit, Sirocco!"

The horse yawned. Richard scrubbed his hands across his tingling scalp. Jesú, the flame-haired girl who drew him like stale darkness to pure sunlight was Llywelyn's daughter!

3

Worcester, England
October, 1278

The autumn wind whistled through the wooden shutters, sending a bitter chill deep into the heart of the Bishop of Worcester's castle. Gwen turned on her back and yanked the coverlets up to her chin.

King Edward's household had been lodged in the drafty old keep for a fortnight, awaiting the wedding of Prince Llywelyn to the King's cousin, Lady Elinor de Montfort.

Gwen had not seen her father since that day at Rhuddlan. It was Einion—sweet old Einion as usual—who had explained why she was to be a hostage.

She'd been frightened to death at first, wildly recalling the tales of her grandfather's confinement as a hostage of King John. Though King Edward was well reputed to have fits of the Plantagenet temper, it was not to the extent of mad King John, and she realized that her father would never put her in danger. She would be brave, and she would make the greatest man in all the world proud to claim her as his daughter.

She had preferred to stay in her rooms, away from the court as often as possible. Windsor overflowed with the English. It mattered not at all that she was a princess. In their eyes, she was a savage, a whore, simply because she came from a land they did not understand.

She thought of the knight called Richard. He represented all she despised, but she could not forget him. Night after night, he haunted her dreams, as real to her as he had been almost a year ago in the stable of Rhuddlan castle.

It was annoying really. He was an arrogant English knight, not at all fit for a princess.

But she had felt so awkward beside him, like she was the servant he'd mistook her for and he was a prince. He was so handsome, and when he'd held her close, she'd thought her heart would come out of her chest.

She'd hoped to see him again in the party of knights who escorted her and the other prisoners to England. Then she'd looked for him at court. But he was gone, as though the stolen moments in the stable had been a figment of her imagination.

Her dreams were strange. Always, a fierce hawk perched upon his arm, its plumage unusual, so dark as to be almost black. Crimson jesses bound its feet and two leashes were attached to it. One dangled free while the other was gripped in the powerful jaws of a golden lion.

Gwen sighed. Why did she let herself think of him?

She was going to marry Rhys ap Gawain. They had pledged long ago to marry each other when they grew up. Gwen toyed with the edge of the coverlet. They *were* grown up now! She was sixteen and Rhys was nineteen.

Would he want to get married as soon as she returned?

The thought was a little unsettling. They'd been friends for as long as Gwen could remember. When she was four and he was seven, he'd carried her around on his back, pretending to be her steed.

They'd spent long hours together; climbing trees, exploring the forest, searching caves for King Arthur's treasure. They'd swam in crystal streams and raced their ponies along the valley floor, they'd fought mock battles with longbows and swords, and planted frogs in the serving women's beds. During all the laughter and childish pranks, they had pledged to be friends forever. It was only natural they marry one day so they could stay together.

But, when she turned fifteen and he was seventeen, they'd realized you didn't marry to be friends.

Rhys had taken her hunting that day. They didn't catch anything because neither of them seemed to have their attention focused on anything but each other. Finally, Rhys had thrown down his longbow and kissed her.

Gwen touched her lips. It had been brief, just a feather-light touch, but everything between them changed. No longer were they just two friends doing the things they'd always done. They were aware of each other on a new level of being, one that was disturbing and exciting all at once.

Gwen never had a chance to find out where that new feeling would have taken them. The war had come and Rhys had gone to fight. Then she was given as a hostage.

And now her dreams were crowded with the image of a tall dark man with eyes of purest silver, a man whose touch had ignited more in its simplicity than ever Rhys's kiss did.

The door to her chamber opened to admit a petite woman with long blonde hair and sparkling eyes. "Gwen! How is it that you are still abed at this hour?" Elinor asked, skipping to the bed. She threw off the cloak she wore over her chemise and darted beneath the covers. "Ooh, 'tis cold in this old castle!"

"'Tis too nasty to get up just yet," Gwen replied, snuggling next to her friend.

"Aye, but I am too excited to sleep any longer! I dared not hope that Edward would ever allow me to marry your father." Elinor sighed and put an arm around Gwen. "Tell me I am not dreaming."

"'Tis not a dream. Today you and I are hostages no longer. We will go home to Wales."

"I would have been there two years ago if Edward had not captured my ship. Jesú, I am too old to be a bride!"

"Five and twenty is not so old. Besides, that is half the age of my father. 'Tis perfect."

Elinor smiled and kissed her on the forehead. "You are such a practical girl. You should be married by now. I would have been married when I was your age if my father had not rebelled against King Henry. Once Papa was killed, there was naught for us to do but flee to France. Poor Llywelyn had no choice but to break the betrothal contract.

"Thirteen long years I have waited. I know Llywelyn only sent for me to irritate Edward, but I am thankful anyway. My father did what he thought was right and he paid for it. But 'twas unfair that I had to pay too."

"It seems to be the English way," Gwen said, twisting a lock of hair around her finger.

Elinor laid her cheek on Gwen's head. "I am sorry. I forgot. We have *both* been paying for our fathers' defiance to the English crown."

Gwen took a deep breath. "'Tis over now, Elinor. I only want to go home and never leave again."

"I am afraid, Gwen. What if Llywelyn does not like me? We've been exchanging letters for years but—but we have met only once and it was so brief—*and* supervised by Edward."

Gwen pushed away and turned to face the other woman. She was about to make a jest but changed her mind when she saw the apprehension painted on Elinor's pretty face. "Do not worry. He will love you, just as I do. You are kind and fair. He will not be able to do otherwise."

"But what if he desires someone younger? What if he takes a mistress?"

"He cannot! You will live by our customs and if you object to a mistress, he cannot take one. Welshwomen are *not* chattel!"

Elinor caught a blonde curl in her hand, examining it carefully. "'Tis lucky you are to be Welsh, Gwen. Mama always told me that I would have little, if any, control over the man I married. I must be ever at my lord's beck and call, ready to entertain him at a moment's notice. I would be his chatelaine and woe if I did anything wrong! Of course she was only preparing me for the worst. She did not object when Papa chose Llywelyn. I wonder if he knew Welshmen were different?"

Gwen leaned back and sighed. "Thank God a Welshwoman may choose her own husband. I would not want to be forced to marry someone I did not like."

"Aye... but come now, let us not be solemn on my wedding day! Get up, lazy bones, and help me prepare!"

Elinor jumped from the bed, giggling. Gwen shot her a look and slowly peeled back the covers.

"I told you all would be well," Edward said, tipping back the cup of wine he held. "Dafydd accepted without complaint the lands I gave him in Cheshire in lieu of a crown, and Llywelyn has been reasonably agreeable."

Richard swirled the liquid in his goblet, staring at the red whirlpool he created. He stifled a yawn. He'd ridden in late last night and his current mistress, Lady Anne Ashford, had kept him awake well past midnight.

Since Llywelyn's surrender at Rhuddlan, the Welsh people had quietly settled beneath the English yoke. There were still border raids—there would always be border raids—but all across Wales, Welshmen presented themselves to English bailiffs and castellans to try their cases and lodge their complaints according to English law. They chaffed under the yoke, but they did not complain... yet.

Richard raised his gaze to Edward. "I still do not trust Dafydd. Better to have given him to Llywelyn to hang than treat him like an English lord."

Edward laughed. "All Dafydd ever wanted was wealth and prestige. He could've cared less about actually ruling Wales. Now that he has his land and money—and an English wife—he'll settle down and plague Llywelyn no more." Edward took another drink. "Indeed, I invited him to come to this wedding I am throwing for Llywelyn and my cousin, but he begged to be excused."

Richard hid his surprise. "'Tis just as well. I doubt Llywelyn would want his Judas here."

"Since when do you care what Llywelyn wants?"

Richard shrugged. "I don't, but I still cannot figure why you summoned me to attend either."

"'Tis simple enough. You are my closest advisor, and I need your counsel." Edward smoothed his hand over the orange velvet of his surcoat. "You know that Llywelyn and our lord of Powys have applied to me to settle a dispute over the ownership of Arwystli?"

Richard nodded. "By the Treaty of Aberconwy, disputes arising over lands in Wales are to be settled according to Welsh law. However," he said, "it doesn't benefit England to allow Llywelyn's judges to rule in his favor since Arwystli borders southern Gwynedd and is strategically important to her defense."

"Precisely. 'Twould be much better served in Gruffydd ap Gwen-wynwyn's hands. 'Tis why I am setting up a special commission to rule whether 'twill be tried according to Welsh or English law."

Richard grinned. "You have no intention of allowing Llywelyn to win. 'Tis merely a stalling tactic."

"Until I can figure out how to circumvent the treaty, 'tis the only option. I am glad you approve."

"Aye, 'tis fitting somehow," Richard said. "But how do you intend to keep Llywelyn in check now that you're giving back his hostages and finally allowing him to wed Elinor? If you give Arwystli to Gruffydd, 'twill surely cause another war."

"I've not yet decided. Something will avail itself of me ere he returns to Wales, I am certain of it." He got to his feet. "Now, I believe there is a wedding to prepare for."

Richard felt a chill run down his spine as he stood. When Ned was in one of his moods, he was capable of anything.

They parted company and Richard returned to his chamber. He lay on the bed and crossed his arms behind his head. He had absolutely no intention of going to the wedding.

He thought of the flame-haired princess and almost changed his mind. She was certain to be there. He'd not seen her since that day in Rhuddlan. When Ned had decided to hold her at Windsor, Richard vowed to avoid going to the royal court unless it was in residence elsewhere.

He knew it was irrational to avoid seeing her. She was only a girl, but she had the promise of great beauty, and Richard was nothing if not appreciative of women's charms.

How much had she grown up in a year's time? He closed his eyes. It would not do to lust after her. She may only be Welsh, but she was also a princess and he could never make her his leman.

No, he was definitely not going to the wedding.

Richard stood in the shadowed recess of the door, watching the crowd. Disgust washed over him. The mere sight of Llywelyn filled him with impotent rage.

He had not been able to stay away, but he still wasn't going in there to watch Llywelyn, his new bride at his side, gloating on the dais, no matter what Ned wanted.

Dancers swirled before his eyes, their clothing a whirlpool of dazzling color. Smoke from the dripping tallow candles curled ceiling-ward, sizzling and sputtering as a draft skimmed across them.

Richard searched the milling groups with a purpose he would not admit. When he found her, he ceased to look elsewhere. Torchlight illuminated her red-gold hair as she glided through the hall.

"Gwen," he whispered, startling himself by speaking aloud. It seemed for a moment that she turned in his direction.

He swallowed, his throat suddenly dry.

She was a beauty. She'd grown. Even from this distance, he could see how she'd filled out, become soft and womanly. He was too far away, but he recalled those cat-eyes, mysterious and golden-green. They were framed in an oval face with high cheekbones and a full mouth the color of ripe summer berries.

Her gown was of vivid blue silk, clinging to her curves with every movement. A small diadem sat atop her crown of curls, a single sapphire winking from it boldly. Her hair cascaded over her shoulders like a flame, red and gold twisting together until the colors were no longer distinguishable, one from the other.

Richard watched her for some moments, unable to tear his gaze away. Men crowded around her, and she slipped in and out of his vision as she moved between them, smiling seductively.

She was Llywelyn's daughter, for God's sake! He should not be surprised that she behaved so wantonly, encouraging the attentions of the men surrounding her. The Prince was completely lacking in morals, ambitious and deceitful. His daughter would be no different.

Richard was not comforted by that thought, though it might make getting her in his bed a bit easier. He frowned. He'd never allowed himself to actually plan on seducing her. Once the idea formed, he knew he would not deviate from it. Besides, it would be a lovely way to anger Llywelyn.

She was accompanied by a blond knight, and they were making their way toward where Richard stood. Slipping back into the shadows of the murky corridor, he waited, unable to leave just yet.

"Is this good, Your Highness?" the man asked when they had walked into the passage.

Gwen stopped and took a deep breath. "Aye. I don't know what came over me. Thank you, Sir Guy," she said, clasping his hand.

Richard felt a sudden and inexplicable anger seize him at the intimate gesture.

"I've wanted to kiss you all night," Guy said, pulling her into his arms.

His head dipped toward her and she turned her face abruptly. "Nay!" she cried as his lips found the hollow of her neck. In the next instant, her slippered foot darted out and kicked him in the shin. He grunted, but didn't let go.

"Unhand the lady, Guy," Richard said, stepping from the shadows. His hand strayed out of habit to his sword hilt.

Guy's face registered surprise, then anger. "The princess is with me. I'll invite you not to interfere if you know what's good for you."

Richard took a step toward him.

Guy backed away, his eyes widening in recognition. "Beg your pardon, my lord. No harm done. I only meant to kiss her."

"If you know what's good for you, you'll get out of my sight. *Now,*" Richard growled.

Guy bowed. "As you command, my lord."

When he was gone, Gwen took another deep breath. She had only meant to thank Guy for being kind to her, but not like that. English bastards always tried to take that which did not belong to them.

She swung around to look at her rescuer. His face was shadowed, but there was something familiar about him, even through the veil of too much wine. What sort of a man could frighten away a knight with only a command? He moved into the light, and her heart began to thump.

"Richard?"

He was even more splendid than she remembered. Tall and darkly handsome. Big. His tunic stretched across his broad chest, molding the hard curves. Her breath shortened when she remembered herself pressed against him.

"Don't you know better than to leave the hall in a man's company and unescorted?" he demanded.

"I only wanted some air to clear my head," she replied, bewildered. Did he not remember her? Somehow it hurt to think so after all the nights she had awakened with him on her mind.

But of course she had only been a clumsy girl when they met, and he was a man. Lord, she still felt like a clumsy girl! Where was all that charm and allure she'd been honing this evening? It was gone, deserting her when she needed it most, just like a fairy illusion.

Gwen smoothed a nervous hand over the bodice of her gown. She didn't notice the way his eyes followed as she caressed the fabric over her breasts, or the tightening of his jaw, or the darkening of his eyes.

No, all she could think was that a man like him would not remember her. She was young and awkward and totally unsuited for one as handsome as he. She'd been a fool to ever think otherwise.

His voice was cool as he spoke. "Or you wanted a tryst and then changed your mind once you got out here. You should not drink so much wine." Her breath caught, but he didn't stop. "But then, that is one of the things you Welsh do best, isn't it?"

"Those are lies spread by you Englishmen! How dare you speak to me that way!" She suddenly longed to prove her worth to him, to see his eyes widen and his words change to ones of respect. She stiffened her spine and fixed him with a regal stare. "Do you know who I am? Princess Gwenllian, daughter to the Prince of Wales, and I will not listen to a mere knight insult me as if I were a chambermaid."

He threw back his head and laughed. "You are sadly mistaken, your most revered and illustrious Highness. I am well aware you are the daughter of that Welsh murderer."

Rage kindled in Gwen's soul. "Murderer? You, an English knight, dare to call my father a murderer? What about all the murders and injustices done to my people in the name of the king?"

"Savages deserve no better than they give," he said, his voice dangerously low.

Gwen clenched her fists and took a halting step toward him. He was not at all as she had dreamed. The illusion was shattered, but at the same time a small corner of her heart leapt that he remembered. "You are an arrogant, vile, English swine!"

He advanced on her with lightning swiftness. Gwen backed away, coming up short when she hit the wall. Before she could move, she found herself pinned against it by his hard body.

Her heart thudded in her chest, her breath shortened, and she lifted her chin to stare defiantly at him. His arms were braced on either side of her head, and he lifted one to brush his knuckles down her cheek. Gwen trembled.

"Don't you realize what could happen to you out here, alone with a man like this?"

"I will scream," Gwen whispered. But her blood surged as his body pressed harder to hers. She felt as if her own body was reshaping itself to mold to his. Every hard angle of him found an answering hollow on her.

Richard smiled. "Nay, I think not, Princess."

"Wh-what makes you so sure?" She sounded breathless, even to her own ears.

"This," he said, lowering his mouth to her exposed throat. Gwen sucked in her breath. She tilted her head back and closed her eyes. Her skin was on fire.

"And this," he continued, running his hand across her breasts so lightly she barely felt it. She shivered. This was wrong and she had to stop it before—before what?

His gaze settled on her mouth when her tongue darted out to wet her lips. She raised her hands to his broad chest, not to push, but to touch.

Slowly, she smoothed them upwards, searching his face as she did so. His eyes glittered strangely, but he didn't stop her. He wasn't wearing chainmail as he had been the first time she'd touched him, and Gwen started at the silken ripple of muscle beneath her palms.

She caught herself wondering what his bare chest felt like, and before she knew it her hand strayed beneath the neck of his tunic. His skin was hot and smooth. She slid her hand over him, encountered crisp hair and hard curves.

He made a sound low in his throat that sounded like a growl. "That's it, Princess. You know what to do, don't you? I should have known you would."

Gwen blinked. He sounded angry and she had no idea why. God, what was he doing to her? Why did she feel dizzy and drunker than when she'd left the hall?

His head descended. Gwen's heart skipped a beat. Right now she wanted this more than anything. When their lips were almost touching, he said, "Kiss me, Princess."

Gwen closed her eyes. Disobedience was out of the question.

4

At the first brush of his lips, a fierce wave of heat surged through her. Gwen swayed into him.

"My lord," came a soft voice. "Is that you, my lord?"

As quickly as it started, it was over. Richard stepped away, and Gwen was left leaning against the wall, dazed and disappointed.

A woman strolled up to him and placed a possessive hand on his arm. She wore a tightly laced gown of shocking red, and a sheer white wimple covered her head. Her blue gaze raked over Gwen, traveling contemptuously up and down her form.

"I expected to find you in the hall, Anne," Richard said, irritation evident in his tone.

"I have been looking for you, my lord," she replied, sidling closer to him.

Gwen felt a sharp prickle run over her spine.

"Well, I see you have managed to find a leman since we last met," she said, tossing a glance at Anne.

"I decided I prefer English women," he drawled.

Gwen drew herself up stiffly, embarrassment seeping into her bones. She'd been witless in his arms and he knew it. And now he was laughing at her.

"If you will excuse me," she said, sweeping them both with a haughty stare before she turned and marched back toward the gathering in the Great Hall. Her heart thumped and her eyes stung, but she refused to let anyone see just how rattled she was. Before she entered the hall, she threw a glance over her shoulder. Richard was still watching her.

Gwen tipped her chin up and glared at him, though inside she trembled from his touch. *No more.*

She swept into the room like a queen, leaving Richard and his leman behind. Damn all Englishmen, especially tall ones with black hair and silver eyes!

Anne smoothed her hand down Richard's arm. "Come to bed and let me take care of you, my lord."

"Aye, wench, I could use a pleasant diversion," he replied, frustration hammering through him. He'd been so close! And the way she'd touched him had set his blood on fire. Even now, he could still feel her slender hands caressing his chest. His skin burned with the memory.

Although it angered him, there was no doubt she was experienced. But what had he expected? The Welsh were known for their lack of morals, as he'd so often been told.

When they reached Anne's chamber, she flung herself at him, her hands working feverishly at the knots and buckles of his clothing as he pushed the door shut. He allowed her to undress him, and when she sauntered to the bed, leering at him hungrily, he snuffed out the candles before joining her.

It was an odd thing for him to do, but he knew if he had to look at her, he'd never be able to go through with it. All he wanted was to forget about Gwen.

He joined Anne on the bed, pulling her against him, his mouth finding her parted lips. She whimpered as his hands trailed down her body, his fingers slipping between her folds to caress the sensitive bud within.

"Now… take me now," she panted.

He rolled onto her, pressing her deep into the mattress, his fingers tangling in her soft hair. In his mind, it wasn't pale, but the color of desert fire.

Anne soon cried out, shuddering beneath him, and he followed her over the brink.

She tried to hold him, but he rolled away and sat up. She sat up behind him, caressing his back, kissing his shoulder.

"Mmm, that was wonderful," she said, tracing his ear with her finger.

Richard jerked away. For reasons he didn't understand, he had to get out. He picked a rush off the floor, walked to the hearth and thrust the tip into the glowing embers to light it, then fumbled about for the candles.

Anne watched him curiously. The tangled strands of her hair fell over her naked breasts as she lay back on the pillows.

Richard began to dress.

Anne bolted upright. "Where are you going?"

"Go to sleep, Anne. I'm not coming back tonight."

He finished dressing and belted his sword into place, then left without another word.

Anne picked up his pillow and threw it. Womanizing bastard! She'd wanted to strangle him when she found him seducing that Welsh bitch, but there was nothing she could do about it.

If she wanted to be the next Countess of Dunsmore, she had to keep quiet and turn a blind eye while he dallied with other women.

She'd been trying to make Richard take her to wife for a year now, since her husband died, but he wasn't as easily convinced as most men.

She was going to be a countess if it killed her! Her looks opened many a door that would have otherwise been closed to the daughter of a burgher.

She had all the things men desired: blonde hair, blue eyes, slender figure, skin the color of new snow. She'd managed to marry a knight in Richard's service, one with a manor of his own. It mattered not at all that he had been several years older than she.

Being known as Lady Ashford was plenty of compensation for bedding an old man and bearing him an heir.

Since Thomas's death, Anne had set her sights even higher. She wanted to be a countess.

And she wanted to be the Countess of Dunsmore because Richard de Claiborne was not only handsome and skillful in bed, but he was also rich and powerful.

Anne yawned. Her body still tingled from the violence of his love-making. He was a devastating man.

Mayhap she was just a tiny bit in love with him. But he was too dark, too moody. He needed no one. To love him, *truly* love him, was to end up with a shattered heart.

Fortunately, Anne loved the money more than the man.

King Edward watched the happenings in the hall with great interest. Why had he not noticed how beautiful Llywelyn's daughter was before now?

He kissed his wife's hand, then patted it absently.

Yes, Gwenllian was lovely, and it seemed as if she had the attention of half the noblemen of England turned on her tonight.

Edward shifted his gaze to the Welsh prince and his new wife. God, how happy they looked. Mayhap Llywelyn would be so besotted with her that he wouldn't plague the English for a while.

Edward chuckled. Wishful thinking, that. The Welsh were contrary to a man and Llywelyn was one of the contrariest. Nay, he still needed a check on the prince. Something to ensure his loyalty.

Edward turned his gaze back to Gwenllian. How old was she now? Sixteen, mayhap? Old enough to be married.

Edward straightened. *Married.* Jesú, that was it! Marry the Welsh princess to an Englishman and tie Llywelyn up even further.

Smiling, Edward drained his goblet and stood. The entire gathering quieted, waiting for their king to speak. He bade them continue without him for a while, kissed his wife on the forehead, and motioned for a page.

"My Lord de Claiborne?"

"Aye?" Richard stopped as the page hurried toward him. Despite the autumn chill, trickles of sweat ran down the boy's skin, staining the neck of his tunic.

"My lord, the king requires you to attend him in his solar."

Richard nodded, following the youth silently. There was to be no hope of avoiding a confrontation with Ned this night.

"Where have you been?" Edward demanded as soon as the page left them. "I've had him searching for you half the night it seems!"

Richard shrugged, taking the seat the king waved at distractedly. He smoothed the crimson fabric of his surcoat before meeting Edward's gaze.

"I was not in my chambers, my liege."

Edward grunted. "In the arms of that wanton, Lady Anne Ashford, no doubt."

"Ah, you know me too well, Ned," Richard said, grinning.

"Well, I cannot blame you. She is a pretty piece and most eager to please too. 'Tis lucky for you that Eleanor is not heavy with child or you would have to share the charms of Lady Ashford with your king."

Richard bowed his head. "What is mine is yours, my liege."

Edward began to pace the spacious solar. A servant came in, pouring them each a goblet of fine Gascon wine, before scurrying out the door.

"I did not see you at the wedding, or in the hall," Edward said, stopping to fix Richard with a penetrating stare.

Richard laughed bitterly. Why did he have to explain to Ned of all people? "I could not be in the same room with that man again for a single moment, much less an entire evening, without crossing swords with him."

"God's blood, Richard! I am the King of England, not you. I've made peace with Llywelyn and I expect you to do the same. I *must* turn my attentions elsewhere. England's laws are in bad need of reform, and I intend to regain my rightful holdings in France. I need you to help me."

Richard gripped the arms of the chair, the carved wood biting into his flesh. "I will do anything for you, Ned, but I will *not* pretend Llywelyn is not my enemy."

Edward tossed his crown on the table. It hit with a resounding metallic thud. "Then you leave me no choice. His daughter is of an age to marry. You will take her to wife."

"No!" Richard jumped to his feet, his steely eyes meeting Edward's hard blue ones. The two men glared at each other for a long moment.

"'Tis high time you took another wife anyway," Edward said.

"I do not want another wife, Ned, especially a Welsh one."

"Jesú, I am giving you a *princess*! Your wife has been dead for two years. You have to think about getting an heir."

Richard closed his eyes as a wave of guilt swept over him. He would not think of Elizabeth and the child that died with her.

He had only wanted to bed Gwen, not marry her. She was Llywelyn's daughter for God's sake!

"Llywelyn is responsible for my father's death. I cannot forget that. Ever."

Edward sighed and rubbed a hand across his brow, sweeping at the dark blond hair that fell in his face. One eye drooped lazily. He had inherited that from his father, but none were stupid enough to believe it signaled weakness in this king.

"The matter of Wales is final. The people will learn to obey English laws and we will move on. I want Llywelyn yoked strongly to my side once and for all."

Richard fingered his sword. "Why *me*, Ned? There are at least a half a dozen others you could choose from."

Edward waved a beringed hand. "You make the most sense. Llywelyn fears you more than anyone. I don't want any trouble out of him the minute my back is turned, and he will remain biddable if you control his daughter and more of his lands. Besides, she is his only child. If my fair cousin fails to bear him any children, then Gwenllian's sons will inherit his throne. She is still a princess, despite her bastard birth, and I want her sons to be half English."

Richard stiffened. "This is not a good idea, Ned. I'll remarry if you wish it, but give me an Englishwoman for God's sake! What makes you think I will even be able to touch the girl?"

Edward laughed. "God's bones, Richard! You forget how well I know you. Once you see her, you'll not fear that ever again. She is most pleasing to look upon."

Richard raked a hand through his hair. He would be able to touch her all right, but he'd rather do it without marrying her.

"Think of the beauty of it. Llywelyn is not known for his ability to sire children. What better way to chafe our Welsh prince than to marry his only daughter and put Black Hawk de Claiborne's sons in line for his throne? I should think that would make you happy, knowing how distressed he will be."

"Aye, but he will not agree to it, Ned."

"'Tis my divine right as his sovereign overlord. He has no choice in the matter." Edward smiled, and Richard heard the implied *and neither do you* as if it had been spoken aloud. "I am the king and he will learn that my edict applies not only in England, but in Wales as well."

Richard expelled a frustrated breath. A king could not force a vassal to marry, but Richard did not need to be forced. Even were it against all he wanted, he would do as he had always done, as he had sworn beside a deathbed in the Holy Land to always do. "As you command me, Majesty."

Edward nodded. "I can always count on you, can't I, Richard?"

"Aye, Ned, you can always count on me," Richard echoed flatly.

"Good. Tomorrow, we will break the news to Llywelyn." Edward lifted his goblet. "Together," he added, ignoring Richard's scowl as he tilted the cup back.

5

"You want to do what?" Llywelyn roared.

Edward swept him with a cool stare. "Not want, Llywelyn. I *am* doing this."

Richard lounged in a chair at one end of the heavy oak table. His eyes followed Llywelyn as he treaded a path back and forth in front of the hearth.

Beneath the solid expanse of the table, Richard cracked one fist inside the other, his gut churning like the sea at full boil.

The worst was yet to come. Edward was forcing him to sign a treaty of friendship with Llywelyn as part of the marriage agreement.

They hadn't gotten that far though. Right now, the Prince was still trying to get over the shock of having his daughter wedded to Black Hawk de Claiborne.

Llywelyn pointed a battle-hardened finger at Richard. His tones were clipped as he spoke to the king. "You intend to marry my daughter to that blood-thirsty barbarian?"

Richard stood slowly and walked around the table. Llywelyn braced his feet apart and waited. Lesser men tucked their tails between their legs and ran when Black Hawk de Claiborne stalked them. If Richard hadn't been so blinded by rage, he'd have admitted a begrudging admiration for Llywelyn's steadfastness.

Edward gripped the table and shot Richard a warning look.

The prince was trying to object to the marriage on the grounds of his daughter's safety, but they all knew what was really at stake. Llywelyn didn't want to give up any portion of his greatly diminished princedom as dowry.

Richard fingered his sword, his voice deceptively mild. "You had no such qualms when you gave her over as a hostage. Why the sudden attack of conscience, old man?"

Llywelyn's eyes flashed. "You're a disrespectful bastard, Black Hawk. But then again I would expect no less from the son of William de Claiborne."

No one heard the singing of steel until the blade was already out of the scabbard. Edward leapt to his feet, his fist crashing onto the table. "Richard! Goddammit, put it away!"

Llywelyn stood rigid with the point of the gleaming sword resting at the base of his throat. Eyes met across a chasm of mistrust; Llywelyn's fearful yet defiant, Richard's malicious and cold.

Richard smiled lazily, but it was forced. "As you command, my liege," he ground out between clenched teeth.

He stepped back and resheathed the sword in one smooth stroke, then gave Edward a curt bow before returning to his seat.

Edward glared at him for a long moment, then sank down into his own chair, smoothing the folds of his blood-red surcoat with great deliberation.

Llywelyn took a deep breath and rubbed his throat. His face was scarlet with fury. "That is precisely what I'm talking about, Majesty. How can you give my daughter to the likes of him? The first time the lass opens her mouth to disagree, he'll skewer her on the point of his sword!"

Richard crossed his hands behind his head and leaned back in the chair. "I'll use my sword on her all right." He smiled. "I daresay she'll enjoy it much more than you just did."

Llywelyn's jaw worked, but he turned to the king and ignored the taunt.

"I am sorry, Llywelyn, my mind is made up," Edward said.

Llywelyn whirled around and began to pace back and forth. "What about Arwystli? What are you going to do about that?"

Edward shrugged. "My commission is busy working on it. We'll hear their findings soon enough."

"Give me Arwystli, and you can have her."

"'Tis not that easy, my friend. I am your king and I am commanding you to betrothe your daughter to my baron. Arwystli has nothing to do with this."

Richard sat back while Llywelyn continued to protest and Edward countered. He thought he might choke on Llywelyn's self-righteousness. First, the man said he feared for his daughter, then he was willing to trade her for disputed land. Richard wanted to kill him even more.

Finally, the raw terms were hammered out: a parcel of land that bordered Richard's, a treaty of friendship, money and sheep, and the succession to the Welsh throne if Llywelyn failed to get any heirs of his own.

Edward leaned back in his chair while Llywelyn crossed to stand by the window. The King winked at Richard and took a swallow of wine.

"Well, shall we send for the lass and introduce her to her husband-to-be?"

Gwen curled in a chair and rested her chin on her fist. She'd not left her room since retreating to it last night. It was small and cozy and far removed from the dark dangers of broad shoulders and silver eyes.

Her heart quickened against her will, her cheeks heating. Richard had been so dangerously handsome in the wavering torchlight. She'd been drawn to him, ready to surrender before he even struck. His smell—spicy, powerful—lingered in her memory, taunting her.

She closed her eyes, leaned her head against the chair. She could feel his lips on her skin, his hands like sweet torture on her innocent flesh.

Gwen had relived the scene a thousand times since last night. It felt so real, even now. She had a sudden thought that if she turned around, he would be standing there, watching her. She pictured him, one corner of his sensual mouth curved in a mocking smile, a smile that told her he knew all of her darkest dreams.

Oh God, would that he had kissed her before that woman came along!

Gwen pressed a trembling hand to her forehead. Why did she think such things about that vile man? He was handsome, yes, but he was English and he was horrible and he was—

"Gwen?"

"Come in, Elinor," she said, more than happy to be interrupted.

The older woman hurried into the room. "Gwen, you must change. That simply will not do."

Gwen looked down at the plain surcoat belted over a white undergown. "Are we not leaving? I have ridden like this before."

"Nay, you are being summoned to an audience with the king. You must change," Elinor repeated.

Gwen clutched her throat. "The king?"

"Do not worry," Elinor soothed. "Your father is with him. 'Twill be all right. Now, let me help you."

She busied herself in one of Gwen's trunks, pulling out a gown of sea-green silk and an ivory surcoat embroidered with silver birds.

"This will do," Elinor said, laying the clothes across a chair before turning back to Gwen.

"Do you know why, Elinor?" Icy fear washed over Gwen's body, rendering her immobile.

"Nay." Elinor grasped her shoulders. "But I do not think he wants to keep you hostage. He gave his word."

Gwen stared into the other woman's hazel eyes for some moments before nodding mutely. She shrugged out of the garments she was wearing and tossed them onto the bed, then donned the others as Elinor handed them to her.

Gwen thought of the leman Anne and the way her tightly laced gown had shown her figure. She glanced at Elinor. The other woman's back was turned, so Gwen tugged the laces tighter, satisfied with the way the gown cinched in her waist and molded her breasts and hips.

If she chanced to run into Richard again, he'd not see a girl, but a woman.

She chided herself for caring what he thought of her, but that didn't stop her from unplaiting her hair and shaking it into a torrent of flame. Elinor knotted a girdle of silk and silver around Gwen's waist, frowning only slightly at the way the gown hugged her curves.

"Mayhap, you should wear a wimple," Elinor said, touching the cloth that covered her own tightly braided hair.

"Nay. 'Tis not the Welsh way."

Elinor shrugged. "As you wish." Squeezing Gwen's hand, she said, "All will be well."

The light that flooded from the chamber's interior seemed unbearably bright when coupled with the murky darkness of the passage Gwen had just come through. She squinted, holding her hand up to shield her eyes.

Unmistakable currents of tension emanated from the three men present. The air crackled with the sparks of their anger, curbed, but not forgotten, at her entrance.

Her father stood at one end of the room. King Edward lounged easily at a table. Her heart started to flutter as her eyes met the third man's.

How, and better yet why, was he here?

"Your Majesty," she said, sinking into a curtsy.

"Come, Gwenllian, sit beside me," Edward beckoned, all smiles as he patted the chair next to him. "May I present Richard de Claiborne, Earl of Dunsmore?" he said sweetly.

Gwen gasped. Oh God—*Gwalchddu!* Only moments before, her fickle heart had been pounding so loud she thought all three men could hear it. Now, it struggled with the effort to beat.

King Edward and Richard de Claiborne.

The Lion with the leash in its mouth. The fierce Hawk he controlled.

The dark knight of her dreams *was* Black Hawk de Claiborne. But Black Hawk was supposed to be cruel and evil and ugly, not handsome and seductive! He was a brutal guardian of the March. Stories were told of him, bards' tales of unspeakable horror chanted in the great stronghold of the Prince of Wales.

Gwen had heard them all. Black Hawk tortured his captives most gruesomely. He drank the blood of newborn babes and devoured children for dinner. He'd sold his soul to the devil and sacrificed virgins regularly on the altar of his masculinity.

Gwen wasn't quite sure what that last part meant, although she had a sneaking suspicion it had something to do with the strange sensations she'd experienced when he'd touched her.

A shiver washed down her spine and she crumpled in the chair Edward offered.

"Are you all right, my dear?" Edward asked, leaning forward to touch her cheek.

"Aye, thank you, Majesty," she replied quickly. "Lord de Claiborne," she murmured, lowering her lashes. She thought of all the Welshmen who had died at his hands, all the women who mourned their husbands and brothers and sons because of him.

Bitter disappointment ate at her. He *was* horrible. She raised her gaze to him, tempered it with defiance and hatred.

The look he returned to her was raw and sensual, and full of contempt. Gwen broke the contact first, stared at her hands clenched in her lap.

"Princess Gwenllian," he replied. His voice was cool and detached. Strangely, it hurt. She dared to look at him once more.

One corner of his mouth crooked in a mocking smile. A dark eyebrow arched upward. Gwen felt her cheeks heating. She lifted her chin and turned to the King as he began to speak.

"Since you are of an age to marry, Gwenllian, it is my duty as your king to find a husband for you. I have chosen Lord De Claiborne."

"No!" she cried, leaping to her feet.

"I am afraid you have no choice, my dear," Edward said, leaning his chair back on two legs.

Gwen took a deep breath. She balled her gown in her fists and told herself there was nothing to fear. "Welsh women cannot be forced to take a husband against their will. I do not wish it."

"You are not a typical Welshwoman, Gwenllian. You're a princess first and as such you are my ward. 'Tis my divine right as your king to arrange your marriage. You will obey me."

Gwen fled to her father's side and grabbed his hand. "Father, you cannot allow this! I'll marry anyone you wish, do anything you ask of me, but do not make me marry Black Hawk de Claiborne," she pleaded in Welsh, her eyes searching his.

He extracted his hand and turned his back to her. He stared out the window, and when he spoke, his voice was cool, devoid of emotion. "I'm sorry, lass, but I cannot do anything about it."

It was happening again. He would not save her. She was being trotted out as a sacrificial lamb, only this time the man who took her was quite capable of slaughter.

Gwen mentally shook herself. She was Llywelyn ap Gruffydd's daughter for God's sake! She was supposed to be a brave Welsh princess, not a coward who would beg for rescue from her duty.

She touched his arm. "I will not fail you like my mother did," she said quietly. He stiffened and she spun around and walked over to the king. Since she had no choice anyway, she would enter into it with dignity, with bravery worthy of her great father. "Very well, Your Majesty. I will marry Lord de Claiborne."

Edward took her hand in his, rubbed little circles in her palm with his thumb. "I'm glad you see it my way, sweet. The wedding will not be for some months yet. Whilst we finalize the terms of your dowry, you may return to Wales."

"Thank you, Majesty," Gwen said. Tears hovered beneath the surface but she swore she would not cry in front of these English bastards.

"Well, Llywelyn, I think we should allow these two a few minutes alone to get better acquainted," Edward said.

Gwen panicked. "Nay, Majesty, please. 'Tis not necessary."

Edward stood and smiled down at her. He was tall, though not quite as tall as Richard, and lean. His face was almost boyish in its handsomeness.

"Ah, are you afraid of my fierce-looking friend, my dear?" He raised her hand to his lips. "Never fear, Richard is tame enough with the lasses. He'll not harm you."

The room seemed deathly quiet when her father and King Edward were gone. The fire crackled and the wind whispered against the stone outside.

She knew when Richard rose from his chair. He had the quiet grace of a cat, but the chair creaked beneath his weight as he stood.

He stopped beside her and she slanted her eyes toward him without turning to face him. He shifted his weight and she let her gaze trail down the long leg that was thrust to one side.

"Why were you afraid to be alone with me, Princess?"

She didn't answer and he leaned toward her until his face was scant inches from hers.

"Afraid you couldn't control yourself, sweet?"

Gwen whirled on him. "If not for the wine, as you pointed out, I would have never allowed you to touch me!"

He grabbed her hand and pressed it to his chest. Gwen gasped and tried to jerk away, but he held her fast. Even through the layers of his clothing, his skin seared her palm.

"Yes, but what made you touch me, sweet? Do you blame that on the wine too?"

Gwen succeeded in wresting her hand free of his grip. She wiped it very deliberately on her dress.

His jaw hardened and he swept her from head to toe with an infuriating glare. "Let me make something perfectly clear to you, Princess. I don't really care how many men you've had before now, but there had better be no more. If you come to me pregnant, I'll pack you off to a convent. I'll not accept another man's brat as my heir."

Gwen's mouth dropped open. "You think I—you mean that—"

He arched an arrogant eyebrow. "I've bedded enough women to recognize desire when I see it, sweet. 'Tis not the sort of thing one sees in an innocent young virgin, at least not so quickly."

Gwen felt a rush of anger so strong it almost blinded her. She didn't even think before reacting. All she heard was the crack of her open palm against his cheek.

And then she was jerked against his body, hard. She looked up at him, unable to tear her gaze away. God, he was so intimidating!

The hard planes of his face seemed chiseled from stone. Black brows drew together over eyes that reminded her of a frozen mountain lake, eyes that bored into hers relentlessly.

Good Lord, *this* man was Black Hawk. What had she done?

Gwen bit her lower lip to cease its trembling.

"I hope you enjoyed that, because you will never do it again, I assure you," he said, his voice washing over her like cool silk. His gaze settled on her mouth and Gwen felt a strange shiver ripple down her spine.

"Did you think of me often this past year?" he asked softly.

"Never!" She tried to jerk away, but it was as if she'd never moved.

"Liar," he whispered.

"Let me go!"

"Not yet, sweet. We have unfinished business, you and I."

Gwen's breath caught as his arm encircled her waist and he pulled her tighter against him. The fury that clouded his features was melting, changing into something even more frightening.

She felt light-headed, dizzy with the speed of her reckless heart, and when his head descended to crush her mouth beneath his, her eyes closed in anticipation.

At the last minute, she clamped her mouth tight against his probing tongue. He let go of her wrists and cupped her head in one large hand.

Gwen's heart hammered in her breast, filling her ears with the sound of her own blood rushing through her veins. The smell of leather and steel, of sweat and horses, of raw power held tightly in check came strongly to her nostrils.

This was nothing like the time when Rhys had kissed her. That had seemed so harmless, so friendly, compared to this.

Suddenly, Gwen wanted to taste the man kissing her, to experience what he was doing. It couldn't hurt, could it?

She softened, melting against him, and his response was immediate. The kiss changed, became less demanding, more seductive. Running his tongue along her lower lip, he nibbled, then sucked it like a sweet. With each soft tug, there was an answering surge of fire in her veins.

When he stopped, Gwen opened her eyes to find him staring down at her.

His eyes were incredible! Moments before, they'd been the color of slate, but now they were almost black.

"Kiss me, Princess," he murmured. Slowly, he lowered his head and slanted his mouth across hers. She opened. The tip of his tongue slipped between her lips, searching, stroking.

Gwen's tongue touched his cautiously. He delved deeper and she mimicked his practised movements, stroking, teasing, tantalizing.

A fire born of his touch kindled in her belly, pulsating, spreading outward and racing along her limbs in a torrent of shivers. She sucked his tongue deeper, tasting him, wanting—what?

Her hands entwined in his dark hair, reveling in the velvety crispness of it. She pressed against him, shock coursing through her at the much harder part of him that pressed into her abdomen.

He groaned, his breathing quickening. Strong hands traced a path of fire down her back, grasping her buttocks and pulling her against the marble hardness of his erection.

She stiffened. Dear God, what was she doing? Another minute and she would prove herself no better than the whore he'd marked her for.

A cry rose low in her throat and she gripped the solid expanse of his upper arms, trying to push away.

Richard lifted his head. "Don't worry, no one will come in here. We're quite safe for about an hour. I would certainly like more time, but that will do for now…"

He buried his lips against the slender column of her throat. He'd never expected her response to send him into such a frenzy of need. But she tasted so sweet, like clover and wild honey, and he wanted her beneath him so he could taste the rest of her.

And he intended to do just that.

"No!" she cried, twisting in his grasp, pushing against him. "Let me go! *Please!*"

Richard marshaled every drop of willpower he possessed to release her. What kind of game was the little wench playing?

She moved to put the table between them. He stared at her, torn between desire and anger. God's bones, she was beautiful! Her face was flushed, her lips swollen from his kisses, her hair in glorious disarray.

Richard ignored the insistent throbbing of his manhood. He let anger take over. "What's the matter, Princess? Afraid you might enjoy it?"

"May you rot in hell, Black Hawk de Claiborne! I will never enjoy *anything* with you! Being your wife will be like never waking from my worst nightmares!"

Richard leaned against the table. "And what makes you think being your husband will be any more of a treat for me? Marrying a Welsh whore is not my idea of a dream come true."

Gwen turned purple. "You—you—vile, disgusting, murdering—"

Before she could discern his intent, he reached across the table and grabbed the front of her gown. He dragged her toward him until she found herself on her back with him leaning over her.

"So full of fire. Did I fail to tell you that I will enjoy you very much when we are in bed together?" His gaze traveled over her breasts and down her belly. "And I can promise that you will enjoy it too."

"Never!"

He brushed his lips across hers. Gwen trembled, despite herself. He did it again, soft, gentle. She watched his eyes darken, felt his hand slide up to mold her breast.

Again, he bent to her, his lips firmer this time. The protest she intended came out as a whimper. Her hands slipped up his arms.

And then he let her go. "Your body disagrees with you, my dear."

Gwen felt her cheeks flame. She hopped from the table and smoothed her gown, refusing to look at him, to meet his mocking stare.

She barely had time to compose herself before he grabbed her hand and led her to the adjoining solar.

Her father and King Edward looked up. Gwen stared at her feet. She'd never been so humiliated in her life. She glanced at the arrogant man next to her. At least she would have a lifetime to pay him back.

Wales, 1281

Prince Llywelyn was in a rage. He sat in the Great Hall of his stronghold on Snowdon and listened as his subjects presented grievance after grievance against the English crown.

Welshmen were being forced to answer to laws and customs that were totally foreign to them. Men were fined heavily for crimes they did not commit. Their woods were cut and timber taken without recompense. Their lands were confiscated and given to English lords.

Merchants were made to sell their goods at the prices the English wanted to pay. If they refused, their goods were seized and the men thrown in jail.

English forest laws were so strict that families could lose everything they had by hunting game in the King's woods. But if they didn't hunt, they would starve.

Llywelyn got to his feet and stalked to his solar. Einion limped behind him. Llywelyn poured a large draught of mead and tossed it back in one swift gulp.

"What are you going to do?" Einion asked.

Llywelyn poured another mead and flopped in a chair. Even though he was more than fifty years old, he hung one leg over the arm and leaned back. "What can I do? Edward has me right where he wants me. 'Tis been over three years and he still stalls on my case against Gruffydd ap Gwenwynwyn."

"I hate to say this, Llywelyn, but witholding Gwenllian hasn't helped. God knows I love that lass as if she were my own, but keeping her from marrying that damned De Claiborne is only hurting you."

Llywelyn laughed mirthlessly. "Aye. When I applied to the Pope for intervention, I'd thought it would be so easy. At the very least, I thought witholding Gwen would make Edward rule on Arwystli! And I had hoped that hothead de Claiborne would've talked Edward into striking by now. Then the Pope would have had no choice but to rule in my favor. Christ Almighty! Since Pope Martin died I've not looked forward to starting over with his successor."

"Black Hawk de Claiborne struck all right. His grip on the border is tighter than ever."

"You know I do not approve of raiding the English. 'Tis pointless. A thousand small struggles will not do what one large effort possibly could. If the clans choose to confront Black Hawk on his territory, then they are fools!"

"But what about the territory he's seized from you lately? Even now, he sits within spitting distance of Snowdon."

Llywelyn ground his teeth together. "I'll get my lands back from the bastard even if I have to face him myself!"

Einion frowned. "I think that's what he wants. And you're not as young as you once were, Llywelyn."

Llywelyn grumbled. Einion was right. He was too old. Black Hawk de Claiborne would hack him to bits on the battlefield.

He stroked the arm of the chair. "I've complained to Edward, but he turns a blind eye. Says he's unaware of any wrongdoing by his Marcher lords."

Einion snorted. "Did you expect him to say any different? De Claiborne is his favorite by all accounts. Edward would let him get away with nearly anything." Einion came to stand in front of him, his old face screwed into a grimace. "You must do something, Llywelyn. 'Tis more than just Black Hawk that's causing trouble. Edward's bailiffs are harassing our people. And Rhuddlan is the worst insult yet!"

Llywelyn's temples hammered. "I know."

"An English town on Welsh soil! And no Welsh even allowed to settle in it! 'Tis gone too far."

"One day, we'll have justice, I promise you. But, for now, I will write to Edward and give him Gwenllian before it gets worse."

"I will send for a scribe."

Llywelyn lay his head back and stared at the ceiling. God's bones, he'd wanted an alliance with Scotland! Well, it was not to be and he would have to find another way to keep Edward at bay.

He swore softly. The Earl of Dunsmore had plagued him for years, first the father, now the son.

With the son, it was almost an obsession.

"A messenger from the King, milord."

Richard looked up from the map he'd been studying. "Bring him."

The knight nodded. Richard stood and walked to the edge of the open pavillion. The canopy swayed in the soft summer breeze, and the haunting scent of roses drifted to his nostrils.

He gazed out across the green meadow. Dandelions and buttercups dotted the grass, vibrant life blazing against a shimmering emerald sea.

And, at the foot of the hill he was encamped upon, roses. Everywhere, roses. They ambled in a thick tangle of prickly vines, choking the hedges, snaking up trees, twisting, grasping, scenting the air with their sweet perfume.

Unforgettable. Just like her. Three goddamn years and he still couldn't get her out of his mind! Why in the hell had he chosen this site for his camp anyway?

The messenger hurried toward the tent on the heels of the knight. He dropped to one knee. "My Lord de Claiborne," he said. "His Majesty sends his greetings."

The man was garbed in chainmail, three golden lions emblazoned on his blood-red surcoat. His face was streaked with grime, and mud dirtied the edges of his mantle. He stood and pulled a sealed parchment from inside his tunic. "The king commanded that I give this into no hands but yours."

Richard took the document and split the royal seal with his dagger. He sank into the chair and spread the paper on top of the forgotten maps.

Jesú, after all this time, he'd never expected it to end so simply!

He raised his head and let his gaze wander through the camp. They'd not had a fight in weeks. The knights lounged on the grass, laughing and drinking. The destriers were tethered under a stand of trees, munching grass contentedly. Squires played mock games of battle, and the women who inevitably attached themselves to traveling knights were doing what they usually did: relieving the men of pent up sexual energy.

Richard thought of his flame-haired princess. God, how he wished he'd never kissed her. One touch of her lips, one brief taste of her honeyed sweetness, and he was drugged.

He dreamt of her.

Often.

He dreamt of her beneath him, sprawling and wild and hot. He dreamt of easing inside her body, dreamt of her clinging and moaning and writhing. He dreamt of her until he woke, hard and aching, and took whatever woman he'd bedded the night before.

Perhaps that was the reason he'd fought Llywelyn's treachery. Perhaps he only wanted to taste her again. Perhaps he wanted it even more than he wanted to thwart her father.

He raked a hand through his hair. What the hell was wrong with him? He had never wanted to marry her in the first place, and now he could think of nothing else.

"Are we going to war, milord?" the knight asked.

"Nay, Edgar." He stood and folded the parchment before tucking it inside his tunic. "Llywelyn yields."

G wen knew she would dream of Richard. It was inevitable, as it had been almost every night for the last three years. Leaving the bed hangings open, she settled into the mattress, reassured by the dim glow of the fire.

She would never admit to anyone that she was frightened of the dark. She had been ever since she was a little girl, ever since she began dreaming of things that came true.

Still, sleep claimed her easily enough, despite the fact she knew who awaited her…

A hand touched her arm and she opened her eyes. Richard lay beside her, his naked limbs entwined with hers beneath the covers.

"You are mine," he said, reaching out to caress her breast.

Fire leapt within her at his touch. "Yes, Richard, I am yours."

He kissed her and she gave herself up to the sweet sensations.

The dream changed.

"The honor will be yours, my love," Richard said, holding his sword out. She took it, then turned to see her victim.

Her father knelt before her, his head cradled on a block.

"Prove that you love me," Richard said.

Gwen raised the sword, then brought it down swiftly. The head dropped to the ground and rolled to her feet.

When she looked at Richard, King Edward stood beside him, holding a crimson leash.

The dream changed again.

Richard stood at the end of the bed where she lay. His armor gleamed in the flickering light of the night fire.

She opened her mouth to tell him to go away. "Lie with me, my lord."

He smiled, unbuckling the sword. "If you help me out of this armor, I will be there sooner."

She crawled to the end of the bed, the cool air raising goosebumps on her naked skin. He pulled at the golden chain attached to a collar around her neck and she found herself in his lap. He stroked her neck, her breasts, her belly, her mound of fiery curls. The roughness of his palm against her skin made her weak, and she laid her head on his broad shoulder.

"You were made for me, for this," he said, his mouth claiming hers in a savage kiss as he pressed her onto the bed. Her breasts were crushed against the hardness of his chest and her mons ached with the desire to have him touch her, to ease the yearning he created.

"Please," she begged.

"First you must tell me if you are virgin."

"I am!"

"I do not believe you."

He left her on the bed and stood once more, fully clothed, at the foot of it. She shivered as the air stirred over her.

He changed into a great hawk, and then she realized she was a hawk too. They were no longer in the bedroom, but soaring high over a green valley. The air was cold and exhilarating as her wings sliced through it.

Together they dove toward a lake, then checked their speed at the last minute to skirt along the top. His talons scooped into the water, lightening fast, and when they came out again, a fish wriggled in his grasp.

She heard his voice echoing in her mind. "You belong to me. Hawks mate for life."

The air felt like ice as they climbed higher and higher. Her teeth chattered.

Gwen jerked awake. The covers lay in a tangled heap at the foot of the bed and she yanked them up to cover her freezing body.

The closer the wedding got, the more intense the dreams became. They were ridiculous, really. She could never love *Gwalchddu*, never betray her father for him.

She went back to sleep, secure in the knowledge she had dreamed the impossible.

Dawn was a slash of seashell pink on the horizon. The color stretched up, fading to different hues of pink, then azure, then black. Stars still dotted the night sky high overhead. Soon, they would be gone, and the sun would command the sky in a blaze of light and color.

It was a perfect day for traveling.

Gwen stood on the walls of her father's keep, huddling into her cloak as she watched sunrise break over Snowdon one last time.

In the courtyard below, men moved about, readying everything for departure. She looked over the trunks fondly. There were at least twenty of them in all. They contained her clothes, linens, silver, and such family heirlooms as her father had chosen to give her over the years—the dragon brooch he'd given her mother, Eurwen's silver hairbrush, a jeweled goblet, and other lesser treasures.

Gwen also had her precious stores of scented soaps and oils, distilled from the mountain's bounty by her own hand. She and Elinor had spent many delightful days making them.

She cast one last longing look around her, then turned in a flurry of silk and wool, and walked resolutely into the castle.

"Gwen!" Elinor cried, hurrying to her side. "I didn't dare think you would try to sneak off without saying goodbye."

Gwen's smile trembled. "Nay, I would not leave without bidding you farewell, dearest Elinor."

Elinor hugged and kissed her, fussing and imparting last words of advice. When Elinor stepped back, Gwen and her father eyed each other uneasily. She understood why he couldn't go with her, but it hurt nonetheless. Elinor's pregnancy was as precious as it was unexpected.

He cleared his throat and picked up her hand, pressing a parchment into it. "Give this to the king for me, lass," he said, holding her hand longer than necessary.

"I will not fail you, Father," she whispered.

"God keep you safe," he said gruffly.

Gwen wiped her eyes, then hurried into the courtyard where a party of fierce warriors waited to escort her to Shrewsbury.

Before they'd ridden very far, a man pulled up beside her.

"Rhys! I thought you'd forgotten me," she said, hurt and relieved all at once.

The morning sunlight shone on his golden locks like a halo. He smiled crookedly. It was a disarming look. "Not on your life, Your Highness."

"Why didn't you just say goodbye before I left?"

"Because I'm not saying goodbye yet."

Gwen could only stare at him. "What?"

"I am accompanying you to Shrewsbury."

Icy dread rose in her throat. "Nay, Rhys, you cannot! 'Tis not a sound idea. Richard is much too dangerous."

Rhys's eyes hardened. "Richard is it?"

Gwen retreated into the folds of her hood to hide her flush. "I am marrying him, Rhys. I imagine he'll expect me to call him by his name."

"No doubt," Rhys said dryly.

Gwen didn't answer. 'Twas the second time she'd ever allowed her betrothed's name to cross her lips. Richard. It rolled off her tongue so smoothly, like a silky caress. That was why she'd vowed not to say it, because it was too damn easy and it felt too damn good.

Regardless of what she told Rhys, she would not call her husband by his name. She would not do anything Richard de Claiborne expected her to do. That was something she had decided long ago. For years she'd tried and failed to please her father. She would not make an effort to please a man she didn't like.

"Please go back, Rhys. 'Twill only complicate things if you are with me."

"He doesn't know who I am. I'm just another one of your men. I won't let him hurt you, Gwen, you may rest assured on that."

She didn't tell him that she was more worried Richard would hurt him. Instead, she said coolly, "Won't you miss Rhonwen?"

He expelled his breath forcefully. "I have needs, Gwen."

"You said you loved me," Gwen accused. And all that time, Rhys had been wenching with the rest of her father's warriors. The knowledge shouldn't hurt, but it did.

"You're marrying another man! What did you expect me to do, stay celibate?"

"Nay," she said quietly.

Rhys sighed, slumping a little in the saddle. "I'm sorry you found us, Gwen."

Gwen colored. She'd gone looking for Rhys late one night when she'd had a bad dream. She didn't like to disturb Elinor and her father, and Alys hadn't been there when she woke.

And Rhys had been busy. She could still hear the woman's husky voice, still see the frantic shaking of the covers. She'd fled, and Rhys had caught up to her before she reached her room. He was half-naked, sweaty, smelling of perfume and another scent she'd not been able to identify.

She'd been surprised to find she was more angry than jealous. She'd immediately thought of Richard and the kiss they'd shared. The thought of Richard kissing other women like that made her stomach turn to ice.

"It's not important," Gwen said, then wondered whether she was answering Rhys or convincing herself she didn't care what Richard did.

Shrewsbury nestled on the banks of the Severn River where it looped into a horseshoe. Thatch-roofed houses crowded within its protective walls, and cattle grazed in the surrounding meadows, tended by young boys who napped beneath trees dressed in the last reds and golds of autumn.

The Welshmen joked about raiding the unsuspecting youths and spiriting the cattle away beneath the king of England's nose.

The town gates were thrown wide, welcoming all who had come to attend the grand wedding. The Welshmen grew silent as the crowd parted to make way for them. They closed ranks around Gwen and glared menacingly at the curious onlookers, their hands falling to their spears. The low murmur of the crowd was barely discernable as people cupped hands to mouths and pointed urgently.

'Twas not the first time Gwen had seen a town, but as always, it struck her oddly. Her father and some of his lords had built castles like those of their English neighbors, but most of the Welsh people lived in concealed homes high above the valleys. Nomads, they had lived that way for centuries, tending their herds of sheep and cattle.

These English, on the other hand, built huts of wattle and daub that looked cold and dank. In bigger towns like Shrewsbury, many of the houses were more than one story and framed in timber.

The road twisted once inside the walls, passing between shops whose hanging signs proclaimed their trade. Shopkeepers leaned out windows, crying their goods to the jostling mass of people. The party rode past a tavern and Gwen heard music drifting from within before harsh laughter drowned out the harp's lilting strains.

Shrewsbury Castle sat at the center of town. It was big, though nothing to compare to Windsor. A thirty-foot high curtain wall ringed the stone keep. Imposing towers glared at the town below, their surfaces pierced with arrow slots at varying heights.

Men walked along the battlements, the chinking of their armor carrying on the wind. A crimson banner with three golden lions snapped in the breeze over the turrets.

They rode beneath the archway and into the outer bailey. Knights practised in the lists as men and women hurried between the outbuildings. Dull pounding came from the armory and the smithy, and the mews rang with falcons' cries.

Extra kitchens had been set up to accomodate the large feast, and an old woman tended the livestock waiting to be slaughtered.

Passing into the inner bailey, Gwen surveyed the scene. Although the castle had to be aware of her arrival, there was no welcoming party fit for a princess. It was just another insult in a long string of English outrages. The Welshmen came to a halt at Gwen's signal.

"Highness," a young girl greeted her, bobbing in a mock curtsy. "The king and queen regret they could not welcome you personally, as the queen is ill. I am to show you to your room."

"Where is the chamberlain then?"

"He is occupied with other guests," she replied, her eyes darting over the fierce-looking men encircling Gwen in stony silence.

Furious looks passed between the Welshmen, and Gwen raised a gloved hand to silence the protests before they could be uttered.

Lord, even the servants felt they were superior to the Welsh!

She had tried to forget the malice the English people displayed four years ago when she rode to Windsor. England had just been the victor in a bloody war with the Welsh, and mayhap tempers had still been high.

But four years of relative peace did not seem to have dampened the hostility.

"Did the king instruct him to ignore me so?"

"N-nay."

"You may tell the chamberlain I shall speak to the king about this."

The girl swallowed and nodded.

"Lord de Claiborne might not be so understanding either," she added as she slid from her palfrey's back. She doubted Richard would care one way or the other, given his opinion of her, but she knew his name would cause a stir.

As expected, the girl paled slightly.

Gwen turned to her men. "Do not allow yourselves to be provoked by these English dogs," she said in Welsh. "Send for me if you have trouble."

"I will accompany you, Highness," Rhys said, swinging a leg across his horse's back to dismount.

"Nay! You will go with the others, Rhys ap Gawain. I will summon you if I have need of you."

He stopped with his leg in mid-air, and she returned his look with a frosty glare.

"As you command, Highness," he said curtly, settling himself on his horse.

Gwen swept up her cloak and turned to follow the girl. Alys hobbled quietly behind.

When Gwen entered the room behind the servant, her breath caught. There was no insult apparent here.

"'Tis to be the nuptial chamber," the girl said.

Tapestries blanketed the walls, some woven, some painted sendal-silk. The floor was strewn with sweet rushes, scented with cowslip and marjoram and cotsmary. A fire blazed in the hearth, throwing shadows over the canopied bed.

The bed. Gwen swallowed. It was huge and hung with royal blue velvet trimmed with gold tassels. And she was going to share it...

She turned away. Two chairs, carved and also cushioned with velvet, sat next to a polished oak table. A narrow window pierced the wall in the center, lined with thick glass rather than shutters. A seat was cut in the stone beneath the window, piled high with plump pillows.

"That will be all," Gwen said, dismissing the servant without looking at her.

"Your Highness," she mumbled, sinking to the floor this time, before she rose and hastened from the room.

"'Tis an outrage!" Alys burst out. "To treat a royal princess so—that chamberlain should have his insolent neck stretched!"

Gwen sighed. "'Tis no use getting upset, Alys. No doubt he feels that the lowliest knight outranks a Welsh princess. I am much more concerned about the men staying out of trouble."

"Oh, I think they will manage," Alys said, her red face twisted in a scowl. "I had better see to the unloading of your trunk. No telling what these curs might do with it. Can I get you anything first?"

"Nay. Thank you, Alys," Gwen replied, sinking into one of the soft chairs. Alys rubbed a hand across her backside, mumbling to herself as she walked out the door. Gwen smiled and shook her head. She removed her gloves, then pulled the cord from her hair, shaking the mass free of the confining braid.

Sweet Mary, she'd not been here half an hour and this place was already working on her frayed nerves. Damn English bastards! She would not let them beat her down. She was a princess. She was Llywelyn ap Gruffydd's daughter!

"Gwenllian?"

She vaulted to her feet. "Majesty," she said, sinking low.

Edward hurried over and reached out a lean hand to raise her. "Nay, no need to bother with the formalities in private," he said, flashing his teeth in a boyish grin.

"Thank you, Majesty," Gwen replied, lowering her lashes at the intensity of his blue stare. She didn't flinch when his hand brushed her cheek.

"I brought you something," he said softly. He held out a small basket. "'Tis from Eleanor. The journey from Windsor has made her ill in her condition, I'm afraid, and she regrets she could not give these to you herself."

"'Tis very kind, Majesty," Gwen said, peering at the two orange spheres. "Forgive me—I do not know what they are."

"Nay, 'tis you who must forgive me. I am so used to having oranges around that I did not think you wouldn't know of them."

"Oranges?"

"Aye. They come from Castile, Eleanor's home. She was but a child when she came to be my bride and she missed Spain so much. 'Tis expensive to import them, but it makes her happy."

Gwen stared at them. "How do you—?"

"I will show you," Edward said, smiling. He led her to the windowseat and urged her to sit next to him. With his dagger, he scored the skin of the orange. Slowly, he pulled the dimpled covering back to reveal the smooth columns of fruit. A spicy smell wafted to Gwen's nostrils and she realized her mouth was watering.

"Close your eyes and open your mouth," Edward said, breaking off a wedge. "Now," he urged.

Gwen bit down. Sweet and sour flooded over her tongue as juice spilled from the tangy fruit, some of it dripping down her chin.

Edward grabbed her wrist as she started to wipe it away. Her eyes flew open to find him staring at her.

With the corner of his tunic, he gently wiped her face, then held up the rest of the slice. Gwen hesitated, opening as he nodded. She jumped when his fingers grazed her lower lip.

"You have grown into a beautiful woman, Gwen," he said, his eyes following the curve of her bosom. He slid closer until his thigh brushed against hers. Smoothing the hair back from her face, he said, "You were always a pretty girl, but now—" He left the sentence hanging as his gaze again flickered over her breasts. "Eleanor is so often with child…"

And then the King of England was kissing her.

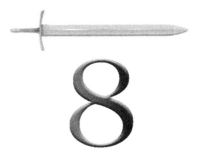

R ichard rode into the bailey of Shrewsbury castle with twenty knights behind him. The chamberlain hurried forward as Richard dismounted.

"My Lord de Claiborne," he said, bowing low. "I hope you are not offended, but I-I was truly busy with other guests when she arrived. I did not slight her!"

Richard stared at the man's balding head, bent low in supplication. "Slight who?"

The chamberlain jerked back. He swallowed hard. A tentative smile brightened his cloudy face. "Your bride, milord. She—"

"She is here?"

The man nodded. "Aye. I thought you knew. She only preceded you by a quarter-hour. I put her in the nuptial chamber, but I did not mean to —"

Richard heard no more. He entered the castle and made his way toward the stairs and the upper chambers. He'd been to Shrewsbury castle so many times that he knew where he was going without asking for directions.

He didn't know why he suddenly had to see her, but he could not have stopped even if he wanted. Three years. Was she still beautiful? Was she everything his mind conjured?

God, he thought of her too much, wanted her too much. Finally, he would see her again and prove to himself that she was only a woman like any other. She did not possess a strange kind of power over him.

The door wasn't fully closed when he reached it. He thought about knocking, but shoved it open before he could do it. She was as much his property, or soon would be, as his horse or his castle. And though it wasn't her fault, he supposed he was angry at her for occupying his thoughts so often.

It was just as well he hadn't knocked.

The little whore was sprawling in the king's arms. Cold fury engulfed him as the world seemed to lose focus for a breathless minute.

"Should I come back later?" Richard asked mildly. It took great effort to keep his voice calm. His bride flinched.

Edward raised his head. "Richard," he acknowledged with cool superiority. "I did not expect you until tomorrow."

"I can see that, my liege."

Edward sighed and stood up. He handed Gwen the peeled orange, then bent to kiss her on the cheek. "Another time perhaps," he murmured.

Gwen scrambled upright and smoothed her gown with shaking hands. Thank God it was over, but why did it have to be Richard who stopped it?

He was glaring at her, his look one of intense hatred. Anger radiated from him, charged the air between them. She could see it in the set of his shoulders, the glint of his flinty eyes, the hard line of his jaw.

Oh yes, he was in a fine rage, and she'd just confirmed every low opinion he ever had of her.

Despite everything, she couldn't help but think how much she'd longed to see him again. He looked the same. No, not the same. Better.

His black hair and beard emphasized the bronze of his skin. He was dark and forbidding in his crimson surcoat with the black hawk emblazoned on his breast. Her gaze darted between him and the King. Edward was tall, nicknamed Longshanks for his height in the saddle, but Richard topped him by a good two inches.

She couldn't keep her eyes off her betrothed, no matter how hard she tried. There could be no doubt he blamed her over this. She wasn't sure why that upset her, but it did. She tilted her chin up and met his stare evenly, refusing to balk beneath his icy regard.

He fingered the hilt of his sword. "Don't let me interrupt you. I can wait outside if you like."

"Come now, do not be angry, Richard. 'Twould not be the first time you and I have shared a woman."

"Nay, but lemans are not quite the same as wives." He looked at Gwen disdainfully. "Then again, when the wife is Welsh…"

Edward smiled. "Aye, Welshwomen are known to be, ah, free with their favors, aren't they?"

Gwen nearly choked on the rage that rose in her throat like bile. She was on her feet instantly, a torrent of Welsh unleashed as she cursed them both with all the eloquence Rhys had taught her.

The king's head cocked to one side. Richard crossed his arms over his chest and listened intently, as if he could figure out what she was saying merely by paying close attention.

Gwen relished telling them exactly what she thought of them in a language they didn't understand, questioning their parentage, their entire ancestry, and their manhood to their arrogant faces.

When she finished, she crossed her arms in a smug imitation of Richard and thrust her nose in the air.

Edward turned to Richard. "What did she say?"

Richard brushed off the sleeve of his tunic. "Many things, Ned, not the least of which was an insult to our manhood. And very colorful, I might add. I would never have imagined such words could cross those delicate lips."

Gwen gaped at him. "Why didn't you stop me?" she demanded in Welsh.

"It was such a pretty speech, I had not the heart," he replied in kind. He smiled, but it didn't reach his eyes.

Gwen swallowed. It was so odd to hear her language on his lips, and yet it seemed so natural, like he had been born to speak it.

Edward laughed. "The lass has spirit, I'll give her that. Probably every bit as stubborn as that old goat Llywelyn, too. What is this news your father promised to send me, sweet?"

Gwen was glad for the distraction just then. She pulled out the letter and handed it to the king.

Edward glanced at the dragon seal, then split it with his forefinger, and unfolded the parchment. He read it quickly, chuckles deepening into laughter as he crumpled it in his fist.

"The randy old goat has gotten my cousin with child," Edward said when the laughter subsided. "Jesú, he has the luck of the devil."

A muscle in Richard's jaw began to tic.

Edward took Gwen's hand and raised it to his lips. "I will give you away in your father's place, sweet princess. Come, Richard. We have much to discuss," he said, releasing her to cross to the door.

Gwen forced her face into a stony countenance when Richard came to stand in front of her.

"I will deal with you later," he said, the softness of his voice a sharp contrast to the hardness of the words.

A wave of fear crashed through her as her eyes swept over him. Elinor had told her that Englishmen could beat their wives. God, he was huge and powerful—he could kill her!

He whirled around and followed the King.

Gwen sank wearily into the windowseat, staring at the orange. 'Twas beginning to get sticky.

Richard de Claiborne was in a dangerous mood. He'd lost count of the number of times his cup had been refilled by the saucy serving wench who even now leered at him from another man's lap. He ignored the invitation, raising his cup to drain it before slamming it onto the wooden table.

'Twas ale he drank this night. Not fine wine, suitable to his station as the King's most trusted advisor, but ale, coarse, bitter, common. Around him, knights and men-at-arms reveled in their debauchery, oblivious to the Earl of Dunsmore's presence. Harsh laughter rang through the air unchecked, mingling with the shrill voices of the serving women.

Oft times he would rather drink with these men than the pompous lords of the realm. It reminded him of the days of his youth, before the Crusade and his elevation to great power.

Power was only achieved at tremendous risk and at first he'd had to be careful, to constantly watch for the jealous lords who sought to tumble him from his perch. Few challenged him these days, however. His reputation for ferocity was unequalled among Edward's barons. When he drank with these men, he could forget who he was for a while.

The girl appeared at his elbow once more, pouring ale into his empty cup. Her long hair had been braided, but as the night wore on had fallen loose, and when it fell across his arm as she leaned forward, he touched it. 'Twas almost red in the glittering torchlight.

"Ye can fondle more than that if ye likes, milord," she said, thrusting her abundant cleavage in his face. Her eyes were bright, her tongue sliding across her bottom lip suggestively.

"And what will you do for me?"

"I can pleasure ye greatly, milord." The girl fairly panted with anticipation. Richard knew the things that were whispered about him, the things that made common serving wenches and noble ladies throw themselves at him with delightful regularity.

He struggled to pull the two images standing before him into one. He tried to imagine himself buried within her, and could not. His body burned for a woman, but only for one woman in particular; a woman as deceitful and immoral as she was beautiful. Llywelyn's daughter.

"Not tonight, wench."

He lifted his mug and took a long drink. Why should it even bother him that he'd found her in Ned's arms? Had he expected any less of her?

Jesú, she was to be his wife in two days and he'd found her seducing the king! Not that he could blame Ned for succumbing to her charms. Gwen had become a very desirable woman, just as Richard had known she would.

Not even his hottest dreams had prepared him for the reality of seeing her again.

She was as exquisite as the first rose in spring. Her body had ripened until all the girlish edges filled out. She was small, but she possessed an abundance of curves that could please any man. He couldn't help but notice the way her breasts thrust upward against the wool of her traveling clothes. He was certain they were full and firm. He'd ached to touch them and find out.

Her scent had stolen to him when he'd stood next to her. Wind and water and mountain heather. And roses, always those damn roses. Would she taste as good as she smelled?

His throat tightened.

And her voice. From the first, he'd thought it sweet and musical, but now it was the sort of voice that dared a man to dream of illicit passion, erotic delights, nights of steamy lovemaking. Husky, breathless.

Richard's knuckles whitened as he gripped the mug. He remembered the last report he'd gotten from the Welsh court.

Princess Gwenllian has a lover. His name is Rhys ap Gawain.

Richard tossed back the remaining contents of his cup, swirling the bitter liquid in his mouth before swallowing it. He shook his head as the serving wench came forward. His stomach roiled from too much drink and too little food.

"'Tis no shame to stop now, milord. If I was you, I'd be saving me strength for the nuptial chamber."

Richard turned to his captain. The burly man's face split into a grin. His mane of brown hair was unkempt, sprouting wildly in all directions, and Richard thought suddenly of the shaggy lions that Ned kept in the royal menagerie. Even the man's toothy smile looked like a lion's.

Richard leaned back and crossed his arms. "Indeed, Andrew?"

"Aye. Had me a good look at that pretty little princess today. Right lusty if ye ask me. I'd say ye got yer work cut out for you with that one. And if I know you, milord, ye'll not let her out of bed fer a fortnight!"

Several men sitting nearby guffawed. Bawdy suggestions were tossed around. One man grabbed a wench and began to demonstrate before she soundly punched him in the ear. Laughter erupted as he yelped and dumped her in the rushes.

The girl scrambled to her feet, red-faced and cursing, and retreated to stand by the wall.

"Don't you know how to please a woman yet, Edgar?" Richard asked, pushing himself to his feet. He swayed but a moment, then walked slowly to the girl. Her eyes lit up as he extended his hand. Richard looked at the eager crowd.

"First," he drawled, "you must get her in your arms—willingly, Edgar." The men roared. "Next, you must kiss her like she's never been kissed before—or at least you must make her believe she's never been kissed like it before."

He bent to place his lips on hers. The room rocked with cheers. Richard kissed her until she went slack in his arms. The girl clung to him for a full minute, staring up at him dreamily, before she let go.

Men patted each other on the back, laughing. Money exchanged hands. Edgar was mercilessly teased.

The wench was not unattractive and Richard desired to bed her, to prove he still could, but his body would not cooperate. He took a deep, cleansing breath.

"Now, Edgar, if you think you can continue where I left off, I'll leave the bedding of this wench to you. As the captain of my guards so thoughtfully pointed out, I must save myself for my wedding night!"

"To Richard de Claiborne, Earl of Dunsmore!" Andrew yelled, raising his mug.

"To Richard de Claiborne, Earl of Dunsmore!" the men echoed, cups raised in unison. "To good health and a stiff prick!" they cried as he strode from the room.

Richard knew exactly where he was going. He wanted his fiery Welsh princess now, tonight. He was consumed with her. Why deny himself? Gwen was no innocent and he would wait no longer.

9

Gwen awoke to the soft rushing sound of water being poured. She lifted her hand and brushed the curtain of hair from her face. A tart smell assailed her nostrils and she realized it was the dried juice of the orange. She had fallen asleep in the windowseat.

"Your bath is almost ready, Your Highness," Alys sang out. She fussed at a steady stream of youngsters who were emptying pails of steaming water into a tub. When the task was finished, she hurried them out the door and came to help Gwen undress.

"How long have I been sleeping, Alys?"

"'Tis well past dinner, but I brought you a tray."

"Jesú! The men—"

"Are fine," Alys finished. "They've been quartered with Lord de Claiborne's knights. I've heard he's threatened his men with beatings if any of 'em so much as blink wrong at a Welshman."

Gwen sank into the tub. She didn't believe it for a minute. "Still, I should send a message to Rhys. Make sure all is truly well."

Alys unstoppered a bottle and dribbled a few drops of precious scented oil across the surface of the water. "I will see to it, Highness."

Gwen breathed deeply the smells of Wales. "Nay, Alys, you are making me feel rotten. I've been sleeping like a lazy cat and you've not had a rest. Please, go to bed. I'll find a page as soon as I've finished bathing."

"I am fine, Highness."

"We're alone now. You don't have to call me that."

"I will see you treated properly whilst we are here," Alys insisted.

Gwen knew better than to argue. She dictated a message and Alys went to find a servant. When she returned, she sank into a chair with a groan.

"Please go to bed, Alys."

The old woman waved her hand. "Nay, nay. I will sit with you until you are finished."

Gwen sighed and picked up the rose-scented soap. Already, this had been a hell of a day. Why had Richard chosen that exact time to come to her room? It disturbed her to realize she'd wanted to see him. Just not under those circumstances.

Gwen lathered herself vigorously, angered that she even cared what he thought. Her lips twitched in a smile. He'd know soon enough she was untouched. What would the mighty Black Hawk say then? She was going to enjoy making him take back his filthy words.

The water was beginning to cool when Gwen finally decided to rouse herself. Alys snored softly, her sewing sprawled across her lap.

Gwen reached for the large drying cloth that lay beside the tub. Wrapping it around her, she crossed to the table to examine the contents of the tray.

She had just finished the soup when she was startled by the insistent rap on the door. Alys jumped out of the chair, her needlework flying as she scurried through the antechamber to answer it.

Gwen frowned. Who would come at this hour?

Rhys! It would be just the sort of thing he would do. She should have sent the message to one of the other men. Any one of them would have had sense enough to send a reply rather than come in person.

All she needed was for Richard to catch her with another man in her chamber. He'd definitely kill her then.

Alys's voice rose desperately. "My lord, you cannot!"

Richard strode into the room, Alys bustling behind him. Gwen stood quickly, her pulse pounding in her ears as she clutched at the wet linen. She glanced with longing at her robe draped over the end of the bed.

Alys's face showed an indignant red. "Your Highness, he would not —"

"'Tis fine, Alys," Gwen said coolly, determined to keep the upper hand in this encounter. "I am certain Lord de Claiborne has pressing business if he needs to disturb us at this hour."

"You may leave us, old woman," Richard snapped.

Alys looked helpless.

Gwen wanted to slap his arrogant face. "I will be fine," she said. The iron gaze holding hers made her think otherwise, but she would not worry Alys. "Wait outside the door, would you please?"

The woman nodded and reluctantly left the room.

Gwen whirled on him. "How dare you come in here and treat Alys so rudely!"

He frowned. "She is important to you?"

"Aye."

"Then I will apologize to her."

Gwen gaped at him. Black Hawk de Claiborne apologizing to a Welsh maid? It hardly seemed believable. "What do you desire of me, my lord?"

Leather and steel stirred against one another as he walked toward her. Instinctively, she moved to keep the table between them, glancing at the sword strapped to his side.

He followed her and she had to will herself to stop. No matter how hard her insides shook, he'd not have the pleasure of knowing he intimidated her.

"Desire is an apt word," he said softly.

Gwen gripped the edge of the table for support. "Do state your business, my lord, and then leave me be. I am not your wife yet. You cannot order me around for another two days."

"You have changed, Gwen," he murmured, his gaze sliding down her body. "In more ways than one."

His breath fanned warmly across her face. Gwen started at the stale smell of ale. She noticed then that his striking silver eyes were slightly glazed, bloodshot.

"You are drunk, my lord."

"Aye, drunk," he agreed, picking up a tendril of damp hair and rubbing it between his fingers. "Drunk with desire."

He allowed his gaze to trace the hollow of her throat. Linen, still damp from her bath, clung seductively to the soft fullness of her breasts. He hardened with hot need.

Richard wanted to carry her to the bed and ravish her. He wouldn't though. He wanted to hear her admit she desired him too. He was going to seduce her.

He traced her jaw, her throat, the ivory skin above her towel. She stared at him warily. Her eyes were mesmerizing. She parted her lips, and he centered on them, remembering the feel of their dewy softness beneath his.

Three years since he'd kissed her. It seemed a lifetime.

In that moment, he knew he stood on the brink of madness with his desire for this woman.

"Did you enjoy Ned's kisses?" he growled, pulling her against his body, all thoughts of slow seduction suddenly gone. Unable to feel her softness through his mail, he groaned inwardly.

"Nay, I—"

"Did you wish him to make love to you?"

"I—"

"None but me will ever touch you. *Ever.* Do you understand?" he demanded, cupping her face between his hands. He did not wait for a reply. He had a sudden desperate need to erase the memory of any kiss but his from her mind.

Gwen opened her mouth to protest and his tongue slipped inside. She heard a soft sigh, and was surprised to realize it had come from her. She was no longer in control of her own body; she was clinging to him, meeting the eager thrusts of his tongue with urgency. It was as if she'd waited for this moment her entire life.

His arms wrapped around her, and he pressed her against him so hard that the steel rings of his mail bit into her flesh. Gwen barely noticed, a tide of conflicting emotions doing battle in her head.

She suppressed a whimper when his mouth found her earlobe. Liquid heat flowed through her, an incredible ache spreading from deep in her stomach to the apex of her thighs in one agonizing leap.

He kissed the hollow of her throat, then moved to the sensitive curve of her shoulder.

An inner voice screamed that she should stop him.

Now.

But she could not. The sweet sensations he was arousing made her bones melt, her legs tremble, her mons ache. She had lost her will to resist from the moment his mouth branded hers.

Her breath caught when he cupped her breasts, squeezing them as he pressed hot kisses along her shoulder. Firelight played across his dark head and she bit her lip, stifling an urge to bury her fingers in his hair.

He straightened, and she tilted her head back to look up at him. His face was a mask of fury and desire, and her heart lurched. She'd never known a man's passion could be so frightening and so breathtaking in its intensity.

"I have waited a long time for this," he murmured thickly.

Deliberately, his hands came up to linger on the top of her drying cloth. She felt the air rush in as he loosened it to slide down her breasts.

Gwen grabbed at the linen. "Nay!" she cried, backing away from him. She was not ready for this, not yet! She still had two days!

"Gwen," he said huskily, cradling her head in one large hand, "what is the harm of letting me taste your sweetness now? 'Tis only a couple of days until the wedding."

"No."

His voice was oddly mocking. "You would withhold from me what you were so willing to give the king?"

"'Tis not true!" She raised her hand to strike him.

"Not this time, wildcat." He caught her arm and propelled her toward him. The kiss was sweet, long, and wet.

Gwen forgot why she was angry. She couldn't think. Her blood stirred and she put her arms around his neck, giving herself over to his heady kisses.

She shivered, though not from cold, as he slowly pulled the cloth down. A distant part of her knew he was baring her body to his sight, but she no longer cared.

The towel slithered to the floor.

Gwen sucked in her breath as his calloused palms touched her bare breasts. His skilled fingers toyed with her nipples, the delicate peaks becoming taut and sensitive beyond belief.

What was the matter with her? She should be screaming at him, telling him to stop, to go away. But dear Lord, even in her dreams she'd never known such bliss was possible. She arched against him, not knowing she was applying pressure to the rigid flesh beneath his armor.

He groaned. "Yes, Gwen. God, yes!"

He dropped to his knees and pressed his lips to the hollow between her breasts, his hands splaying over her back and buttocks.

Gwen teetered between fear and pleasure. His mouth closed over her nipple and she cried out with the shock of it. The sensation was exquisite. Her fingers threaded through his hair.

And then he swept her into his arms, his lips fusing to hers as he carried her to the bed. Fear won the battle as she realized just exactly what he was about to do. He was big and savage and he thought her experienced. He would not be gentle.

"Stop!"

He stopped, one knee on the bed. "What is wrong?"

"I-I am not ready—I cannot—"

His eyes hardened. "You mean will not. Christ almighty, you're a goddamn tease!" He dropped her on the bed.

Gwen scrambled for her robe, her cheeks flaming. "Get out of my chamber!"

He smiled then, a feral, savage smile. "This will not be your chamber in two days. It will be ours. And nothing will save you on our wedding night."

She wrapped the robe tightly around her and climbed from the bed. "'Tis not yours yet, so get out," she snapped.

"Consider yourself lucky this night, Princess. I'll not take by force what you so willingly offered only minutes ago."

Gwen tilted her chin up and stared at him imperiously. "I never offered you anything."

His voice was deadly soft. "Do not make me prove the lie, Princess. You desire me, whether you admit it or not."

Damn the man! He was arrogant and insufferable beyond reason. And right, damn him. She was not about to admit it though. "I most certainly do not desire you, my lord."

He gripped her chin in an iron fist and crushed his mouth to hers. Gwen forgot to fight. She opened, moaning as his tongue stroked hers.

"Liar," he taunted.

Voices came from the antechamber. Welsh voices. Gwen's heart leapt to her throat as she recognized Rhys's. When she looked at Richard, his eyes were ablaze.

"Expecting a lover? 'Tis no wonder you wanted me to leave, sweet."

Rhys burst through the door. Gwen shook her head in warning. But she knew Rhys would not back down. He stared at her and Richard, missing nothing. She crossed her arms self-consciously as Rhys's gaze lingered on her silk-clad form.

One glance at her betrothed told her he had noticed too. And she knew a storm was brewing in that black heart, a storm of great power and violence.

She held out her hand in a desperate attempt to silence her childhood friend. "No, Rhys!"

"What has the bastard done to you, Gwen? I'll kill him if he's hurt you!"

Richard's face darkened. A muscle in his jaw started to tic.

"So, this is Rhys ap Gawain," Richard said in Welsh.

Rhys's eyes widened.

Richard swept her with a menacing glare. "You are braver than I thought, Princess, to bring your lover to your own wedding."

"Rhys is not my lover!"

He continued as if she'd never spoken. "'Tis sorry I am to disappoint you, sweet, but he cannot come to Claiborne castle. I may not have been the first, but I *will* be the last."

Rhys put a hand to the dagger at his waist. "If you've hurt her, I'll—"

"You'll what, boy?" It came out as a growl. Gwen shivered. Black Hawk de Claiborne was capable of horrible, brutal things. He would kill Rhys without the slightest provocation.

Gwen grabbed him as he started to move. "Please, my lord, I beg of you. Leave him alone."

"Why?"

"He means no harm. We grew up together. Rhys has always been protective of me."

"Do you love him?"

Gwen hesitated. "He is the brother I never had."

Richard didn't believe it for a minute. The golden-haired young man glared at him, his knuckles white on the hilt of his dagger. Hardly a brother.

But her eyes were luminous with unshed tears, her face hopeful and expectant. Her hair had started to dry and a stray tendril hung over her shoulder. It was like a flame against the sky-blue of her robe.

Richard longed to twirl it around his finger.

One tear trickled down her cheek. His blood ran cold. She'd defied him at every turn, angered him without regard to the penalties he could exact, but when her lover showed up, she became all weepy and submissive.

He started to set her aside, but she clung to him suddenly, one hand gripping his surcoat so hard he thought she'd rip it.

"Please don't kill him," she whispered.

Richard struggled with his temper for a long moment. She actually believed he would kill her lover. He wanted to, God how he wanted to! He took a deep breath. "Very well, I will honor your request, sweet. *This* time."

"Thank you, my lord."

She sagged against him, and his anger surged anew.

"If I catch him here again, I will not be so easily persuaded. Now get rid of him," he bit out.

Gwen wiped her hand across her eyes as she turned to Rhys. She used her most formal tone. "Rhys ap Gawain, you will go back to your quarters immediately. Do not disturb me again."

Rhys's blue eyes were murderous. "Gwen—"

"'Tis an order! Now, go!"

"Not until you tell me all is well."

"I am fine, Rhys. Please go," Gwen added softly.

Rhys bowed. "As you command, Highness." He shot a look of pure hatred at Richard before stalking from the room.

"It seems your chamber is a popular destination today," Richard said coldly. He stopped in the door where Alys stood pale and wide-eyed.

He raised her hand to his lips. "Forgive me, Alys. 'Tis your mistress's place to give you orders, not mine. I am sorry if I frightened you."

Gwen stood in shock for a long time after he'd gone. She'd never actually believed he would keep his word. Alys stared at the back of her hand and blushed.

A few minutes later, a clanking and scraping sounded outside the chamber. Alys went to investigate. Low voices came from the other side of the open door, then there was silence.

"What is it, Alys?"

"Guards, Highness. By order of Lord de Claiborne."

10

A lys's ruddy face contorted in a grimace. Gwen dropped the lock of hair she'd been furiously twisting and clasped her hands together.

"You'll ruin it if you don't stop," Alys said, hands on hips.

"It won't happen again." Gwen started twisting the end of her chemise. Two days had passed with alarming speed. Today she would become the wife of Black Hawk de Claiborne.

And tonight, he would make her his wife in deed as well as name. Tonight, she could not escape him.

Gwen shivered.

Alys worked in silence, twisting Gwen's curls around her fingers until small ringlets fell in a thick tangle of molten fire.

When she finished, Gwen stood. Alys nodded appreciatively at the way the white silk of the chemise clung to the soft curves of Gwen's body.

"Your handsome lord will certainly enjoy seeing you in that, Highness."

Gwen pouted even as she felt the color rising in her cheeks. Since Richard had kissed Alys's hand, the woman had nothing but praise for him. "Nay, Alys. The English completely strip the bride and groom before the bedding."

Alys's eyes widened. "Barbarians!"

Gwen nodded, pleased she knew something Alys did not. Elinor had explained *that* particular custom to her.

Alys helped her into a red silk undergown, buttoning the sleeves at her wrist. Next came a forest green overgown, embroidered with the red dragon of Wales. Fitted at the waist and bosom, the skirt draped softly over her hips, swaying seductively when she walked.

The long sleeves trailed almost to the floor and Alys knotted them to keep the velvet from getting soiled, then retrieved a golden girdle studded with precious gems. She wrapped it around Gwen's waist, arranging it so its gilded chains tinkled musically with every movement.

When Gwen had donned the jeweled slippers and flowing green mantle, Alys settled a golden circlet on her curls. "You are sure to take any man's breath away today, child. I wish your mother were here…"

Gwen swallowed. She gazed into the polished silver mirror the King had provided. Touching one of the crimson dragons emblazoned on the velvet gown, her fingers lingered over the fine needlework.

"'Tis just you and me, Alys," she said softly. "Like always."

The cathedral entrance was blocked from Gwen's sight as King Edward led her up the human path that magically cleared before them.

Onlookers thronged the grounds, waiting for a glimpse of the bride. Every man, woman, and child in Shrewsbury was here today, and others besides. 'Twas not often a town got to host a wedding for the highest nobility.

Leaden clouds blanketed the sky in misery. The wind was slight, but chilly. A lock of Gwen's hair lifted, fluttering across her face.

In the distance, she heard the lowing of cattle and the bleating of sheep. She focused on the cathedral. Stained-glass windows adorned the gray facade. The arch above the door was in the new Gothic style, suggesting the church had undergone a recent renovation.

Richard waited in the entryway, his face impassive. Gwen's feet felt like standing stones. She forced them to keep moving.

He extended his hand without a word. He did not smile, or lift an eyebrow, or show any emotion of any kind, and that disappointed her.

Perhaps she'd hoped for some sort of comfort from him, some sort of camaraderie. After all, neither of them wanted this marriage. She supposed he had every right to be sullen.

When their hands touched, a lightning bolt of sensation rippled along her nerve endings. She looked at him in surprise. If he'd felt it, he wasn't showing it.

His presence filled her senses. He wore crimson and black, as usual. The hawk device was embroidered over his heart and the great, jeweled sword was strapped to his hip.

He towered over her, and she schooled herself not to look up at him. Her face burned just remembering what had passed between them.

The bishop's voice droned in her ears and she let her mind wander. It didn't go far, just to the man beside her.

Who was this man called Black Hawk anyway? Standing next to him in this setting, it was almost hard to believe he was capable of the violence attributed to him. Why could he not be ugly, with a wart on the end of his nose and a fat belly to boot?

Mayhap evil always used beauty as a facade. If so, then this man was full of ugliness. Gwen closed her eyes.

His hand was warm on hers. He smelled of soap and spice and danger, always danger. When he spoke, his rich voice slid over her like a velvet caress.

From a great distance, she heard her name, but it was not Richard's voice that spoke it. Her eyes shot open.

"Princess Gwenllian?" the bishop was saying. "Your vows?"

The crowd murmured. Richard squeezed her hand. She looked up at him then. Fury masked his handsome features.

Gwen turned and stammered her vows. The noise of the crowd trickled off.

Richard accepted the ring the bishop handed him, then turned to her. His voice was clear, but Gwen sensed the hard edge of anger beneath the surface.

"With this ring I thee wed." He slid it over the tips of the first three fingers of her right hand. "And with my body I thee worship."

Gwen felt a chill ripple over her.

"And with all my worldly chattels I thee endow." He slid it onto the third finger of her left hand. "In the Name of the Father and of the Son and of the Holy Spirit, Amen."

She tilted her face up to accept his kiss. The contact was brief, but at the last moment his tongue darted over her lower lip. Gwen shuddered.

The horde of onlookers cheered.

Richard led her into the church for the nuptial mass. They knelt side by side before the bishop as the gathered nobles filed in behind them.

The air was cooler inside the cathedral than out. The vaulted chamber soared high overhead. The sounds of people shuffling in and talking quietly rose to become a dull humming. The light of thousands of candles flickered, seeming lifelike in their joyful dancing. Despite whatever recent work had been done, the church still smelled old. Not musty exactly, just old, as if the air was subdued by the solemn stones surrounding it.

A hush fell over the gathering as the bishop began to speak. His voice rose, distinct and clear, to float disembodied over the crowd.

Gwen slanted a look at her husband from beneath her lowered lashes. His face seemed carved from a block of stone, the short beard doing little to soften the chiseled angles. She caught herself thinking she was glad it didn't cover half his face. Instead, it hugged his jawline, emphasizing the rough masculinity that was his alone.

His midnight hair shone blue-black in the candlelight. Gwen remembered the feel of it between her fingers. Soft. Crisp. Velvet. It was shorter than most men's, not even reaching his shoulders, but she found she liked that too.

It occured to her that his profile did indeed resemble the hawk he was called after. Fierce, proud, and noble.

Her stomach fluttered. For a moment, she felt like the young girl who had been smitten with the handsome knight. And, if she dared admit it, this was exactly what she had wanted back then.

But that was so long ago, and he was not who she'd thought he was. She felt a little pang of remorse for her lost dreams.

Her gaze trailed down his body to his hand. It hung at his side, motionless. Gwen shivered. It was powerful, containing the strength to choke the breath from her if he so wished it.

And yet it was beautiful. Well-shaped from large palm to tapered fingers, sinews capable of great strength now lay still in silent supplication to God.

Gwen knew the feel of his hands already. Knew the palms, calloused from battle and strenuous training. Knew the smooth fingertips, capable of eliciting pleasure where she had never experienced it before. She blushed and glanced at his face.

He was watching her. One corner of his mouth quirked in a mocking grin. She jerked her gaze away, staring at the floor and cursing herself for getting caught.

When at last the mass was over, Richard stood and then bent to help her up. His hand clamped over her elbow and when he raised her, he pulled her to him.

"Was that desire I saw on your face, my sweet?" he whispered.

"Definitely not!" Gwen prayed he couldn't hear the thundering of her heart.

"I'm going to enjoy proving you wrong."

The husky tone of his voice sent her stomach fluttering again. She turned and started down the aisle ahead of him. She stumbled, but his strong hands closed over her arms.

"Is something wrong?"

"Nay, my lord. My legs ache, but I will be fine. You may let me go."

"As you wish," he said.

Gwen's legs buckled again. This time, Richard swept her into his arms. There was a collective gasp from the crowd. Gwen buried her face in his shoulder.

Cradled against his chest, she felt the steady beat of his heart, felt taut muscle flexing beneath her as he carried her down the aisle.

She expected him to put her down when they got outside, but he did not. "I can walk, my lord."

"Nay, I think not."

"My lord, you must not carry me all the way to the castle."

"The peasantry does not seem to mind."

Indeed, they did not. People cheered, patting each other on the back and pointing as the Earl of Dunsmore stood on the steps with his bride in his arms. Many of them had jostled for a position all morning, hoping to catch a glimpse of the bridal couple as they left the cathedral. They'd been too far back to witness the ceremony, surging forward as the lords and ladies entered the church for the nuptial mass.

"What is the matter, Richard?" the King asked as he came up behind them. He was resplendent in royal purple. A jeweled crown sat upon his head, tilting jauntily to one side.

"That bishop is an interminable bag of wind. The mass was too long. Even my legs ache."

"Poor child," Queen Eleanor said, laying her hand on Gwen's arm. "Why don't you ride in the litter with me? 'Twill be more comfortable."

Gwen opened her mouth to answer, but Richard cut her off. "Nay, I will carry her, Majesty. The crowds have waited all day to see the bride and groom together. We must not disappoint them."

Eleanor smoothed a hand over her protruding belly. "Aye, you are right, Richard. Please help me to the litter, Edward."

"I shall do better than that, my love," he said, reaching for her. "I shall carry you, too."

A great murmur arose as the king lifted his wife in his arms. "You are so romantic, Edward," the queen said softly.

Gwen recognized the glow that lit the queen's face. She'd seen it often enough between her father and Elinor. What surprised her was that Edward had the same look.

Why had he kissed her when he was in love with his wife? She thought of Rhys and his admission he had bedded other women while he was in love with her. Good Lord, men were horrible.

"Jealous?" Richard growled, his eyes darkening. "Just because Ned isn't immune to your charms does not mean he doesn't love his wife. But you'll not have another chance to seduce him, that I can assure you," he whispered fiercely.

Gwen's eyes widened. "You bastard," she hissed. "Put me down!"

His grip was like iron and once again she was reminded of the raw power lying just beneath the surface. "Such crude language for a princess, my dear. If you do not stop struggling, I shall drop you on your lovely behind in front of all these people."

Gwen stilled. She had no doubt he would delight in humiliating her. She would not give him the pleasure.

"Shall we, Richard?" Edward asked when he had finished whispering in his wife's ear. Eleanor's pale face glowed pink. Her gaze did not stray from her husband's face.

"Aye, Ned," Richard replied.

The two men began the descent to the street. Guards formed around them and the crowd parted easily as they made their way toward the castle.

Word spread before them, rippling through the gathered masses like a banner in the wind. By the time they reached Shrewsbury castle, men and women thronged the bailey, cheering wildly.

The minstels' gallery struck up a tune when they entered the Great Hall. Richard carried Gwen to the dais, setting her on her feet beside the table.

She refused to look at him. Instead, she allowed her gaze to wander over the elegant hall.

Fine white linen was draped over the trestle tables, and the smell of a delicious feast hung thick in the air. Servants bustled through the room, laying out trenchers for the guests filing in.

The walls and ceiling were freshly whitewashed, and the King's banner hung behind the dais. Scented rushes were scattered on the wooden floor and roaring fires blazed in the center and surrounding hearths.

Richard took her hand and led her to their place at the high table. His thigh brushed hers as he joined her on the bench. She tried to slide away but he grabbed her wrist.

"You will act the happy bride today, Princess."

Gwen glared at him. "If 'twere any but you—"

"Aye, but I am not Rhys ap Gawain."

"Pity," she said flippantly.

His hand tightened on her wrist. "You are my wife now. You will do as I tell you from now on. One of the very first things you must learn is that you do not use that insolent tone with me."

Gwen flashed him a pretty smile, tilting her head to one side. "It must be an incredible bore, what with people always bowing and scraping in your presence."

The pressure of his hand changed. He stroked the inside of her wrist and palm. She'd expected anger, but his mouth curved in a smile. "I don't expect you to bow, sweet. All I need from you is for you to keep your mouth shut and spread your pretty legs—though not at the same time. I certainly don't mind if you wish to scream in bed."

Gwen snatched her hand away. Fortunately, she was saved from a reply when trumpets heralded the beginning of the feast.

Edward and Eleanor took their places at the center of the table, and the servants began their steady stream from the kitchens.

A girl poured wine into a single goblet. Gwen was dismayed to realize she and Richard would share it, as well as the plate of silver before them. A bowl of warm rosewater was placed between them and a servant stood ready, holding a fresh linen towel.

The king and queen were served first, then the newlyweds and important guests, and finally the rest of the hall.

Richard took a silver-handled eating knife from his belt and carved into the roast venison. The smell was heavenly.

He made quick work of the meat, tearing it into small pieces. He chose one of the juiciest morsels and held it out. Surprised, Gwen took it from the tip of the knife.

When he held out the next piece, it was in his fingers.

"Open for me," he said. His fingers lingered over her lower lip, and she found it strangely exciting.

Gwen swallowed quickly. "Will you not eat, my lord?"

"Only when you have finished."

She reached for the goblet, but he got to it first. She hesitated when he held it to her lips, then sipped. The sweet wine warmed her insides. Or was it the look in his eyes as their gazes locked over the top of the cup that caused it?

The afternoon wore on, the courses becoming grander with its passing. There were endless dishes of meat and game, birds delicately roasted and then made to seem lifelike when their feathers were painstakingly put back into place, stuffed fish, lamprey eels, dishes of stewed vegetables, and baked pears sweetened with honey.

Musicians walked through the hall, playing their instruments gaily, clad in brightly colored cloaks. There were lutes and timbrels, a harp and bladder-pipes. A minstrel regaled the high table with a tale of warriors and dragons.

"Do you not like the story?" Richard asked.

Gwen started. She'd not realized she was frowning. "I was just thinking a Welsh bard would be better."

Richard smiled. "A poor English minstrel can't compare, eh?"

Gwen fixed him with a haughty stare. "Nothing English can compare, my lord."

If anything, his smile widened. "Oh, we shall see about that… eventually."

Damn the bastard, he was making her blush again! Gwen reached for the goblet, but he was there first. She kept her eyes downcast as she drank.

"What are you doing?" she asked when his other hand threaded through her hair.

"They expect a happy bridal couple," he said, jerking his head toward the hall. He set the goblet down and leaned forward to kiss her.

Gwen parted her lips out of sheer instinct. Yes, that had to be the reason. She certainly hadn't done it because she wanted to kiss him.

She vaguely heard the cheers of the crowd through the pounding in her ears. When his tongue stroked across hers, she answered, meeting him with a hunger she hadn't known she possessed.

He pulled away and she gazed up at him. He was much too handsome for comfort. She could drown in those eyes of liquid silver.

"How does that compare?"

"Huh?" she said. He smiled and she jerked away, her cheeks flaming. "It will do, I suppose."

She hoped it sounded the same as if he'd asked her something trivial, like how the wine was, or how she thought the venison tasted.

Richard only laughed.

As dusk approached, the torches were lit and a portion of the floor cleared for dancing.

"We must lead the first dance," Richard said in her ear, his hot breath sending a tingle down her neck.

Other couples joined them as the musicians began to play. They moved down the line, changing partners, until the pattern came full circle again.

The music stopped and the dancers clapped. Richard pulled her against him.

"Not yet, my boy!" someone said. "You've a long way to go until the bedding!"

People laughed. Hands were suddenly on their shoulders, tearing the newlyweds apart. William de Valence, Earl of Pembroke and the King's uncle, clapped Richard on the back and steered him off the floor.

Gwen turned as male voices clamored behind her for the next dance. And found herself face to face with Dafydd ap Gruffydd.

"Niece," he said, holding out his hand.

She regarded him icily, intending to sweep him aside. He grabbed her hand before she could act. "Let me go!"

"Not until you dance with me." Although much younger, he resembled his brother. His hair was darker, with not a strand of gray, and his eyes were a mossy green.

But the shape of his face, the handsome lift of his mouth, the arch of his brows—those were the same as Llywelyn's.

Gwen stood stiffly, refusing to move. The other dancers were waiting, and rather than make a scene, she acquiesced.

"You are as lovely as your mother was, Gwenllian."

"Thank you."

They moved through the steps in silence. She could feel Dafydd watching her. Unable to stand any more, she snapped, "What do you want from me?"

"To warn you."

Only the pressure of his hand kept her moving. "About what?"

"Your husband. Watch him, Gwenllian. Be cautious. He's a dangerous man."

"*Gwalchddu* you mean. I'm well aware of it. But why do you care?"

"Because of Eurwen. She would never have approved of Llywelyn doing this to you."

He was hitting too close to the mark. Gwen stared straight ahead. "'Tis none of your business! He does what he must to preserve Wales."

Dafydd's bark of laughter startled her. "Aye, 'tis what he says all right. Mayhap he thought the same thing when he sent Eurwen away, too."

Gwen halted. The dance was over, but she hadn't noticed. She clutched his hand. "What do you mean, Dafydd? What are you talking about?"

He bowed and kissed her hand. "Thank you for dancing with me, Gwenllian."

And then he was gone. Gwen started after him, but she was stopped by a wall of people. She'd always been told that her mother had abandoned her and her father, chosen to return from whence she came.

Faceless men stepped up to her, asking for a dance. Gwen accepted, one by one. Her mind whirled. Dafydd ap Gruffydd was a liar and a traitor. But what if he wasn't lying this time?

"Where are you going, Richard?"

Richard turned back to the knot of men. "I think you have managed to keep me from my bride long enough, don't you?"

William de Valence chuckled. Red Gilbert's face twisted in a knowing smirk. "I am sure you will make up for it once the door to the nuptial chamber closes."

"Aye, likely to keep us all awake with the lass's screams of pleasure ringing through the castle till the dawn," said Henry de Lacy, Earl of Lincoln and Salisbury.

Edward's brother, Edmund of Lancaster, Derby, and Leicester, affectionately called Crouchback, glanced furtively at Eleanor seated out of earshot, but lowered his voice anyway. "The way I hear it, Richard and Ned fucked their way through every whorehouse between here and the Holy Land. He'll wear her out long before dawn, then he'll start on the serving wenches!"

The men guffawed. Gilbert slapped Edmund on the back, forcing him to spit out the wine he'd just drunk. Edmund coughed, wiping his mouth on his velvet sleeve. Edward sauntered over.

"What's so funny, brother?"

Edmund looked up, tried to speak, then broke off in a fit of giggles. The other men laughed. Edmund sank to the bench and found himself on the floor. He looked around for a moment, startled, then started laughing again.

"Christ almighty, Edmund, 'tis by the divine grace of God that you were not born first," Edward said, rolling his eyes in mock disdain.

Edmund blinked, giggling. "Amen, brother. I'd not want your crown for anything."

Edward turned to Richard. "What's got him so tickled?"

Richard lowered his voice. "He was chronicling our exploits in the finest pleasure houses of Christendom."

"Ah, it seems it must be nearing time for the bedding then, eh? Talk always seems to turn to sex when people are anxious to proceed with the ceremonies." His brows drew together. "Who is that young Welshman your wife is talking to, Richard?"

Richard turned to follow Edward's gaze. They were the only men in the room who could see over the crowd. "Rhys ap Gawain," he said, moving before Edward could reply.

"The Earl of Dunsmore has many enemies, does he not?"

Anne jumped. She turned to glare at the newcomer. She did not like being startled, and she did not like sharing her plans.

The man let his gaze wander down her body, then back up again. Anne tingled. He was handsome, with his dark auburn hair and beard, and his green eyes. He wasn't tall, not like Richard or the king, but he was lean and hard. "What makes you think I am his enemy?"

"'Tis written on your face, my dear. You hate him." He walked behind her. Anne stood still, waiting. Her heart quickened. Then she felt the press of his hard body against her back and his hot breath in her ear. "Jilted you, did he?"

Anne stiffened, furious. She spun around to face him. "Who are you?"

"Your color only confirms it," the stranger said, laughing. He took her hand and pressed it to his lips. "Dafydd ap Gruffydd, at your service."

Anne felt a rush of desire at his touch, saw the answering look in Dafydd's eyes. "Well, well, a Welsh prince," she said.

"Mayhap you will go for a walk with me. I hear the gardens are lovely at night."

Anne extracted her hand. "There are no gardens, Highness."

Dafydd smiled. He was really only a lord here in England, since Edward recognized Llywelyn as the Prince of Wales, but he was still a prince by birth. "You've not told me your name," he said as she started to walk away.

"Lady Anne Ashford."

"Ashford. I am familiar with Ashford Hall. Mayhap I will drop in one day."

Anne lowered her lashes and shot him a coy glance, then turned and walked away. Dafydd ap Gruffydd. As much as she wanted to stay and flirt with him, she already had other plans for the evening.

"You are supposed to help me, Rhys!" Gwen cried.

Rhys's eyes flashed. "I'll not help you find Dafydd. He's a traitor to our people!"

"That's really rich! You deliver me into the clutches of Black Hawk de Claiborne, yet you won't help me find Dafydd?" She'd been looking for her uncle since she'd managed to get away from the dancing, but he was nowhere to be found.

Rhys gripped her shoulders. "I'd not have brought you if you had even once asked me not to do it! I'd have taken you away and to hell with everything."

Gwen shook him off angrily. "Fine, if you won't help me, I'll go alone!"

"If you leave the hall, I will follow. Your husband will think we are trysting."

Gwen's eyes widened. "You wouldn't!"

"I would. He already thinks we are lovers. How do you think he will react knowing you've gone off with me on your wedding day?"

Gwen's jaw worked but no sound came out. How dare he! After all she'd done to keep Richard from killing him, this was how he repaid her. Her hand cracked across his cheek.

He stared at her without speaking. Red bloomed where she'd slapped him and Gwen was instantly contrite.

"Oh, Rhys, I am sorry," she said, caressing his cheek.

His expression softened and he covered her hand with his. "That doesn't hurt half so much as knowing you will be in his arms tonight when you should be in mine."

He kissed her palm, then released it. Gwen bit her trembling lip. "You were the best friend I ever had!" she said, throwing her arms around his neck. "I will always love you for that."

He hugged her tight, rubbing his face in her hair. "Let go before he sees you," Rhys said softly, though his arms tightened for a second.

Gwen planted a quick kiss on his mouth, then turned and hurried away. She scrubbed the back of her hand across her eyes, crying out when she collided with something solid.

She stumbled back, her breath catching.

Richard held out his hand.

She threw a quick glance over her shoulder. Rhys was gone. Her hand trembled as she slipped it into Richard's. He led her to the dais and nodded to the King.

"'Tis time for the bedding!" Edward announced. The crowd cheered. Gwen sagged against her husband. Only the two of them knew it was he who kept her on her feet.

11

"**D**rink this, dear," Queen Eleanor said, placing a goblet of spiced wine in Gwen's icy hand before dismissing the servant.

"Thank you, Majesty."

It was almost time. Gwen gazed at the gigantic bed, its velvet curtains drawn open, the bedding turned down and strewn with rose petals. *Rose petals!* Where on earth had they gotten those this time of year?

A log crackled in the fireplace, the fragrant scent of herbs twining with the smoke. Gwen thought she smelled rosemary and mint. She took a deep breath, trying to keep her mind on anything but what was about to happen. It wasn't working.

She couldn't think about Rhys or Dafydd, just Richard and the look on his face when he'd found her. She couldn't get over the gnawing feeling he had seen her and Rhys. His eyes had glittered with a note of challenge when he'd held out his hand. She'd almost felt like he was daring her not to take it.

Eleanor glided to a chair and sank into it gracefully. Even at this advanced stage of pregnancy, she was elegant. "You must drink it all. The first time is better if you are relaxed."

Other voices piped up, quickly agreeing with the queen. Gwen looked at the faces of the ladies who had volunteered to prepare her for the bedding. They had only been introduced to her today, these wives of Edward's barons. There were so many people attending the wedding that she knew she'd not seen even a third of them.

God, how she wished Elinor were here!

"Well, ladies, let us prepare this lovely bride for her husband," said Catherine de Lacy, clapping her hands impatiently. She unclasped Gwen's mantle and handed it to Alys.

Gwen stifled a smile. Alys's face was redder than usual, her jaw set stubbornly. Gwen knew Alys was grumbling beneath her breath at having these highborn ladies intruding upon what should be her job. The old woman shook out the cloak, then retreated to the antechamber to hang it.

Mary de Clare, wife of the Earl of Gloucester, lifted the circlet from Gwen's head, then began to delicately reshape any curls that had fallen flat. Mary seemed rather shy, and Gwen guessed her to be not much older than herself.

"You have glorious hair, Lady Gwenllian," Mary said, her voice so soft Gwen barely heard her.

"Thank you, Lady Mary."

Catherine stripped Gwen of her surcoat. "'Tis odd to think of Richard de Claiborne married once more. 'Tis been so many years since Elizabeth died, I was certain he would remain unwed. Certes, he's had too much fun corrupting married women. 'Twas high time Edward forced him to take another wife!"

Margaret de Valence tittered. Mary blushed. Eleanor turned purple. "Catherine, you should not speak so in front of the Earl's new bride!"

Catherine blinked. "Oh! Forgive me, Lady Gwenllian. I do not think sometimes. Henry always tells me I should think before I speak, but I can never manage to do so."

Gwen's heart dropped. Richard had been married? None of the stories she'd ever heard mentioned that. Had he loved his wife? What had happened to her? "'Tis forgiven, Lady Catherine. I am well aware my husband has a reputation. Our marriage was made for political reasons and not for love."

Catherine smiled. "Aye, but that doesn't mean you cannot enjoy the pleasures he can give you this night."

"Do not mislead her, Catherine. The first time is not usually so pleasant. The second is much better," Margaret said. "Do you not agree, Mary?"

Mary stammered her agreement, her face losing color. Her hands shook as she twisted a curl into place. No one else noticed Mary's discomfort, but comprehension dawned on Gwen with chilling clarity.

Life with the Red Earl of Gloucester wasn't pleasant. He was a big man, not so much tall as broad, and Mary was tiny compared to him. He must ravish her brutally.

Gwen shivered. Good Lord, Richard was far bigger than she. And she'd angered him plenty since she'd arrived. Would he hurt her like Gloucester hurt Mary?

"Finish your wine, Gwenllian, and the first time will not be so unpleasant as these ladies would have you believe," Eleanor said. "I was but thirteen when Edward took me to bed the first time, although we had been married since I was ten, and we drank wine until we were both giddy. 'Twas not at all unpleasant."

Margaret spoke first. "And we know the King has never displeased you, Majesty. How many children is it now?"

"Twelve," Eleanor said, patting her belly. Her eyes lost some of their sparkle. "Though only half my babies have lived."

"God grant you a son this time, Majesty," Mary said.

Gwen, Catherine, and Margaret spoke as one. "Amen."

Eleanor wiped away a tear, then stood. "You are as lovely as a bride should be, Gwenllian. Ladies, remove her chemise."

Panic seized Gwen as they lifted the garment from her body. Cold air caressed her skin, goosebumps rising where it touched. Soon, Richard would touch her. That made her shiver even more.

Margaret dusted her with scented powder while Catherine daubed her with perfume. At last, they slipped a woolen robe over her naked body.

"Take her to the end of the bed. Catherine, Margaret, be ready to remove her bedrobe. Mary, you stand by the door," Eleanor said, waving her hand. When all were in place, she turned to Alys, who held a long-handled pan. "Please warm the sheets, Alys."

Alys nodded and picked up a set of tongs. She selected a few glowing embers from the fireplace and dropped them in the pan.

Gwen forced her breath to come slowly, steadily. Her heart raced. From anticipation? From fear? Perhaps it was both.

Men's voices came faint at first, growing louder with each passing second. They were on the stairs, moving ever closer. Their voices rose, becoming more distinct, more individual.

Eleanor took the goblet, nodding in satisfaction at its emptiness. "Do not be frightened, my dear. Hold your head high. The inspection will take but a moment and then we will put you in bed. I am afraid you will have to endure listening to their crude jokes for a short time, but I am sure Richard will get them out quickly."

Gwen returned the Queen's smile and took a deep breath. She could handle this. She was Llywelyn ap Gruffydd's daughter.

"I want this over with quickly, Ned," Richard growled in the king's ear.

"Patience, Richard. You'll have the lass to yourself soon enough. Let these men have their fun."

Edmund and Gilbert reached the chamber first and pounded on the wooden door. When it didn't open immediately, men at the rear of the party began to holler how best to breach a stubborn entryway. Soon, the entire party had taken it up, suggestions ranging from ramming it swiftly to penetrating it slowly.

Richard grated his teeth together. He'd never liked these damn ceremonies, although he conceded the necessity for them. How else to make sure the bride and groom were free of flaws? But it always seemed that the poor bride was the one to suffer from the pop-eyed scrutiny and bad behavior of so many drunken men.

He was in no mood for this tonight. He clung to the edge of his control by the barest thread. Seeing his wife with her lover had frayed his temper badly. He'd stifled an urge to break up their lovers' quarrel, intercepting Gwen when she hurried away. He'd immediately pulled her to the dais and signaled the king to announce the bedding-down revelries. The sooner he was alone with her, the better.

While the ladies had left the hall to prepare, Edmund and Henry de Lacy had plied him with drink, thinking it would be funny to see him pass out on his wedding night. He'd drank only half of what they'd given him, pouring the rest onto the rushes.

The wine had merely fostered his rage until he was ready to burst with it. He recalled none of the conversation, none of the ribald comments of his peers.

The door opened. Mary de Clare paled when she saw her husband at the forefront. Richard felt sorry for the tiny woman. He knew Gilbert was hard on her. Edward knew it too, but there was nothing to be done about it. A man's wife was his property, and he could treat her however he saw fit.

Mary stepped back to allow the men to enter. Richard was pushed through first, Edmund and Gilbert on his heels.

"My lords," the queen said, motioning to the bed.

But Richard was already staring. He searched Gwen's face, looking for fear, for contempt. Her glorious eyes glittered, but she held her chin high. If she was afraid, she hid it well.

Hands were on him suddenly, removing his clothes. He did not resist, did not help, merely stood. When they had stripped him to his chausses and braies, he stopped them with an upraised hand, ignoring the protests that arose.

Gwen returned his heated stare. From the moment his broad chest was bared, she could not tear her gaze away. A few scars criss-crossed the hard muscles, silent testament to a life spent wielding a sword. Black hair spread across his chest, tapering to disappear beneath the waist of the braies that rode his narrow hips.

When their gazes again locked, his eyes were aflame. But was it desire or anger? Her heart beat faster.

Catherine and Margaret grasped the edges of the robe and pulled it from Gwen's body. Voices raised in merriment died to a murmur, then hushed altogether.

Gwen fought to remain still. She knew the others stared too, but she could only look at Richard. The intensity of his stare, the darkening of his eyes from slate to pewter, the coiled tautness of his muscles made her weak at the knees.

He took a step forward. Eleanor held up her hand. "Do you find a flaw, my lord?"

He stopped, swallowed. "No," came the husky reply.

"And you, my lady?" Eleanor asked, turning to Gwen.

Dear Lord, like she would even know what she was supposed to be looking for! "Nay," she replied, her voice trembling.

Eleanor nodded to the ladies. They put Gwen in bed, then placed a lit candle in one of the niches of the headboard and pulled the bedcurtains closed.

Richard paid no attention while the ladies took their leave. His thoughts were only for the woman waiting for him. His one glimpse of her two nights ago had been so brief he had begun to wonder if he'd only imagined the creamy silk of her skin, the uptilt of her breasts, the rosy crowns of her nipples.

It seemed he had waited for this night for four years and he was suddenly impatient to get on with it. Exasperated, he turned, barely listening to the bawdy jokes that flew through the air. How to tame a wild Welsh filly and how to furrow a ripe field were only a couple of the suggestions offered.

Richard clenched his jaw, meeting Edward's gaze. One corner of Edward's mouth quirked. He held his goblet up, calling for silence.

"My lords, it seems our most beloved Earl of Dunsmore is impatient to attend to his bride, so let us drink to his success and be gone!"

"Hear! Hear!" they said, lifting their drinks as one.

"Dunsmore, you're worse than a ram in rut! But not that I blame you after what we have just witnessed." Red Gilbert clapped him on the back, laughing.

"Out." Richard's voice was hard-edged with leashed fury. "Now."

They all stared at him. Edward cleared his throat, breaking the silence. "I do believe, my lords, that this is the first time this King of England has ever been dismissed by a vassal! Ah, but if I had not seen the lovely prize awaiting him, mayhap I would be angry. As it is, I cannot find fault with his command." Edward smiled, motioning the men toward the door. They grumbled about the fun ending before it had begun, but filed out peacefully.

When Edward was the only one left, he winked at Richard. "Try to get some sleep this night, eh?"

Richard grinned suddenly. "As you command me, so shall I do."

Edward returned the grin, then disappeared through the door after the others. Richard bolted it, knowing from his past attendance at weddings that men delighted in bursting in on a couple who had forgotten to bar the door.

Now that he was alone with Gwen, the anger he'd been holding in swelled to fruition. He stalked to the bed and threw open the hangings.

Gwen gasped. The golden light of the fire licked over his immense frame, caressing the crests and hollows of hard muscles. Her pulse raced. His face was livid.

He was on the bed in a flash, gripping her arms. "In England, a man can beat his wife for less than what you did to me tonight."

His eyes glittered like cold steel. Gwen no longer cared what happened. He didn't even know her, just made assumptions based on his own narrow-mindedness. She was not going to take his bullying anymore.

"Do it then!" His eyes widened. A growl rose low in his throat. Goaded beyond reason, she cried, "What are you waiting for, my lord? Do it!"

He released her and she braced herself for the blow, but it did not come. He left the bed, stopped to remove his chausses, then walked to the table and poured some wine.

Gwen stared openly. She could not stop herself. She had never seen a man's body unclothed before, had never known one could be so beautiful. His braies rode low on his narrow hips, hiding his bottom and his male sex.

She wanted to see it—and yet she did not. She jerked her gaze upward. When he turned to face her again, her breath caught. He was supple and graceful, a lion stalking his prey, and she realized in that moment how lucky she was that he had not hit her.

"You play dangerously close to the edge, sweet," he said. "But tonight I can think of better things to do than beat you."

He slammed the goblet down. He had desired her since the first day he'd seen her. He would deny himself no longer.

But he must be careful. After all, she could be carrying her lover's child. He would not spill his seed in her until he was certain she did not.

There would be no subtle stoking of a virgin's passions. First, he would make love to her like a storm over the Irish Sea, and together they would explore heights untouched. When they had come down from their initial passion, he would start again, slowly awakening her body to sensations she had never experienced with a man as young and green as Rhys ap Gawain.

Richard stripped off his braies, gritting his teeth when she turned away in silent rejection. All the women he'd ever bedded always wanted to see his manhood, to touch it, to feel its great size in their hands before he filled them with it. Well, he would melt her defenses soon enough, and then she would beg him for it.

His blood pounded in his ears as he reached for her. She stiffened and his control snapped. He crushed his mouth to hers. She'd wanted him before. He would make her want him again.

Perversely, she started to fight, pushing at him, pulling his hair, twisting beneath him as his entire length pressed down on her, flesh searing flesh. Richard found it strangely exciting. She was challenging him, trying to deny the attraction that burned like a flame between them. He vowed she would beg him for fulfillment before he was finished.

"Go ahead and fight me, wife, for it will make no difference," he whispered against her lips. "Once you are mine, you will never again desire a green boy like Rhys ap Gawain."

"No! He is not my lover!"

"He never will be again," Richard said fervently. She stilled, her eyes widening as his hard length pressed against her abdomen.

She sucked in a strangled breath and began to fight with more fury than before. "No!"

"Oh yes, my sweet," Richard said hoarsely. He forced her legs apart, settling himself between them.

Panting from her exertions, she ceased struggling. Crystal tears glittered in her golden-green eyes.

Richard almost stopped, almost started over, but he was too far gone. He'd wanted her for much too long to stop now. Besides, she would forget all about Rhys once he was inside her, caressing her secret woman's place.

He stroked her hair, kissed her neck. He would enter her slowly until she begged him to sheathe his entire length inside her. Then they would burn together.

He pressed against her entrance. She was impossibly tight and he shuddered. He checked himself. His need was great and he was dangerously close to thrusting to the hilt. She quivered beneath him and he felt a surge of triumph. His Welsh bride was as affected as he by the joining of their bodies, whether she admitted it or not.

He pressed his lips to her ear, murmured encouragement to her in Welsh, swallowing heavily as he slipped into her folds. So tight.

"Open for me, Gwen," he said in a husky whisper. She was so small he feared he might hurt her.

"I know not what you mean," she replied.

"Sweet Christ, do not tease me now, woman!" He pushed deeper still, then froze. "Oh my God," he groaned. It couldn't be—it just couldn't be!

Richard rolled off her, his mind trying to adjust to this startling revelation. There was no mistaking the barrier he had encountered. His wife was no whore.

"I told you so you great black brute!" She scrambled onto him, clawing, slapping. With a quick movement, he pinned her arms to her sides and pressed her onto her back.

The sheet had tangled, coiling around her body and separating them by a thin sheaf of linen. Her breath broke on a sob. She wasn't quivering with desire. She was shaking with fear! Jesú, he was no better than men like Gloucester!

He wanted to hold her, comfort her, make everything right again. "I did not know. I thought..."

"I know what you thought, you vile English bastard! I hate you!" she said tearfully.

Richard flinched. He deserved her hatred and more for the insults he'd dealt her. He had refused to see her as anything but a whore from the moment he learned she was Llywelyn's daughter. Nay, that was not true either. He'd considered her for a leman the very instant he slipped off her hood in the stables of Rhuddlan castle.

Her underlip quivered and he couldn't stop himself from kissing her once more. He coaxed her to part her lips, sliding his tongue over them lightly. He wanted to reassure her, prove he could be gentle.

But kissing her, even so tenderly, was enough to start his shaft pulsing again. When she felt it, she jerked away like a rabbit trying to escape a fox. "Please, my lord, please don't hurt me," she said in a rush.

Richard lifted his head. Her eyes were wide, their depths a mixture of fear and loathing. With a sigh, he buried his face against her neck, breathing deeply of her sweet scent. "I won't hurt you," he said thickly. And then he let her go.

Slipping into his clothes, he was siezed by a primal joy that she had known no other man. And he, like some kind of crazed animal, had almost raped her. That left a sour taste in his mouth. He'd never forced his attentions on a woman before, had never needed to.

Returning to the bed, Richard pushed the sheet back and pulled his dagger. He ran the finely-honed blade across the underside of his forearm.

Gwen gasped. "What are you doing?"

"There must be blood on the sheets tomorrow."

"But…" She looked up with wondering eyes.

"I've treated you badly this night. I'll not touch you again until you wish it." Clenching his fist, he held his arm over the linen until a few drops had fallen, then wiped the wound on his tunic. "Sleep well, Princess."

He unbarred the door and called for Alys. "Lock it behind you."

He waited until he heard the bolt slide into place before he moved.

A lys came rushing into the chamber. "What on earth happened? You've not been in here long enough for—" She stopped when she took one look at Gwen.

"I don't want to talk about it, Alys," Gwen said quietly.

"Did he hurt you, child?"

"Nay. Leave me. Please."

Alys sighed and gathered her blankets, then retreated to her pallet in the antechamber.

Gwen stared at the ruby red drops staining the sheet. It should have been her blood, but it was his. She straightened the coverlets and sank back onto the pillows. She felt strangely empty inside. Sleep would be a long time coming.

Richard didn't know where he was going until he came to the door leading to the battlements. A walk in the cold air would do him good. He found himself alone on the castle walls, the guards having presumably retired to some corner to dice and drink.

Richard leaned against a merlon, propping his foot in an open crenel. Lights blazed in the town. Revelers' voices stole to him on the night air. The celebration, *his* celebration, was in full swing in the Great Hall far below.

How in the hell could he have been so wrong about her? His hand strayed to his sword hilt and he caressed it out of habit. The weapon was as much a part of him as his own soul, the need to carry it deeply ingrained from years spent in the unforgiving borderlands.

He swore softly. Instinct had told him she was untouched when he went to her room two nights ago, but he had pushed it away. She was Llywelyn's daughter for God's sake! She was *supposed* to be immoral!

She could have been currying favor with Ned, though he doubted it. The King could not resist a beautiful woman. Richard should have known who was seducing whom, but he'd been too blinded by rage, too willing to believe the worst about his Welsh bride.

He slumped against the wall, sickened by his own misconceptions. She hated him and he deserved it.

The night grew still, the laughter and music gradually fading. He heard the clattering of horses' hooves in the bailey as some of the guests departed for their lodgings in town. Many would be bedded in the hall below. Others, the important ones, would have their own chambers.

The castle lay in absolute silence when Richard finally decided to rouse himself. He had no idea how long he'd been there, but he threw back his head and laughed, the sound all the louder because it was the only one on the chill air.

What the hell was the matter with him? His wife was a virgin! He was going to be first and last. He should be celebrating his good fortune, not sulking in the shadows like a cat.

But first he must make this night up to her. She desired him. That much was plain in the way she'd responded to him in the past. His groin tightened. He would seduce her slowly, deliciously, until she could no longer resist.

He laughed. It shouldn't take all that long. He was very skilled in the art of seduction.

She didn't stand a chance.

He wound his way through the castle, heading for their chamber. Someone moved in the passage ahead. He stopped, drawing his dagger. The blade gleamed in the torchlight. He shrank into a shadow and waited.

Soon, a blonde head came into view. He sighed and sheathed the knife, stepping into the light once more.

"Jesú, Richard! What the devil are you doing here?"

"I might ask the same of you, Ned."

Edward glanced at the door next to them. "Tired of your new wife already? Find a serving wench."

Edward tapped on the door. A woman with pale hair answered. "Majesty," she breathed, opening the door to admit him.

When Edward was well inside the room, she swept Richard with a knowing look. "So the little witch wasn't worth the wait after all? 'Tis a pity . . ."

"Anne!" came Edward's impatient voice from behind her. She smiled and closed the door.

Gwen slept badly, as she had known she would. She awoke several times after what seemed only to be minutes. Richard had not returned. Finally, she got up and wrapped her bedrobe around her.

The fire had burned down until only a soft glow remained. Alys snored on her pallet in the antechamber. Gwen crossed to one of the chairs and sat down.

She knew where Richard was. He had found another bed, one with a welcoming woman. She twisted a lock of hair.

Well, it was not as if she cared. The bastard had damn near raped her. She was glad he was gone.

But she couldn't stop thinking about him. His raw male beauty nearly stole her breath away. She almost wished she had glimpsed the mysterious male organ, but she had been too frightened to look at it when he removed his braies. She tingled with the remembrance of where he had put that male weapon.

It was irritating actually. Why had it not felt as good then as the thought of it did now?

She had not expected him to stop when he did. Black Hawk de Claiborne was a cruel man. He should not have stopped. Jesú, it would be easier to hate him if he had not!

A soft tap came on the door. Gwen crossed to the entryway. Alys would never hear his knock.

She slid the bar from its cradle, then opened the door slowly. Richard slipped in and closed it behind him. She could barely see him in the murky antechamber. His dark form seemed but a shadow in the night, shapeless, a demon come to haunt her. Her worst nightmare.

Alys snorted.

Gwen jumped, nearly screaming.

The old woman coughed, then turned on her pallet, oblivious to all but her dreams. Gwen pressed her hand to her chest.

"You should have asked who it was," he growled.

Gwen bristled. "Who else would be sneaking into this chamber in the wee hours of the morn?"

He went and sat in a chair, then poured wine from the flagon on the table. Gwen stopped just outside the antechamber, unsure of what to do next.

He watched her for some moments. "What are you doing out of bed?"

"I could not sleep."

"Come here."

Gwen hesitated.

"I won't hurt you," he said softly.

Rushes crackled under her feet, the faint scent of marjoram rising from them. She stopped in front of him. He pulled her onto his lap, tucking her into the bend of his arm before settling his mantle around her.

"'Tis too cold for you to be out of bed."

"I am not cold, my lord."

"Richard."

"Richard," she repeated. In truth, the heat he gave her was welcome. Discreetly, she snuggled closer.

"Drink some wine. 'Twill warm you," he said, raising the goblet to her lips. She sipped, gazing at him over the rim.

She saw the passion flare in his eyes, felt it stir in his loins. Gwen pushed the wine away and tried to slide from his lap. He wrapped his arm around her, holding her tight.

"I cannot help how my body responds to you any more than the sun can help rising and setting. I gave you my word I would not touch you. Just sit awhile and it'll stop, I promise."

Gwen stilled. In a way, it thrilled her to know she caused such a reaction in him. "Where were you all night, my lord?"

He searched her face. "Where do you think I was?"

Gwen chewed her lip. She shouldn't have asked. Now he would think she cared what he did. "I think you were probably with your leman," she said imperiously.

He laughed softly. "Jealous?" His silver eyes seemed like smoke in the dim light of the chamber.

"Nay, of course not!"

"I do not believe you, Gwen."

Gwen turned her head to escape his scrutiny. He was so infuriating! He put a finger under her chin and pulled her back.

"I am not jealous," she repeated firmly.

"You would not have asked otherwise. Women always want to know just where it is a man has been when they care very much where he has been."

"I do not know what you are talking about. I am not—"

"I want to kiss you," he interrupted, setting the wine on the table. "Will you let me?"

Gwen lowered her lashes. She should tell him no. "Aye," she said softly, raising her eyes to his once more. Her heart started to thunder. Yes, God help her, she did want him to kiss her.

His expression was unreadable. Slowly, his head descended. Gwen closed her eyes. Excruciating seconds passed.

His lips grazed hers.

She waited, expecting more, wanting more.

He did not return.

She opened her eyes reluctantly. "Why did you stop?" she asked, a touch breathless.

"You did not tell me I could keep going."

"Oh."

"Would you like me to kiss you again?"

"Yes."

He kissed her harder, longer. Her heart pounded. He stopped, kissed her chin. "Again?" he whispered.

"Yes." This game was sending coils of heat spiraling through her. The logical part of her brain was trying to tell the rest of her that this was madness, that she was playing with a fire that threatened to rage out of control and consume her.

His mouth became more demanding. His tongue caressed her lower lip. He stopped. "Again?"

"Yes," she moaned, unable to stand the torture any longer, ignoring the warning signals in her mind.

His mouth descended. She parted her lips and his tongue slipped inside. He shuddered. His manhood came to life, bucking insistently against her. Gwen shifted, part nervous fear, part curiosity.

He groaned, kissing her harder, deeper.

She wound her arms around his neck. Their tongues met, stroked, melded. Just when she thought the fire would consume her, he stopped. He kissed the hammering pulse in her throat.

"I cannot keep kissing you," he said thickly.

Gwen bit the inside of her cheek. She wasn't sure she wanted this to end just yet. "Why not?"

His shaft leapt beneath her. "That is why. I am in danger of breaking my promise."

Sweet Mary, she almost wanted him to. But she'd not give in so easily because it was exactly what he expected. What was the tale? Sacrificing virgins on the altar of his masculinity. Gwen took a deep breath. She was never going to do the things he expected. "Mayhap you are right then."

His eyes narrowed for a second, then he sighed. "'Tis almost dawn, Gwen. We must get in bed before the women come to inspect the sheets."

"We?"

"Yes, *we*, sweet. Do not worry, the only thing I will do is sleep."

Aye, he needed sleep because he had been out bedding some other woman all night. Not that she cared, of course.

He stood with her still in his arms and carried her to the bed. She waited until she was under the coverlets before she shed the robe and tucked it under her pillow.

Richard's eyes twinkled with amusement as he began to strip. Gwen watched him, breathless, then turned away at the last second, flushing at his low chuckle.

The mattress shifted as his weight sank onto it. Gwen had to hold on to keep from rolling into him. Her skin tingled with his nearness. She could actually feel him breathing!

And then she felt him behind her. His body didn't touch hers, but he was close enough that his heat scorched her anyway. She stifled a gasp when his lips touched her shoulder. His fingers traced a searing path down her side—shoulder to curve of waist to flare of hip to thigh. Gwen felt a tremor of excitement wash over her.

"Good night, Princess," he murmured in her ear. Then he turned on his side, and promptly fell asleep.

For a while, Gwen did not think she would be able to do the same. Her body was on fire. Her breasts tingled, and the damp heat between her thighs pulsed. It was a very long time before the rhythmic sound of his breathing lulled her into a sleep that was troubled by dreams of him touching her in those places that burned for him.

Gwen awoke, still enclosed in the cocooned semi-darkness of the bedcurtains. A sliver of light cut through a narrow opening, caressing Richard's body from the waist down. She waited, but he did not move.

It was odd, waking up beside a man. He lay on his back, one knee bent to the side, his head turned away from her. She could feel the heat coming from his body and she longed to curl up beside him. She wanted to see what he looked like and what he felt like.

Curiosity began to get the best of her the longer she lay there. What did he look like down there anyway? She wormed her way toward him, easing across him to look at his face. His eyes were closed.

She lay back, exhaling slowly. Now, all she had to do was lift the covers and the mysterious male sex would be revealed. She took a deep breath. Slowly, she lifted.

The black hair that had tapered down to the waist of his braies branched out again, hiding what she sought. She frowned. Maybe if she sat up a little. Her face flamed at her brazenness.

Gwen clenched her stomach muscles, raising herself.

"Can I help you find something, sweet?" His voice was drowsy, but amused.

She dropped the coverlet and fell back. "I was just going to get out of bed."

"Then why did you not get out on your side?"

Gwen could think of nothing to say.

Before she realized what he was doing, he rolled her beneath him, making sure the sheet separated their bodies. Gwen gasped. It wasn't enough. She felt every excruciating inch of his skin as it burned into hers.

"I want to kiss you," he whispered.

"No." She couldn't allow him to steal her senses as he had last night. Whenever he kissed her, she was in danger of losing herself, of drowning in him. She had the upper hand now. His guilt would not allow him to touch her without permission. She was going to make sure he paid for all the horrible things he'd done to her.

"You don't mean that," he murmured, nibbling her ear.

Gwen closed her eyes. *Sweet Mary!* If this was how life with him was going to be, she would never endure it. Her body betrayed her without a trace of remorse, awakening to the hot ripple of his breath in her ear.

"Let me kiss you," he whispered again, fiercely, urgently. She turned toward him, seeking him.

Her answer was lost as his mouth descended, claiming hers. In a rhythm she now knew well, she parted her lips, moaning as their tongues met.

Even as she felt his manhood growing and stretching, her body responded. The sweet ache tortured her, begged her to join her body with his. As if he knew what she was thinking, he ground his iron maleness against her, rubbing slowly. She sucked in her breath as sensation bolted through her, then raised her hips to meet him.

He groaned, and for a minute she thought she'd done something wrong, but then he was trailing hot kisses down her neck, whispering against her skin, words she only half caught.

He dragged the sheet down, exposing her breasts. Her breathing quickened as his tongue flicked across her nipple. When she thought she would die from the anticipation, he took it in his mouth, licking and sucking. The sharp tingle reached all the way to her toes.

"Richard," she whispered. "Oh God, Richard."

"Let me taste my name on your lips." His voice was throaty, masculine.

"Richard," she whispered again. He crushed his mouth to hers. She succeeded in wrenching her arms free of the tangled sheet, and she wrapped them around him, stroking the hard muscles of his back, drowning in a whirlpool of sensation.

Dimly, she heard voices. She decided her mind was playing tricks when the sound abruptly ceased.

"My lord?" came Alys's voice beside the bed. "My lord?"

Richard raised his head. "Go away, Alys."

"My lord, the ladies are here to inspect the sheets."

"Send them away. They can come back later."

"I already have. Twice, my lord!"

"Then do it again."

"They have brought the queen this time, my lord."

His eyes flashed in the dim light. Gwen squirmed beneath him, her passion ebbing when he was no longer mastering her senses. God above, whenever he touched her she behaved just like the whore he'd accused her of being!

He looked down, realized she was fighting him, and rolled away. Colorful Welsh curses issued from his lips as he threw open the hangings and grabbed for his braies and chausses. "Jesú, if it's so pressing, tell them they can inspect the goddamn sheets!"

13

Gwen sat up, feeling beneath her pillow for the bedrobe. She tugged it over her naked body, heat suffusing her face. The women had been sent away twice. God only knew what sort of a sex-crazed Welsh whore they thought she was.

Richard pulled on his underclothes, then turned and held out his hand. "Ready, sweet?"

Gwen took a deep breath. "Aye."

The queen and her ladies waited. Richard let her go, and she shrank against the wall, desiring to be anywhere but here.

He strode out in front of the women. He was bare from the waist up, his braies riding low on his hips. Margaret de Valence gasped. Last night it had been part of a ceremony, but this morning was a different matter altogether.

Catherine de Lacy merely gaped at him.

A smile played at the corners of Eleanor's lips. "Richard de Claiborne, you are incorrigible."

Richard bowed. "Majesty. Ladies. If you had not insisted on interrupting my sleep I am certain I could have found the time to dress properly later. *Much* later."

Eleanor waved a hand, silently bidding the women to carry out the task. Alys stood in the entryway, her hand covering her mouth. The corners of her eyes crinkled.

"Really, Richard," Eleanor said. "You must eat sometime."

He didn't answer, his mouth crooking in a lazy grin. Eleanor shook her head.

Gwen stood quietly, hoping to avoid any attention. Fortunately, Richard was drawing most of it. Catherine and Margaret found the stain and called the Queen over. For one irrational moment, Gwen thought somehow they knew it wasn't really her blood.

But the three of them merely nodded. Catherine smiled at her, winking, and Gwen prayed the floor would swallow her up.

"We will expect you at table soon," Eleanor said over her shoulder as they walked out the door.

Richard turned to her. Her breath shortened. Even in the full light of day, he was magnificent. If his chest was not so broad and his arms not so big, he would almost be a little boy with his mussed up hair and mischievous eyes.

Gwen gasped when he picked her up, holding her so he had to look up at her. His arms wrapped around her bottom and she held herself up by pressing down on his shoulders.

"You have only glimpsed the surface of things to come, sweet. There is much yet to learn of passion between a man and a woman."

He swung her around, laughing, then slid her down his body until their eyes were level. Gwen was mesmerized. What had gotten into him?

He stared at her for so long she thought she would melt. His voice was soft when he spoke. "If I were Rhys ap Gawain, I'd have never let you go."

Gwen wasn't even aware he had set her down until he walked away. Her heart sped dizzily and she leaned against the wall for support.

"Dress warmly. We ride for Claiborne castle today," he said, tugging on the rest of his clothes.

"How far is it, my lord?"

He came to her, his gaze penetrating hers once again. His finger brushed her cheek. "Have you forgotten my name so soon, Gwen?"

"Nay."

"I know how to make you say it," he said softly, reaching for the edge of her robe. Gwen jerked away. He laughed. "If you forget it again, I may have to." He went to strap on his sword. "'Tis a day's ride to Claiborne, sweet, no more. I will be in the hall with the king. Come as soon as you are dressed."

He left and Gwen was thankful. She needed a chance to catch her breath and quiet her racing heart. Sinking down on the edge of the bed, she stared at the small stain of blood.

Alys returned, flashing Gwen a knowing look.

"Not you too, Alys," Gwen said, groaning.

Alys giggled as she hurried about her business of readying for the journey.

The hall was almost as lively as it had been the night before. Gwen paused in the entryway, scanning the crowd. Elinor had once told her that feasts sometimes went on for days. This one might also, but Richard had chosen to leave today. In a way, she was glad. Not that Claiborne castle was the ideal destination, but at least the English court wouldn't be there.

She wanted to search for Dafydd, but Richard picked her out, his gaze following her as she wound her way through the room. He frowned when she took her seat beside him.

"Where is your wimple?"

Gwen touched her thick braid. "Welsh women do not wear them."

"In England, only virgins and the queen herself may wear their hair uncovered. From now on you will cover your hair as befits a lady of your station."

"I will not do it," she said, glaring at him.

"What?" His voice was hard, dangerous.

Gwen swallowed. God, it was like baiting a tiger. But she wouldn't back down. "I am Welsh. You've taken all I have but you cannot take that from me. I will not pretend to be English."

His face darkened. "You will do as I tell you."

"You have the advantage of strength over me, my lord. Mayhap you should beat me into submission. Or worse…"

Richard curbed his fury. He probably deserved that remark last night, but not now. He'd shown restraint with her and he'd certainly not pressed his advantage when he could have. His voice was controlled. "Now is not the time, Gwen. I will discuss it with you later."

King Edward turned to them, his eyes twinkling. "Sleep well, Richard?"

"Aye, Ned," Richard said more curtly than he intended. "And you?"

Edward beamed. "Like a baby."

Richard grunted.

A servant brought oranges to the queen. "Do have an orange, Gwenllian," she said, leaning forward to catch Gwen's attention.

"Thank you, Majesty," Gwen replied.

"Richard, you will have to start getting oranges for your wife. She has fallen in love with them," Eleanor said, peeling the fruit deftly.

Richard's jaw tightened. "Indeed?" He turned back to Gwen. "Was one lesson enough, or do you need me to peel it for you?"

Edward coughed.

"I can manage," Gwen snapped.

Richard drew in a deep breath. He'd regretted it the instant the words crossed his lips, but it was too late to take it back. God's passion, how she aroused his anger! And other parts of him.

That was the problem, he decided. He was unused to this state of frustrated sexual arousal. He was going to have her, soon, or he was going to find comfort elsewhere.

She didn't look at him while she fumbled with the orange. Tired of watching her struggle with it, he grabbed it. She ignored him, picking up a piece of bread instead.

"You must both come to London for Christmas," Edward said.

"Oh yes!" Eleanor echoed. "I will be delivered of our son by then. You must come and celebrate."

"Thank you, Majesties. We shall," Richard replied, handing Gwen the peeled orange. She took it, snatching her hand away when his fingers brushed her palm.

Edward sat up straight. "God's bones, where is my mind this morning! Richard, I want you to escort Lady Ashford to her estate on your way back to Claiborne."

"Why does she want to return to Ashford Hall?" Richard asked, suspicious of anything that put Anne in close proximity to him.

Edward shrugged. "She has been at court for six months. She wishes to visit her son."

Richard frowned. "I plan to travel quickly. The lady will only hamper me with her baggage."

"One night in Oswestry will not hurt you. You can make it that far. Mayhap you will find something of the brigands that have been waylaying pilgrims to Holywell."

"I already have. I think they're using one of the caves in the Cambrian foothills for their base. I intend to hunt them down when I have seen my wife settled at Claiborne."

"Jesú, Richard! One night will make no difference. I have promised Lady Ashford escort and you will provide it."

The woman was up to something, of that Richard was certain. She was vain and spoiled and not in the least bit happy living in the March. Did she think to come to Claiborne and try to insinuate herself as his mistress again? He wouldn't put it past her, though if she did, she would not find the task easy. Besides, he'd slaked his thirst at that well too often to want another taste.

Still, there was nothing he could do except obey. Richard inclined his head. "As you command, Majesty."

Gwen stood in the bailey with Alys, waiting for the last of the horses to be loaded with Lady Ashford's things. Good Lord, the woman had a lot of trunks! Thankfully, her own trunks had gone straight to Claiborne when they'd descended from the mountains. She looked around for a sign of the elusive lady, but saw nothing to indicate she had appeared.

Pewter-tinted clouds hung low in the sky. It had not rained yesterday and Gwen prayed it would wait. She did not look forward to riding in a downpour.

The inner courtyard hummed with activity. Richard's knights checked their saddles, ran their hands over their horses legs to feel for any injuries —bone splints, swollen tendons, cuts—and when satisfied, mounted gracefully despite the bulk of their armor.

They were a splendid looking group. She counted twenty of them, all turned out in crimson and black, and carrying helms that sported plumes of white and black feathers. One man bore a blood-red banner with the hawk emblazoned in the center of it.

Black Hawk's men were frightening enough just standing here. Gwen imagined they were downright terrifying when they rode you down in battle.

A group of horsemen caught her eye. "Rhys!"

She lifted her skirts and ran across the bailey, dodging puddles and animals. An old woman shook her fist when Gwen nearly ran into her. Gwen gave her a hasty apology and kept on going.

The bay stallion tossed his head impatiently as she ran to Rhys's side and gripped his calf.

"Were you going to leave without saying goodbye?" she asked breathlessly.

"I would not dream of it, Your Highness." Rhys's mouth lifted in a boyish smile, a smile that contained a hint of sadness. "Are you well, Gwen? Did he hurt you?"

Gwen fixed her gaze on his leg. "No, he did not hurt me," she said softly. Rhys touched her hair and she raised her eyes to his.

"If he ever does…"

"Have you seen Dafydd?"

"Nay, I have not." Rhys glanced in the direction she had come. "Be careful of him, Gwen."

Gwen nodded, unsure if he meant Dafydd or Richard, and unwilling to ask. She stepped away, forcing herself to smile.

"Take care, Rhys ap Gawain."

"I will." He studied her for a moment, his blue eyes keen. "If you ever need my help, I will be there."

She reached for his hand. "Oh Rhys—"

He shook his head. "No tears, Lady de Claiborne."

"No tears," she repeated, smiling past the glitter in her eyes. She knew he'd emphasized the title on purpose. She needed that reminder of her new life before she broke down and cried like the frightened girl she was.

The Welshmen who had brought her to Shrewsbury sat their mounts quietly. They all watched her, waiting. A lump formed in her throat. "Farewell to you all. Tell my father and Elinor I am well."

Without waiting for a reply, she turned on her heel and hurried away. She would surely cry if she allowed herself to wonder whether she would ever see any of them again.

Richard had emerged from the armory and stood beside Alys, a scowl on his face. He wasn't looking at her and she turned to follow his gaze. Rhys held the bay in place, returning Richard's stare.

Gwen's steps faltered momentarily. She forced herself to walk toward her husband. He was menacing in his chainmail. Covered from head to foot in leather and steel, the only splash of color was the crimson surcoat embroidered with the hawk device. Gwen shivered. He looked murderous.

His face was framed in metal, his eyes like silver-ice. He didn't utter a word when she stopped beside him.

A groom came from the stable, leading a huge black stallion. The horse pranced, snorting and neighing, and the boy's face turned white.

Richard jerked his gaze from the retreating Welshmen and whistled an intricate five-note call. The horse's ears pricked, then he quieted, stepping quickly. Gwen turned to stare at her husband. 'Twas a falconing call he had used.

The boy handed over the reins with shaking hands. Richard spoke to the horse in soothing tones, words Gwen could not quite hear although she recognized them as Welsh.

'Twas almost odd the way he used Welsh so naturally. But he had probably lived in the March his entire life and had learned it as a boy. It was a musical language, very suited to calming nervous animals. Or women. Awareness pricked her as she watched him smooth his hands over the stallion's neck.

Sirocco's body quivered. Gwen looked away suddenly. Had she trembled beneath Richard's hand too?

"Which horse am I to ride?" Gwen asked. The mare she had ridden to Shrewsbury was unsaddled and tied to a line of packhorses.

"You are riding with me," Richard said without looking at her.

Gwen fisted her mantle. "I am not a pampered English woman, my lord. I am capable of handling a horse."

He turned to regard her for a moment. "The March is dangerous. You ride with me." His tone did not invite argument.

Gwen fumed.

"Mount up!" Richard cried to the party. He turned to one of Lady Ashford's servants. "Girl, tell your mistress if she does not get out here now, I will leave without her."

"Aye, milord," the girl replied, sinking into a curtsy before running toward the castle.

Richard grasped Gwen by the waist and lifted her sideways onto Sirocco, then swung into the saddle behind her. Locked within his iron embrace, she wasn't afraid of falling from the tall stallion.

"Are you comfortable?" he asked.

"Well enough, my lord."

"I thought we had settled that," he said dryly.

Gwen refused to answer. A woman emerged from the castle and Gwen's jaw slackened. 'Twas the leman, Anne!

What the hell had she expected? Richard was an Englishman. He did not need his wife's permission to keep a mistress.

But the worst part was he thought so little of her that he would take no pains to hide it. It hurt to think the things he had done to her—the words he whispered and the way he touched her in places no man ever had—were nothing more than the skilled actions of a man well accustomed to lying with women.

Gwen bit back the bitter tears of betrayal that stung her eyes. She knew what kind of man he was. All men were horrible, and this one most of all.

Gwen shifted. She was much too aware of him, much too close to him right now. She did not think she could endure being held between his powerful thighs league after league.

She half-turned toward him. "Please," she begged. "Please let me ride my own horse."

He looked down at her and frowned. "What is the matter with you? I've not hurt you and yet you always want to get away from me. Do you truly find me so unpleasant?"

Gwen stared at the castle gates. No, not unpleasant. Just unnerving.

He stiffened when she didn't answer. Sirocco began to dance beneath them, his ears swiveling backward as he awaited his master's signal.

"Are you ready, Lady Ashford?" Richard asked irritably, his warm breath stirring past Gwen's ear.

"Aye, my lord," Anne replied.

As Sirocco surged forward, Gwen was pushed against Richard's chest. That woman was Lady Ashford? She glanced at the lady perched delicately on a small grey palfrey.

Envy flared in Gwen's soul. Anne was the court ideal, the one the romances sang about. Pale blonde hair peeked from under her headcovering, her skin was as white as snow, and her eyes were the blue of the sea. It was no wonder Richard wanted her.

But if she was not his leman, then he must have another one waiting at Claiborne castle. Gwen's spirits sank even further.

Richard kept Sirocco to a brisk walk until they reached the open country. Once outside the town gates, he signaled the company forward, and Sirocco leapt beneath them, eating the ground with long strides.

Gwen tried to forget where she was for a little while. The wind blew in her face, cold and exhilarating. The raw power of the horse beneath her was breathtaking, and she realized Richard was holding the stallion back so the packhorses could keep up.

Sirocco eventually settled into a smooth rhythm, and Gwen's eyes began to drift shut. She tried to keep them open, but she finally gave up and fell asleep against Richard's chest.

Richard turned to look at the train stretched out behind the company of knights. He'd had to call for a walk long ago. Anne's baggage could not keep up with knights on the move. Jesú, at this snail's pace they would never make Oswestry! He could not see the sun for the clouds, but he guessed it to be past midday.

He cursed Anne under his breath, and Ned for making him bring her. Though he doubted her reason for this journey, mayhap he was wrong. She'd not cared for her husband much, but her son was growing up quickly and would be lord of Ashford Hall in another few years. How old was Tristan now? Eight or nine, surely.

Sir Thomas of Ashford had been many years older than Anne when they married. When she had given him a son, Thomas was overjoyed, but then the poor man died in a border skirmish, as so many of the men living in the March did.

For a time, Anne had hoped to better her station by marrying him. In the end she'd had to be satisfied with being his mistress. He felt no guilt over it. Anne would spread her legs for any man with money and power. She had benefited as much as he from the pleasurable hours spent in bed together.

But even had he wanted, he could not have married her. She was a burgher's daughter and a knight's widow. She did not have rank, or land, or money—the things an earl needed in a bride, the things Elizabeth had when he married her.

Ned had found a way around Dunsmore's lack of wealth when they first returned to England. He had given Richard an heiress with land and money almost equal to that of Gilbert de Clare.

Richard squinted into the distance, trying to push away the memories of his first wife. On one side of them rose a tall forest of oak and evergreen. On the other were open fields of hay and, in the springtime, heather. Up ahead the road branched, one path leading into the forest, the other through the fields.

They would stick to the open country. With Anne's belongings screaming their presence, 'twas better to stay in the open, even though the forest path was the quicker.

Richard squeezed the reins, bearing down until the mail gauntlet bit into his flesh. Poor Elizabeth. He had never done right by her. He had married her for her possessions, and she knew it. She had loved him anyway, even though he didn't love her. He'd failed her in the end, just like he'd failed his father.

Richard looked down at the sleeping woman in his arms and had a sudden feeling that even had she possessed nothing, he would have married her anyway. He shook his head. It was a fanciful notion brought on by his feverish desire to have her. Once he'd made her his wife in deed as well as name, he would no longer have such ridiculous ideas.

Her hood had fallen back to reveal her face. Richard studied her. He could look as long as he liked and she'd never know. And he did like to look at her.

Long dark lashes feathered softly against pale cheeks. Tendrils of autumn-colored hair had come free from her braid and ringed her face in loose, spiraling curls. Her generous lips were parted like the petals of a blushing-rose, tormenting him with remembered kisses.

Her body was soft in sleep, molding to him so trustingly. Richard shifted in the saddle as he thought of her naked and in his arms just like this. Nay, not like this. Better. He pictured her beneath him, her body molded intimately to his, his masculine flesh surrounded by her silken heat. He shifted again. Chainmail and saddles were not designed for a man's comfort when aroused.

A fat droplet of rain smacked against Richard's helm, echoing in his ears. He snapped his head back. The sky was black. He swore vehemently. "Andrew!"

The captain of the guard reined his horse in beside Richard. "Aye, milord?"

"We have to find shelter. The women cannot ride in a storm." He paused, scanning the treeline. "We're still too far from Oswestry. Llanwell cave is near, is it not?"

Andrew grimaced, then nodded. "Aye, milord."

The wind began to swirl around them, the raindrops falling faster. Gwen stirred as the water hit her face. Richard tightened his arm about her waist. "We'll have to take a chance on it then!"

14

The company changed direction, leaving the road and threading through the dense forest. The trees deflected the rain somewhat, but the force of the storm grew greater with each passing minute until even the trees no longer protected them.

Gwen pulled her hood down over her eyes. Forest smells of evergreen and lichen hung in the air, mixing with the smell of wet horse. The cold wind pressed fingers of ice into her skin. She clung to Richard for warmth, but his armor prevented most of it from reaching her.

After what seemed like hours, they finally stopped. Richard sent a handful of knights forward. They returned a short time later, reporting that the cave he sought was empty.

It was located at the rear of a small clearing. The ground sloped gently uphill to the entrance, littered with leaves and fallen branches. The opening was wide enough for two men to pass through side by side, and tall enough for the tallest man, which she supposed had to be Richard.

They sheltered the animals beneath a stand of thick trees close to the entrance. Richard dismounted first, then held out his arms. Gwen slid into them, and he carried her inside.

The cave was large, much bigger than any she and Rhys had explored on Snowdon. Straw littered the floor and a pit had been dug in the center, the remains of charred logs still lying in it.

The ceiling was not very high. Spikes of rock hung from it like daggers, and Richard had to duck more than once. A man returned from the depths and reported that nothing was to be found before the cave dead-ended. Richard dismissed him and turned to the man at his side.

"We'll have to build a fire, Andrew."

"Milord, 'tis not a good idea."

"I know." Gwen clung to him, shivering. "Do it anyway. The ladies will freeze otherwise."

"Aye, we've enough of us to protect 'em, I suppose."

"We'll never make Oswestry at the pace we've been going, even if the storm subsides. We stay here tonight."

"Aye, milord." Andrew turned on his heel and went to direct the men.

"What does he mean, protect us?" Gwen asked.

Richard set her down. "'Tis the borderland, Gwen. There are always things to be protected from."

It was an odd thing to feel a tremor of fear here in the March. Even though clans waged war against one another, Gwen had always felt safe atop Snowdon.

"Once we've set up, I'll make sure you get to change into something dry."

Gwen nodded and he left her to join the men.

Alys hurried over. "We must get you some dry clothes, Highness," she said, rubbing her hands up and down her arms.

"I am fine, Alys. Take care of yourself. We will change and warm ourselves by a fire soon enough."

Anne Ashford sauntered over, her two maids close on her heels. "Well, my dear. We meet again it seems."

Gwen clamped down on her chattering teeth. "Indeed."

Anne removed her sodden wimple. "I remember you well. You're all grown up now, and such a pretty thing too. Aye, it makes me wonder what it is you lack that would send Richard to my door on his wedding night." She shook out her pale hair until it hung, straight and smooth, to her hips.

Gwen's stomach turned to ice. "I really do not care as to my husband's whereabouts. 'Tis of no concern to me."

"'Tis good then, since he is a man of immense appetites. He could never be faithful to you, dear."

Gwen flipped her hood back, then concentrated on wringing out her sleeves.

Anne laughed softly. "No doubt you are remembering his passion in the marriage bed. 'Tis so short-lived, passion. It takes much more than that to keep them interested once the new has worn off."

When Gwen still did not answer, Anne shrugged. "'Tis no concern of mine, but I will offer you some advice anyway. Don't lose your heart to him. He'll give it back to you in pieces."

Gwen raised her head, strangely sympathetic at that moment. "Is that what he did to you?"

Anne laughed gaily. "Oh no, of course not. Richard is a very interesting bed partner, but not the sort of man a sensible woman would fall in love with." She flashed her teeth in a condescending smile, then moved away, her maids behind her.

"That woman is a witch," Alys hissed.

"Aye," Gwen said. "But no doubt she tells the truth. I cannot blame her for that."

Alys merely looked at her, disbelieving.

"Where else could he have been last night? He was gone for most of the evening. I let him in myself shortly before sunrise."

Alys shook her head. "I still do not believe her. She seeks to unsettle you with all that talk. You should not listen."

Gwen put her hands on her hips. "You are entirely too taken in by him. He is not the kind man you think he is. He *is* Black Hawk!"

Alys turned red. "I know what is said of him, but I also know what my eyes tell me, child. I always trust my eyes. Words lie, the eyes do not."

Gwen knew Alys would not be convinced. Ever since Richard had apologized to her, Alys was his champion. The woman who had been a mother to Gwen for most of her nineteen years had been stolen from her by smooth words and a winning smile.

Gwen turned away, angry that he left no part of her life untouched. He wouldn't be satisfied until he'd taken everything.

Gwen stomped over and sank down against the wall. She already intended to pay him back for so many things. This was just one more item to add to the growing list.

In a very little while, the men had a fire going. They cordoned off an area of the cave with ropes, securing them on the daggers of rock hanging from the ceiling, then hung blankets to section it off for the women. Thankfully, they created two rooms. One for Gwen and Alys, the other for Anne and her maids.

Gwen was glad for that. She did not want to spend the entire night in the same room as Anne. Of course, mayhap Richard could have lain between them, gifting them each with a kiss and a caress from time to time. Gwen did not find the thought very amusing.

She slipped into a silk chemise and wool overgown, then donned a thick mantle lined with fox.

When she emerged to stand beside the fire, Richard came to her side. Water dripped from his surcoat and pooled at his feet. His helm was gone and his face was streaked with dirt. He no longer wore his gauntlets. Rusty water trickled from under his mail sleeves, staining his wrists and hands.

"Aren't you cold in all that metal?" Gwen asked.

Amusement lit his features. "Aye, sweet, I am."

"Why do you not take it off then?"

His voice was husky when he spoke. "Promise you will say that to me when we reach Claiborne castle."

Gwen blushed. She turned back to the fire, hoping she could blame the red glow on the heat. Why did the damn man affect her so?

He laughed. "As much as I would like, if I were to take it off here, who would protect *me* from cutthroats?"

"I never thought of that," Gwen admitted.

The storm whipped through the trees, whistling and blowing, for hours. When at last it quieted, darkness had settled in for the night.

Gwen went to bed when Richard joined his men at watch, only awaking when something big lowered itself beside her. The scream died in her throat as a hand clamped over her mouth and eased her back.

Her heart slowed as her sleepy senses registered Richard's familiar scent. He removed his hand carefully.

"You scared me!" she said. "Where is Alys?"

"With Lady Ashford and her maids."

He climbed beneath the blanket and stretched out beside her. He still wore the mail, but at least he was dry.

"I did not mean to wake you," he said.

"What time is it?"

"'Twill be daylight before too long."

"Do you ever sleep, my lord?" Gwen asked. Had he been with Anne just now, too?

He pulled her into his arms. Gwen did not protest, even though his armor was hard and cold. "Sometimes," he breathed.

He nuzzled her hair. Gwen shivered. God, it would be so easy to believe he was sincere in the things he did to her. But she could not, because that was the object of his game. A notorious ladies' man, Elinor had once told her.

"Are you cold?" he asked.

"Nay."

"Then why are you shaking?"

"I am not shaking," she lied.

"You're afraid of me."

Gwen started to deny it, but stopped before the words could form. She *was* afraid of him. Afraid of the way her heart quickened when he was near. Afraid of the way her body responded when he touched her, despite knowing who and what he was.

The fire burned softly in the middle of the cave, casting a buttery light into the makeshift chamber. His face was shadowed, but she caught the glint of an eye when he moved his head.

"I've not given you much reason to be anything other than frightened, have I?" He released her. Gwen felt a twinge of disappointment. It was kind of nice to be held close in the middle of the night when the world was dark and still. Reassuring somehow.

She reached for him, touched his hand. It happened so quickly that she did not realize she had done it until it was too late. "I... I know you will not hurt me."

He let his breath out on a long sigh, then turned on his side to face her. "Are we truly in danger here, my lord?"

"I would hear my name on your lips," he said, tracing her lower lip with his finger.

Gwen turned away. He gripped her chin gently and pulled her back. She gasped as his lips brushed across hers.

"Y-you did not ask," she said.

"I forgot," he whispered. His kiss was soft, gentle. Gwen's heart pounded furiously. When his tongue sought entrance, she did not deny him.

But it was different this time. Not the hot, almost desperate stroke of tongue on tongue, but a slow sensuous glide that wreaked havoc on Gwen's senses.

When she was certain she could take no more, he stopped as if he knew it, then traced a burning path down her neck. Her hands stole to his hair.

He lifted away and she opened her eyes to find him watching her. "My lord?"

He brushed his lips across hers. "Say it."

"W-what?"

His tongue caressed her lower lip. She shivered. "The way you said it before," he whispered.

She stiffened. "I—"

"*Say it.*"

"Richard," she said on a sigh.

Softly, he claimed her mouth, deepening the kiss with each passing second. Gwen was breathless by the time he terminated the contact.

"See, 'twas not so hard, was it?"

"Nay."

This was not the way it was supposed to be. He was supposed to be cruel and evil. She'd even been prepared to martyr herself. To submit to him, to his cruelty, to always know the pain he inflicted upon her was through no fault of her own. God, it would be so easy to hate him if he would only *do it!*

And yet he was a different man in the quiet hour before dawn. The hard edges were softened, almost gone. He was gentle somehow, a flesh and blood man with hopes and dreams.

She could almost believe him capable of love in these moments. But nay, his heart was as black as his name. She must not ever forget it!

He traced her jaw. "There is always a chance in the March that we will come across a hostile raiding party. Or a band of brigands. The road to Chester is full of travelers making pilgrimages to Holywell. Robbers hide out in these caves, emerging to waylay them and make off with the jewels and money they have brought for offerings."

Gwen shivered. This was something she knew a little about from listening to her father's councils. "My father does not sanction the raiding parties. He says the might of England cannot be stopped with small bands of Welshmen striking haphazardly through the March."

Richard's finger stilled. When she looked at him again, his eyes were hard and cold.

"'Tis almost amusing to hear you say so, my dear. But you see, I know better. Your father is as murderous and dishonest as the Sultan of Egypt was."

Gwen wanted to deny it, started to deny it, but could not. The pain in his voice was too real, too raw. Instead, she said very quietly, "Why do you say that?"

"Of course you could not know," he said half to himself, then louder, "My father was killed in a raid. All the men in his party were massacred, except one. That man swore Prince Llywelyn led the raid."

"Nay," Gwen whispered. She grabbed his hand. "He would not do it. I *know* he would not. 'Tis not possible!"

Richard jerked his hand away. Of course she would defend her father. But he couldn't say why it felt like a sword thrust to his heart. "Do not tell *me* what is possible, Princess. I have fought too many battles, seen too many English corpses, to not know what the Welsh are capable of."

"And you have slaughtered countless Welshmen in retaliation for what you believe!"

He gripped her arms suddenly. "What would you have me do, daughter of Llywelyn? Should I let them terrorize English towns? Burn out farmers and peasants? Steal their cows and pigs?"

Gwen stared at him through wide eyes, her face only inches from his. "I-I do not know. But there must be a better way."

"Jesú, why did you have to be Llywelyn's daughter?" He let her go, then sat up and raked his hands through his hair. "Nothing good will ever come of this union. To you I am an evil murderer, and to me—" He took a deep breath. "To me, you are a living reminder of the man I've sworn to kill."

Gwen scrambled upright and grabbed two fistfuls of his surcoat. "You cannot kill him! You signed a treaty of friendship. I'll not let you do it!"

"Nay, Princess, I cannot kill him yet. But one day, he'll do something to break that treaty and then—"

"You are wrong! He did not do it! Where is this man, this survivor? How did he know it was my father?"

"He knew," Richard growled.

Gwen felt like a kitten that had gotten a tiger by the tail, but she wasn't about to let go. "I want to speak to him! I'll prove he's wrong!"

"You cannot." His teeth flashed white as he bared them in a cruel smile. "He's dead."

Gwen fisted his surcoat tighter. "I do not believe you."

"I am sorry, sweet, but 'tis true. He died before I got back from Crusade."

Gwen let him go. She sank back on her heels, staring at the floor. The man was dead. Richard would never believe her.

Black Hawk de Claiborne was going to kill her father. She felt the hot trickle of tears as they washed over her cheeks. When she raised her head, Richard was watching her, his expression unreadable.

"Gwen..." He lifted his hand, then dropped it again when it was halfway to her face. Shoving himself to his feet, he muttered a curse, and stalked into the night.

G wen smacked at Alys's hand, mumbling, then finally opened her eyes. The pain that rocked through her head almost made her collapse back on the blankets.

She swallowed, the ache in her throat but another agonizing reminder of the night she had passed. God how she wished she had some willow bark.

"Water, Alys. Please," Gwen said, tucking an errant lock of hair behind her ear as she climbed to her feet.

When Alys returned, Richard was with her. He frowned. "You are unwell?"

Gwen gripped the cup, her knuckles turning white. She wanted to scream. She'd cried herself to sleep after he'd gone. This was his fault and he stood there like some kind of a god, demanding to know if she felt well. "Whatever made you think that, my lord? I am quite well, thank you."

He glanced at Alys, then put a finger under Gwen's chin. She jerked away, stung by his touch. He dropped his hand to his side, his brow furrowing.

Alys mumbled an excuse and disappeared.

He clasped his hands behind his back and planted his feet apart. "I am sorry if I upset you. I said things I should not have. 'Tis not your fault for the things your father has done. I do not blame you."

"How noble of you," Gwen said dryly. "And I can assure you I do not need your insincere concern over my well being, my lord. Please do not strain your tongue by uttering things you don't mean."

He spoke as if he'd never wronged the Welsh in his life, as if all the blame could be laid at her father's feet. A distant part of her realized he was apologizing and that it was probably a thing he was unaccustomed to doing, but she didn't care.

He straightened to his full height, his eyes glittering like mountain ice. "You really push the limits of my patience, wife. I'll not have you behaving like the barbarian you were brought up to be. In England, a wife knows her place. I expect you to learn yours."

Gwen spat a Welsh curse at him. On impulse, she tossed the contents of the cup in his face. Her blood pounded in her temples as his features hardened. He was on her in a split second, pinning her between the cave wall and his chest.

Water trickled down his surcoat and flowed between them, seeping into her gown. Gwen pressed her cheek against the cool rock, squeezed her eyes shut, and braced herself for the blow he would surely give her this time.

Breathless seconds passed. She felt him brushing her hair back over her shoulder and she opened an eye warily. His warm breath tickled her ear as his lips pressed into the soft flesh below it. A tingle rippled down her spine.

He seized her earlobe between his teeth, nipping it gently while she bit her lip to keep from moaning. His mouth made a mockery of her resistance when he swept hot kisses across her throat. Her fingers dug into the rock to keep from clasping his head.

His voice was soft and velvety when he spoke. "Know that I can take what is rightfully mine whenever I wish. I could have done so many times over by now, but I have not. Would you like it right here against this wall with my men listening to your cries? They'll not help you. If I choose to beat you afterward, none will come to your aid."

One hand snaked beneath her loosened neckline. Gwen gasped as his thumb brushed her nipple, ashamed she couldn't control her reactions when it beaded beneath his touch.

"You like this," he murmured.

"Nay!"

"Aye," he said, pushing her gown aside and lowering his mouth to her breast. Gwen moaned. His tongue made delicate forays around the sensitive tip until she knew she would go mad. The trickle of cool water over her heated skin did not dampen the desire. In fact, it made the sensation more erotic.

She couldn't stop herself from saying it. Nay, moaning it. "Richard..."

The insistent pressure of his body, the hot feel of his mouth, the cool water dripping off him, and the scent of his maleness were all gone. Gwen opened her eyes to find him watching her, his face hard and distant. She yanked her gown closed.

He'd just made a fool of her. He'd provoked her desire until she responded, then backed away and left her reeling with a flame in her gut. Clutching the gown, her face flaming with indignance and shame, she lifted her chin and looked him square in the eye.

"I hate you." She'd meant it to come out forcefully, but it sounded more wounded than anything.

"So you've said before." He wiped his face on the edge of his mantle. "But it matters not. I do not need your love, only the sons you will give me. And I think I've proven you will be more than eager to give them to me. Now get ready, we leave shortly. I will come for you when 'tis time to go."

He walked out and Gwen flung the cup at his broad back. It missed, glancing off the hangings instead. The arrogant, no good, vile, insufferable English swine! She spun around and kicked the cave wall, then sank to the floor and clutched her foot in both hands.

Alys returned, frowning as she bent to retrieve the cup. "Men can be beasts sometimes." She began to fold the blankets and stow them for travel.

Gwen looked up in surprise. "Aye."

Pushing at the curtain of hair that fell across her face, she picked up a brush and started to work out the snarls. When she had straightened her clothes and put on her shoes, she stepped into the open cave.

The knights and their squires hustled around, breaking camp with the efficiency of men long used to hard lives in the wild.

Gwen walked to the entrance. Richard stood beside his stallion, his back to her, tightening the fastenings of the saddle.

The ground was icy where the rain had frozen in the night, spangled like stars sprinkled across the earth. Gwen's breath curled in the frigid air. She thought of Snowdon and the early snows that would have claimed the slopes by now. She hoped Elinor and her father were well. She would have to write to them when she got to Claiborne.

Would Richard allow her to write her father? Even if he did not, she would find a way.

She wandered into the clearing, breathing deep the forest smells of evergreen and autumn. The sky was heavy with fleecy clouds. The first snows would come soon here too. Gwen reached for her hood, shaking off a sudden feeling of uneasiness.

Within the space of a heartbeat, she heard a high-pitched whistling sound, then a sickening *thunk* and a man screaming. She dropped the hood, instinctively searching for Richard.

He was not in the same place he'd been only moments before. Men and horses scrambled everywhere. Voices shouted in alarm. She thought she heard someone calling her name but she did not turn around.

She caught sight of Richard as he swung into the saddle, his dark head towering above the rest. Relief flooded her. He unsheathed his sword with a quick movement and settled the large shield with the hawk device in front of him. Sirocco's ears pinned to his head, his nostrils flaring with the scent of battle.

All the knights who had managed to mount galloped toward the woods, charging the brigands' position in an attempt to drive them back. Arrows whistled through the air, the sound eerie and inhuman. Gwen turned to run. Her gaze lighted on the man who had screamed. She stopped, pressing a shaking hand to her mouth.

The arrow was embedded in the knight's chest, the shaft sticking out of the steel as if it were Excalibur buried in the stone. His life's blood seeped from his body, a crimson stain spreading across the frozen ground.

Only an arrow fired from a Welsh longbow could pierce a knight's armor as if it were an egg. She shuddered, scanning the treeline. The archer would have needed to be fairly close to fire such a deadly shot. The impact of the longbow was much greater at close range. At hand-to-hand range, it was deadly.

Oh God, Richard! She took a faltering step forward, searching for him again.

An arrow slammed into his shield, burying itself. Gwen sank to her knees, unaware she had screamed. Richard shouted at her, but she couldn't move. He spurred Sirocco toward her, placing himself and the huge stallion between her and the onslaught of arrows.

Breathless minutes passed before the arrow fire ceased as abruptly as it had begun. Next would come the charge with spears and swords and war cries. Gwen waited, but nothing happened. Mayhap the Welshmen realized they were out-numbered among so many armored knights.

Richard yelled a command. Within seconds, several knights galloped off in pursuit.

He dropped his shield and jumped from Sirocco's back, falling to his knees beside her. "Are you hurt?" He ran his hands over her, his gaze following quickly.

"Nay," she whispered, staring at the clearing. Arrows scattered the ground. Some were buried in the earth until only the feathered tips protruded. There were no other bodies and for that she was thankful.

He flung himself to his feet, then jerked her up by the arm. His grip was not gentle as he propelled her into the cave.

Alys huddled with Anne and her maids. Tears streamed down her face as she ran to Gwen.

"Why did you not come when I called?" Her hand shook as she smoothed it over Gwen's arm. Gwen opened her mouth. Something told her she should apologize, but no words would come out. Richard spoke first.

"'Tis over now, Alys. Your lady is fine. Sit with Anne and her maids a while longer and dry your tears."

Alys bit her lip and nodded, then returned to the group of women.

Richard hauled Gwen deeper into the cave until they rounded a corner and were out of sight of the others. He whirled her to face him.

"You stupid little witch! What the hell were you thinking?"

Gwen blinked, barely conscious of him. "They were Welsh," she said woodenly.

"Of course they were Welsh!" His eyes narrowed. "How did you know?"

"The knight... the longbow... the arrow—" Tears trickled down her cheeks.

"Christ," he whispered, pulling her against him. She clung to him, the tears spilling soundlessly. He stroked her hair, her back. "You should not have seen that."

He smelled of sweat and steel and rust. Gwen gripped his surcoat, pressing her nose against it, inhaling him. The sound of his breathing was reassuring, and for a while she could pretend he was still her knight from Rhuddlan castle.

He held her for a long time and Gwen realized he would not break the contact first. She stayed in his arms longer than necessary, enjoying it even though she should not. For a time, it did not matter who and what he was. She had feared for him and he was safe and he was holding her and it felt good.

But it could not last forever. She dried her eyes on her sleeve and tried to move away. He tightened his arms around her. "You could have been killed. Never leave safety so foolishly again."

Gwen traced the outline of the hawk over his breast. His concern did seem genuine, whether it was or not. She decided to pretend it was. It felt nice. "Yes, Richard," she said softly.

He tilted her face up and kissed her. She melted against him, clung to him like he was an anchor in a fierce storm. He pulled away first.

Pressing his forehead to hers, he said, "We cannot leave until Andrew returns. I have much to do until then."

He took her hand, gently this time, and led her back to the others. When she sat next to Alys, he went to join his men.

Anne shot her a smug look. "Not doing so well, are you dear?"

Gwen was not in the mood for Anne Ashford. She ignored her, hoping the woman would take the hint. She did not.

"Richard is not difficult to please. Demanding, certainly, but not difficult. Of course, if you had managed to satisfy him, he would not be so hard on you now."

Gwen raised her head slowly. Anne smiled. Gwen's voice was low when she spoke. "You should be careful, Lady Ashford. You know what is said of the Welsh. We are savages, barbarians. There is no telling what we might do."

Anne's smile faded. The two maids' eyes widened. Alys glared at them, punctuating Gwen's meaning.

"Come, Alys." Gwen stood, brushed the folds of her gown, and walked away with her chin in the air. Alys trailed behind her. Gwen could hear the woman chuckling under her breath.

"That was telling her, my lady," Alys said when they sank down closer to the entrance.

Gwen smiled. "Sometimes, 'tis an advantage to have the English think us barbarians."

Richard reentered the cave, and her eyes were drawn to him. He was every inch a commander. His men listened to him with admiration and respect, then hurried to carry out his orders without question. And yet he also seemed to be listening to them, accepting their advice, and acting accordingly.

Gwen clasped her hands together to keep from fidgeting with her cloak. When the Welsh had attacked, she'd had no thoughts for her countrymen. She'd only been afraid Richard would die.

But wasn't that what she really wanted? If he were dead, she could go home. She would not be forced to be his wife, to bear his touch. Her heart cried out at the thought of him dead, the same as she had cried out earlier.

No, she did not wish him dead, especially after what she had seen today. She would wish that on no man.

Almost an hour passed before the knights returned. Andrew rushed in, his panting breath frosting quickly in the frigid air, his words coming out in half-gasps.

"Got away, milord. No sign of others."

Richard smacked a mail-clad fist inside his hand. "God's bones! We can't stay to track them. I've got to get the women out of here."

"Me an' Matthew can do it. Leave half the garrison an' we'll catch 'em, milord."

Richard rubbed his face absently. It was a good idea under normal circumstances. He glanced at Gwen, then shook his head. "Nay. I need every man to guard the ladies and the baggage. We'll make Claiborne by the end of the day, then we will return on the morrow."

"Aye, milord," Andrew said, dipping his chin to his chest in salute.

Richard's gaze strayed to his new wife. Jesú, he did not want to leave her so soon, but he had no choice. Duty called.

He went to her and held out his hand. "We are leaving now, sweet."

He wasn't angry with her anymore although he should be. When he'd seen her standing in the clearing amid all that arrow fire, his heart had dropped to his feet. And when he'd pulled her inside and confronted her, he'd had to fight himself not to shake her until her teeth rattled.

But then she'd turned to him for comfort and like some poor besotted fool, all his anger fled. In that moment, all he'd wanted was to hold her close and protect her.

She slipped her hand in his and he helped her to her feet. Her hand was so small, so soft and delicate; so out of place in his large, battle-hardened one.

Her sweet scent wrapped around his senses, tormented him with remembered dreams. God how he wanted her! He barely stopped himself from crushing her to him and burying his face in her silky hair.

Outside, Sirocco stamped his feet, snorting and twitching. The battle had excited the stallion and he was eager to gallop. As before, he quieted instantly when Richard spoke.

He turned to lift Gwen onto the horse. She was watching him, but her gaze darted away, her cheeks flushing light pink. With the instinct of a man who knows the strength of his attraction to the opposite sex, Richard knew she had watched his hands skim Sirocco's neck, had remembered them skimming her body.

The knowledge sent a surge of triumph through him—and a desire so strong it nearly took his breath away.

His hands spanned her waist and he found himself thinking how slight she was. For an instant, he wondered if she could withstand his passion. Surely he would break her in two if he weren't careful.

He pulled her to him, held her against him longer than necessary. Their gazes locked, and she suddenly turned her head away.

"Look at me," he commanded softly.

She did and he touched his lips to hers. Unable to stop at such a brief taste, he deepened the kiss. Her response was both innocent and passionate, and his loins ached from want of her.

"Jesú," he swore.

"My lord?"

He traced a finger from her forehead to her jaw. "I was just wondering if the rest of you will taste as sweet."

Her color deepened. He lifted her onto Sirocco's back, then donned his helm and buckled the straps securing it to his hauberk. When he'd pulled on his mail gauntlets, he climbed behind her.

"Where is he?" she asked as they began to move.

"Who?"

"The dead knight."

"His body is tied to his horse. We must take him home and give him a proper burial. I shall have to tell his wife." He cleared his throat. "Hugh had two children."

Gwen swallowed past the raw ache in her throat. She wanted to cry for Hugh, for his wife, for his children, but she had no tears left. She didn't know him, but the senselessness of it all appalled her.

Would this bloodshed between Wales and England never end?

Richard obviously cared about his men. It was the sort of thing her father would do, personally telling the wife of a fallen soldier instead of sending a messenger. It was noble and honorable.

Gwen relaxed in the iron embrace of the man behind her. Black Hawk de Claiborne had just risen a notch in her estimation.

When at last Claiborne castle rose in the distance, Gwen squinted as though she could see it better by doing so. They'd long ago parted company with Anne, who was on her way to Ashford Hall with some of Richard's knights for escort. Gwen prayed that was the last she would see of Richard's lover.

Beyond the castle, the River Dee slashed through mountain rock on its course to the Irish Sea. Claiborne perched on an escarpment high over the river valley, the crimson banner with the black hawk waving from its turrets.

It loomed larger and larger with each passing second. Gwen swallowed a bubble of fear. This was Claiborne castle, castle of cruelty, castle of death. It was the last, the mightiest castle between the March and Snowdonia.

A small village clustered onto the hillside below the castle. Daylight waned as they approached the town. A cry went up from the watch and the heavy gates creaked open slowly.

A dog barked somewhere. Chickens scattered, clucking noisily, as the big destriers disturbed their pecking. The mingled smells of food and filth permeated the air.

The road was muddy. Thatch-roofed houses lined the street on either side. The shops were closed, their windows boarded up until tomorrow. Smoke rose from holes in the ceilings, carrying the smell of stews and meat. Gwen's stomach growled.

Riding steadily upward, Gwen was amazed at the sheer size of the castle. It was ringed by a second curtain wall that boasted no less than six towers. Two of the massive towers rose up on either side of the gates. Peppered with arrow slots, they looked like faces with hundreds of probing eyes. Chains clanked somewhere within the walls and the iron portcullis raised its sharp teeth. Behind it, heavy wooden gates swung open and yet another portcullis stood beyond, slowly cranking upward.

When they rode beneath the arch, Gwen looked up. The sharp spikes of the portcullis stared back at her, and murder holes gashed the ceiling.

Boiling oil would be poured on the unsuspecting enemy who managed to make it beneath the arch.

They halted in the bailey and Richard slid from Sirocco's back, holding out his arms for her. He set her down and she smoothed her skirts, ignoring the needling pain in her limbs caused from so many hours spent in the saddle.

Torchlight illuminated the curious faces around her. Gwen regarded them with apprehension. She was Welsh and they were English. It reminded her of her days at Windsor, and she suddenly longed to disappear.

"'Tis good to see you home, milord."

Gwen's head snapped up. The man had spoken in Welsh. A short stocky man of advanced years bowed to Richard. His long gray hair was tied back with a thong and he had a shaggy beard that reminded her of Einion's.

"Owain, this is the new Countess of Dunsmore," Richard said, pulling her forward by the hand. He had removed his helm, and Gwen was struck anew by the raw beauty of his features.

Owain's face split in a toothy smile. "Ah, Lady, you are even more lovely than I imagined. Be well come to Claiborne castle. I am Lord de Claiborne's steward and I look forward to serving you."

Gwen stammered a thank you, momentarily caught off guard. The man was Welsh! She glanced at Richard. Black Hawk de Claiborne left a Welshman in charge of his household?

"We'll not dine in the hall tonight," Richard said. "Send food and bathwater to my chamber."

Owain bowed again, smiling. "As you wish, milord."

Gwen thought he winked but she wasn't sure.

"And fetch Father Stephen. Hugh de Lydford has fallen in battle."

Owain's face grew solemn. "Shall I send a messenger to Lydford manor?"

Richard shook his head. "Nay," he said, sounding suddenly very weary. "I am riding out on the morrow. I will tell Lady de Lydford myself."

Gwen's heart sank. He was leaving her here alone. Not that being with him was a comfort, but at least she knew him. Her gaze skittered over the crowd.

Owain frowned. "You cannot leave. You have only just arrived. What of your bride?"

Gwen liked this Owain already. And at least he was Welsh. That made her feel somewhat more at home.

"I must, Owain. You will take care of Lady de Claiborne in my absence."

Owain stepped closer, his voice an angry whisper. "You push yourself too hard, Richard!"

Gwen stared at the two men. This old Welshman dared to speak to his English lord as though he were an errant child. She expected Richard to explode.

"I do what I must do," Richard said stiffly.

"You have proved yourself a thousand times over. Send the knights like the other Marchers do."

"Owain," Richard growled.

The Welshman stepped back, drawing himself up. "Milord," he said curtly.

Richard took Gwen's hand and led her into the castle. He hustled her through the Great Hall so fast she barely got a look at it.

What she did see would have been enough to give Elinor fits for a year. The room was dingy from the smoke of the heating fires. She couldn't tell if the rushes were fresh, but she doubted it since dogs trotted between the tables, begging handouts from the seated knights.

Serving women looked more like whores than anything, their clothing disarrayed and stained with wine and handprints. Gwen even thought she saw a man and woman coupling on one of the benches, but she wasn't certain.

Even if she hadn't, there were enough wenches seated on men's laps as to leave no doubt to the sort of things that went on in Claiborne castle.

They passed through without stopping and Gwen realized with dismay that Richard wasn't going to introduce her to his household as his new wife and countess. How was she supposed to command any respect if he showed her none?

He stopped in front of a large door and pressed her back against it. "I have wanted to do this for hours..." Dipping his head, he claimed her mouth in a hungry kiss.

Gwen's hands splayed across his chest in a defensive gesture, but his kiss was so intoxicating that she was powerless to end it. "Wh-where are we?" she asked when he finally released her.

"Our chamber," he said, smiling his cool predator's smile.

"B-but I thought I would be staying in the women's quarters, f-for now."

He opened the door, then caught her in his arms before she tumbled backward. "Silly wench," he teased, picking her up and stepping over the threshold. "Even the naivest of virgins knows a man and woman must be in the same room if they are going to make love."

16

"You promised!" Gwen cried as he set her down in the middle of the room.

A devilish smile lit his handsome face. "Aye, I've not forgotten. But, how am I ever supposed to get you to agree if I stick you in another part of the castle?"

Gwen hadn't counted on that bit of logic. It never occurred to her that he would still try to seduce her. She moved away from him, then stopped when she realized she was walking on a tapestry. She whirled to face him. "I am sorry, my lord. I did not know it had fallen on the floor."

Richard laughed. "You have done nothing wrong. You can walk on it." She looked down, saw that he too stood in the middle of the colorful cloth. "'Tis from the East. The Saracens use them. 'Tis called a 'carpet'."

Gwen took a step, testing the fabric. She had heard that the queen used carpets in her private apartments, but she had never gone there when she was a hostage at Windsor.

It was not unpleasant. It would most certainly feel better on her naked feet than rushes did. She looked around the room in disbelief, finally noticing the difference between it and the rest of the castle. 'Twas the exact opposite of everything she'd seen so far!

The master chamber reflected the tastes and personality of the man who dwelt here. It was large and furnished with the most basic of elements. The only exotic thing was the carpet.

A stone fireplace lay against one wall, a massive wooden tub sitting next to the hearth. Three large windows, all with glass, looked out on the river valley. A table with several plain chairs stood to one side of the room. The walls were white, painted with red lines to resemble bricks, and a large tapestry hung facing the canopied bed.

Gwen swallowed hard. Two hawks, one larger than the other, soared side-by-side high over a lake. The larger one gripped a fish in its talons.

Richard followed her gaze. "'Tis beautiful, is it not?"

Gwen nodded.

"'Tis also from the Holy Land. 'Tis the male and female. They mate for life, you know," he said softly.

"Aye," she replied, pressing a hand to her throbbing temple. Where was she going to get some willow bark?

Servants came bearing trays of food, and hot water for the bath. When they had filled the tub and laid the food on the table, Gwen found herself alone with Richard once more. She did not know what to do, so she waited for him to move first.

"'Tis a wife's duty to undress her husband and bathe him," he said, coming to her.

"You are wearing armor," Gwen said, studying her feet.

Richard chuckled. "An Englishwoman would know how to remove her husband's armor."

Her head snapped up and she glared at him. He drew off his gauntlets and tossed them on the table, then unclasped her mantle and let it drop to the floor. She stood very still as he pulled the tie from her hair and moved behind her. His fingers deftly loosened the braid, shaking it out until her hair fell to her waist in a silky cloud.

Gwen's heart was in her throat. "W-what are you doing?"

"Since you cannot attend me, I will attend you." He reached for the girdle at her waist and unknotted it smoothly.

"I do not need your help, my lord," she said, trying to pull away from him. "What of your promise?"

"Jesú, you are so worried about that, aren't you?" A lazy grin spread across his face. "I can promise you, my sweet, that when I make love to you, 'twill be with your complete permission. In fact, you will ask me— nay, beg me—to do it."

Gwen stiffened. "You are outrageous."

"Some might say so." He stripped her down to her chemise, and she breathed a sigh when he turned and shrugged out of his hauberk.

Rust stained his quilted gambeson orange. He laid it out carefully beside the shirt of mail and continued to divest himself of the armor until he was clad only in a tunic and chausses.

Gwen watched him out of the corner of her eye as he took her hand and led her to the tub. His mouth curved in a smile as he lifted the bottom of her chemise. She held her arms rigidly to her sides, stopping his progress.

"Come now, love," he coaxed, "the sight of your beautiful body gives me much pleasure. Would you deny me when I will be gone for God knows how long?"

Gwen relaxed slowly. It was just this once and she was the one with the say so. It couldn't hurt to allow him this much.

He eased the chemise up, caressing her hips, her waist, the sides of her breasts, before lifting it off.

"Jesú," he breathed, his eyes darkening. She crossed her arms over her breasts and he reached up to undo them. "Let me look at you."

His gaze traveled down her body, slowly, slowly. Gwen resisted the urge to cover herself. Her nipples tightened, and he murmured his appreciation. He lingered so long on her triangle of flaming curls that she wondered if he'd forgotten the rest of her.

Her eyes flickered over him, widening at the bulge straining against his clothes. She looked up in time to see him swallow hard.

"Get in," he said, his voice low, intense.

Gwen obeyed. Warmth flowed down her spine like honey as she settled into the water. God, it was wonderful after the cold ride through the March! She closed her eyes and leaned her head against the edge.

Mayhap she could forget that Richard was staring at her like she was a cup of wine and he was dying of thirst.

"I think there is room enough for two in there."

Her eyes shot open. He was removing the rest of his clothes. "You promised!"

"I said nothing about baths, Gwen, only making love."

This time she could not tear her eyes from him. She would see his male sex even though she was terrified of it. Her heart lodged in her throat as his clothes peeled away.

He was beautiful, every last inch of him. Flame and shadow licked over his bronze body. His manhood only emphasized what she'd already seen. And it was every bit as big as she'd thought it would be.

Weapon was an adequate word. It stuck out like a knight's lance, and beneath it was a sac much like a stallion's. Black hair curled around the base, the same black hair that trailed from his chest to the juncture of his thighs and down his legs.

Her mouth dropped open. That thing was supposed to fit inside her. Elinor had told her so. It was the only thing Elinor had told her, but she'd assured Gwen it would work.

"Do you like what you see, sweet?" Amusement tickled the corners of his mouth.

Gwen turned away, her face hot.

Richard chuckled and stepped into the tub. The water rose considerably beneath his bulk, some of it splashing over the sides to soak the beautiful carpet. He seemed not to care.

He sat at the other end, facing her, his legs stretching along either side of hers. "'Tis heavenly, is it not?"

Gwen glanced at him. "Aye." She crossed her hands over her breasts, trying to ignore the feel of his skin against hers. He reached for the soap and a cloth.

"Come here."

"I would rather not, my lord."

"Back to that, are we? Come here, Gwen. Have I hurt you yet?"

"Nay," she admitted reluctantly. She scooted forward until he could reach her. He uncrossed her arms and ran the lathered cloth slowly over her breasts. Gwen closed her eyes.

Why did it not feel the same when she did it? It glided over her breasts, her neck, her face. Her skin warmed beneath his touch, then chilled when he moved on.

He washed her arms, then moved lower, down her belly, down—

"Nay!"

"'Tis only a cloth, Gwen." He slid it over her mons again.

Gwen bit her lip at the delicious sensation. Mayhap he did not know the feeling it caused when he touched her there.

"See, 'tis only a cloth," Richard said huskily. "It does not hurt, does it?"

"Nay," she whispered, watching him, her entire body quivering with each brush of the cloth against her womanhood. When he stopped, she almost asked him not to, then caught herself at the last second.

He turned her until her back was to him. She hesitated, then did as he directed. He lathered her hair, massaging her head with sure fingertips. She leaned further and further into him until she brushed against his stiff member.

Richard groaned, and she jumped. He rinsed her head gently, then handed her the cloth. "Your turn," he said.

Gwen's jaw dropped. She retreated to the far end of the tub and turned to face him. "My lord, surely you do not expect—"

"Aye, I do." He had the audacity to grin.

She took a deep breath and moved toward him. She touched the cloth to his chest, hesitantly at first. His silver eyes glittered. She rubbed harder. It was a stretch to reach him. She got to her knees and moved closer.

The dirt from his armor washed away, leaving the handsome face that had haunted her dreams for the last four years.

He shifted and the unexpected motion threw her off balance. He caught her as she fell against him.

Gwen gasped. The hair on his chest was rough against her breasts, and deliciously erotic. He pulled her closer until her torso was pressed to his, his manhood straining between them.

"You torment me, Gwen," he whispered. "You've tormented me for years."

He crushed his mouth to hers. Gwen opened to him like a rose to the first morning light, responding to his caresses with feverish intensity. He trailed wet kisses down her neck, and she threw her head back, arching into him. His hands moved over her, shaping her.

She gave a little cry as his mouth closed over her nipple, pleasure bolting through her like a tongue of fire.

He teased the hard bud, and then he was sucking on it, nipping it. When he stopped, Gwen thought she would burst, but he took the other nipple in his mouth and began again. Her fists curled into his shoulders.

His hand glided down her body. He cupped her mound, his fingers stroking the hot flesh. A tremor shook her when his thumb brushed across the nub of her womanhood.

Liquid heat flowed through her veins. Every nerve ending in her body came alive as his hand moved over her again and again. This was madness. Every caress, every shudder, inescapably bound her to him.

It had to stop.

His mouth closed over hers, his tongue probing urgently. One hand splayed across her back, crushing her against his hard chest.

He picked her up and when she sat down again, her legs were over his thighs and his swollen manhood pressed against her mons. He grasped her buttocks in both hands and slid her upward along the length of it.

Gwen tore her mouth from his as fear welled up inside her. "Nay!" she cried, pushing against him. He was a big, brutal warrior. His mating would be savage, feral, uncontrolled.

"I want you," he breathed against her neck. "God, how I want you! Do not deny me, Gwen." His voice was hoarse, almost pleading.

Indecision washed over her. It was happening too fast. Her body ached for him even while she feared him. He was her husband and it was only right she give in. And yet if she did, she knew she would be lost—hopelessly, irrevocably lost. He would demand nothing less than total surrender, and when he was done he would leave. She was just another conquest, and she couldn't bear it.

"I-I cannot," she said.

His arms tightened around her briefly, and then he shoved her away. His eyes flashed in the firelight. "I'll not wait forever, wife."

Gwen looked away, crossing her arms over her breasts as he stood and stepped from the tub.

When she finally stole a glance at him, he was nearly dressed. His face was hard, savage. The muscle in his jaw twitched.

Gwen knew despair in that moment. He would spend the night in some other woman's bed, touching her, kissing her with all the passion that should be Gwen's.

"Ask Owain for anything you might need while I'm gone. I will instruct him to teach you how to administer a castle in your lord's absence. I doubt you had much training for that in your father's household."

Gwen gripped the padded edge of the tub. "When will you return?"

"Do you care?" he asked harshly. He rubbed a hand over his brow, his voice softening. "I don't know. It could be days, maybe weeks."

Gwen's heart sank. She almost changed her mind, almost asked him to make love to her, but the words were too foreign.

He scooped up the armor. "'Tis best if I sleep elsewhere this night. I will send Alys to attend you."

Gwen's blood roared in her temples. "You mean you will spend the night in another woman's bed."

His face darkened. "You'll not question me, wife," he growled. "I'm a man. I have needs. If you cannot meet them, 'tis your own fault if I spend myself on another."

He left and Gwen smacked her hand against the water. Fat droplets splashed her face, trickling down her neck to wash away the lingering sensation of his kisses.

Richard strode into the Great Hall. A pretty wench eyed him and licked her lips. He watched her, undecided. His body throbbed. This girl was new. He'd not taken her before.

She swung her head toward the pantry. Richard nodded. He followed, closing the door behind him. The pantry was deserted, as she must have known it would be. Loaves of bread, and the remains of prepared dishes from the kitchen, were laid out on the shelves and tables.

The girl lifted her skirts, smiling. Richard swallowed. Goddamn his flame-haired bitch of a wife to hell! He would not wait for her to give him the release he sought. It was her fault she drove him to this.

A niggling voice told him he'd gone too fast with her. He'd let his need spiral out of control and he'd frightened her. If he went back and started over, plied her with sweet talk and gentle caresses, she would surrender to him, he was sure of it.

But going back would mean humbling himself. Richard clenched his jaw. He would not beg a woman for her favors, especially when there were others willing to appease him.

He'd wanted to deny her accusations of infidelity, but anger and pride prevented him. She would learn her place and she would learn not to question or accuse him.

Richard eyed the wench doubtfully. If he did this, it would put Gwen in a bad position. He shook his head. He was the lord of this castle. The servants would obey Gwen because she was his wife, whether he tumbled serving wenches or not. The lord always kept lemans.

Despite the display of legs and female attributes, his shaft was flaccid. Richard closed his eyes and thought of Gwen. He pictured her in his tub, her creamy skin glistening with moisture, her green eyes wide, her lips parted in discovery.

His manhood cooperated. He was going to do this. He was going to prove, to himself and to her, that he would not be ruled by any woman.

He released the drawstring of his chausses and braies. The girl smiled and licked her lips.

Richard swallowed again. "Like this," he said, turning her so she was bent face first over a table. Her round bottom wiggled, inviting him to sheathe himself within the glistening pink folds of her womanhood.

He shoved all thoughts of Gwen from his mind and stepped closer, gripping the girl's hips.

"Aye, milord, aye," she panted.

The sound of her voice, high-pitched, not throaty and musical like Gwen's, shattered his single-minded concentration.

Richard backed away, his stomach twisting. "Not tonight."

Bloody hell if he wasn't losing his mind. His hands were actually shaking as he fastened his clothes!

He turned away when the girl faced him. Her skirts dropped into place with a swish. She waited, as if he might change his mind.

"Get back to the hall," he snapped.

"Aye, milord." The door closed behind her and Richard leaned against a table, bracing himself with his hands.

God help him, he couldn't do it. He couldn't leave Gwen to face a servant he'd recently bedded. They might obey her, but they'd laugh behind her back.

He should have taken the time to introduce her in the hall tonight. Now she would have to forge her own way with the staff. Owain would help her, he would see to it.

He almost succeeded in convincing himself that was the only reason he'd stopped.

A s dawn sent its first pink shards skyward, Richard rode through the gates of Claiborne and into the valley below. Ten knights accompanied him, breaking into a gallop at his signal.

Frost covered the rippling hillocks. The morning air stung his throat and lungs. Mist hung over the Dee, cloaking it in ghostly raiment.

Sirocco, sensing his master's grim mood, cocked an ear backwards. Richard patted the stallion's shoulder. Horses were a damn sight easier to understand than women.

Richard had spent the night on a bench in the hall. He'd not had the energy to find another chamber. He'd had to listen to the grunts and moans of satisfied lovers mating beneath blankets on the floor. It had not helped his temper in the least.

He could have sent Gwen to the women's quarters, but somehow the thought of sleeping in his bed without her was too much to bear after the brief taste he'd had of her.

God, the night they could have had if she'd only let it happen! His body hardened as he remembered the silken feel of her skin beneath his fingers, her startled gasps as she'd discovered her sensuality, the way her wet hair had clung to her neck when he'd brushed it aside to kiss her throat.

It would be a long ride if he kept thinking of his wife.

The morning sun quickly disappeared behind a blanket of thick clouds, yet it was still early when they reached Lydford manor. The villagers stared as they rode through. 'Twas not often Richard rode out to his manors. Patrolling the border took up all of his time, so he left the management of his fiefs entirely to his estates steward.

Richard noted with satisfaction that the houses were well thatched and the walls stout. No holes in the wattle and daub. Pigs and chickens ran freely. Dogs barked. Some loped along beside the destriers, wagging their tails. Others stood and watched them pass, too busy or too lazy to join in the chase.

The villagers raised hands in greeting, calling out to Lord Black Hawk. These people knew the value of their overlord and they told him so with their grins and waves. Not only did he provide them the means to fill their bellies and those of their families, he also kept the borderland safe so they could prosper in peace.

Laughing children with dirty faces ran behind the knights, gaping at the giant warhorses and the armored men who sat atop the beasts. Black Hawk de Claiborne was a legend come to life and they followed him all the way to the gates of Lydford manor.

The men rode into the courtyard. The laundress looked up from her trough of linens. She wiped her wrist across her face, her solution of wood ash and caustic soda forgotten for the moment.

Isabelle de Lydford rushed from the keep. She wore a plain brown surcoat and chemise and her hair was hidden beneath a woolen wimple. A smile lit her plump face as her gaze searched eagerly over the men. The smile died slowly as Richard dismounted.

"W-where is Hugh?"

Richard clenched his fists, the mail biting into his skin. God, how he hated this! He'd told wives before that their husbands were dead, but each time was like the first. The pain was always the same. "Lady de Lydford, I wish to speak privately with you."

Isabelle's face paled. Her back stiffened and her chin lifted bravely. "I would hear what you have to say now, my lord."

"'Twould be better if--"

"Nay! I cannot bear to wait. Tell me now, my lord, please."

Richard took a deep breath and stepped closer. "Hugh served me well, lady. 'Tis no greater honour than to die in the service of your lord, and of your king."

Isabelle's eyes filled with tears. She began to shake and she pressed her hands to her face. "I thought I could bear it, but I cannot," she whispered.

A scream rent the air as she fell to her knees. She beat her fists into the dirt, wailing. Richard bent to lift her up but she jerked away from him. He stooped beside her, the edge of his scarlet surcoat pooling like blood at his feet.

"Lady de Lydford, please, for your children's sake." He never knew what to say or how to comfort the women.

Always, he thought of his father. Had William de Claiborne felt like this when his wife died? Richard swallowed. Jesú, to love someone so much that the loss was like having an arm or a leg ripped off. It was frightening.

Isabelle's body shook beneath the weight of her sobs. She looked up at him finally, her eyes red-rimmed, tears streaming down her face. "What…will…become of me…and—and my children?"

"Your son is heir to the fief Hugh held for me. You are under my protection until he comes of age."

She turned away, nodding, her body still shaking with sobs. Richard stood. His men were looking the other way. Some of them fidgeted with their reins, others sat stiffly. Each man knew that it could have been him, or that he could be next.

The village priest hurried forward. Richard remounted. "Take care of her, Father," he said, gathering his reins and signaling his men forward.

The men rode in silence to the crossroads where Andrew awaited them. Richard thought of Isabelle de Lydford long after they'd left the village and manor behind.

Loving too much was dangerous. His mother had been the lucky one. She'd gone to her grave loved and loving. It was his father who remained to bear all the pain. And him.

That was why he swore he would never love anyone again, especially a wife. Women died in childbirth all the time. Elizabeth had, and the babe with her. What was to stop his newest wife from doing the same?

Gwen awoke all alone in the strange bed. She damned herself for even thinking Richard might have come back in the night. His bed was not unpleasant, but it had certainly evoked provocative dreams of him.

Easing from the big bed, she slipped on her robe. Alys bustled into the room, her face a very indignant red.

"You would not believe, my lady!" Her hands gestured wildly in time with her mood. "These English heathens have no fresh bread or pastries. The cook says 'tis mutton and cheese and stale bread, or nothing! And that I only gathered by his pointing and shouting. He speaks not a word of Welsh or French! Just that vile, guttural, grating-on-my-ears English!"

Gwen groaned inwardly. English. It had never occurred to her that these people wouldn't speak French. In all her time in the king's household, she'd never had a problem because all the servants spoke court French.

Even in Shrewsbury she'd never encountered a servant she could not converse with. But this was the March, a border castle at the edge of the Welsh wildlands. There would be scant need for Richard's servants to speak French.

How could she have overlooked something so vital? Even Elinor had never thought of the possibility. She had been raised in exile in France, and was unaccustomed to English households.

Damn Richard for leaving her to this!

"'Tis all right, Alys. Help me dress and I will straighten these barbarians out. First, I will find that Owain. Mayhap he speaks this crude English." She would not let her husband beat her down!

Alys brightened at the suggestion. "Aye, he can give that cook the tongue-lashing he deserves!"

"Now for my dress. Nothing too grand, and nothing too plain. I must look noble, but not too far above them. Wool, I think. 'Tis too cold for silk, and velvet will be too pretentious."

"Aye, my lady," Alys replied, heading for the antechamber. She heard Alys flipping through her trunks and she retrieved her brush.

When Alys returned, she had a black chemise and a red surcoat. Gwen grimaced. "Crimson and black, Alys?"

The woman nodded. "Think about it. 'Tis the perfect reminder that you are the Countess of Dunsmore. If I'd thought of it before, I'd have embroidered hawks on some of your gowns."

Gwen took the garments. "Nay, Alys, no hawks. I've enough reminders without wearing them myself."

Alys shrugged. "As you wish, but 'tis a good idea."

Gwen dressed and went looking for Owain. Alys followed, grumbling about English heathens the whole way. Gwen stopped a girl and asked in French if she knew where Owain was. The girl blinked. Gwen moved on. She asked two more women who looked at her like she had ten heads. Gwen's patience snapped on the fourth.

"Owain!" she shouted. "Take me to Owain! I don't care whether you understand another word, you understand *Owain*." She motioned for the woman to start and incredibly she obeyed, taking Gwen and Alys right to the old Welshman.

"Milady," he said, rising from his seat and bowing. "What may I do for you?"

Gwen walked into the room, her jaw dropping. It appeared to be the family solar. It was quite large and well furnished, though the furniture looked as if it hadn't been polished in years. A fire burned in the hearth and smoke stained the rocks of the fireplace black. Dusty tapestries hung from the walls, which were wainscoted and painted, though dull from lack of cleaning.

The cushions on the chairs were worn, the velvet cracked and faded. Gwen shook her head. Richard de Claiborne was wealthy. This was ridiculous. An earl of his standing should have a well-kept castle, not one that oozed neglect from the very foundations.

She whirled on Owain. "What is the meaning of all this?" she asked, sweeping her arms wide.

Owain's fuzzy white eyebrows drew together. "I do not understand, milady. The meaning of what?"

Gwen sighed. He was a man. This whole castle was full of men. The only women were the serving women and they wouldn't be interested in keeping the castle clean if no one made them do it. Richard had said he doubted she had much training for administering a castle. Well, she was about to show him.

Dear Lord, if this mess was what the English thought keeping a household was all about, it was a wonder they'd ever managed to find their way out of the rubble to defeat the Welsh.

"First, I want you to gather all the chambermaids. I will give the orders and you will translate. Then we will see to the rest of the staff."

Gwen sank into a chair while Owain did as she bid. When he had gathered the women, Gwen proceeded to outline their duties as she'd heard Elinor do. Owain listened, his eyes widening at first. After he got over the initial shock, a grin spread across his features and he translated with what Gwen would have said was glee.

The women glared at her, no doubt not relishing the tasks of waxing furniture, beating rugs, sweeping out the rushes, scrubbing the flagstones, setting out fresh rushes and scenting them with herbs, and scrubbing the walls until they were no longer dingy. Their faces brightened when she promised an extra day's wages for a job well done.

Owain frowned at that, but said nothing.

The women hurried off, chattering amongst themselves, but not before dipping into a deep curtsy for their new mistress.

Next, Gwen told the serving wenches in no uncertain terms that they were to dress more modestly and conduct themselves with better behavior while they served in the hall.

She gave sweeping orders for the hounds to be removed to the stables immediately and for the knights and men-at-arms to not lounge unnecessarily.

A search of the storerooms revealed yards and yards of velvet and trimmings for reupholstering the chairs and making new bed hangings. Alys got to work immediately.

"Take me to the kitchens, Owain," Gwen said.

"As you wish, my lady," he replied, grinning from ear to ear.

The kitchens were at the rear of the castle. The wooden building was large, housing two hearths and several workers. Heat radiated through the structure as cauldrons of soup and meat bubbled over the fires.

Gwen spotted the master cook before Owain pointed him out. He stood next to a spit, deep in conversation with the girl who turned the meat. Every now and again, he would wave a hand or issue a command that sent men and women scurrying.

The furtive glances of his staff alerted him something was amiss. He turned quickly, his eyes widening. His wrinkled face glowed red from the heat, as did his bald head.

He directed a stream of grating English at Owain, gesturing at Gwen the whole time. Gwen drew herself up in her best princess manner. This man was going to be a handful.

"What did he say, Owain?"

Owain cleared his throat. "Uh, he doesn't like you in his kitchen, milady. Says he's not about to take orders from a slip of a girl."

"Tell him he is dismissed."

"Milady, Oliver has been at Claiborne for thirty years. You cannot dismiss him just like that."

"Yes, I can. Tell him he is dismissed. And this is *my* kitchen. Tell him that also."

Oliver turned even redder as Owain spoke. He shook a fist at Gwen, spouting in English.

"What did he say?"

"He said he will only obey Lord de Claiborne. If Lord de Claiborne dismisses him he will go, and not until."

Gwen chewed the inside of her lip. She decided to be bold. She'd seen her father bluff his way through meetings with his chieftains. She would use the only weapon at her disposal. "Tell him he does not share Lord de Claiborne's bed, I do. And what does he suppose Richard will do when he learns his cook has been rude to his new bride? I can't imagine Richard will take kindly to such an insult."

Owain translated. Oliver paled, his gaze flickering over her doubtfully. Gwen brushed her hair from her face in a pretty gesture, studying the far wall with interest.

Oliver wiped his hands on his tunic before speaking. Owain turned to her, barely able to contain his smile. "He asks the countess to please reconsider dismissing him and says he will serve her well and faithfully."

Gwen toyed with her girdle chain. "Very well. Tell him he may stay. From now on, the menu is to be discussed with me."

Oliver bowed when Owain finished translating. Gwen took a quick inventory of the kitchen. She instructed Oliver to prepare lighter fare in the morning, followed by a large mid-day meal, and ending with a light supper.

By the time she and Owain departed, Oliver seemed more than eager to bake confections and roast tender gamebirds for her pleasure, though he grumbled under his breath the entire time.

Gwen smiled to herself. Elinor would be proud.

When they reached the solar, Owain was beaming at her. "Is there anything else I can do for you, milady?"

Gwen pushed a lock of hair over her shoulder. "Yes, Owain. You can teach me how to speak English. I can't have you translating for the rest of my life."

"'Twill be my pleasure."

"We will start tomorrow then. I am too tired for much else today." Judging by the shadows creeping across the room, it was almost dusk. Gwen realized she was exhausted. She'd had no idea her first day at Claiborne would take so much out of her. Damn Richard! She would succeed in spite of him. "I think I will retire now, Owain."

"Shall I send a tray to your chamber?"

"Aye." Gwen turned to go, then stopped. "Thank you, Owain. For everything."

He smiled in answer.

Later, Gwen lay in bed and thought of the day behind her. Thank God Owain had not balked at her orders, or she would never have gotten as far as she had.

Tomorrow promised to be just as interesting. There were still the outbuildings to be toured, and mayhap the village, and then...

She was asleep before she could complete the thought. Alys pulled the hangings shut and retreated to her pallet.

The knights set up camp once the shadows of night darkened the sky. They'd found a set of prints at Llanwell cave and had followed the trail all day without rest.

Andrew walked over to where Richard sat against a tree. "'Tis odd is it not, milord?"

"Aye," Richard said, lifting his flask to his lips. He took a long drink of the bitter ale, then wiped his mouth across his mantle.

"Welshmen usually head straight for the mountains. Do ye think they mean to lead us astray, then double back?"

Richard shook his head. "'Tis not like a Welshman to go so deep into England."

"Ye mean to say ye thinks they're English? What of the weapon?"

"Edward is having English archers trained to use the longbow. 'Tis more effective than our crossbow and if ever Llywelyn tries to rebel again, he'll get his own weapon used against him."

Andrew looked thoughtful. "Well if they weren't Welsh, why'd they attack us, I wonder."

Richard had been thinking about that too. "I'm certain 'tis the same brigands who have been robbing travelers on the road to Chester. They must have been using Llanwell cave as a hideout and were probably taken by surprise to find us there. I don't think they planned the attack. They retreated too quickly once they found out they were outnumbered. Welshmen would have fought harder."

Andrew nodded. "Aye, yer right about that. The Welsh don't give up so easily."

The men took turns at watch during the night. Richard rose sometime after midnight to take his turn. He leaned against a tree to rest the weight of his mailed body.

Against his will, he thought of Gwen. Richard was not at all accustomed to allowing a woman to dominate his thoughts, but he couldn't seem to get this one out of his mind.

God how beautiful she had become! If anything, her hair was more glorious, her eyes more breathtaking, her body more desirable than ever before. He knew an overwhelming urge to possess her, to mark her as his woman forever. He thought of Rhys ap Gawain and the urge became even stronger.

Rhys loved her. It was obvious from the way he looked at her. Did Gwen love him too? Richard was certain she did. It didn't matter though. She was his. She was going to sleep in his bed, bear his children, keep him company on cold winter days. Him, and no one else.

A sudden thought struck Richard—there were many ways to make love to a woman and not all of them involved penetration. He was amazed it had never occurred to him before now.

He slammed an iron-clad fist into his hand. The mail chinked dully. By God, she'd not deny him again! 'Twas no wonder she'd responded to his foreplay. She was accustomed to being touched that way, just not to the sex act itself. Richard knew a murderous desire to castrate Rhys ap Gawain.

Slowly, the red mist of rage lifted. What did it matter if she were experienced in other ways? Her virginity was intact so she could not be carrying her lover's bastard. Surely that was all that mattered.

Richard breathed out between clenched teeth. Seduction was still the best course of action. He would use her body's response against her until she was too blinded by passion to say no. He vowed he would have her as soon as he returned to Claiborne castle.

18

I t was more than a fortnight since Richard had gone. Gwen stared out one of the large windows in his chamber. *Their* chamber.

A light blanket of snow covered the valley below. The River Dee cut through the white landscape like a knife. Jagged mountain peaks rose beyond the valley. Owain had told her that the highest and furthest was Snowdon.

Every day she looked for it, and every day she was thwarted by the steamy clouds clinging to the mountain range. She sighed and turned away.

Alys sat beside the fire, humming a melody while she sewed. Gwen's gaze drifted to the huge bed.

She'd come to think sleeping in it was torture. The covers, the pillows, the sheets—they all smelled of Richard. It was like lying in his embrace, and yet it was not.

"I am going for a walk, Alys," she said, sweeping on a heavy velvet mantle lined with white ermine.

Alys looked up from her sewing. "Is aught amiss?"

Gwen shook her head. "I just need to get out of this room 'tis all."

"He will return safely."

Gwen swallowed. "I was not thinking of my husband, Alys." In truth, she had thought of nothing else for days.

Alys shrugged and bent her head over her sewing. Gwen hurried for the door.

Claiborne castle was huge. Gwen wandered with no real destination, moving from room to room in silence. Servants bowed or curtsied when she passed. She smiled her acknowledgment.

Without thought, she trailed her hand along tabletops and woodwork, searching for a trace of dust. There was none, and that pleased her.

Gwen scanned the faces of the chambermaids and serving wenches she passed, wondering which of them Richard had spent the night with before he'd left.

It didn't matter. His attempt to belittle her with his servants had not worked, thanks to Owain's cooperation. She'd had to suppress a desire to be harder on the women, certain all their chattering in a language she couldn't comprehend was about her. Even if it was, they still obeyed her orders.

There had been a few problems at first. Servants who were asked to do things they'd probably never done before complained bitterly. One woman refused outright to scrub the smoke from the walls. She'd been sent packing only to return the next day humble and ready to work.

Rushes crackled under Gwen's feet as she walked, the scent of marjoram and roses rising from them. Some of the smaller rooms were carpeted in the same manner as Richard's chamber. The carpets had been dragged outside and beaten until not a pouf of dust came from them. The wainscoted walls shone with fresh paint. Some were white, others green, some gold.

In the Great Hall, a mural of Richard's coat of arms commanded the wall behind the dais. Now that it was washed, the colors leapt out and made the hawk seem alive somehow.

As far as Gwen was concerned, they could have left it dulled by smoke.

The hall was orderly these days too. The knights had rebelled at first. Gwen had had to threaten them in the same manner as she'd threatened Oliver. For them, she'd worn silk and velvet and made sure it was tightly laced.

The humor of it hadn't escaped her. A virgin pretending to be a siren. Just keeping her color down while she'd strutted in front of them and spoken of Richard's devotion to her had taken all of her willpower. Owain had not needed to translate for them because the knights spoke French as well as English. It had been satisfying to finally be able to speak for herself.

She stopped at the passage leading to the women's quarters. She'd considered taking a room there, but the idea of leaving Richard's chamber had disturbed her for some reason. His bed might be torture, but she didn't want to give up the feeling of being with him. It was ridiculous, but she actually felt safe in his room. Safe in Black Hawk's lair.

What had Elizabeth felt when she lived here? Gwen chewed her lip. She wanted to ask Owain about Richard's first wife, but she couldn't bring herself to do it. Owain was close to his lord. He would likely tell Richard all she'd said and done since he'd left anyway. Having Richard know she'd asked about Elizabeth was too much.

Gwen turned away from the passage. It was a good thing Owain had not suspected her true purpose when she'd insisted on touring every last inch of the castle. She'd searched all the rooms for a sign of a kept woman. If Richard had a leman, she wasn't at Claiborne.

She thought of Anne again. Ashford Hall was less than a day's ride away. Richard could come and go with ease if he so desired. Mayhap that was where he was now. He'd probably caught the Welshmen the first day out and was avoiding his wife.

Gwen was fuming by the time she found Owain in the Lesser Hall. His face lit up when she approached. "How are you today, milady?"

"Very well, thank you," she replied stiffly. Owain frowned. Gwen's anger crumbled. "I'm sorry, Owain. Mayhap I am feeling a bit restless."

She took a seat and studied the bright walls with satisfaction.

Owain followed her gaze. "'Tis as grand as ever it was when Lord de Claiborne's mother was alive. You've done an admirable job."

Gwen smiled. Owain had told her about Richard's mother and how the castle had flourished in her day. "Do you think so?"

"Aye."

She twisted a curl around her finger. "'Tis a grand castle. And big." It was strange, but she'd come to appreciate Claiborne castle. It had a wild, untameable quality about it that reminded her of its lord.

Owain nodded. "Aye, 'tis. King Edward's master builder Sir James added onto it a few years ago. Refortified it and enlarged the rooms. 'Tis more grand and fearsome than ever it was in milord's father's day."

"'Tis hard to believe you've been here that long."

"Aye, 'tis for me sometimes, too. But I served William de Claiborne since before Lord Richard was born. Richard is eight and twenty and I was here two years before that."

"What clan do you come from?"

"I am from Gwent, Lady, in the Black Mountains."

Gwen nodded. "I thought you spoke the south."

Owain smiled. "After all these years 'tis still obvious?"

"Aye." She toyed with one of the golden chains hanging from her girdle. "Owain?" He waited, his eyebrows raised. "I...I was wondering why you continue to serve him. He is an enemy of our people."

"He does what he must to serve his lord, the king. His father would have done the same had it been commanded of him."

"But you are Welsh! Does it not bother you?"

He took her hand and squeezed it lightly. "Some ties are stronger than others, Lady."

Gwen cleared her throat. "What was he like? I mean when he was a little boy?"

Owain sat in a chair opposite her. His mouth curved in a smile that was oddly like Richard's. "Much the same as now. Stubborn, headstrong. Once when he was four, his mother told him he could not go with his father into the borderlands. Do you think he cried? Nay, he snuck into the stable and would have been out the gates if he could have reached the horse's back. He came to me to ask for help and I had to talk him out of it."

"Why didn't you tell his mother?"

Owain chuckled. "I would've eventually, but it was easier to talk him out of it first. Even as a boy, he had a damnable amount of pride. Probably would have never forgiven me if I'd hauled him to his mother."

"How did you manage it?"

"It wasn't easy. I had to promise to sneak sweets from the kitchen and be his target for sword practice. Thank God his sword was only a stick!"

Gwen laughed. She tried to picture Richard as he was then. She could not. He was too dangerous, too forbidding, to ever imagine him as a little boy.

"Did you teach him to speak Welsh, too?"

"Aye. He has always been good with languages. He learned very quickly." Owain shot her a calculating glance. "Mayhap he can teach you English better than I... if the two of you find the time."

Gwen blushed. Owain had been present for every lecture she'd given about how Richard was besotted with her. A sudden thought struck her. What if he did tell Richard the things she had said? Richard would probably laugh and denounce her in front of everyone.

"Is he usually gone for so long?" she asked, changing the subject.

"'Tis never the same, milady. Sometimes days, sometimes weeks."

Gwen almost dreaded his return. When Richard was back, he would be the lord and master of Claiborne castle. He might not let her make decisions or continue doing things the way she had been.

She twisted the chain furiously. Damn if she would give up without a fight! She felt useful, needed, and she would not let him take it away.

After she checked on the progression of the afternoon tasks, she returned to the master chamber. The windows drew her, as always, and she pressed her hands to the thick glass.

Snow whispered past to cover the ground below. She tried to make out the individual patterns of the white flakes as they fell. Eventually, her eyes registered movement far off in the valley.

What shepherd would have his sheep out in this weather?

She pressed her nose to the glass, then wiped impatiently at the steam that sprang up. She hurried to the next window, and the next, each one steaming in turn.

She wiped the window with her sleeve and peered into the valley again. Horses. Knights. The crimson and black banner of the lord of Claiborne castle.

"Richard," she whispered, pressing her fingers to the glass. She turned from the window and ran to the door. There were a million things to do.

"Rub him down good and walk him until he's cool, Edwin," Richard said, handing over Sirocco's reins.

"Aye, milord," Edwin replied. He led the sweating stallion toward the stable, petting his nose and talking softly.

"Are ye ready for a pint o' ale, milord?" Andrew asked, drawing alongside him.

Richard smiled. "Among other things."

The two men trudged across the bailey together. "Aye, I reckon ye can't wait to see that dainty wife o' yours. I intend to find me a bit of womanly company too. Christ, 'twas some hard ride!"

"Aye," Richard said. He stifled a yawn as he and Andrew climbed the stairs of the forebuilding. He stumbled as they entered the hall and Andrew reached out to steady him.

"Mayhap ye should skip the wooing and go straight to sleep, milord. Ye should ha' stayed in Shrewsbury for a night or two."

Richard looked at his captain's bloodshot eyes. "Mayhap we should both skip the wooing til we're better rested."

Andrew grinned. "I'm not so tired I can't lay on my back and let some wanton female take advantage of me."

Richard's smile faded as he let his gaze wander over the hall. "My God…"

Owain came up to him. "Milord," he said, bowing. His tunic was spotless with not a wrinkle to be found.

"What the hell is going on here?"

Owain grinned. Andrew's jaw hung open. Richard walked into the hall and stopped. He turned around slowly. The walls had actually been whitewashed! The tables were draped in white linen and the men seated at them talked quietly.

The serving wenches were laced up to their necks. One of the knights laid a familiar hand on a wench's bottom. Richard gaped as she slapped him and stormed away.

And where were the hounds?

He stared at the mural. Jesú, he didn't remember it being so bright, even when his father had had it painted. The little wench had turned his castle on its head!

Owain came up beside him. "Your countess has made some changes."

"I can see that," Richard growled. His head was spinning. The changes weren't bad, just shocking for a man who was used to routine. How in the hell had she managed it? And, better yet, where was she? Why wasn't she waiting for him? Surely she'd known he was coming. The whole damn castle knew he was here before he'd even ridden through the town gates.

"Your wife awaits you in your chamber, milord," Owain said, as if discerning his thoughts.

Richard felt a tension he'd not even known was there drain from his body. "Send food and bathwater."

Owain's smile broadened. "She has already ordered them for you."

Richard brushed past him and headed for the stairs at the other end of the hall. Tired as he was, the muscles in his groin tightened. He clamped down on his desire. He was too weary for seduction and she would not come willingly.

He hurried to his chamber and flung open the door. Gwen whirled to face him, her hair swirling around her like liquid fire. Richard stared. Why had he ever wanted to make her wear a wimple?

Her golden-green eyes were wide as her gaze flickered over him. Richard swallowed. Jesú, she was radiant. Her pale skin was like flawless cream against the blue velvet of her gown.

He wanted to gather her into his arms and feather kisses across her face. Impatiently, he pushed off his chain-mail coif. His hair was matted with sweat, and he raked a hand through it. The crimson surcoat with the hawk device was torn and dirty. The great sword hung limp at his side, no longer shining and fierce.

"'Tis good to see you, my lord," she said.

"Is it?"

Gwen blinked. "Aye," she said, lowering her gaze. It really was good to see him. She hated to admit she'd missed him. Even tired and dirty, he was handsome. She was drawn to him as only a woman could be to a man.

He stripped off his gauntlets and tossed them aside, then came to stand before her. He picked up a lock of hair.

"You have not been wearing a wimple, have you?"

"I said I would not."

He dropped the flaming tendril and entwined his fingers in the hair at her temple, running them through to the ends.

"We will compromise then," he said softly. "You do not have to wear one except when we go to court. Agreed?"

Gwen looked up in surprise. He watched her expectantly. "Aye, my lord," she said, gifting him with a smile.

He sighed. "Will you never call me by my name without my reminding you?"

Gwen stared at his chest. She loved his name, loved to say it over and over. How many times had she lain in bed and said it to herself just for the pleasure of hearing it on her lips?

She raised her eyes to his. He'd just given her something she wanted, so she would give him something in return. "I will not forget again, Richard."

The smile he gave her was heartstopping. He ran his fingers lightly over her cheek. "'Tis like sweet music when you say it."

"Shall I help you out of your armor?"

His eyes glittered. Gwen swallowed. She saw herself in the depths of his silver gaze, saw what he was thinking at that moment. It was something she'd thought about for the past fortnight.

She didn't know why she'd gone to the armorer and insisted he teach her how to armor a knight. It had seemed like a good thing to know at the time. Now she was glad she'd done it.

"Aye, show me what you have learned."

She stood on tiptoe to reach the laces of his coif. She managed to unbuckle it from the hauberk and he bent over so she could pull it off. Flakes of rust drifted to the floor.

She frowned. "Is it ruined?" The headcovering was heavy and she carried it over to a trunk and laid it on top.

"Nay," he said. "Bruno will make it shiny as new."

Gwen returned to his side. "How?" She lifted the bottom edge of the mail shirt to get at the buckles beneath. He watched her, his brows drawing together as she found the buckles and laces with sure fingers.

"He will roll it."

Gwen stopped. "Roll it?"

"Aye, he puts it in a barrel with sand and vinegar and rolls it around. The vinegar eats the rust and the sand washes it off."

"Oh. Bruno didn't tell me about that."

"You've been talking with Bruno, sweet?"

"Aye, 'twas he who explained how to remove the armor. It wasn't easy to get him to talk, but once I did, he was most thorough."

Richard laughed. "Aye, 'tis Bruno all right."

Gwen finished unlacing the mail stockings. She pushed them down his hips and he stepped out of them. She bent to pick them up, dropping them when they were only halfway off the floor.

"Mayhap you can help with the clothes underneath," he said. He started to unbuckle his sword, but Gwen was there first. She laid it aside, then removed his surcoat. She thought he winced as he shrugged out of the heavy hauberk, but she wasn't sure.

He picked up the leather and metal in his right arm and carried it to the trunk where she'd laid the coif.

She helped him out of the gambeson and tunic, gasping at the ugly black bruise snaking across his left shoulder. Her fingers skimmed over it. "My God, what happened to you?"

"Axe," he said. " 'Tis much better than it was. Christ, I thought he'd severed my arm when it happened."

Gwen felt the color draining from her face.

Richard cupped her chin. "I am fine, Gwen, truly. I forget how delicate women are sometimes. Forgive me."

She batted his hand away. "I am not a mewling Englishwoman!"

He grinned. "Nay, more like a Welsh spitfire." She turned away and he grabbed her arm. "You're not finished yet."

His undergarments! How could she have forgotten those? She took a deep breath. Her hand strayed to the drawstring waist. His shaft strained against the cloth and she hesitated.

"I told you before, 'tis you who causes it. You do not have to worry, Gwen. As much as I wish it were otherwise, I am far too tired to try to make love to you."

She worked at the string, her heart fluttering. She had lain awake nights, remembering how he had touched her, knowing that if he did so again she would be powerless to resist. She almost wished he would touch her.

She slid the garments from his body, sucking in her breath when his manhood stood up proudly. What did that male weapon feel like? She wanted to trace her finger along the ridge and find out. Heat unfurled in her belly. She closed her eyes and turned away, her ears suddenly hot.

"Jesú, 'tis not as bad as that, is it?"

"Get in the tub, my lord—Richard," she said faintly. How was he ever going to fit that inside of her?

The water splashed. He sighed. Gwen pushed up her sleeves before gathering the soap and a washing cloth.

His eyes widened. "You are going to attend me?"

She busied herself so he wouldn't see the color staining her cheeks. She reasoned that it was because he'd ridden so far and so hard, and because he looked so tired, that she complied.

"Isn't that what I am supposed to do?" she asked lightly, careful not to look into the tub as she dipped the cloth in the water.

"Only if you want, Gwen. I'm not so spent I can't do it myself."

Gwen didn't answer as she stroked the cloth over the refined angles of his face.

"It feels so good." He closed his eyes and settled back, trusting her as a child might. Dirt and rust washed away easily. The dark circles beneath his eyes did not.

She frowned, moving down his neck. She washed his shoulder gently, then held up the cloth and squeezed it. Hot water trickled over the bruise, and he groaned.

"Does it hurt much?" she asked softly.

"Like hell."

"You are sure nothing is broken?"

He opened his eyes. She caught his briefly questioning look, the hint of vulnerability that was quickly veiled. "Aye, I am sure. 'Tis stiff and somewhat sore, but will heal. I've had worse."

Gwen bit the inside of her cheek. "You caught those men?"

"Aye."

"What did you do with them?" she asked, focusing on the bubbles on her hand.

"What do you think I did?"

Gwen raised her gaze to his. She sensed that what she did or didn't say was very important somehow, but still she could not answer.

"You think I spitted them and left them to rot. Or that I hung them or mutilated them, don't you?"

"Nay," Gwen whispered. The bubbles popped, tickling her flesh.

He let his breath out slowly. "I took them to the king's justiciars in Shrewsbury."

"They will hang," Gwen said dully. How many Welshmen would die before King Edward was satisfied?

"Aye, but they weren't Welsh, Gwen."

Her head snapped up. "But, the longbow—"

"English outlaws. The king has been training English archers to use it."

Gwen frowned. "Aye, Rhys told me so."

Richard's eyes hardened. Gwen cursed silently. Suddenly desiring to escape his cold glare, she stood.

His body relaxed as she ran her fingers through his crisp black hair. She massaged his head, delighting in his little groans of pleasure. Lather dripped down her arms when she finally bid him to lean forward and rinse.

She came to his side again and dipped her hand in the water. She rubbed the cloth across his chest, lingering on the hard muscles. The darkness of his skin made her hand seem like purest ivory in contrast. The tips of her fingers grazed his breast and heat curled within her. She glanced at him. His eyes were the color of smoke.

"There is more to me than that," he said in a husky voice.

Gwen swallowed and moved downward, over his ribs, his abdomen. Something touched her and she jerked away. Slowly, she returned.

This time when that part of him touched her, she did not move. Her heart beat wildly. Their eyes met as she closed her hand over solid male flesh.

Richard groaned. "God above, Gwen, I do not have the strength to do it the way you deserve."

Gwen let him go, ashamed for acting so boldly. "I-I'm sorry, I shouldn't have—"

Her protest was cut off as he grabbed her arm and pulled her down until their mouths touched. She kissed him back, her lips parting, her tongue seeking his. Fire leapt in her breast and flowed to the apex of her thighs.

She whimpered when he pulled away. His eyes searched hers. "I want you so much I can taste it, but trust me when I say the pleasure would be all mine. I promise you once I've rested, I'll devote myself to your pleasure as well as my own."

Gwen nodded, unable to believe what she was agreeing to.

He smiled. "Now get away from me before I lose control of my lustful desires."

Gwen stood and went to the window. The snow was falling heavier now. Cattle shuffled through the fields, nosing for shoots of grass buried beneath winter's first offering.

Her cheeks burned and she pressed her face against the cool glass. He was barely returned and her body throbbed for him. And she had just agreed to let him make love to her.

Gwen shivered. It was going to be an earth-shattering experience, she was certain.

She heard Richard climb from the tub. She waited until she was sure it was safe before she turned around.

He had slipped on a black tunic and was seated at the table, whipping the covers off the dishes. Gwen's eyes widened as she watched him. He wolfed down the roast pheasant and peas with saffron, two meat pies with onion and garlic, half a loaf of bread, cheese, and a flagon of wine.

When he was finished, he took a deep breath, then stood, stretched, and walked to the bed.

"Wake me in time for supper," he said, falling onto the mattress.

Gwen's jaw dropped. Surely he was joking.

19

When Richard awoke, the sky beyond the windows was dark. He pulled himself up and looked around. The soft orange light of the fire bathed the room in a warm glow, and a delicious smell assailed his nostrils.

Curiosity got the best of him. He stretched, shrugged his stiff shoulder, and climbed from the bed. Gwen was curled in a chair by the table. Her head lolled to one side, the fiery curtain of her hair spilling over her arm to trail to the floor.

Something very like tenderness spread through him as he went to her. He ignored the smell coming from the table and knelt beside her. A fierce, primal hunger surged in his veins. He was going to make her his.

Now.

Tonight.

She'd not see another dawn without knowing him as a man in the most intimate sense of the word.

It surprised him he was in no hurry. After burning for her for so long, he was content to watch her for a little while. He brushed a strand of hair from her face, tucking it behind her ear carefully. How had Llywelyn ever managed to sire such a beautiful creature?

She was so innocent, so angelic in sleep. Richard felt a pang for the lost innocence of his own youth. When had he ever not known the depths of despair the soul was capable of sinking to?

Richard pressed his lips softly to hers. She stirred, but did not wake. He did it again. She mumbled something and swatted at him. Richard smiled.

This time he kissed the exposed skin of her neck. She sighed. He nibbled her ear and she jumped.

"Richard!" she cried, leaping to her feet. He sat back on his heels, chuckling.

Gwen rubbed her ear. His soft breath had sent a chill all the way to her toes. "I did not mean to doze off. I'm sorry."

"'Twas my pleasure to wake you." His gaze traveled down her body. "There are even more interesting ways to awaken. I shall delight in showing them all to you in our life together."

Still smiling, he stood and removed the covers from the dishes.

Gwen heard the intake of his breath. "How in the hell did you get old Oliver to make *blankmanger*?"

"I told him, of course," she replied.

"Jesú, he complained so bad whenever I told him to do it, I ceased telling him. Says it's too damn time-consuming." He stared at her for a minute. "'Tis not just Owain and Bruno then, you've enchanted Oliver too." He shook his head. "Go away for a fortnight and a Welshwoman conquers my castle without even one siege-engine. Have you eaten yet?"

"Nay."

He sat down and beckoned her over. When she went to sit beside him, he pulled her into his lap. Gwen's heart fluttered. His eyes were breathtaking. They drifted slowly from her face to her breasts and back again, as though he was undecided whether to taste the food or taste her. He made her so very aware of herself—of her desires and her inexperience.

He dipped a spoon into the *blankmanger* and held it to her lips.

"'Tis good?" he asked.

Gwen nodded. The dish was rich and almondy and she tasted the slight flavor of anise.

He fed her another spoonful before trying it himself. "Mmm, you're going to have to tell Oliver to make this more often."

"If you wish it."

His eyes narrowed playfully. "I have to wonder just what you did to the poor old man."

Gwen looked away, trying to hide her blush.

Richard laughed and held a goblet to her lips. "'Tis lucky for you that he is an old man, or I might just wonder about the state of your purity."

Gwen sucked in her breath. It was too much like the old accusations to ignore the memories it brought. "You—"

His arm tightened around her, his expression sobering. "I am teasing, Gwen. 'Twas a poor choice of words. Do not doubt that I fully appreciate the gift you're giving me." He held the goblet up again. "Drink."

Gwen relaxed against him, the warm glow of the wine spreading through her limbs. He drank after her, then teased her with a light kiss.

When they had finished off the dish and shared more wine, Gwen waited for him to try something else.

He pressed his mouth to hers with barely restrained hunger.

"What of the rest of the meal?" she asked breathlessly.

"I'm not hungry for food, Gwen."

His voice rippled smooth as velvet over her spine. A thrill of anticipation shot through her and she shivered. It was finally happening. His hand closed over her breast. Even through the layers of her gown, his touch branded her like a hot iron.

He bent to kiss her again and she wound her arms around his neck, careful not to touch his left shoulder. Eventually, he moved down her throat, licking and kissing until she thought the ache between her legs would consume her.

His shaft bucked beneath her, pressing into her bottom. He pulled her gown up and caressed her knee. Stroking his fingers along the inside of her thigh, he moved slowly upward. When he was almost to the apex, Gwen clamped her legs tightly together.

He leaned back. His eyes probed hers with such force she felt as though he had looked into her soul. "You want it as much as I do, Gwen. Just let it happen."

She turned away, feeling the loss of his mouth and hands acutely. She burned so hot for him it hurt. "I'm frightened," she whispered.

He kissed her cheeks, her forehead, her eyelids, the tip of her nose, then pressed his brow to hers. "I won't lie to you. 'Twill hurt at first but I promise it gets better very quickly."

Their eyes locked, and she ran the back of her hand down his cheek. "Show me how to please you, Richard."

"I will," he promised, lowering his mouth to hers. He kissed her for a long time, making no move to touch her anywhere else. He took her from soft, feather-light kisses to intense, soul-searching ones, and back again. When his hand slid up her thigh a second time, she didn't protest.

She gave a little gasp when his fingers stroked her curls. He parted her folds and found the tiny bud within, his thumb circling slowly. She whimpered and he slipped a finger inside her.

Gwen jumped. His mouth slid to her ear and he began to suck on her earlobe. Her insides melted.

"Richard… you must… stop."

"Why, love?"

"'Tis sinful," she said, gasping as a tremor shook her.

"Nothing I will ever do to you is sinful, Gwen." He slipped another finger inside her, stretching her. She threw her head back and he tongued her throat.

Gwen cried out when he removed his hand. What he did to her was wicked, but God how she loved it! He unknotted her girdle and let it fall to the floor. Next, he undid the laces of her surcoat and raised her up to slip it over her head. Soon the rest of her clothes lay in a heap on the floor.

Richard took a deep breath to steady himself. The glow of the fire licked over her body, bathing it in sensual light. He ran his fingertips down the silken skin of her belly. She shivered.

"God, you are more beautiful than I could have ever dreamed," he said. Her skin gleamed like fine pearls, her nipples puckered, and the flaming curls between her legs beckoned him to lose himself in the delights of her body.

He wanted to carry her to the bed and ravish her, but he knew he must go slowly. In this moment she trusted him and he would not break it.

He slid his tongue around a firm nipple. She gasped and he sucked it into his mouth. He caressed the silk of her mons, and she arched into his hand, urging him.

Richard sucked harder. Her moan sent a surge of raw male power spiraling through him. She was unbearably sweet and he thought he might never get enough. He was very aware of his own effort to breathe, of his desire to take her now, hard and fast and deep.

He slipped a finger inside her again. She was incredibly tight, so wet and hot, and it no longer mattered to him whether she had done this before. He swore she would never remember any lover's caresses but his. He would do everything to her, worship her body with his, teach her all he knew of loving until anyone else paled by comparison.

When he was finished with her this night, she would know that no one else could ever take his place. He took her other nipple in his mouth, reveling as it hardened beneath his tongue.

She writhed on his lap, and he knew her body was building to a feverish peak. She wanted him. The knowledge thrilled him like it never had with any other woman.

"Stand up," he commanded.

Gwen stood. Her body pulsed as he rose and removed the black tunic. He wore nothing beneath it and her eyes widened at the sight of his thick shaft protruding from the nest of charcoal curls.

She swallowed heavily. He would never fit inside her. He was going to hurt her.

He pulled her against him and skimmed his hands along her spine. "You've no idea how many times I've dreamt of making love to you."

Gwen fought a rising tide of panic. She was awkward and unskilled. He would be disappointed. "I do not know what to do."

"I will show you everything, my sweet."

He bent to kiss her, pressing his hand into the small of her back and bringing her abdomen against his hard shaft. She marveled at the feel of his naked body against hers, hard against soft, unyielding against yielding.

He lifted her against him, still kissing her, and sat down on the chair. Her knees pressed into the cushion on either side of him, and she was almost amazed he had gotten her into that position without her realizing it.

"I'm going to let you do it, love." He reached for the flagon of wine and poured some into the goblet they had shared. "First you must drink this. 'Twill help you relax," he said, holding it to her lips. She swallowed, then leaned back and dared to glance at the vermilion head of his shaft cleaving up between them.

Tentatively, she touched it. He grabbed her hand and her heart turned over as their eyes met. Dear Lord, he was so handsome, so dark and beautiful, so… carnal.

"Do not," he said hoarsely. "Not this time."

The gravity of her situation—what she was about to do and the man she was about to do it with—rolled through her mind unheeded. Right now, she wanted him more than she'd ever wanted anything else in her life.

He cupped her breasts in his hands, suckling each of them in turn. Watching him made her weak at the knees.

His thick shaft brushed against her mons. Gwen bit her lip. Was that her making those noises, those little mewling cries, those whimpers?

"Richard…"

He trailed wet kisses between her breasts, up her throat, her chin. She sought his mouth eagerly, opening, coaxing his tongue deep.

She wanted him badly, wanted to experience all the things he would do to her, the promises his touch invoked. She stroked the hard muscles of his chest, kneading his flesh beneath her hands. His skin seared her fingertips. He was supple and hot and exquisite to touch.

He growled his pleasure and Gwen suddenly knew that more than anything she wanted to please him.

He moved his hand between them and rubbed her cleft. It was never enough, only a light teasing pressure that darted away as soon as she felt herself building to an unnameable peak.

"Richard, please," she begged, unable to stand the exquisite torture a moment longer. "Please."

"There is only one way to ease the ache," he murmured against her cheek. He leaned back and she saw that his eyes had gone black with passion. "You must take me inside you."

She glanced at his thick shaft, disappointment and fear welling within. It was the moment of truth and she didn't know if she was ready. "It will never fit. 'Tis too big," she said.

"Oh yes it will, sweet," he replied, slipping a finger inside her. Another finger joined the first. Her eyes widened as a third finger slipped in. He flexed them, stretching her, sending waves of pleasure along the walls of her sheath.

"'Twill feel a hundred times better than that. Soon, you will be glad it isn't smaller, I promise."

She looked at him doubtfully.

"Do you trust me?"

Slowly, Gwen nodded. It was strange, but she did trust him, at least in this. He moved the tip of his shaft within her folds, stroking her as he'd done with his fingers.

Gwen sucked in her breath at the intimacy of it. He urged her up until she was poised over him. "Take me inside you, Gwen," he whispered urgently.

She swallowed, then gripped his biceps and eased herself down.

"Yes, that's it," he murmured, encouraging her with his eyes.

She took a deep breath and tried again. A sharp pain rocked through her as the tight barrier of her virginity refused to stretch. "I cannot go any further," she said.

Richard swallowed heavily. "'Tis what I told you about. You must get past it." He held himself perfectly still, his groin tightening in anticipation.

"I cannot do it," she repeated.

Richard stroked a hand over her breast. A fine sheen of sweat broke out on his brow. "I thought Welshwomen were braver than that," he said softly.

She glared at him. She gritted her teeth and sank lower, sucking in her breath sharply. Richard's blood pounded in his ears until he could hear nothing but the beating of his own heart. God, what price he was paying for restraint!

"I don't want to do this anymore," she said, her eyes filling with tears. "It isn't going to work."

Richard knew he had to take her now, quickly, or lose her. "Forgive me, Gwen," he said as he gripped her hips and drove upward in one smooth, clean stroke.

She cried out, her eyes dilating with pain. He hugged her tight to prevent her from escaping. "'Tis better to get it over with," he soothed.

Gwen held her breath. He had lied. The pain was unbearable. She wanted nothing more than to end his invasion of her body but his arms clamped her too tight.

Within the space of seconds, he eased his grip on her. Gwen started to move away, then realized with a shock that the sensation had changed.

She was full of him. He was hard and throbbing within her, and when she moved, sensation streaked from her scalp to her toes.

"You understand now, don't you?" he asked, his voice thick with the effort his control was costing him. His face was hard, feral, and his eyes glinted with something very near to anger. Gwen realized it was the same fierce passion she had glimpsed on their wedding night. A sudden thrill shot through her. She would be the recipient of it all—and she *wanted* it all.

"Oh yes, yes I do. Make love to me," she whispered.

"God in Heaven, I intend to," he vowed. Richard fused his mouth to hers, mastering her with his kiss as he intended to do with his body. He broke away, gathered her against him, and stood. She was still impaled on him and she wrapped her legs around him as he placed his hands beneath her buttocks.

She buried her face in his neck, kissing, licking, sucking. "Richard, Richard…"

All his good intentions fled him. He had meant to be gentle, handle her with a light hand, but her heated response made him crazy. Her sheath gripped him like a glove and exquisite vibrations shot through him with every step he took toward the bed.

There would be no holding back the stormy passion raging through him. He would give her all—and he would take all.

He slipped out of her as he laid her on the bed. She clutched his arm, protesting the loss.

"Shh, my sweet," he murmured, fanning her hair across the pillows before taking her mouth in a searing kiss. When he covered her body with his, she spread her legs instinctively.

"Yes, Gwen, that's it," he said thickly. "We're going to burn together, you and I..."

Her heart lurched at the look of pure animal lust on his face. He poised over her for one breathless moment, then drove into her swiftly, setting her insides on fire.

She clung to him helplessly, let him lead her where he would. He made love to her like a summer tempest; fast, furious, hard. She quickly learned to meet him, to arch into him, to thrust up when he thrust down.

The sensations were cataclysmic, blinding. They fused their mouths together, momentarily silencing the cries echoing in the chamber.

The pressure built within her until she knew she would explode. He sensed it and quickened his movements, then ground his hips against her at the last second.

Gwen cried out as the world shattered into a million multi-colored shards. She spiraled through light and darkness until it pieced slowly together again.

He remained still, whispering to her, kissing her softly, drinking his name from her lips as she said it over and over. Every nerve ending in her body quivered and she was certain the aftershocks had made even her eyelashes sensitive.

He still throbbed inside her and she realized he had not achieved his own release. He began to move, slowly at first, then with the same fury as before. He thrust into her a dozen more times and she felt the hot spurt of his seed even as he cried out.

He did not withdraw immediately. He murmured endearments to her in Welsh, stroked her hair, her moist brow, her lips.

Tears trickled from the corners of her eyes to spill on the pillow below. He brushed one aside with his thumb.

"God help me, I wanted to be gentle," he muttered. "I'm sorry, Gwen, I did not mean to hurt you."

"Nay," she whispered. "You didn't hurt me." She let her gaze wander over his face, memorizing him as if she didn't already know every last detail. How could she tell him—this man, this *stranger*—that he had just made her feel more alive, more wanted, more needed than she had ever felt in her life? "'Tis just that it... it was so beautiful."

He cradled her face in his hands. "It will always be so between us, I promise you," he said, and then kissed her.

Gwen slipped a hand into his damp hair. Her other hand stroked his back. She felt him begin to grow and lengthen inside her. Her heart quickened.

"You are ready again?"

"Yes," he said, slipping from her as he trailed kisses over her breasts and down her belly. "But 'tis better if we wait. You will be sore enough as it is."

Gwen sighed her disappointment. She shivered. The air was cool against her moist body without him to warm her.

He smiled, then got up and went to get wine. Gwen rolled onto her stomach, sprawling across the soft bedding, her body tingling with new awareness.

When she heard him coming back, she turned over. He watched her, his eyes darkening.

"Get beneath the covers, love," he said huskily. Gwen pulled the coverlets up from the bottom of the bed and accepted the wine he handed her. He slipped in beside her, then took the goblet and held it to her lips.

She sipped, letting the cool liquid soothe her parched throat. When she raised her eyes to his, he was watching her intently.

He turned the goblet and drank from the same place she had, then lowered it and bent forward to kiss her. The taste of wine on his lips and tongue had the unbelievable effect of arousing her.

She leaned into him, attempting to deepen the kiss, but he only backed away. "Was it everything I promised?" he asked, his beautiful eyes searching hers.

Gwen trembled all the way to her toes. "More," she breathed softly.

Richard smiled, caressing her cheek with a long finger. "'Tis only the beginning."

Lord, what more could there be? And yet she knew she wanted to find out. She wanted to experience it all with him. She decided in that instant she would hold nothing back when he made love to her.

When they had finished the wine, Richard yanked the hangings closed and settled into the bed with a sigh, pulling her against him.

Gwen molded to him without protest. She wanted to explore him, to find out more about his body, but she was too shy to do it now. She buried her face in the curve of his neck and pressed her lips to his throat. His arms tightened around her.

Why did she feel so happy? She knew she shouldn't, but she didn't want to analyze it right now. The fact was she felt wonderful lying in his arms. His scent mingled with hers, reminding her of the beautiful intimacy they had just shared. If being with a man was always this way, it was no wonder the castle wenches were so eager to bed the knights.

No doubt they'd been just as eager to bed their lord. She shoved the disturbing thoughts aside and concentrated on the man next to her.

What would her life be like now that he was home? She'd come to enjoy the independence she felt in managing a household. Would he take it away? It was in his power to do so. He could order her to stay in this room and perform for his entertainment during the day, and when the day was over, he could order her to perform for his pleasure.

That last thought was not without merit.

"You have made some changes," he said suddenly.

"Aye, it seemed for the best."

"I've only been in the hall. Will I find the rest of my castle as changed?"

"Aye," she said softly. "You are displeased?"

He was silent for a moment. "I was at first. Just a little," he added when she stiffened. "I thought you'd had no training, being Welsh. It was quite a shock."

For once, Gwen was not offended. She laughed. "Ah, but you forgot about Elinor. 'Twas she who whipped my father's hall into shape. I could not help but be influenced."

"'Tis been a long time since things were in order around here. 'Tis not a high priority for fighting men."

Gwen wanted to ask if Elizabeth had kept the castle properly when she was alive, but she could not bring herself to utter the name during this new closeness.

"'Twould not have been possible without Owain," she said.

"I told him to obey you as he would me, but I think he would have done it anyway. He's taken a liking to you."

Gwen stroked the side of his face, unaware of how tender the gesture was, or of the hidden things it stirred within him. "You told him to obey me?" she asked.

He had not forgotten her! He'd made sure she would have Owain. Without thinking, she turned his face and pressed her lips to his.

He cupped her cheek. "Aye, I did. But tell me, love, how did you manage to get Oliver to do what you wanted?"

Gwen's heart quickened. "I threatened him."

"You threatened him? With what?"

"I threatened to dismiss him."

Richard chuckled. "I cannot imagine Oliver believing such a threat."

Gwen smiled against his throat. "He didn't at first." She raised herself to look down at him. There was still enough light that she could see his features. She decided to take the plunge. "He said he would only believe it if you said it. So…"

"What?"

"You might get angry."

He brushed her cheek with his finger. "Tell me anyway."

"I asked him if he wanted to gamble on who had more influence with you, him or me. He decided not to take the chance."

Richard laughed. "You must be mighty convincing if he found thirty years service lacking against your claim."

"Well, I didn't exactly play fair. I suggested that since our marriage you found certain… ummm, pleasures… with me that would very likely influence you in my favor."

Gwen swallowed. There, she'd said it. Now he wouldn't have to hear it from anyone else. She thought her heart would stop beating while she waited for his response.

He pushed her back on the pillows, his kiss as sensual as hers had been tender. Gwen's arms slipped around him.

"You could just be right about that, sweet," he murmured thickly.

His manhood pressed against her abdomen and she tried to shift beneath him, wanting him deep inside her. When they had been joined, she had felt his strength coursing through her as if it were her own, and she wanted to know that feeling again.

"'Tis too soon," he said, sucking her nipple into his mouth.

Gwen moaned and arched into him. "Please, Richard..."

"I'll hurt you..."

"Nay..." Her hands closed over the taut muscles of his buttocks.

He groaned. "God, you really don't play fair, my sweet. Are you certain you want me?"

"Yes."

"I don't want to hurt you."

"You won't. Please, Richard..."

"'Tis selfish of me, but I cannot deny my own needs when you are asking me to do it." He shifted downward. She spread her legs and lifted her hips. They both groaned as he slid inside her.

If she'd had any doubt the sensations she'd experienced had been real, he proved it to her again in exquisite detail.

They fell asleep much later, bodies sated, clinging to each other in sleep as they had in passion.

20

Despite having spent weeks in the saddle, resting infrequently and riding hard, Richard was awake at dawn. It was the warrior in him, ever used to arising at first light when the enemies' camp was beginning to stir as well. Men didn't stay alive by letting the enemy catch them in their beds.

His body ached. He'd made way too many demands on it. First, the ride through the borderlands, then the night spent indulging in pleasure. He started to stretch, then became aware of the small form clinging to him. At the same time, his sleepy senses recognized the sweet scent of roses.

Gwen.

Richard brushed aside the riot of fiery hair. She was beautiful. He hardened instantly. God help him, he wanted her again.

There was nothing unusual in that, but he acknowledged it was much too soon. He doubted she'd welcome him once she became aware of the soreness that accompanied losing her virginity and making love half the night.

She lay partially across him, her head nuzzled against his shoulder, an arm thrown over his chest, a leg nudging his groin. In short, she clung to him as if her life depended on it. Richard smiled.

He'd awakened with a woman at his side so many times in his life that it should not seem a novelty. But somehow this was different. Was it because she was Llywelyn's daughter? Did he feel a certain amount of triumph that he'd spent the night filling her with his seed, the innocent daughter of his enemy?

Even as he asked himself, Richard knew it was none of these things.

He brushed his lips across her forehead. She sighed and shifted, her leg causing him an exquisite amount of torture before it stilled. Carefully, he extracted himself from her arms. He had to leave before he rolled her on her back and indulged in his lust.

Once he was fully clothed, he returned to the bed to stare down at her, though he told himself he should not. He tucked the fur coverlet around her, his heart beating faster than usual as he relived in finite detail every glorious minute of their lovemaking. Her every curve, her every quiver, sigh, and moan was imprinted on his brain forever.

Richard ran his hand through her russet curls, then straightened and pulled the hangings shut before he was tempted any further.

Alys was in the small solar that adjoined his chamber. The old woman dipped in a curtsy. "Good morning, my lord."

"Aye, 'tis good indeed." He took a deep breath. Why did the morning air seem so alive, so fresh and new?

"Can I do something for you, my lord?"

The old woman was looking at him, waiting for him to speak. Richard realized he'd been standing there for some moments. "Umm, yes, Alys. I don't want Gwen awakened. Let her sleep as long as she wants. You can bring a tray up for her later."

Alys smiled. "Aye, my lord."

Richard had the distinct impression he'd not fooled the woman for a minute.

Light pierced the depths of the curtained bed. Gwen rubbed the back of her hand across her eyes and propped herself on an elbow. She turned to the man at her side, but he was gone.

It was disappointing to wake up without him. She frowned. Disappointing? Irritated, she reached for the hangings and threw them open.

The table had been cleared of the previous night's half-eaten meal. Likewise, the pile of discarded clothes was also gone. Gwen blushed clear to her toes. What on earth must Alys think?

The tender ache between Gwen's legs reminded her of the things that had happened last night. She couldn't stop herself from smiling. She and Richard had finally made love—and it had been glorious! She couldn't imagine why she'd waited so long.

Now she understood the secretive look in Elinor's eyes. It was a look born of the pure joy of joining with a man in an act as beautiful as it was mysterious.

Guilt followed quickly on the heels of Gwen's happiness.

Richard was her father's enemy, *her* enemy. He was Black Hawk de Claiborne, despite his melting caresses and heart-stopping kisses. And he'd told her he intended to kill her father one day.

Gwen furiously twisted a lock of hair. Why should she feel guilty? She couldn't have kept Richard from claiming his privileges forever. He was too much man, and far too dangerous, to prevent him from taking what he wanted.

And it was not as if she could ever love Black Hawk de Claiborne. Her father would always come first, there was no fear of that.

Gwen flipped the coverlets back and shrugged into her robe. She would never allow Richard to kill her father. Somehow, she would stop him.

Alys came in, carrying a basin of water for Gwen to wash with. She set it on a stand beside the bed. "Good morning, my lady," she trilled. "I thought I heard you call for me last night, but then I didn't think it was my name you said after all. Was everything all right? Did you sleep well?"

Gwen's face was ablaze. She remembered what name she said, and the circumstances under which she had said it. She lifted her chin and looked Alys in the eye. "Aye, thank you, Alys. I must have been dreaming."

Alys smiled broadly. "Aye, no doubt you were." She cleared her throat. "Lord de Claiborne seems in good spirits this morning, I must say."

"He does?" Gwen cursed herself for sounding too eager. Shrugging, she said, "'Tis nice, I suppose."

She waited, but Alys did not speak. Gwen sighed. Alys would offer no more information than Gwen asked for.

"Where is he, Alys?"

"I last saw him in the hall." Alys's eyes strayed to the bed. She sucked in her breath, her brow furrowing.

Gwen followed her gaze. The sheet was crisp and white, like newfallen snow, marred only by the few drops of blood strewn across it like precious rubies. She met Alys's questioning look.

"'Tis not time for your flux. I've been counting."

Gwen crossed her arms. "Nay, I… we—that is, he…"

She let the sentence trail off. She couldn't finish because one thought kept winging through her brain—the amount of blood was almost exactly the same as Richard had put on the sheets at Shrewsbury. It was a painful reminder that what he had done with her last night was nothing new to him.

The things she had thought so special—the way he touched her, the way he kissed her, the way her name sounded on his lips while he was shuddering his release—were things he had done with countless women. She was just another of his conquests.

At least he'd gotten her name right.

Alys straightened the covers. "'Tis extraordinary. He waited until you were ready. Do you have any idea how lucky you are, child? Most men would not wait."

Gwen turned away, tears pricking her eyelids. Aye, she was lucky all right. He'd almost raped her that first night, then stopped when his own guilt prevented him, not because of any concern over her feelings.

And now Alys was more firmly on his side than ever before, believing him to be some kind of sainted man among ordinary mortals.

Gwen hugged herself tight. Just as he'd done in the cave, Richard had once again proven she was unable to resist his smooth seduction. She'd given in gladly, willingly, wanting him with a fierceness she'd not known was possible.

'Twas no wonder he was gone when she awakened. It hadn't meant the same thing to him as it had to her.

How could she face him again when he would turn his cold silver eyes on her and laugh because he had won?

She ate very little of the food Alys brought. She took care with her appearance, her stomach knotting as she ran a brush through her hair, shaping the red-gold curls.

She wanted to see him, and yet she did not. She rejected the first three gowns Alys chose, finally settling on gold samite. Gwen knew the color suited her hair perfectly. She chose a simple girdle of gold and silk to complement the dress, then pinched her cheeks until they glowed soft pink.

She descended to the hall, telling herself it mattered not at all if Richard looked at her indifferently.

She hesitated when she saw him. Richard stood at the other end of the hall, deep in conversation with Owain. She started to flee back up the stairs, but he looked up and saw her before she could go. Their eyes locked and he moved toward her.

Gwen could only stare, her heart doing flips in her chest. She remembered him as he had been last night—all virile, hungry male. He had joined his magnificent body with hers and shown her what it meant to be a woman.

A small shiver washed over her and she knew all her careful composure was for nothing. If he looked at her with contempt or indifference, she would die.

"Did you sleep well?" he asked, taking her hand and pressing it to his lips.

"Aye," Gwen said, unable to meet his eyes. Why did he have to be so handsome? Her heart accelerated as she waited for the setdown that was sure to come.

She started when his lips brushed her palm, and then she was imagining them elsewhere on her body, kissing, sucking, arousing. The sweet ache between her legs tortured her with memories of his possession.

Hot. Complete. Breath-stopping.

Gwen closed her eyes.

"'Tis the same for me," he said in a thick voice. "I cannot stop thinking of you, or of last night."

Gwen met his heated stare. How did he know?

He drew her close and lowered his mouth to hers. Gwen responded, dimly hearing the cheer in the background. Before she could drown in him, he lifted his head. His eyes were smoky as his hand stroked her cheek. "Jesú, I could take you back to bed and make love to you for the rest of the day."

"Yes," Gwen whispered, mesmerized by the stark need in his eyes.

"My sweet wife, you tempt me beyond reason," he said, twisting a stray curl around his finger. "Unfortunately, I've far too many things to do today."

Gwen stared at the floor, momentarily embarrassed by her own boldness. Richard still wanted her! The knowledge sent a wave of relief washing over her.

"Are you certain I did not hurt you?"

He sounded so concerned, and she couldn't stop herself from touching him, from running her hand down his perfect jaw. His eyes grew intense. "'Tis a mild pain, nothing I cannot handle. I suspect it hurts far less than your shoulder."

He laughed. "Aye, I suspect you are correct."

"I am disappointed, though."

His brows shot up. "Disappointed?" He looked so disconcerted she wanted to laugh.

"Yes." She slid him a sideways look. "You promised to wake me."

Richard grinned. "I was right about you, wasn't I? You are a tease, and a wicked one too."

He tucked her arm in his and led her from the hall and out into the wooden forebuilding. Cold air blew up the stairwell from the bailey below. He turned to her, drawing her against him once more.

"*Un cusan,*" he said, lowering his head.

One kiss. Gwen slipped her arms around him, running her hands up his back. If he meant the kiss to be brief, it was not. His mouth was like velvet, his tongue silken torture. Gwen moaned, meeting him, urging him.

The need to taste him, to feel him, was all consuming.

Desire unfurled in the pit of her stomach. It raged through her like wildfire and she pressed herself tighter to him, thrilling at the answering hardness of his loins.

His right hand splayed across her back, his left brushed her neck, her collarbone, the soft swell of a breast. He cupped the firm mound, squeezing softly.

Gwen ran her hands over him, imprinting the feel of him on her fevered brain, giving in to the urge to touch the proof of his desire for her.

He shuddered and pulled her tighter. Footsteps echoed on the stairs below, and they broke away reluctantly.

Andrew's head appeared in the stairwell. "There ye are, milord. Bruno's waitin' for ye in the armory like ye said." He looked at Gwen. "Good mornin', milady." His gaze darted between her and Richard, taking in the ruffled hair, rumpled clothes, eyes that kept seeking each other rather than him. "Excuse me, milord, milady," he mumbled, retreating the way he'd come.

Richard backed toward the stairs. "Tonight," he said, his hand stretched behind him, feeling for the rail. When he came in contact with it, he stopped, his eyes never leaving hers. Gwen waited for him to say something else, but he whirled around and disappeared down the stairs without another word.

She leaned against the wall and touched her lips. Richard still wanted her, and it was a relief.

Gwen joined Owain in the family solar for her English lesson. She sat in a window seat and peered out into the bailey. Thinking she spied Richard's dark head in the lists, she pressed her hands to the glass and squinted.

Surely he wouldn't engage in sword practice or jousting with his injured shoulder. Sighing, she turned to Owain. From this distance, she couldn't tell who it was.

"You're looking well today, milady," Owain said, raising his head from his account books. His mouth curved in a smile. "Could it have anything to do with the return of our beloved lord?"

Gwen turned back to the window, blushing. She couldn't exactly deny that Richard was her beloved after all the things Owain had heard her say to the staff. She cleared her throat and fixed him with her best princess stare.

Owain chuckled. "Very well, I won't say another word."

Gwen pulled at a loose thread on one of the pillows. Finally, she thrust the pillow away and said what was foremost on her mind. "Please tell me about Elizabeth."

Owain leaned back in his chair, his face creasing in a frown. "I think you should ask Richard, not me."

"Please, Owain. I-I cannot ask him." She grabbed the pillow and twisted the thread around her finger, staring at the purple blotches that arose when she pulled too tight.

Owain sighed heavily. "He should tell you about her, but he probably will not see the need. He has always been stubborn like that." He paused, staring out the window. "Lady Elizabeth was a kind woman. She was quite young and very shy when she first came here. She had not your beauty or your boldness, but she learned to get along. She loved Richard, but then most women do."

Gwen looked at the old man sharply, but he seemed lost in his own thoughts. She knew he had not said it to hurt her. He was merely speaking the truth as he saw it. How many hearts had Richard broken? "Did he love her?"

Owain continued to stare out the window, speaking in that dream-like state of one who is lost in thought. "I think he was fond of her."

Gwen felt the hair on the back of her neck prickle. It was unreasonable to be jealous of a dead woman. "How did she die?"

"Birthing his son. The babe was stillborn and she died soon after."

"Oh," Gwen said quietly. A wife and a son. *Did you love them, Richard?* "He must have been devastated."

"Aye, I think so, though he wasn't here when it happened. He was with the king at Kenilworth, planning the war against your father. When he returned, he spent a long time in the crypt. He never spoke to me about it." Owain sighed. "I was beginning to worry if he would ever remarry. He needs an heir, a son to leave Dunsmore's holdings to."

Gwen smoothed her hand over her belly. Could she give Richard the son he needed? Did she even want to?

When she looked up, Owain was watching her, a smile softening his face. Embarrassed, she clasped her hands in her lap.

"Of course," Owain said, "'tis possible your son will have so much more than just Dunsmore to rule. I was rather surprised your father agreed to let Richard's sons in line for the throne. But then again, if your stepmother gives birth to a boy, it will no longer matter."

Gwen's heart dropped. "What?"

"Jesú, you did not know," Owain said, his voice filled with dread.

"Nay," Gwen whispered.

He let out a long breath. "Richard will kill me for this."

Gwen took hold of her seething emotions. "There is no need to tell him, Owain. For all he knows, my father told me."

Owain nodded. "Aye, if you wish it then."

"I do." Why had her father not told her? Sweet Mary, Black Hawk's son on the throne of Wales!

Her son.

'Twas no wonder Richard made love to her with such enthusiasm! He wanted to put his babe in her so he could claim the throne one day.

God, how stupid she'd been not to realize why he seemed to desire her so much!

A flash of comprehension sent icy horror washing down her spine. Black Hawk de Claiborne would not wait past the day she delivered a healthy boy. Once it was done, he would take an army to Gwynedd to kill her father.

Then he would claim Wales for their son.

21

The shadows of late day stretched dark fingers across the solar. Gwen fancied that the dark fingers also closed over her heart, gripping her in an unshakable melancholy. The dinner bell rang, and she rose from the windowseat.

She would not succumb to Richard's smooth charm ever again. She had been a fool to believe the things he said. They were lies, all lies.

He was nothing but a cold English barbarian who thirsted for revenge and wouldn't balk at using her to achieve it. He would stop at nothing to get what he wanted. There was nothing he would not say, nothing he would not do.

She wasn't about to help him in his quest. He would get a surprise tonight when he tried to bed her. She would not give in so willingly ever again.

Gwen shoved aside thoughts of the previous night, the way she'd felt lying in his arms, beneath him, taking him inside her and—

She would *not* give in. But why did it have to hurt so much, knowing that Richard was using her for his revenge? Had she expected any less from a man as evil as him?

Gwen dashed away a tear as she entered the hall. Servants and knights smiled and nodded as she passed. Gwen acknowledged them all, but she had eyes only for Richard. He stood on the dais, his impressive height emphasized by the raised platform.

She wondered if he knew the effect he had. Anyone walking toward him would have the feeling they were puny and weak while he appeared powerful and larger than life.

Einion had once told her that kings and queens did this sort of thing on purpose. They sat on huge thrones at the end of long, vast halls so that all who approached felt humbled in the presence of greatness.

Was Richard proclaiming his mastery over her?

He truly was magnificent and she almost hated him for it. One look from his predatory eyes made her want to forget all she had resolved.

He was dressed entirely in black for a change, and she thought wildly that the devil himself would look no different if he were to appear before her at this very moment.

Behind him, the crimson and black coat of arms screamed the brutal legacy of the lord who ruled here.

When she reached the dais, he took her hand and drew her close. Gwen flinched as a coil of heat uncurled within her. She fixed her gaze on his chest, certain if she looked in his eyes she would be lost.

She learned she was to have no choice in the matter as he lifted her chin with a finger. His eyes narrowed. "What is wrong?"

"Nothing," Gwen whispered.

"Then why wouldn't you look at me?"

Gwen felt her lip begin to tremble. She dug her nails into her palm. There was no way she was going to cry over him. "I am looking at you now, my lord," she said coolly.

He frowned. Hurt crossed his features so quickly she almost missed it. His eyes hardened to silver-ice. "I am so relieved we settled that," he said, taking his seat.

Gwen sank next to him. How was it he managed to make her feel horrible when he was the one in the wrong? God, what an idiot she was! She had to suppress an insane desire to beg his forgiveness, to do anything to see the warmth return to his eyes.

She forced herself to smile throughout dinner. She thanked the servants, sent her congratulations to Oliver, and talked pleasantly with Father Stephen while Owain darted puzzled looks between her and Richard.

Richard remained dark and closed. He attended her dutifully but never spoke a word to her. He ate heartily, drank wine with dinner, and then switched to ale before dessert was served.

The girl who filled his cup was buxom and pretty. Gwen figured the wench was perhaps a year or two older than she was. Her black hair was twisted in a braid and a few strands dangled over her shoulder. Her bosom strained against the rough wool of her gown as she leaned in front of Richard.

The girl spoke in English, and Richard answered. Gwen understood *I* and *you* and the girl's name, *Maude*.

Richard smiled at Maude, his gaze lingering on her abundant chest. Maude slanted him a seductive smile in return. Gwen felt a hot shard of jealousy prick her.

This wench had to be the one he'd bedded before he'd ridden after the outlaws!

Gwen knew suddenly that he would not even attempt to bed her tonight. Once had probably been enough to get her with child. He would spend the night where he really wanted, which from the looks of it was in Maude's bed.

Gwen jerked away when he turned in her direction. She let her gaze wander over the crowded hall. People engaged in raucous conversations, laughing, slapping backs, drinking toasts to health and success.

She tapped her fingers on the table. 'Twas all a stark contrast to the heavy silence between her and Richard.

After dessert was served, Richard leaned toward her, his breath tickling her ear. "Go up to bed, Gwen." He tossed back the ale and motioned for Maude.

Gwen stared at him in disbelief. He *was* going to bed that wench and he could care less if she knew it. By God, she'd be damned if she'd stand for it! She threw her eating knife on the table and shoved herself to her feet. "If you touch one—one!—woman, I will cut off that which you pride so much and—"

"And deprive yourself too, sweet?" He laughed and she felt a chill run down her spine at the lack of humor in it. His voice had a hard, bitter edge to it as he said, "You'll not do it and I'll tell you why—because if you did you'd not get to scream my name to the heavens as you did last night when I was buried within you."

Gwen's eyes bulged. She flew at him. He caught her wrists and jumped to his feet. His eyes flashed pewter, his jaw tightening. "I told you before, *never* again," he said from between clenched teeth.

"You are a bastard, Black Hawk de Claiborne!"

"Aye, so I am." He picked her up and swung her over his shoulder. The hall erupted as the knights and men-at-arms cheered their lord. Gwen beat her fists against his back in impotent fury, screaming Welsh curses at him.

She barely heard herself above the din. English barbarians!

He kicked open the chamber door, then walked over to the bed and threw her down. For a minute, his face was so savage she thought he was going to rape her and she was appalled at the surge of heat between her thighs. Dear God, her traitorous body *wanted* him to loose his passion on her!

He turned and strode to the door, leaving her breathless and disappointed.

Gwen scrambled off the bed. "English bastard!" she screamed, running after him.

He slammed the door. She started to fling it open and follow, then stopped.

St. Dafydd's bones, she was not going to chase him like a lovesick little girl! She crossed to the window and threw herself in the seat, staring out at the darkness beyond.

She didn't care what he did or who he did it with.

A sob escaped her trembling body. She brought her knees up and put her face in her hands. For the last damn time, she was not going to cry over him!

Richard downed another cup of ale. The hall had long since cleared of women, except for the serving wenches, and the men diced and drank with abandon. Occasionally Richard joined in their games.

He was beginning to want things he had no right to, things he did not deserve. Was it too much to want a woman who accepted him for what he was, a woman who could see past all the tales to the man beneath?

Jesú, he didn't even know who the man beneath the hardened exterior was anymore. How long since he had buried his self under an avalanche of honor and dedication to duty?

And God help him, he'd wanted Gwen to be the woman he could share his inner self with. But she wasn't and he found that sorely disappointing.

He laughed. Hell, who was he kidding anyway? Men like him didn't deserve happiness. Men like him only knew war and killing and blood. Endless, endless blood.

What woman would ever see beyond that? They flocked to him, because of his face and his position and his reputation, but none ever cared what, if anything, lay beneath their preconceptions.

"To lowest hell with all women," he muttered.

A young knight raised his cup in agreement. "Aye, m'lord, women's tricksome, they are. Always sayin' one thing, an' meanin' another." The boy's head slipped to the table, cradling on his outstretched arm. He was snoring within seconds.

Richard sighed, saluting the lad with his cup. "Aye, tricksome."

Out of the corner of his eye, Richard watched Andrew move across the room to intercept a pretty wench. The captain bent to whisper in her ear. The girl shook her head, covered her mouth and giggled.

After a little more coaxing on Andrew's part, they disappeared into the pantry.

Richard scanned the room, looking for Maude, then dismissed the thought of lying with her as quickly as it had come.

He wasn't capable of it, not any longer. From the first moment he'd glimpsed Gwen in Shrewsbury, he was unable to get aroused by anyone else, no matter how comely or skilled.

Richard tightened his grip on the goblet until the beaten metal started to crumple. He opened his fist and dropped the mangled cup on the table.

She was playing games with him, the Welsh bitch! All women did it —they learned it from the goddamn cradle!—but he had not expected it from her. Her response seemed so genuine this morning, but it was all a lie.

She was just like the rest. He'd seen the same trick hundreds of times. Hot one minute, cold the next, all in an effort to confuse and bewitch some poor unsuspecting male. He'd never fallen for it before and he was not about to fall for it now.

He swiped his arm across the table, knocking the cup to the floor. It hit with a dull thud, bounced, and rolled into the rushes. Several of the knights glanced up, then turned back to their dicing.

Richard bounded to his feet. Goddammit, if she wanted to play, he'd play! Why should he deny himself anyway? She would be all soft and womanly now, begging him to make love to her. The trick was always the same.

He took the stairs two at a time, then flung open the door with such force that it slammed against the wall.

Gwen jumped from the windowseat. Her hair tumbled to her waist in a glorious blaze of color, her eyes flashing with an unholy green light. The golden cloth of her gown shimmered and danced in the fireshine like an illusion born of faery magic.

Richard blinked. Winter howled in the mountains and valleys of the March, but he had captured autumn within the walls of his castle. She stood before him now, gazing at him with all the splendor and fury that was hers alone. His body hardened to the point of pain. He took a step toward her.

She held up her hand and he saw that it shook. "Don't you come near me," she said, her voice low and menacing.

Richard grinned. Good God, she was challenging him! It wasn't what he had expected, but he was not in the mood to show any mercy. "You should realize I will always do whatever I wish," he growled.

He moved slowly, deliberately, the hawk closing in on his prey. She backed away like a hunted animal.

She collided with the wall, then planted her feet defiantly. "Do not touch me."

Their eyes locked and he reached for her. "Let me go!" she hissed, jerking her arm away.

Richard grabbed her again, his hand tightening around her like a vise as he pulled her to him. He cupped her breast with his free hand and smoothed his thumb across her nipple. The pouty flesh thrust upward at his touch and he smiled. "I want to feel you beneath me again, *cath wyllt*. And you want it too, don't you?"

"No! Never again!" she cried, twisting in his grasp, clawing and fighting like the wildcat he named her. "Don't you touch me! Don't you dare touch me you filthy swine!"

He pinned her against the wall, one knee thrust between her legs, his engorged member pressing into her abdomen. His hands gathered silken fistfuls of hair. "You want me, Gwen. Admit it."

"No!"

Gwen gasped as he lowered himself and rubbed his manhood against her sensitive flesh. She'd not counted on him assaulting her senses this way.

"Your body betrays you," he said thickly.

"I hate you, *Gwalchddu*, truly hate you."

His grip tightened almost painfully. Gwen knew an instant of fear before his mouth descended to crush hers beneath it.

She smacked her open palms against his chest. It was as useless as slapping solid rock. But his bruised shoulder, however...

She doubled her fist, hesitating an instant before slamming it into him. He didn't stop, or cry out, or reel in pain, because the blow landed harmlessly on his chest. She couldn't bring herself to hurt him.

"No!" she cried when his lips moved down her neck. "I'll not have you after you've been with another woman!"

Richard stopped. Her eyes flashed green fire and he thought he had never seen a more desirable woman in his life. He could not help but tell her the truth. "I swear to you I've not been with anyone else."

"You lie!" she screamed, pushing against him. "You're a lying Englishman!"

"Is that what this is all about? Christ, I want no one but you!"

"I saw you stare at her! You were with her!"

"No! I've been with no one!"

"Liar!"

"By God, I'll prove it to you then!"

He crushed his mouth to hers again. Despite everything Gwen promised herself, she felt her body responding. Why had she chosen to dwell on his attention to another woman, rather than his plan to kill her father?

It made no sense, but she couldn't think of that right now. All she could think of was him. He tasted of ale and fury and desperation, and he touched her with an urgency that fired her soul.

I want no one but you.

It was a lie, but God what a sweet lie. All rational thought fled her. Her squeals of protest changed to moans of pleasure. Hands that beat against him now clutched his surcoat, lips that pressed together tightly now opened, muscles that stiffened now relaxed and melded to him.

"Yes, Gwen, give yourself to me," he whispered against her lips. "I'll lay the Heavens at your feet, I swear it. *With my body I thee worship.* I vowed it when I wed you. 'Tis a vow I intend to keep."

He was a demon. Only a demon could say such things and make her want them so much she'd give her soul to have them. It was madness. *He* was madness.

"Richard..." she whispered as his mouth claimed hers. His hands slid down her body, gripped her buttocks and pulled her against the hard proof of his desire. Gwen quivered from the inside out.

Her fingers found the clasp of his mantle. The garment fell to the floor with a soft sigh.

Later... she would hate herself later.

She unbuckled his sword belt and let it fall. His hands came up to undo the fastenings of her clothes. Slowly at first, then with increasing urgency, they shed their clothes until their naked bodies pressed together, hard to soft.

Richard dropped to his knees. Gwen's fingers entwined in his hair as his lips traveled over the sensitive flesh of her breasts and belly.

"You are perfect," he murmured against her skin. "So soft, so sweet." His fingers stroked her cleft, found her wet with need. "So full of desire."

Gwen shuddered. Why had no one ever made her feel this way? Why did it take the one man she should hate most to show her how belonging could feel like?

Gwen's fingers tightened in his hair. Oh God, what would this feel like if there was love between them? Her knees buckled with the intensity of her longing for something that could never be.

He swept her into his arms and carried her to the bed. He laid her on it, then stood above her. There was something else reflected in his face, something she could not name.

Vaguely, she thought of her nudity and that she should be blushing under his hot stare. But she wasn't embarrassed. She felt beautiful, totally uninhibited, when he looked at her like that.

Rising to her knees, she came to the edge of the bed and pressed her palms against his flat stomach. He shuddered. Inspired, she closed her eyes and tasted his bronze skin the way he'd done to her. She was rewarded with a groan.

He joined her on the bed, pushing her back, his huge form hovering over her. He stared at her, not touching her, his fists pressed into the bedding on either side of her head.

"Kiss me," she pleaded, her hands skimming up his belly, curling against his chest. He didn't move. Her gaze trailed to his shoulder. How had she ever thought of hitting him there? With a little cry, she raised her head and touched her lips to the bruise, softly, gently.

"God, Gwen."

She licked him and he shuddered. Her hands traveled up his sides, down his arms, while she tried to heal him with the gentle touch of her mouth. She lay back on the pillows.

"Love me, Richard," she entreated.

"Jesú, I've never wanted a woman as much as I want you." It sounded like a confession before the onslaught of a storm that left one wondering whether they would still be alive at the end.

Gwen pulled his head down. "Show me."

The dam within him broke and he suddenly came alive. She melted as his mouth sought hers with fierce, demanding kisses. She ran her hands through his hair, over the planes of his face, touching, feeling.

Her lips were bruised and swollen when he finally gave them up to drag kisses down her neck and over her breasts. Her breath caught as his tongue made lazy circles around her nipple.

She writhed beneath him, aching, wanting him to fill her and be done with this madness. But he didn't. Instead, he teased her nipples until she was certain the next touch would make her scream.

And then he was moving down, his hot mouth blazing a trail of delight over her flesh. When he pressed a kiss into the curls between her legs, Gwen thought she would explode from the anticipation.

She half sat up, reaching for him. Dear Lord, he wouldn't *really* kiss her there would he? He slipped from her grasp as he moved down her thigh. A mixture of relief and disappointment washed over her. If he'd done that, she didn't think she would survive it.

He pushed her legs apart and ran his tongue up the inside of her thigh. Gwen gasped his name.

He raised his head. His eyes were glazed, drugged with passion. "I love it when you say my name like that. It sounds like a wicked invitation. I promise I'm going to make you say it again and again."

He threaded his hand through her curls and stroked her bud with his thumb. Gwen closed her eyes, moaning as sensation spiraled through her like molten steel.

When she thought she could take no more, he replaced his thumb with his tongue.

"Oh my God! Richard, you cannot—"

She sank back on the pillows, powerless to stop him. He stroked and licked and sucked, and all the while she was convinced she was dying the most exquisite of deaths.

Wanton and shameless, she rocked her hips against him, begging him for fulfillment in a throaty voice she barely recognized. The instant before she reached her peak, he thrust his searing tongue inside her.

"Richard!" she cried, clenching handfuls of bedding in her fists. Her stomach muscles spasmed with the violence of her climax, raising her off the pillows.

He loomed over her, then surged into her while she still convulsed. The walls of her sheath contracted, gloving him tightly.

"Oh my God," he said, closing his eyes and going completely still. He bent to kiss her and she tasted herself on his lips. It was shocking and intimate and wonderful.

Slowly, he started to move. Gwen welcomed the ache his possession caused. The feeling was deeply sensual, knowing that the man who made love to her now was the source of both the pleasure and the pain.

She wrapped her legs around his waist and sank her teeth into his good shoulder, nipping him with every stroke of his body within hers.

"That's it, *cath wyllt*. Let yourself go," Richard whispered. He sucked her neck and earlobe, then raised himself on his palms to look down at her. It was a strain on his shoulder, but he didn't care. He had a deep male need to see her response to his lovemaking, to watch as he possessed her body with his.

Her molten hair spread in a wild tangle over the pillows. Damp strands clung to the sides of her face and her glorious eyes were so dark and sensual that he was reminded of stormy Mediterranean seas.

He'd had women from one end of England to the other, from France to the Holy Land, and none had ever seemed so beautiful or roused his lust so completely as this one.

Richard shuddered with the force of the passion he felt for her. How many times had he pictured her like this in his dreams?

He licked her full underlip. She raised her head to meet him, seeking his mouth urgently, protesting when he lifted himself away.

"Nay, love. I want to look at you. I want to know you're mine."

"Aye, yours," Gwen whispered without thought. She ran her palms down his chest, over the taut peaks and hollows of his muscles. Her gaze trailed from his face to where their bodies joined together, and she marveled each time he disappeared inside her.

Impulsively, she reached between them to touch him. He groaned. "God, Gwen, you make me feel—"

His hand found hers and turned it until she was touching herself. Gwen gasped. His fingers guided her until she was panting with the need he strummed into her.

He pulled her hand away and lowered himself. His tongue plunged into her mouth, matched the heated rhythm of his body.

She ground her hips against him and he angled to catch her most sensitive spot. Her whole body tensed, then exploded. She clutched him tight with arms and legs as the spasms racked her. He drank her cries into his mouth, then returned them when he could no longer hold back the driving need of his own body.

He bathed her face in soft kisses, then rolled so she was on top. Gwen laid her head on his chest, caressing his side lazily.

He stroked the curve of her back, the rounded form of her buttocks. For a long time, neither of them spoke.

Richard broke the silence. "Making love is much better than fighting, is it not?"

Gwen raised her head to look at him. Tendrils of her hair clung to his chest and throat. She smiled. "Mayhap fighting is not so bad if it always ends up like this."

Richard laughed. "Aye, mayhap not." Sobering, he smoothed the tangled mass from her face. "I've been with no other woman since I first saw you again in Shrewsbury."

Gwen lowered her lashes, unable to meet his brilliant stare. He gripped her chin and forced her to look at him.

"You don't believe me, do you?"

"Why should I?" she whispered. She'd seen enough of men and their tangled notions of love. If the king could not be faithful to his wife, and Rhys could not be faithful to her, how then could this man, who felt no love, be faithful? But God how she wanted to believe him!

In the silence that followed, the fire snapped as it burned through a pocket of sap in one of the logs.

"Yes, why should you?" Richard said. In truth, he could give her a hundred reasons, but he was not about to do so. He wanted her to believe him because she trusted him.

That surprised him. If her trust was what he wanted, then he'd set himself a hell of a task. What right did he have to even ask her for it?

Her face fell a little and she laid her head on his chest again. He thought she mumbled something about men.

"Do you love Rhys ap Gawain?" he asked suddenly. He wanted to know, needed to know. He was aware of a tightness inside his chest, a flame that burned hot, a flame that was ready to consume him.

She looked at him sullenly. "That can hardly matter now, can it? I am married to you."

"Tell me anyway," he commanded.

Gwen pushed herself up until she was sitting astride him. His eyes swept over her and she felt him begin to harden inside her. She smoothed her hands over his chest and abdomen, encouraging him. Some instinct made her grind her hips against him. His shaft pulsed in answer.

"Mmm, my lord, you are wicked."

"Tell me," he growled, gripping her wrists, his eyes flashing fire.

Gwen tossed her hair over her shoulder, but it spilled back anyway, enveloping her breasts in a silky cloud. "Are you jealous, my lord?" she teased in a husky whisper. His shaft bucked.

His voice was strained when he answered. "Mayhap I am. Mayhap I just don't like the idea of making love to a woman who has given her heart to another."

A thrill coursed through Gwen. Richard *was* jealous. Jealous over her. The knowledge made her feel powerful, wicked, wanton. With a boldness she'd never dreamed she possessed, she lowered her head and traced his nipple with her tongue.

"Christ almighty," he breathed, his erection filling her to bursting.

Gwen gasped as a delicious tremor shook her. "Mmm, do not worry yourself, my lord, because my heart is my own. I will give it to no man."

Richard released her wrists, the tightening in his chest dulling somewhat. He gripped her hips and drove into her, showing her the rhythm before he eased back and let her take over. She threw her head back as she rode him, abandoning herself to the pleasure.

Watching her was exciting beyond belief. She suffered no inhibitions over her body or her state of arousal. She used him for her pleasure, unaware or uncaring that he watched. He enjoyed indulging her. He was definitely not one of those men who thought women were supposed to be meek and submissive in bed.

He held back his release until he thought he would explode. When her movements quickened and her muscles started to contract, he let himself go.

As the last of the tremors shook him, she collapsed on him, locking his head between her hands and fusing her mouth to his. Her hot tongue plunged between his lips, demanding his cooperation. He was only too happy to give it.

"Shameless wench," he said when she lifted her head.

She smiled. "Did I do it right?"

Richard gazed up at her. He'd been haunted by those cat's eyes for years. "Aye, you did everything right, more so than you know," he said, rubbing his thumb across her kiss-swollen underlip.

Slowly, she lowered her head, her expression softening. She traced his lips with her tongue, then kissed him, hot, wet, open-mouthed. Richard pulled away when he felt the familiar tightening in his groin. Christ, he hadn't been hard this much since he was a green lad!

"Did I do something wrong?" she asked, frowning.

Richard laughed. "Jesú, no! But I cannot keep doing this, Gwen."

"Why not?"

Richard thought he had died and gone to heaven. Would she always be like this? God's bones, 'twas every man's dream come true—a beautiful woman who was also insatiable.

"Because I just returned yesterday and my body still aches from being in the saddle for so long."

Her brow furrowed. "Oh! I am sorry, I did not mean to keep you up. You need your rest. I understand."

Richard tried not to smile. Yes, she was keeping him up, and in more ways than one. She started to move away but he clamped his arm over her and held her in place. "Stay with me." He yawned and pulled the coverlet over them. "I'll wake you in the morning. Unless you wake me first…"

22

Gwen was a traitor. She knew it as soon as she awoke and saw the man lying beside her. She could not resist his lovemaking, even if it endangered her father and her country.

She started to wake him, but had not the heart to disturb him. She climbed from the bed and slipped on her chemise along with a fur-lined cloak for warmth.

Richard lay on his side, his dark head a sharp contrast against the white pillow. His eyes were closed and he snored softly. He stretched his arm to where she had lain, groping for a moment before stilling.

Gwen watched him, confused at the tangle of feelings he caused within her. She would stop him. Somehow, she would stop him.

Unwilling to dwell on it now, she turned and stole to the window. The Dee was the only thing moving in the entire landscape. The snow had stopped falling and the valley was covered in a white so new, so perfect, that it seemed as if the world were new and perfect also.

Gwen pressed her hand to the cold glass, half wanting the iciness of it to shock her back to reality. She glanced over her shoulder at Richard and a wave of longing swept through her. Lord, would she never get over it?

She stared out the window for a while longer. Someone tapped on the door and Gwen went to answer it. Alys waited on the other side, her ruddy face creasing in a smile. "I didn't know if you'd be awake yet."

"Aye. What's that?" Gwen asked, motioning to the tray in Alys's hands.

"I thought maybe you and Lord de Claiborne would not wish to go to the hall this morning."

Gwen smiled. "You're a gem, Alys."

"Nay, my lady, not at all," the old woman said, bringing the tray in and setting it on the table. She regarded Gwen with knowing eyes. "All is well between you?"

Gwen nodded. She wanted to say *no, all is not well, all is wrong, I feel things I shouldn't be feeling*, but she couldn't.

Alys glanced at the hearth. "The fire has gone down. I'll get someone to tend to it."

As soon as she left, a chambermaid hurried in. When the fire roared with renewed life, the girl curtsied and hastened out the door, closing it behind her quietly.

Gwen flipped up the cloth covering the tray. Oliver had prepared pastries sweetened with honey and costly sugar. Flagons of water and wine were there also, as well as the usual bread and cheese.

Gwen returned to the bed and sat next to Richard.

The covers had slipped down to his hips, revealing his broad chest. The ugly bruise was purple, yellowed around the edges. It made her heart ache.

He was scarred in places, fine lines marring his perfect golden flesh. Despite his warrior's marks, he was still beautiful. She touched one of the scars on his side, tracing it along his ribcage. Had a Welsh sword caused it?

The thought didn't give her the satisfaction it once would.

Catching her lip between her teeth, she slipped the covers farther down his body. The part of him that gave her such pleasure was different this morning. Always before it had seemed huge and overwhelming.

How extraordinary it changed so much when he was aroused!

Just the mere thought of him ready to sheathe his hard length in her body excited her.

Gwen swallowed, pulling the covers up, then slid down and propped her head against her pillow. She watched him sleep, reaching out once and a while to touch him or to brush his hair from his forehead.

She lay next to him for a long time, never tiring of looking at him. When he finally opened his eyes, he was facing her, and she was struck by the incredible clarity of his gaze.

He gave her a breathtaking smile as his eyes flickered over her chemise. "How long have you been awake?"

Gwen smiled. "A long time."

"What have you been doing?"

"Watching you," she said, her traitorous heart singing.

He pulled her into his arms. His mouth slid over hers, shaping her lips, demanding surrender. Gwen melded to him without the slightest hesitation. "You forgot to wake me," he murmured against her mouth.

"Nay," Gwen said, breathless, "you needed to sleep."

"I need something else even more now," he said. Gwen became aware of his pulsing arousal as his hand slid down her spine and brought her against his loins. Her breath caught. Dear God, he wanted her again. She was more than willing.

He grasped the end of her chemise and slipped it up her body. Gwen helped. When it was off, he stared down at her, his eyes turning smoky. "Jesú, you are going to be the death of me."

"Do not say that!" she blurted, her hands curling into fists against his chest.

His brows drew together. "I was not serious, Gwen."

She touched his face, ran her fingertips over his lips. He kissed them, and her heart lurched. What would it take to stop him from killing her father? What would be the price?

"I know," she replied, shivering suddenly.

She saw that hint of vulnerability flicker through his eyes, and then it was gone, making her wonder if she'd imagined it in the first place.

Before she could dwell on it any further, he was kissing her, stoking the fires of her passion, loving her until they cried out together with the sweetness of their joining.

Alys tripped into the family solar with the light step of a girl half her age. Owain rose at her entrance. His face was marred by a frown. Alys couldn't help but think he'd been handsome when he was younger. Sweet Mary, he was still a fine figure of a man.

"Well, how goes it?" he asked.

Alys cleared her throat and pushed aside her wanton thoughts. A woman her age for heaven's sake!

"My lady said all was well between them. And they've not emerged yet, so one can assume they are, er, getting along…"

She thought Owain's ears were red when he turned away. " 'Tis good then. I was afraid…"

Alys went to him, laid a hand on his shoulder. "Don't fret. Gwenllian is stubborn, but sensible all the same. It came as a shock to her, was all."

Owain took her hand in his. "Richard needs a woman who'll stand up to him for a change. He's entirely too used to being lord and master of all he surveys."

Alys squeezed his hand. "I should be going. I have a million things to do."

Owain cleared his throat, then brushed off his tunic self-consciously. "Stay a while, Alys. If all is indeed well with the young ones, they'll not emerge for some time being newlyweds and all." He coughed, his ears going red again.

Alys smiled. There was nothing she would like better than to stay and talk to this handsome Welshman. "Very well, Owain, I imagine I can spare a minute or two."

Richard sat at the table and pulled Gwen into his lap. Her coppery curls spilled over her shoulder and he brushed them back, kissing her. He thought if he wasn't careful, he might never stop kissing her. "I love the way you look in the morning with your hair all wild and tangled."

She combed her fingers through his hair, smoothing it in place. "And I love the way you look with yours sticking up."

"My what sticking up, sweet?"

She flushed. "You are positively wicked, my lord!"

"Aye, you bring out the worst in me." He broke off a piece of pastry. "Open for me."

She did, just as trusting as a baby bird. He fed her without any thought for himself, his finger tracing her lower lip after every morsel. So soft, so tempting.

Finally she pushed his hand away. "I cannot eat another bite. Will you not let me attend you now?"

"If you wish," he said.

She fed him a piece of the pastry, tracing his lips in imitation of what he did to her. He sucked her finger into his mouth. Her breath caught. She pulled her finger away slowly, trailing it over his lower lip and down his chin.

Richard threaded his fingers in her silken hair and pulled her down to kiss him. Christ almighty, he was getting aroused again! She really was going to be the death of him if he didn't regain his control.

"I don't understand this," she said quietly, shaking her head.

"Don't understand what, sweet?"

She raised her lashes and he saw it. Desire—naked, unadulterated, consuming.

Richard took a deep breath. Hell, he was hard pressed to understand it himself. It was too intense, nearly maddening, and impossible to stop. He shifted her on his lap until she felt him. Her eyes widened.

"Yes, I feel it too." He raised her hand to his lips, pressed kisses into her palm and across the back of her wrist. "Passion is a beautiful thing. 'Tis not meant to be questioned or understood." He pushed up her sleeve, his lips following. "It should be enjoyed, appreciated, encouraged."

A knock sounded on the door. Richard ignored it. He sought her sweet mouth, fully intending on taking her back to bed and assuaging this maddening passion.

The knock came again, stronger this time. Gwen pulled away. "Shouldn't you answer it?"

"Do you want me to?"

Her arms were around his neck, pulling him to her rather than pushing him away.

"No," she said truthfully. She eased her hold on him with a sigh. "But it might be important."

"Enter," Richard said, never taking his eyes from her face.

"Milord?"

It was Owain's voice.

"Yes?"

Owain cleared his throat. "I beg your pardon, milord, but your estates steward has been waiting to see you for quite some time."

"Tell him I'll be down soon," Richard replied.

"Yes, milord," Owain said. Something in his voice made Richard turn. Owain was grinning from ear to ear. Richard stared at the closed door for a second, wondering what the hell had gotten into the old man.

Richard sighed, his gaze sweeping over his wife with longing. "We must wait, it seems." He brushed aside a lock of hair that had fallen in her face. "Promise you will behave no differently when next I see you."

"I promise," she replied softly.

"A kiss to seal the bargain?"

"Is it safe?"

Richard laughed. "I doubt it, but let's try anyway."

Their lips touched. It was like igniting a fire. At the last minute, when he felt his sanity slipping away, Richard managed to set her away from him.

He stood and smacked her on the bottom. "Get dressed, temptress."

She shot him a look of pure indignance. "Temptress? 'Twas you who insisted on a kiss!"

"Aye, but only because you tempted me."

He pulled on his clothes and belted his sword in place before going to her. She stood with her back to him, running a silver brush through her tangle of curls.

He took the brush and stroked her hair a couple of times, then tossed it on the bed and threaded his fingers in the silken mass.

"Jesú, you manage to seduce me with a hairbrush, wench. Do you have any idea how desirable you are?" He bent to kiss her neck, pulling her against him so she felt his arousal. "Mmm, would that I could stay. At this rate, you'll be breeding in no time."

He turned and walked out the door. Gwen curled her hand around the bedpost and leaned against it numbly as silent tears slipped down her cheeks.

"Milord?"

Richard jerked his gaze to Sir John Frost, his estates steward. John was going over the manor accounts with him, telling him how much revenue he had collected, how much was still due, which estates had produced which goods for their lord.

Richard knew John was fleecing him to line his own pockets. All estates stewards did it. The trick was in finding one who wasn't too greedy. Richard figured he'd done just that. As far as he could tell, the amount was fairly insubstantial, and the man was efficient if nothing else.

Richard set his wine cup on the table. "I'm sorry, John. My mind is elsewhere."

John smiled. "'Tis understandable, milord. What with being newly wed and all."

"Aye," Richard said. It did seem as if being newly wed was muddling his brain. He'd thought of nothing but Gwen all morning, barely paying attention to John's recital. No, he was not himself, not at all. He forced her image from his mind. "You were saying, Sir John?"

"I have put together a tentative expense list for the Christmas festivities, my lord."

"You must take that up with Owain. I will not be in residence at Christmas."

"You are going to London?"

"Aye." Richard stood, ending the audience. "Owain will find you suitable quarters."

John got to his feet and bowed. "Aye, milord. Thank you, milord."

Richard made his way across the hall, gripping his sword unconsciously. Why couldn't he keep his mind on business? All he could think of was Gwen. He would have even sworn he could feel her presence, as if she were a vital part of him.

He wanted to drop everything and go to her right now. He wanted to make love to her, of course, but he also wanted to talk to her, hear her laugh, learn more about her.

He stopped. Jesú, there were a million things he didn't even know about her! Did she have a favorite food or a color she preferred over all others? Did she like a particular jewel? Hell, did she even like jewels?

Richard gripped the sword hilt tighter. Since when had he ever cared about such things? Wives were for keeping households and getting heirs. He made sure she had plenty of money in her own purse. If there was something she wanted, she could buy it. She did not have to go without.

A niggling voice told him how pleasurable it would be to give her gifts, how beautiful her face would look when she bestowed her smile upon him, how grateful her body would be when he finally loosened her gown and made love to her.

Richard shook his head. He was a warrior, not a courtier for God's sake! He didn't have time to chase around the countryside looking for pretty baubles just to put a smile on his wife's face.

There was one place in this castle that would bring him to his senses.

The chapel was at the far end of the fortress. It was a cool place, not too large, and set with stained glass windows that cast rainbow light onto the stone floor. Richard didn't come here often, despite Father Stephen's reproving lectures on his immortal soul. Richard rather figured his immortal soul was lost anyway. He'd done way too much killing in his life to ever be forgiven.

But the chapel was not his destination. His destination lay beyond the sanctuary of God. He stepped into the crypt and let the cold air envelop him. There was a small window high overhead that sent a shaft of light into the stillness.

Six sarcophagi greeted him in stony silence. There was his grandfather, Henry de Claiborne, the first Earl of Dunsmore. Awarded the earldom by King Richard the Lionheart for bravery in the Holy Land.

Richard had always thought it ironic that his own position also came from service to a Plantagenet in a faraway land.

His grandmother, Isobel, lay beside the first earl. They had both been dead when Richard was born. His father had spoken often of Henry's gallantry and Isobel's beauty.

Richard touched an ornate sarcophagus. His father, William. Another only son. Perhaps a better one, too.

He turned, traced the raised stonework of Catrin de Claiborne's resting place. Died too soon.

Richard thought the same thing he'd always thought: *Would that I had known you better, Mother.*

But that was not why he was here. Taking a deep breath, he turned. The last two tombs were the ones he was most responsible for. Elizabeth, and beside her, a tinier version.

His son, Matthew. She'd named him, their dead son, before she'd slipped into the sleep that was not a sleep.

She'd named the boy, and Richard had not been there for either one of them.

He sank to his knees beside her and pressed his forehead to the cold stone. Dear God, he had no tears to give. He'd never had any, not for either one of them. And he should have, goddammit!

He smoothed his hands over the lifeless marble. "I'm sorry, Elizabeth."

He always said it. Always, and she never answered, never gave a sign. The only sound was the hollow echo of his own voice.

He tried to picture Elizabeth, to see again her doe-eyed gaze as she'd stared at him with utter devotion. But he couldn't see her. All he could see was a woman with autumn hair and mysterious eyes, a woman who made him feel more in the little time she'd been his wife than he'd ever felt for Elizabeth.

Guilt stabbed through him, twisting dagger-like tentacles until he wanted to cry out from the strain of bearing it. He squeezed his eyes shut and gripped the cold stone. "You deserved more, Elizabeth. More than I ever gave you."

Richard shoved himself to his feet and exited the crypt. He was half-way to the lists when he realized he'd never even thought of his father or of Llywelyn.

23

"Milady, there are men riding into the bailey."

Anne looked up from the game of chess she was playing with her son. "What sort of men, Gena?" she snapped.

Witless woman! *Men.* What kind of a description was that? How was a lady to know whether she should run and hide or play the gracious hostess?

Gena swallowed, and wrung her hands. "Knights, I think, milady."

Tristan shot to his feet. "Knights, Mama! Mayhap Lord de Claiborne has sent for me at last."

Anne's hand fluttered to her throat. Richard? Had he returned to her?

Gena shook her head. "Nay, 'tis not Dunsmore. The heraldry is wrong."

Tristan's face fell. His blue eyes, so much like his mother's, showed his disappointment. At nine years old, he should have gone to Claiborne castle to begin his training. He would train as a squire, then he would become a knight, then he would return to rule Ashford Hall.

Anne refused to let her own disappointment show. It angered her she could still be vulnerable to Richard after all this time.

A servant rushed into the solar and bowed. "A man to see you, milady. He wouldn't give his name, but said to tell you he is a prince."

Anne's heart quickened. "Show him in."

The man bowed again. Gena followed him out. Tristan turned to his mother, his brows drawn together in a look that was not meant to grace a boy's face.

Anne squeezed his hand. She had never wanted to be a mother. She'd not enjoyed her son very much when he was smaller, but now that he was growing up and resembling her more and more, she felt a certain fondness for him. "'Tis all right, Tristan. 'Tis only a friend. I will introduce you to him, and then I wish you to find your tutor and see about your lessons."

Tristan returned her smile. "Aye, Mama."

The door to the solar opened. The servant who had announced the visitor held it until the man entered, then closed it behind him.

"My lord," Anne said. "Be well come to Ashford Hall. May I present my son, Tristan?"

Tristan stepped forward. "Be well come to Ashford Hall, my lord."

"You may call me Dafydd," he replied, clasping the offered hand. His gaze locked with Anne's and she felt a tremor pass through her.

"Run along now," she said to her son.

"Aye, Mama."

When Tristan was gone, Anne sank into a chair. "What can I do for you, my lord?" she asked coolly.

Dafydd ap Gruffydd sprawled in the chair Tristan had occupied. "My men and I would like lodging for a night. Or mayhap two…"

One corner of his mouth lifted in an insolent grin. Anne let her gaze sweep over him slowly, measuring his abilities.

When she met his stare, he showed no hint of irritation, only amusement. She crossed her arms over her breasts. "Why should I even consider it? I've had the favor of powerful earls, and even the king himself. What could I possibly have to gain by allowing you… lodging?"

Dafydd shot out of his chair and pulled her to her feet. His mouth crushed down on hers. Anne couldn't stop her response. She melded to him, returned his kiss with a hunger that had not been eased by the attractive young knight she'd recently taken to her bed.

Dear God—finally—a man. A man who knew how to please a woman. Her arms slipped around him, her breasts flattening against his chest, her woman's center unerringly finding the hard evidence of his desire for her.

His grip tightened as she rubbed against him. Even through the layers of cloth separating them, his fingers managed to tease her nipple into aching arousal.

Her hand slipped between them to close over his hardened manhood. She expected him to groan, to lose control, to undress her and slide deeply into her body. Most men did.

It was men like Richard, like King Edward, who resisted and tormented and teased until she was a quivering mass of desire.

And men like Dafydd ap Gruffydd. Anne shuddered.

Dafydd lifted his head. "We have a common enemy, you and I. We both wish to see Richard de Claiborne brought to his knees. I propose we work together to achieve it."

Anne disengaged herself from his arms. Revenge on Richard. It sounded so sweet. And was there nothing she would not do to achieve it?

"What do you have against Richard?" she asked, partly to prolong the anticipation of lovemaking, partly to learn if his reasons were good enough to ensure dedication.

Dafydd's eyes hardened. "Let us just say he owes me a crown. If not for him, I would be sitting in my brother's place."

Anne crossed to the door and slid the bar home. Her hands strayed to the laces of her gown, loosening them with great deliberation. "Very well, Dafydd ap Gruffydd, but you'd better make it worth my while."

His eyes softened, swept lazily from her feet to her head, leaving her with no doubt as to the thoroughness with which he would also peruse her naked body. "You can count on that, my dearest Anne."

Richard shrugged his sore shoulder as he walked into the hall. Andrew was beside him, still laughing about the young knight who'd gotten knocked off his horse during jousting practice.

"He'll learn, Andrew. I'll wager you and I both fell off our horses a time or two when we were still learning."

"Aye, yer right about that," Andrew admitted.

It was almost dinner and the hall was crowded. Richard scanned the knots of people, frowning when he didn't see Gwen. Owain stood behind the dais, intent on a conversation he was having with a woman Richard couldn't see. When Richard approached, the two stepped apart.

"Milord," Owain said, rubbing his forehead absently.

Richard turned to Alys. "Where's Gwen?"

Alys's face seemed redder than usual. Her eyes widened and she clutched her gown. "I thought she was with you, milord."

Richard bit down on the shred of unease curling around his heart, reminding himself not to lose his temper with Gwen's maid. "When did you last see her?"

Alys stole a guilty look at Owain. "Two, maybe three hours ago."

Richard forgot his patience. "Christ, woman! Are you always in the habit of leaving her alone?"

Alys paled. Owain started to speak, but she cut him off. "Nay, Owain! He is right. I-I shouldn't have left her. I'll find her now, milord."

Richard raked a hand through his hair. "My apologies, Alys. Gwen is a grown woman. You shouldn't have to watch her."

In a move he'd not have tolerated from anyone else, Alys took his hand and patted it like she would a boy's. It was a strangely endearing quality she had, trying to mother him years too late. "I'll find her for you, milord."

Richard's voice was soft when he spoke. "Nay, Alys. She's probably still upstairs. I'll get her."

Richard took the stairs to the master chamber two at a time. He swung the door open and entered. The room was quiet. "Gwen?"

He checked the bed, then went to the small adjoining solar. Next, he checked the family solar. When he made his way back down to the hall, his heart was beginning to hammer.

Alys and Owain hurried forward, both of them frowning.

"She's not upstairs," Richard said. "Do you have any idea where she could have gone, Alys?"

Alys's fingers dug into her gown. "Nay, I—"

Richard spun around and motioned for Andrew. "Gather some men and start searching the outbuildings and bailey for any sign of my wife."

"Aye, milord," Andrew said.

Richard considered having him question the guards at the gate, but found he couldn't even think of what that would imply. She couldn't leave him, could she? A tingle of apprehension slid down his spine.

"Owain, start searching the keep." Owain nodded and moved off to issue orders. "Is there anywhere else you can think of, Alys?"

"Nay, I… yes! The walls, milord. At her father's stronghold, she went up there sometimes."

"You stay here in case she shows up." Alys sank onto a bench, her face pale and drawn. Richard squeezed her shoulder. "I'll find her, Alys, and when I do, you may have to stop me from paddling her backside."

"Nay, milord, I'll help you," the old woman vowed.

Gwen huddled against the stone battlements and stared at the valley. She'd come up to the walls to think, and stupidly lost track of time. The sun had not been out in days, so all she saw was a dulling of the lead tinted horizon. When she'd turned to leave, she'd realized the white glare of the snow had thrown off her perception of time. Night had fallen.

Shadows, blacker than the night itself, yawned across the battlements, but if she kept her eyes on the snow, it didn't seem as dark. It was childish to be afraid, but she was.

How was she going to get down? There were no torches lit in the stairwell. The logical thing was to feel her way along the passage, but she was too scared to do it.

She'd yelled into the bailey for help, but she was too high up and the wind carried her words away before they could fall.

Her eyes stung with tears and she wiped at them impatiently. Some Welshwoman she was! If her father could see her now, he'd probably disown her. She was the daughter of a great man and she was weak, spineless, simpering.

'Twas no wonder she was such a disappointment to him.

Dear God, what would Richard think? She laughed then, a frightened, hopeless sound. The mighty Black Hawk wouldn't want a woman such as she to be the mother of his sons. He was strong and brave, all the things she was not.

The joke would be on him when she gave him his heir.

She leapt to her feet as the door to the stairwell banged open. A torch burned in the wall sconce, silhouetting a man's shape against the opening.

"Richard!" she cried, throwing herself in his arms, burying her face against the broad expanse of his chest. She was shivering—from cold, from fear, from relief.

His arms tightened around her, then he thrust her away. "What the hell are you doing up here? I've got Andrew and Owain tearing up the place looking for you!"

"I'm sorry," she mumbled, threading her arms around his waist and pulling herself close once more. "I'm cold. Can we go inside now?"

He drew her into the stairwell and unclasped his mantle. "Why didn't you come down if you were cold?" he said, wrapping it around her.

Gwen sniffled and kept her face downcast. "I-I couldn't."

He didn't say anything for a long moment and she sensed he was studying her. She dreaded his next question, knowing what it had to be, and wondering what answer she could give.

"Come, I'll get Alys to prepare a hot bath," he said, taking her hand.

When they reached their chamber, Gwen folded herself into a window seat, vaguely hearing his rapid orders to a waiting page.

She huddled into his cloak. It smelled of him, and she found that comforting. Closing her eyes, she buried her nose in the fabric.

Her knight had rescued her from the shadows.

She turned away when he came to her. Sitting beside her, he took her chin in his fingers and turned her face to his.

"You've been crying," he said. "Why?"

"'Tis nothing," Gwen replied, dropping her eyes.

"It must be something."

"Nay."

Richard stood. He looked down at her for a moment, then unbuckled his sword and set it aside. Christ, he had no idea how women thought!

What was he supposed to do? He was surprised to realize he was even thinking about it. In the past, he just walked out when a woman behaved irrationally.

But why had she been crying? It ate at him until he was suddenly struck with a horrifying thought. "Was it something I did?" he asked just a little too sharply.

Her eyes widened. "N-nay."

Richard wanted to pursue it, but Alys hurried in with the first of the servants bearing steaming water.

He sat back while she chastised Gwen. He'd never seen the maid behave with anything but deference for her lady, but right now she looked like an angry mother. Gwen bore it all with quiet, almost embarrassed grace, nodding now and again.

Richard studied his wife. It bothered him she was upset, and it bothered him even more that she wouldn't share it with him.

He knew he should have spent time with her today. Why had he denied himself the pleasure of her company?

The pleasure of her company? Since when had he ever considered a woman's company to be a pleasure unless it was in bed?

When the tub was filled, Alys started to help Gwen undress, but Richard stopped her. "I'll take care of her," he said.

Alys's eyes widened briefly, and then she curtsied. "Is there anything else you will require, milord?"

"Aye, I don't think we'll be dining in the hall tonight. Please send something up."

Alys curtsied again, then retreated from the room.

"Will you come to me, wife? Or must I drag you from your perch?" he teased.

When she stood before him, he began to untie the knots of her girdle. Her hand, small and white and still cold, settled on his.

"'Tis not necessary for you to attend me. I can do it," she said softly.

"I want to," he answered, equally as soft.

Silence suspended between them like the soft beat of butterfly wings. He took his time, removing each garment with care. When she was naked,

Richard knew a moment of pure physical lust when he thought he might spread her beneath him on the carpet and drive endlessly into her.

He sensed she needed more from him right now and he took a deep breath, fighting for control. It was hard won, but he seized it and held on firmly.

She sank into the tub, and Richard thought he was insane. Was he truly jealous of the water caressing her silken skin?

He picked up the soap and knelt beside her.

"I can do it," Gwen said.

This time he gave in. "'Tis probably a good idea, love," he said, then wondered if his voice was as unsteady as he felt. He retreated to a chair to watch, his body throbbing as though he'd not made love to her in years rather than hours.

She lifted a slender arm and slid the washcloth from her fingertips to her shoulder. Candlelight illuminated the trail of liquid that ran down her chest and dripped off her breasts. Her nipples beaded as wet skin met cool air. A single drop of water fell from the tip of one rosy crown.

Richard closed his eyes. He would have loved to lick away that drop of water, and any others that wanted to cling to her delicious body. "Alys told me you used to go up to the walls of your father's castle."

"Aye."

"I might not have found you otherwise. What would you have done then, since you couldn't come down?"

She didn't answer and he opened his eyes to find her head bowed.

"Gwen?"

She turned to him, her lower lip caught between her teeth.

"Why couldn't you come down, Gwen?" he prodded softly.

"I had no candles." Her reply was so soft he had to strain to hear. Did she say candles?

"Why didn't you go to one of the towers?"

She threw the cloth to the end of the tub. It smacked against the water, then sank beneath the surface. "You don't understand! It was dark and I—" She stopped and pressed her hand to her forehead.

Richard went to her, knelt beside the wooden tub. He brushed his knuckles down her cheek. "Tell me, Gwen. Tell me why."

"I've never told anyone," she whispered. "Never."

"Never told them what, *cariad*?" Richard realized he'd slipped into Welsh, called her *love*, a term he'd used often when coaxing women, but never in Welsh. It must have been because she was Welsh that he'd done it.

She fixed him with her golden-green stare. Richard cupped her cheek, swept his thumb across her lower lip. "You can tell me, *cariad*."

She lowered her lashes. "I cannot. You will think—"

"I will think what?" he asked when she stopped.

She took a deep breath. "I-I don't like dark places."

He saw the flush creep into her cheeks, the slumping of her shoulders, the quivering of her lip. Jesú, this woman who had stood up to him from the first minute he'd known her, who had dared him to beat her and thrown water in his face, who had faced arrowfire without blinking, was afraid of the night! And afraid what he would think of her for it.

Richard wanted to hug her to him and laugh at the absurdity. But he didn't because he knew she would think he was laughing at her. "Is that all?" he asked lightly. "And here I thought it was something serious."

Her head snapped up. Her eyes flashed, daring him to pity her. "Didn't you hear me? I said I was afraid of the dark. I couldn't walk around the walls because I was too scared to move!"

Richard shrugged. "We'll just have to make sure you carry a torch the next time, won't we?"

Gwen slumped against the back of the tub and studied the ceiling. "I am not brave like you or my father. 'Tis weak and childish."

"I think you are very brave. And I see nothing childish about you."

Something in his tone made Gwen look at him. He tried to hide it, but his gaze flickered over her body, lingering on the tips of her breasts peeking out of the water. Heat surged between her legs as surely as if he'd touched her with his hands rather than his eyes.

"Why didn't you come see me today?" The words popped out before she could stop them. Gwen fervently wished she could call them back.

He met her gaze. "I wanted to."

On impulse, she closed her hand over his where it gripped the edge of the tub. His fingers laced through hers, then he brought her hand up to his cheek.

"I thought of nothing but you all day," he confessed. "Dozens of times I stopped myself from coming to you."

"Why?" The word came out as a whisper. She wondered if he'd even heard it.

He rubbed his jaw against the back of her hand, slowly, deliberately. "Because I have duties, Gwen. Because what I want comes second."

A candle sputtered as a glob of tallow fell against the flame. Their eyes met. Something pulsed between them, something so strong and bewildering that Gwen felt as if her heart would burst from her chest at any moment.

"What do you want right now?" she asked breathlessly.

He let go of her hand and leaned forward until their lips were almost touching. Gwen closed her eyes in anticipation.

"You," was the word he whispered, the word that seemed to tickle her skin with its promise before his mouth claimed hers.

When Gwen thought his kiss might consume her very soul, a knock sounded on the door and he pulled away to answer it. She sank down in the tub until only her chin was visible while two serving women brought in the dinner Richard had requested.

"Are you warm enough now?" he asked when they had gone.

"Aye," Gwen replied.

He came to her and held up a towel. Gwen stood. His eyes darkened as rivulets of water trailed down her pinkened skin. Wordlessly he dried her off, then wrapped her in white ermine, despite her protests it was too expensive to use as a blanket.

She followed him to the table. He pulled his chair close to hers and proceeded to attend her as if they were dining in the hall. He gave her the best portions of meat, feeding her every bite from his fingertips. He held her goblet, only drinking or eating when she insisted.

Gwen decided she loved the attention. No one had ever done such things for her before. She realized she'd never wanted anyone to do such things. And now she wanted him to do them, only him.

He was close, so close. His lips frequently brushed her ear. He whispered words to her, beautiful words, and she translated them all into English.

"Dengar."

"Alluring."

"Hardd."

"Beautiful."

"Trysor."

"Treasure."

"Dymuniad."

"Desire." Gwen shivered. Richard held the goblet and she drank. Silence fell between them and Gwen's mind wandered.

It seemed such a private thing they did, but she wanted to ask, *did you do this for Elizabeth? Did you share times like these, times when you said not a word but still spoke in ways that made her heart sing?*

Oh God, did you love her, Richard?

"What is wrong, Gwen?"

She looked at him then, focused on his striking eyes, his midnight hair, his firm jaw, and she smiled to hide her discomfort. In truth, she dreaded the answer to that question. "Nothing at all. I fear I have drunk too much wine though."

"Indeed?"

"'Tis your fault. 'Twas you who held the cup."

He laughed. "Mayhap I wanted to get you drunk so I could ravish you."

"You need not get me drunk for that," she replied, her cheeks heating.

"Wanton wench," he teased.

"That, too, is your fault."

"Aye, I fully accept the blame." He rose and pulled her up with him. "And now, if you do not object, I think I might like a demonstration of your wantoness since I have thought of nothing else all evening but your naked body underneath that fur."

Gwen spread her hands over his chest. "How can I refuse my savior?"

His hands tightened over her arms. "Nay, Gwen, not for that. Never for that. Do it because you want *me*."

She said the only thing she could say, the thing she knew instinctively she had to say. "I want you, Richard. 'Tis because I like the things, umm, the things…" She dropped her chin to her chest, her ears growing hot.

He laughed softly. "Ah, sweet, you are absolutely the most uninhibited recent ex-virgin I've ever known, but you can't say the words, can you? You can't say that you like it when we make love, that you like the way it feels when I'm deep inside you, or the way I touch you, or the way my tongue feels on your hot flesh."

A fire raged in Gwen's body, but she still couldn't look at him.

"It makes a man crazy when a woman tells him the things she likes about his lovemaking."

She raised her head. "Truly?"

He put his hand over his heart. "I swear it." His brows drew together thoughtfully. "There is perhaps another English word I should teach you. Owain wouldn't dare, and mayhap I should not either, but I don't think I can resist the temptation."

He smiled mischievously and Gwen's curiosity was piqued. "What, Richard? Tell me, please? I want to know."

"'Tis a vulgar word."

"I know how to curse! Rh—my father's warriors taught me." She watched him for a sign he'd picked up on her near slip. He didn't mention it and she was relieved.

"You cannot repeat it to anyone."

"Very well," she replied impatiently. "Tell me!"

"Fuck."

"Fuck? What does it mean?"

"To make love."

Gwen considered it for a moment. Richard watched her, one eyebrow quirked upwards, a lazy grin tickling the corners of his mouth. She sensed there was more to it than that, but she didn't know what it could be.

"'Tis a rather strange word. But then, English is a strange language, I've found. So how do you use it? Do you say…?" She went through every combination she could think of, starting with 'I want' and ending with 'will you'.

Richard led her to the bed while she rolled the foreign words over her tongue. His eyes glittered while she continued to talk.

Finally, he picked her up and laid her before him, spreading the white ermine to reveal her naked body. "Jesú, you are a delight. You've just managed to say things even a London harlot might think twice about."

Gwen propped herself on her elbows. "Why you—!"

Richard pounced on her, pushing her back into the mattress. "Ah, *cariad*, 'tis incredibly exciting to hear such words cross your sweet lips. Forgive me, but I could not resist."

Gwen wanted to be angry, but his smile was so disarming that she started to giggle instead. He laughed too, and Gwen caught herself thinking how much she loved the sound of his voice. "You are truly depraved, my lord," she said, wrapping her arms around his neck.

"Aye, I am indeed," he replied, burying his mouth against the hollow of her throat. "And I'm going to make you every bit as depraved as I am. I want you to tell me what you like, and what you want me to do, and where you want me to touch you. I want you to tell me everything."

Gwen cupped his face between her hands. "I like it when you laugh," she said softly.

He smiled. "That was not the sort of thing I meant, but I'm glad you said it. I will laugh more often if it pleases you."

"Aye, it does."

"What else pleases you, my lady?"

"You please me."

"Take my hand," he said, holding it up. "Now, put it where you want it most."

Gwen hesitated only a moment before setting his open palm on her breast. Before he could do anything, she slid his hand downwards, over her belly, and settled it between her thighs.

Her breath caught as his finger slipped into her cleft.

"Tell me you want me," he growled.

"Yes, yes, I want you…"

His lips touched the skittering pulse in her throat, and Gwen was lost. She chanted his name as he trailed kisses down her body, then back up again, his garments rasping against her flesh, the touch of the cloth both erotic and maddening.

She tugged at his surcoat, aching, needing to feel his hot skin next to hers. She whimpered when he grabbed her hands.

He pressed his lips to each palm. "'Tis torture, is it not, *cariad*? But, is it not also exciting, having a man make love to you with all his clothes on?"

In truth, it was very arousing to lie naked before him while he remained fully clothed. She was open, vulnerable, and it made her realize she trusted him, at least in this. He wouldn't harm her, her handsome knight, the man who had saved her.

Gwen's hand found his hard length, rubbed it through the layers of cloth. She was rewarded with a low groan. He was less in control than he pretended, and that excited her even further.

"'Tis maddening, my lord."

He closed his eyes. "And your touch is exquisite, my lady."

Her nipples thrust against his tongue as he drew each one into his mouth and taught her the raw, hungry depths of desire.

By the time he knelt between her legs, she was moaning his name, begging him for fulfillment. Holding her breath, she watched as he fumbled beneath his garments to release his chausses. She couldn't even see his male weapon when he lifted his tunic and fitted himself to her, entering her body in a long, slow glide.

All she could feel was him—pure, hard, rampant length, filling, filling. And then he was moving and she was riding the sweet waves of intense pleasure, taking him in, differently at this angle, but still wonderful, so wonderful.

She barely remembered the English words, but she managed to say them, and he groaned, thrusting into her even harder.

Wild excitement coursed through her at the sight of him, fully clothed, kneeling between her legs and giving her the same pleasure as if he were naked and lying on top of her.

His hands cupped her bottom, raising her to meet him. Gwen clenched her lower lip between her teeth. She had no idea it was her fingers that toyed with her nipples, or that the sight was driving him mad.

"My God, you are beautiful," he said, his gaze locked on hers while she took all he had to give. His eyes finally drifted shut and his head tilted back, his breathing coming faster and heavier.

Then he leaned forward and braced himself over her, driving into her with hot fury. Gwen went with him, over the edge, tumbling headlong into the sweet, wild place she'd only recently discovered with him.

It was a long time before they were coherent, and an even longer time after that when Gwen helped him shed his clothes so they could crawl under the coverlets together.

"We can leave the hangings open a bit, if you like," he murmured in her ear.

Gwen snuggled closer and yawned. She couldn't believe how tired she was. It made her tongue loose, but she didn't care. "Nay, I am safe as long as I'm with you."

"I will protect you, *cariad*. Always, I promise."

24

"Chess is like battle, Gwen. The object is to outflank the enemy. You must think carefully on your next move."

"I am thinking," she grumbled. Richard was the enemy. That was the easy part. Beating him was the hard part. She frowned and reached for her bishop. Before her fingers closed over it, she glanced at her husband.

He watched her intently. She hesitated, then grabbed her queen instead. Too late, she saw the mistake.

"Checkmate," he said, blocking her king. "If you'd went with your first instinct, I'd not have won."

Gwen leaned back in her chair. "I'm not any good at this."

"Yes you are. Your problem is you allow yourself to jump to the wrong conclusion too quickly. If you learn to take your time, you will be much better."

Gwen picked up her king and toyed with it. A fortnight had passed since he'd brought her down from the battlements. They spent more time together now, making love, talking, going for long walks. "Who taught you how to play?"

"My father. He was very good." His eyes became clouded, distant. Gwen's heart lurched. She wanted to go to him, soothe him, chase the clouds away.

"My father never taught me anything," she said suddenly. Dear God, what had made her admit that? She never spoke of her father to him. She cringed, waiting for his condemnation of the man he hated.

"'Twas his loss," Richard said quietly.

Gwen shrugged it off. Some wounds were still too raw to share with anyone. "'Tis all right. I had Alys and Einion. My father had Wales." She wisely left Rhys off the list.

"Who is Einion?" he asked, his eyes flashing.

"My father's seneschal."

Richard relaxed. "You mean the old man with the white hair?"

"Yes. Owain reminds me of him sometimes."

"Owain is a good man. He's been with my family for years."

"Aye, he told me."

"What else did he tell you?"

Gwen's eyes widened. She knew him well enough to know this was a demand. "Nothing, my lord. Should he have?"

Richard rubbed his temples. "Nay, of course not. Forgive me for snapping at you."

Gwen rushed to his side. Standing behind his chair, she replaced his fingers with hers. "Of course I forgive you," she whispered.

He sighed and leaned his head back, his eyes drifting closed. His lashes were so thick and long that Gwen had to resist the urge to touch them, to feel their silkiness beneath her fingertips. She laid her cheek on top of his head, rubbing it against his hair. God above, she cared for this man too much, and she couldn't stop. More than ever, she wanted to share his life, wanted to know him and be a part of him.

Her fingers traveled in slow circles. "Did you grow up here?"

"Aye," he said. "Here and London. The coast sometimes. I have a castle on Mor Iwerddon. We shall travel there in the spring. You will love the beaches and cliffs."

Gwen smiled. The Irish Sea. She loved the way he used Welsh so naturally. She could almost pretend she'd married a Welshman and settled in Wales.

They usually conversed in French, but whenever they made love, he inevitably slipped into Welsh. She didn't think he was conscious of it. It was so natural, so intimate, something Anne or Elizabeth could never have shared with him.

"What of your mother and father?" she asked. "What were they like?"

"My father was a warrior, one of the best. He remained loyal to King Henry during the Barons' Revolt when so many of them followed Simon de Montfort."

Gwen swallowed. "I-I'm sorry he died. You must miss him terribly."

He stiffened, then relaxed just as quickly. "Aye," he said on a sigh.

"And what of your mother? What was she like?"

"I don't remember her very well. 'Tis terrible, isn't it? But she died when I was five, and 'twas so long ago that I remember little beyond the fact she was beautiful and sweet. My father never got over her death. He used to call for her sometimes, long after she was gone. Then he'd remember and Owain would have to lead him to his chamber. I'd hear him crying and..."

Gwen's fingers stilled. She pressed her lips to his forehead. "What, Richard?"

He clasped her hand and laid it against his heart. "Nothing, *cariad*. I am talking too much. You are terribly full of questions today," he said, pulling her into his lap.

Gwen brushed a lock of hair off his brow. "'Tis not unreasonable for a wife to want to know her husband."

"Nay, I suppose not."

"Sometimes I feel as though I've known you forever," she said, caressing his cheek. "Other times, I feel as if I know you not at all."

He caught her fingers and kissed them. "Your eyes are the color of the Mediterranean where it kisses the shores of Corfu," he said, his voice soft and silky. "'Tis all gold and green, hardly blue at all."

"Where is that?" she asked, breathless.

"'Tis one of the Greek Isles."

"You've been many places, haven't you?"

"Aye. Wondrous places. Horrible places."

"Tell me about them."

"We started in Southampton," he murmured against her mouth. "We stopped in France..." He nibbled her earlobe. "Then sailed around Spain..."

Gwen's breath caught. His voice was low, passion-drunk, indelibly male. Little shivers of delight raced along her spine.

He fanned fiery kisses along her throat. "Portugal…"

His fingers had been working her laces and he pulled her gown aside to kiss her shoulder. "Gibraltar…"

"Mmm, Richard," she gasped, her body tingling with arousal.

"Morocco…" he said, his lips as hot as the Sahara itself whispering along her collarbone. "Sicily…"

He dipped into the valley between her breasts. "Italy… the Greek Isles…"

He opened her gown enough to reveal a soft nipple. Gwen's hands strayed to entwine in his hair. His tongue traced a lazy circle around the little bud, then he sucked it into his mouth.

Gwen moaned her pleasure.

"And the Holy Land," he said before attending to the other pouting nipple.

"Mmm, Richard. I don't want to talk any longer."

"Why not?" He leaned back and closed her gown.

"Don't stop now!"

"You must learn to savor your pleasures, sweet. Think how many times more exciting it will be if we wait."

Gwen pouted. "I don't want to wait!"

"We must. 'Tis almost time for the evening meal. If we are absent from the hall one more time, people will talk."

"Stubborn man!" she said, hopping from his lap. "They are already talking. And besides, mayhap I will not wish to make love later."

An irritating grin spread over his handsome features. "You want me, Gwen. You'll not deny me."

"Oh, you are a devil!"

His grin widened. "Aye, mayhap so."

Gwen eyed the chessboard. Tease her would he! She'd show him she wasn't so easily rattled. "Let's play again," she said. "I'll beat you this time, I swear it."

Richard laughed. "All right, *cath wyllt*. We'll see who still has their wits about them."

Gwen leaned forward to gather her pieces. Her gown was still unlaced and her breasts threatened to spill free.

"You are doing that deliberately," Richard said.

Gwen blinked innocently. "Doing what?"

"Trying to tempt me."

"Are you tempted?"

"I'd be lying if I said no. But you can't have your way with me that easily, wench. It'll take more than that to seduce me."

Gwen straightened. "And just what will it take?"

He smiled. "Tell you what, if you win this game, I will do whatever you command me."

"Anything?"

"Anything."

"Then prepare to lose."

Gwen threw herself into the game with relish. She ignored his hot gazes when he was trying to distract her, and managed to distract him once or twice when she opened her dress to reveal a naked breast. He would swallow and try to remember his move, and she would smile demurely and say "Sorry."

Still, she was surprised when he lost, since his skill was the greater. But she didn't dare question her good fortune.

He sat back and laced his fingers behind his head, grinning lewdly. "Ask and ye shall receive."

"Bar the door."

When he returned, she stood and pressed against him. "Kiss me," she whispered.

He did, blindingly. Gwen had to remind herself she was the one in control. If she weren't careful, the seducer would become the seduced. She pulled back and put her hands on his chest while she caught her breath.

"You'll have to do better than that," he said, inching her gown up her body.

"Nay!" Gwen cried, pushing away from him. "You must do what I say. Now, undress."

"Demanding little hussy, aren't you?" he said, smiling as his hand went to his sword belt.

Gwen licked suddenly dry lips as his clothes peeled away. His bronze body was hard, magnificent, breathtaking. When he stood only in his braies, Gwen couldn't stop admiring him. She wanted to touch him, wanted to feel the tremors beneath his golden flesh when she explored him with her mouth and her hands. "All of it," she said.

"What about you?" he asked as his braies dropped to the floor.

Gwen shed her clothes in a heap. When she went to him, she said, "I want to touch you."

His eyes darkened. "*Cariad*, you are supposed to make me do things to you, not the other way around."

"You said anything, remember? And this is what I want," she finished, standing on tiptoe to press her lips to his neck.

"You seek to torture me," he murmured.

"Nay, I seek to pleasure you." She circled his nipple with her tongue, smiling against his skin when he sucked in his breath. Her hands roamed over him, delighting in the solid muscle and the quivers rippling through it. He was like a hot-blooded stallion, well trained to the saddle but dying to break free and run.

Gwen closed her eyes, feathered kisses down his chest, over his abdomen. Her hand closed over his thick shaft and he groaned. "Does it hurt for me to touch you like this?"

His laugh was strangled. "It will hurt if you stop."

Emboldened, Gwen traced it with her finger. It was a curious weapon, with a life of its own it seemed as it bucked beneath her touch.

Gwen had a sudden thought. When he touched her with his tongue, it nearly drove her mad. Would it be the same for him?

Tentatively, she licked him. His eyes shot open, his entire body stiffening. "Oh God," he said, swallowing.

Gwen laughed. Oh yes, he liked it. She swirled her tongue around the tip, down the length of him, finally taking as much of him in her mouth as she could. His hand came up to cup the back of her head, guiding her, tightening in her hair until he moved away abruptly.

Then he pulled her to her feet and kissed her. "My turn," he whispered huskily. Before she could voice a protest, his arm swept across the table, knocking the chessboard to the floor. Then he bent her over, face first, and slammed into her from behind. Gwen gasped, her fingers clutching the edge of the table.

The polished wood was cool on her sensitive breasts, a sharp contrast to the scalding heat of the man bending over her. Shivers raced along her nerve endings, multiplying, finding new erotic points of impact along the way.

"Tell me what you want," he commanded in a husky whisper.

"Touch me."

His hands came up beneath her, cupped her breasts, his fingers teasing her nipples. "Like this?"

"Yes, oh yes…"

"And this?" he asked, one hand moving down to stroke the swollen bud of her arousal.

"Yes, yes!"

"Jesú, it had best be soon, sweet. I won't last much longer."

But he needn't have said it, because at that moment, all the nerve endings in Gwen's body built and shattered, leaving her gripping the table and crying his name as the incredible sensations rocked her.

He grabbed her hips and impaled himself to the limit—once, twice, three more times—before her name left his lips in a harsh cry of fulfillment.

He collapsed in a chair and pulled her down on top of him. He nuzzled her neck, his breath heavy in her ear. "Your mouth is magical, Gwen. I don't think I've ever come so hard in my life."

She put her arms around him and sighed. "Aren't you glad I won?"

He kissed her throat and laughed. "I think we both won, sweet."

It was a week later when Gwen stood on a stool, a length of cream velvet draped around her, as Alys pinned and tucked and mumbled to herself.

They were leaving for London within another week and Alys was frantically trying to finish the new gowns she'd insisted Gwen must have.

"Be still, my lady," Alys said, straightening and putting her hands on her hips. She tilted her head from side to side, studying the lay of the cloth.

"Sorry," Gwen replied, fidgeting. It was impossible to get comfortable with all these pins sticking in her!

Richard had acquiesced to the old woman's whim, and had even accompanied her and Gwen into the village to buy cloth of silk and velvet.

Gwen remembered his hot eyes on her as Alys had held up bolt after bolt of different color fabrics. "Oh yes, definitely that one," he would say when a color struck him.

Alys had hummed and clucked to herself, preoccupied with her task, but Richard's gaze had told Gwen far more than mere words.

The devil was letting his prick decide and she'd told him so when they finished. He laughed and said, yes, but it had good taste. Gwen got him back then. She told him, yes, it did taste good.

"Be still, my lady," Alys mumbled over the pins in her mouth.

"Sorry," Gwen said. It had been very satisfying to watch Richard's eyes darken with longing, to know it was her he desired.

He was so much different than she'd once thought. She no longer believed the awful tales about him. Richard was a warrior. He did what his king ordered, the same as any of her father's warriors would do if Llywelyn commanded it.

And she didn't really know he would make war on her father if she bore him a son. Still, she prayed every day Elinor would give birth to a boy so she would never have to find out.

Alys removed the cloth. "There."

"Thank heavens," Gwen said. Alys frowned. "I'm sorry, Alys, 'tis just that I've been standing here for so long. I need to go for a walk."

Alys waggled a finger. "Nay, 'tis to find that handsome husband of yours. Gracious, it's a wonder the two of you ever leave the bedchamber."

"Alys!"

The woman laughed. "'Tis the way of young love. Soon, we'll have a castle full of children."

Heat prickled Gwen's skin. She knew she should keep her mouth shut. "You are wrong, Alys. I do not love him. I cannot."

"And why is that, pray tell?"

Gwen uttered the words that were like a litany to her. "He is my father's enemy."

Alys sighed. "You don't live with your father, you live here. I've been around long enough to recognize love—"

"I don't want to talk about it!" Gwen realized she was clutching her chemise in her fists. She smoothed the material over her body with shaking hands, then retrieved her gown and slipped into it. "I'll be in the hall if you need me," she said calmly.

Alys sank into a chair and bent over her sewing. "Aye, my lady," she said, her voice clipped.

It was all Gwen could do to keep from running out of the room. She needed to be alone for a while, needed to think.

It wasn't true, was it? Wouldn't she know if she loved him?

She loved the way he made her feel, the things he did to her, but that did not mean she loved him any more than he loved her. And he did not love her, of that she was certain. Not once had he ever said it, not even in the throes of passion when he slipped into Welsh.

No, what he felt for her was desire. Passion. And one day it would fade, just like Anne had told her it would.

25

Gwen didn't know what it was that drew her to the stable. She strolled between the horses until she found Sirocco. He nickered to her, shoving his nose in her stomach. She laughed and began to scratch him behind the ears. "Such a beautiful boy," she murmured.

"Do you always affect savage beasts so?"

Liquid heat surged in her veins as the velvet voice slid down her spine. She whirled to face him, her breath catching high in her throat.

"Richard," she said, her voice a husky whisper. "You frightened me."

"I'm sorry, *cariad*. I saw you coming in here and I had to follow."

He would be menacing if she didn't know him. He was big and covered by a mantle black as night. His silver eyes gleamed in the dim light of the stable, flickering over her so slowly that her stomach fluttered in anticipation. He moved and the hilt of his jeweled sword peaked out from beneath his cloak, adding to the restrained danger of him. Her senses were heightened by his nearness, her breathing more rapid.

"'Tis as if time were reversed, except that you are even more beautiful to me. Mayhap I should do to you now what I wanted to do then."

Gwen shivered. "And what was that?"

He stepped closer until they were separated only by an arm's length. He caressed her throat then slid his hand to the soft swell of her breast. Her insides melted. "I wanted to toss you into the hay and make love to you."

The aroma of hay and horse filled her nostrils. Her breath frosted in the cold air. His hand lay palm open over her breast and she knew he could feel the flutter of her heart. Gwen closed her hand over his, shutting out everything but him.

"Do it now," she said, wanting to be close to him, wanting to know he needed her in some way.

His eyes darkened. He pulled her to him and she tilted her head back, expecting his mouth to claim hers.

He stroked her hair, his eyes searching her face. When he spoke, his voice was low, rapid, almost regretful. "Nay, you are too fine and too special to be tumbled in the hay like a commoner. You deserve silk and furs and jewels. You should be closeted in a luxurious palace and waited on hand and foot by adoring servants. Edward should have found you a prince."

"Nay!" Gwen cried, frightened by his strange turn of mood. She gripped his surcoat. The black hawk crumpled in her fists, mingling with the crimson. "I want to be with you! I-I..."

"What, *cariad*?"

Gwen swallowed hard. She had been about to say she loved him. Damn Alys for suggesting it! She desired him, certainly; cared for him, probably; but loved him?

"'Tis nothing." She slipped her arms around him and buried her face against his chest.

"I held you like this that day," he said softly. "Except I don't believe you held me as tightly then as you are now."

Gwen squeezed her eyes shut. She *did not* love him. Dear God, she *could* not. Her father was depending on her. Her loyalty was to him.

"You're shaking," he said. "Why?"

Gwen resisted his efforts to push her away so he could see her face. He gave up when she wouldn't budge easily, lowering his cheek to the top of her head. "'Tis my fault. I'm sorry for frightening you. I will never let you go, *cariad*, never. Don't you know that?"

"I'm not sure what you would do," she whispered against his chest.

Richard's fingers entwined in her hair. She didn't resist this time, and he tilted her head back and kissed her. Stable-sounds roared in her ears: the munching of hay, swishing of tails, low nickers and snorts.

Something tugged on her mantle and she broke the kiss. Sirocco nibbled on the velvet cloth. Richard didn't try to stop her when she disentangled herself from his arms to pet the stallion.

"Ridiculous beast," she cooed, combing his forelock with trembling fingers.

"You treat him like he's a lovable pet instead of a warhorse," Richard said. "You should never forget he is dangerous."

Gwen laughed. If he noticed the near hysterical note in her voice, he didn't show it. "As if I ever could," she said softly.

He pressed a kiss to her forehead. "Let's go for a ride. Sirocco needs to stretch his legs a bit."

"Yes, I'd like that," she replied.

She was surprised when he began to saddle the stallion. She'd thought an earl would call a groom for such menial tasks, but then she realized Richard was a warrior, a man very capable of looking after himself.

"I can saddle my own horse, too," she said.

He put his hands on his hips. "Princesses don't know how to saddle horses."

"This one does," she said smugly.

She retrieved a saddle, struggling to hold the leather frame. It was too heavy, so she dropped it and started to drag it toward her horse. Richard laughed and picked it up with one hand.

"Nay, woman, I'll do it. What kind of a husband would I be if I let you do it yourself?"

"I really can," she grumbled.

"Fine. I'll set it on your palfrey's back and you can do the rest. Agreed?"

Gwen returned his smile. Sweet Lord, he was too beautiful when he smiled like that. "Aye, Richard."

He settled the saddle in place and stepped back. "How long have you had this mare?" he asked, patting the horse's neck.

"Since I was five, I think."

"Mmm, almost fifteen years. How old was she then?"

Gwen stopped in the middle of tightening the girth. "I don't know. I've always had Gwynt. I never stopped to think how old she might be."

Richard was smiling. "Gwynt?"

Gwen's face grew hot. She turned away and tugged the strap. "Aye. When my father gave her to me, he let me name her, so I chose Wind. I know she does not look like much, but to a five year old she was fast."

"Aye, I know. I named my first horse Gwynt."

Gwen turned. "You did?"

Richard nodded. "Aye." He checked the cinch while she slipped the bridle in place. "Jesú, 'tis tight enough!"

"Of course it's tight! There's a trick to it, you know."

"Indeed?" Richard asked, barely containing his smile. He knew there was a trick to ensuring a saddle was tight, but he'd have never thought this slight wife of his would know it.

She waved her hand airily. "Oh of course. You bring your knee up and nudge the horse's belly just enough to get him to let out his breath. Then you pull the strap tight."

"I shall remember it," he replied. It was worth pretending ignorance when she turned her smile on him.

They led the horses into the bailey and he hoisted her into the saddle. Taking a small escort of men, they rode through the town and into the valley. Crisp snow crunched beneath the horses' hooves, the air filling with snorts and the jingling of reins as the animals tossed their heads.

Richard rode beside his wife while the men hung back far enough to give them privacy. He told her how the valley would look in the spring, pointed at a place where wild roses grew in profusion.

He didn't tell her those wild roses had reminded him of her, that for four years he'd ridden out here and walked through the perfumed air, thinking of the Welsh girl he couldn't forget.

His gaze kept straying to her face. She already seemed to love this valley almost as much as he did. Her enthusiasm was genuine and that pleased him immensely.

They brought their horses to a halt on a rise overlooking the river. Her breath caught as she gazed at the rippling sheet of pristine snow stretching before them.

"'Tis beautiful, simply beautiful," she said.

"Aye," Richard agreed. But he wasn't looking at the river below, or the naked trees encased in crystal ice, or the endless sea of white undulating across the hills.

He tapped Sirocco with his heel and the well-trained stallion side-stepped until he was rubbing against Gwen's palfrey. She turned to him, her eyes sparkling with delight, her cheeks flushed with delicate color.

Richard felt a throbbing pain in his heart. He supposed it should have been frightening, but he found it unbearably sweet instead. "I want to show you something else," he said quietly, his finger tracing the curve of her face.

She smiled, catching his hand and threading her fingers through his. "I will follow you anywhere."

The pain in his heart swelled. "I don't want you to follow," he said, "I want you beside me. Will you stay beside me, Gwen?"

"Aye, Richard, I will."

They stared at each other, her smile fading, softening, turning to a look of such pure, sweet beauty that Richard wanted to grab her and hold her close. He didn't feel the icy wind blowing his cloak open, didn't hear the soft rushing of the river, or the piercing cry of a lone hawk high above.

He cupped the back of her head and bent to kiss her. She met him with such warmth, such hot passion, that his insides melted.

Richard groaned. "I should have taken you to bed."

She pulled away, smiling mischievously and admonishing him with a wagging finger. "'Tis too late now, my lord. You must show me this other thing first."

"Tease."

"Lecher."

He grinned. "You win, my sweet. Let us proceed."

They turned and skirted along the silvery river, then entered the forest, winding through the trees until he stopped before a sheer rock face that soared skywards.

Gwen dismounted and followed him toward the wall, gasping when he disappeared inside a fold in the gray rock.

A hand reached out and grabbed her, pulling her into the cave entrance.

"Richard! You scared me disappearing like that," she scolded, her heart racing.

He brushed his lips across hers. "You're always so concerned for me, worried over every bruise and every battle. Does that mean you care for me?"

"Nay," she lied, pushing away. She kept her back to him. "'Tis just that I'm afraid the next man King Edward gave me to would not be so skillful in bed."

Richard laughed. "I've spoiled you, eh? Mayhap I should just worry about my own needs from now on and forget about yours."

She whirled around. "You would not!"

"Nay, you are right. I'm only teasing you, my beauty. Never fear, your pleasure is so entwined with my own, I'd not get anything out of it if you didn't also."

He stepped into the cave and she followed. It was too dark to see anything. "Richard," she whimpered.

His hand found hers. "I am here, love. I won't leave you. Hold on to my mantle while I light a torch."

Gwen gathered a fistful of cloth, pressing herself tight against his back.

Long seconds passed, and then light suddenly flooded the cavern. Gwen gasped. A thousand—no!—a million shards of multi-colored light were reflected from the mirror-like surface of the walls.

"'Tis beautiful, is it not?" Richard stabbed the torch into the soft ground. "I found it when I was a boy. I used to come here often, searching for King Arthur's treasure."

"Rhys and I used to search for the treasure!"

"Do not say that name to me," he said quickly. "Not now, not here."

"I'm sorry. I did not mean—"

"Shhh," he said, slipping the hood from her head and entwining his fingers in the silken waterfall of her hair, "not now, *cariad*." He looked at her for a long moment. "I think I have finally found a treasure," he murmured before kissing her.

Gwen melted against him, lost in his embrace. Nothing else existed outside of here and now. So much for loyalties and heirs and dead wives. She was hopelessly trapped in the spell he wove.

"Would that it were summer," he said in her ear.

She clawed her way back to sanity. "Why? Surely it looks the same no matter what time of year."

"Nay, 'twould look a thousand times better if I could undress you and make love to you beneath these sparkling walls."

"Wh-what makes it look like this?" she asked, stepping away from him.

He shrugged. "'Tis crystal. It shines so when reflected."

"Oh," she said, spinning around and staring at the ceiling. She twirled until she was almost dizzy and the brilliant lights merged into one streak of color.

"Gwen."

She stopped, her gown swirling around her. His voice was so raw, so naked. The look on his face frightened her.

"Richard?" She took a step toward him, her heart pounding, her vision still swimming.

"Sweet Christ, if ever I were to see a fairy princess, she would look just like you." He crossed the distance between them and molded her to him, cupping her cheeks and tilting her face up to his. His look was unguarded for once, his eyes mirroring some turmoil within. "Fairies have a nasty habit of abandoning their mortal lovers. Say you won't abandon me, Gwen."

"Nay, Richard, never," she replied, and meant it.

He kissed her possessively. Gwen buried her fingers in his hair, lost herself in the silken heat of his mouth. She wanted to be as close as it was possible to be, wanted him to touch her deep inside, wanted to feel their hearts beating as one.

She wanted to remember this moment forever.

"Take me, Richard. Now, here," she breathed against his lips.

And then he was pressing her against the wall, shifting their clothes, fitting his body to hers, sheathing himself within her moist heat. Dear God, never had she felt more alive than when this man made love to her. It was more than physical, more than man and woman.

She *needed* him. Needed him in order to breathe, to live. She tightened her legs around him, met his mouth ravenously.

After they'd exploded together and drifted back to earth, Richard held her against him, his breath heavy in her ear. "I have no control when I'm with you."

"I like you uncontrolled," Gwen whispered, easing her legs down his body until she was once again standing.

"I've never shown this place to anyone," he said. "You are the first."

"I'm glad you shared it with me. 'Tis beautiful."

"Aye, 'tis one of the few treasures of my heart." He traced her cheek with a finger. "We will come again in summer, when we can linger."

"I will look forward to it," Gwen replied, slipping her hand into his as they left the shelter of the cave.

The men rejoined them at the edge of the woods and they rode back the way they'd come.

Claiborne castle sat on its formidable perch, cowering the valley into meek submission. Gwen was surprised to feel a sense of belonging, of home. Where once the sight of Claiborne had made her cringe, she now thought it perhaps the most beautiful castle in all of Wales and England.

They passed into the village and up the steep slope to the castle. As they rode into the bailey, Gwen leaned over her mare's neck, petting her and speaking words of praise for a pleasant ride.

When she looked up again, there was a large party of newcomers milling around the inner bailey. Her heart plummeted to her feet. In the party's midst, a lady with blonde hair sat atop a white horse. Her gaze flickered over Gwen, then landed on Richard. The smile she gave him said, *I've missed you, lover.*

"What the hell are you doing here, Anne?" Richard bit out.

"Now is that any way to greet an old friend?" Anne said, her lips pursed in a ridiculous pout as she rode forward to meet them. She swept her hand toward her party. "It seems as though you have forgotten your duty to my son, my lord. I have brought him to begin his training."

Richard's voice could have cut through steel. "I've forgotten nothing. I will send for him in the spring when the snows thaw. You may return to Ashford Hall first thing tomorrow."

Anne opened her mouth to protest, but a boy rushed forward then, his face lit with admiration and awe.

"Greetings my Lord De Claiborne! 'Tis been a long time since you have been to see us, but Mama said you wouldn't mind if we came to Claiborne instead. I've been looking forward to learning to be a squire. I promise to study very hard."

He broke off, looked up at his mother, then at Richard. Gwen had a difficult time reconciling the fact that this boy was Anne's son. She hardly seemed the motherly type, but the boy's face shone equally for her and Richard.

"You've grown, Tristan. I am certain you will make a fine squire," Richard said. "In the spring—"

Gwen tugged Richard's sleeve. For some strange reason, she couldn't bear to see Tristan disappointed. Richard turned, the annoyance on his face softening only slightly. Lowering her voice, she said, "You cannot send the boy home, my lord. He's waited too long, and 'twould break his heart if you sent him away now."

"He will begin in the spring. He can wait that long."

Gwen shook her head. "Nay, he cannot. Richard, please."

His hand closed over hers. "Why do you care so much, *cariad*?"

"I—" She glanced at the boy. "I do not know, exactly, but mayhap 'tis because I know what it feels like to be disappointed."

His expression grew distant. "Disappointed because you had to marry me instead of the man you really loved."

Gwen gripped his hand as though her life depended on it. "Nay, I've never loved any man—"

But you.

She bit the inside of her cheek, suddenly confused by the emotions inundating her.

He waited, his eyes flickering over her face. When she said nothing more, he sighed. "For you then." Turning back to the boy, he said, "I believe my captain's squire is soon to be made a knight. You will begin training to be Sir Andrew of Carrick's squire."

"Thank you, my lord!" Tristan cried, his face breaking into a wide grin.

Anne's gaze went from her son to Richard to Gwen. Her eyes narrowed for only a second. Gwen returned her stare evenly. "We are pleased to offer you lodging, Lady Ashford, until you can begin your return journey. I will have Alys find a room for you."

"Thank you, Lady de Claiborne, but I shan't be returning to Ashford Hall. I wish to accompany you and Lord de Claiborne to London for the Christmas festivites."

Gwen felt insane panic rise in her stomach. She turned to Richard, waiting—praying—for him to say no.

He didn't acknowledge her. "You are welcome to travel with us, Lady Ashford," he said politely, all traces of his anger gone.

Gwen's heart split in two.

26

Gwen whirled around as the door to the solar opened. Richard entered, stripping off his gauntlets and throwing them on a table. His hair was windblown, his cheeks and nose reddened by the cold. He flashed a smile, and Gwen sank into a chair, no longer able to hold herself up.

Unconsciously, she pressed a hand to her thundering heart. Surely, even at this distance, he could hear how loud it beat for him.

"I did not expect you so soon," she said.

"Are you disappointed?" he asked softly.

"Nay. I-I missed you."

He laughed. "I was but making sure Tristan was settled in with Andrew and Justin. I've not been gone *that* long, wench."

Gwen stared at her lap, willing the ridiculous tears she'd been holding back to go away. She heard him move, and then he was at her side, kneeling and clasping her hands between his.

"I had to say yes, Gwen. As much as I would rather refuse Anne, 'tis better to take her away from the March. She prefers life at Edward's court and will not wish to return with us."

Gwen nodded, unable to meet his gaze, unable to speak for fear of crying.

Richard squeezed her hands, then framed her face and forced her to look at him. "What is it, Gwen?"

When she didn't answer, he searched her face, his eyes widening. "You think she is still my mistress."

After a moment, he stood and went to the other side of the room, his back to her.

Yes, God help her, she was afraid Anne was still his mistress. She should have known today had been too perfect to be real. Richard was a man, like the king, like Rhys.

Gwen stood, one hand still clutching the chair arm for support. "She told me you were with her on our wedding night."

He whirled around, his face taut, hard-edged with anger. "And you believed her?" he asked incredulously.

Gwen stared at the floor. "Why should I not? You are English. You don't need my permission to keep a mistress."

She looked up, found him staring at her intently. She thought he was going to say something but then he crossed the room in a flash, dropping to his knees in front of her.

It happened too quickly for her to respond with more than a surprised squeak. She would have stumbled backward and fallen in the chair had he not wrapped his arms around her waist and held her tight. He pressed his face to her breasts, and when he spoke she could feel his hot breath through her garments.

"I swear to you—on my life, on my honor, on everything I hold sacred—that I have been with no other woman since I first saw you again in Shrewsbury."

Mute shock stilled her vocal cords for long seconds. She wasn't sure what she had expected, but this had definitely not been it. Slowly, she entwined shaking fingers in his hair and clasped him tight. When she found her voice, it was barely a whisper. "I believe you. Oh God, I believe you."

He tilted his head back. "There is only you, I swear it."

Gwen cupped his face and pressed her lips to his. The kiss was long, infinitely sweet, perfect. Her heart sped dizzily.

He put her off guard, twisted her insides with his nearness, made her want things it was impossible to have.

She tore away from him and went to stand in front of the fire, suddenly chilled. Another minute and words would have poured from her lips unchecked, words she was not yet certain she was ready to say.

She heard his breath leave him on a long sigh, and she peered over her shoulder. He still knelt, his arms limp at his sides, his chin bowed to his chest, his eyes closed. She turned away when he lifted his head.

The scraping of his sword against the floor told her he was rising. Gwen prayed he would not come to her. If he took her in his arms one more time, she would be lost.

She strained to hear his movements, but there was only silence.

"Gwen?"

"Yes?"

"What do you want?" he asked softly.

She turned, searched his face. His eyes were intense, his features so impossibly beautiful he stole her breath away. *I want you to love me, to need me the way I'm beginning to need you.*

"I-I am not certain," she whispered, her vision growing fuzzy around the edges. "'Tis too soon…"

He raked a hand through his hair. "I have some things to do before dinner." He retrieved his gauntlets and tucked them in his sword belt. "I will see you in the hall tonight."

He was already out the door when Gwen started forward.

"Richard, wait!" He turned, watched her expectantly. "I…" But she faltered, not knowing what to say.

He smiled and leaned against the doorframe. The tension still evident in his body was strangely at odds with the casual stance. "Miss me already, wench?"

Gwen couldn't help but laugh. It was either that or cry. "You are impossibly conceited, my lord."

"Aye." He straightened and let his gaze sweep her from head to toe. "Now why don't you take a nap, love? I have a feeling you won't be getting much sleep tonight," he drawled.

And then he was gone. Gwen sank into the chair. Oh God, what was wrong with her? What was this feeling that heightened and swelled in his presence, then refused to give her a moment's peace even when he was gone?

"Sweet Jesus, milord, ye nearly took my arm off with that one!"

"Sorry, Andrew," Richard said.

Andrew got to his feet and grabbed his sword from the floor. He flexed his arm, arcing his weapon back and forth and grumbling to himself.

"Shall we go again?"

Andrew's head snapped up. "What, are ye crazy?"

Richard grinned. "I promise to go easy on you this time."

"Easy? Ha! Ye fights like a woman! I was only bein' kind when I let ye win."

Richard's laughter echoed off the walls. "Then you won't mind fighting me again," he said, clashing swords with the other man before he could reply.

Servants hovered in the doorways, watching the contest between warriors. Knights leaned against the walls, shouting encouragement.

Owain had stared at him like he was a madman when he'd ordered the Lesser Hall stripped of furniture. But the old Welshman had made sure it was done, mumbling something about stubborn fool noblemen Richard only half caught.

The fires had been banked, but sweat dripped down the inside of Richard's tunic, plastering the garment to his skin. His hair clung to his head and his muscles screamed their agony with every movement.

He blocked a thrust from Andrew's sword, then whirled away before the captain could redirect. Indeed, Richard felt like a madman, but he couldn't stop. He needed this mind-numbing exercise, needed it to stop thinking about one beautiful Welshwoman.

But it wasn't working.

All he could remember was that one moment of blind desperation when he would have done anything to erase the doubt from her eyes.

He had fallen on his knees and sworn to her, sworn as though what she thought of him was the most important thing in the world. Christ, it still shook him up!

But it was important, so important it scared him.

He sent Andrew backwards with a mighty heave, then rushed in, his battle cry on his lips. He'd never knelt to anyone but Edward, never been willing to swear away his very soul to gain the trust of a woman. Why now? Why her?

His sword caught the hilt of Andrew's, stripping it from the captain's hand.

Because he wanted her. Because he wanted *all* of her, her body, her heart, her soul. No one had ever made him feel the way she did.

No, this could *not* be love! He refused to let it happen!

Love was deadly. It weakened warriors, toppled empires, left nothing but the destruction of lives and hearts in its wake. He would not love any woman, ever!

Gradually, Richard became aware of the men standing around him. They called to him, their eyes wide, their faces pale. He blinked.

"Richard."

He felt Owain's hand on his arm and he turned.

"Drop the sword, Richard," Owain said quietly.

Richard looked down the length of his blade. Andrew lay on the ground, the tip resting against the base of his throat. Blood and sweat pooled in the hollow above his breastbone.

Richard flung the sword away and knelt beside his captain. "Jesú, Andrew, are you all right?"

Andrew gulped in air. He rubbed his neck, smearing the blood. It still welled up from the wound Richard had inflicted, but fortunately it was only a scratch. "That's the last time I accuse ye of fightin' like a woman," he choked out.

Richard offered his hand and Andrew clasped it. The men loosed a cheer as Richard helped him to his feet.

The cheers heightened when Richard told Owain to let the ale flow freely. The men hustled from the room, heading for the Great Hall and the entertainment awaiting them.

Richard scrubbed a hand through his matted hair. Owain retrieved his sword and handed it to him. The steel sang as it slid home in the scabbard.

"Can't be easy, keepin' a mistress and a wife in the same castle," Owain said, shooting Richard a disapproving look. "Course, 'tis no reason to kill one of your men."

Richard glared at the old man. "I told you years ago not to interfere in my life," he growled.

Owain snorted. "I promised your mother I'd look after you. And that debt is more important than any you would lay upon me."

Richard accepted a mug of ale from a serving wench. She curtsied, eyeing him appreciatively. He winked out of habit.

"Be about your duties, wench!" Owain barked. "And stop twitching your arse! His lordship cares naught!"

The girl rushed from the room, red-faced. Richard lowered the ale. "What the hell was that all about?"

"If you want to scatter your seed to the wind, then do it elsewhere! I'll not sit by and let you make a fool of your wife! Can't you see how it would hurt her?"

Richard let his breath out in a rush. "Jesú, must you always assume the worst of me? But why not, since Black Hawk de Claiborne is a ruthless bastard? He destroys all he touches, isn't that right? He's incapable of caring about anyone but himself."

Richard drained the mug and flung it in the rushes, then stalked from the room.

The Great Hall was boisterous tonight. The men from Ashford Hall presented new opportunties for dicing and gambling. Richard's knights ate with relish, anticipating the aftermath of the hearty meal. Many of them were already deep in their cups, as proved by their coarse language and behavior.

Gwen took a big swallow of wine and set the goblet down before Richard saw her. Her head hummed pleasantly, and her stomach was warm and tingly. She glanced down the table at Anne, her nerves scraping raw when Anne laughed at something someone said.

Gwen slanted a look at Richard. He was angry with her. 'Twas the only explanation for his moodiness. She touched his sleeve. When he turned to her, she was startled by the sudden racing of her heart. How was it he managed to catch her off guard when she was the one who initiated the contact?

The lines of tension in his brow worried her. She reached up to stroke his jaw. "You are beautiful," she said. It wasn't what she had wanted to say, but it suddenly seemed the only thing she could think of.

His face softened, then he pressed his lips to her palm. "I have naught but a pretty face. You are the one who is beautiful, both inside and out."

"'Tis much more than your face that attracts me to you," she said, swallowing hard.

The look he gave her was intense, full of longing. He traced her lower lip with his thumb. Just when she thought he was about to say something, he shuttered his emotions and a teasing smile spread across his lips.

"What other parts of me are you attracted to, Gwen?"

Gwen took a sip of wine to drown her disappointment. "You are trying to make me blush."

"Am I succeeding?"

"Not yet."

"Well in that case, I cannot wait to get you on your back... or mayhap your hands and knees."

Gwen smiled. He was not going to win this one. She pulled his head down and whispered in his ear. "I will fuck you any way you wish, my lord."

He shuddered. His voice was a raspy growl when he spoke. "God's blood, you make me harder than all of the marble in Westminster Abbey."

"Really? Let me see." Gwen slipped her hand beneath the table and slid it up his thigh. His eyes glittered as she found him. "Oh yes, 'tis big and hard," she said, rubbing her hand along his length.

"Keep doing that, wench, and there will be no need for lovemaking this night."

"Then let us go up now." Touching him, feeling the proof of his desire, sent liquid heat surging in her veins, pooling where she burned hottest.

"We have guests. 'Twould be rude to leave before dessert is served."

"I have dessert for you, my lord."

His gaze lingered on her breasts, then dipped down to the juncture of her thighs. "Aye, that you do. And I'll wager you taste sweeter than any of Oliver's confectionary monstrosities. Of course I will need to do extensive tasting to be sure..."

Gwen sucked in her breath when he touched her earlobe with the tip of his tongue.

"Did you know 'tis possible to come without even being touched down there? No? Well, 'tis. I'd love to make you so hot for me that you—"

The outer doors swung open and men rushed into the hall crying, "Milord!"

Richard shot to his feet.

A man dressed in a thick wool tunic and cloak ran to the dais and gripped the edge of the table.

"My lord earl," he panted. "Signal fires. To the south. Village attacked. Welshmen."

"To arms!" Richard cried to the now quiet hall.

"Nay!" Gwen yelled at the same time, jumping to her feet.

But Richard did not hear, or if he did, he ignored her. He leaped over the table and ran for the door, not once looking back. The hall emptied behind him as the knights raced for their horses and armor.

Gwen started after him. Owain grabbed her arm, pulling her up short. "Come, milady. I will take you to your chamber."

Gwen turned to him, her heart racing. "Nay! I must see him before he goes!" Richard couldn't leave without saying goodbye! What if—?

"He will not have time, milady. 'Tis not unusual for this to happen. He will return in a day or two, never fear."

Gwen tore away from Owain and ran for the bailey. Richard was facing Welshmen, and Welshmen carried longbows. She remembered the unholy horror of seeing a wooden haft protruding from steel. It defied logic, and yet it had happened.

She clutched her skirts and raced down the stairs of the forebuilding and out into the snow-covered bailey.

Confusion reigned. Men shouted to each other across the yard. Horses were hurriedly saddled and led from the stables. Young grooms held them ready until the knights were armored.

Torches illuminated the figures of the men, casting huge shadows against the stone walls of the castle. Squires worked frantically, throwing hauberks and coifs on the knights. Nimble fingers buckled and cinched like lightning.

Gwen ran between the warhorses, dodging hooves and teeth. She didn't stop until she found Sirocco's gleaming black hide. A groom fitted the crimson and black trapper lined with hardened leather over the stallion and cinched it in place.

Richard stood beside the horse while his squire buckled his coif. Torchlight rippled across his hauberk as he turned to her, the shiny metal glittering like the iridescent scales of a sea monster.

"Holy Christ! What the hell are you doing out here, Gwen? Get back inside before you get hurt."

"Richard—you must be careful—I—"

"Get inside. Now, woman!"

Wiry arms wrapped around her waist, pulling her backwards. "I'm sorry, milord," Owain said. "She got away from me."

"By all that's holy, get her out of here!" Richard grated from between clenched teeth. His gaze held hers for an instant before he turned his head.

"No!" Gwen began to fight, kicking and twisting in Owain's grasp. Despite his age, Owain was strong and his grip on her was tight. She could not escape. "Richard!"

The squire finished and stepped back. Richard glanced at her a last time, then turned to mount.

Gwen clawed at Owain's arms. Richard was leaving and she might never see him again. She pictured him lying limp across Sirocco's back, an arrow protruding from his chest. Her breath broke on a sob.

"Richard!" she cried. "Richard!"

He stiffened, gathering his reins and ignoring her.

"Oh God—Richard—I love you!"

She slumped against Owain. There was no time to consider the implications of her confession. All she knew was if something happened to

Richard, her life would be useless and empty. She couldn't let him leave without knowing it.

She heard the swift intake of his breath as he turned around. Owain let her go. She flung herself into Richard's arms. He crushed her to him, kissing her fiercely.

She loved him, loved his smile, his eyes, his mouth, the way his hair felt between her fingers. She loved the things he did to her, the silky glide of his voice when he whispered wicked things in the privacy of their bed. She loved *him*. He was hers, had been hers since the first moment she'd seen him at Rhuddlan castle.

She wound her arms around his neck, sobbing. A steel barrier stood between them. He was shielded from her, and she didn't think she could bear it.

"Richard... oh, Richard..."

He reached up to caress her cheek and could not. His hand hovered, then dropped. Even they were encased in chainmail. He gave an agonized groan, then tried to push her away.

"You must go in now," he said, his voice soft, almost pleading. "I will return soon, *cariad*, I promise."

"No," she said, clinging to him. "No. You cannot leave me."

Richard pulled her arms from his neck and pushed her away, motioning for Owain to take her. "I must, Gwen."

Owain's strong hand wrapped around her arm. She stood, stubbornly refusing to move. Wasn't he going to say anything else?

"Do not make this any harder on him," Owain whispered in her ear. "Come."

Gwen brushed at the tears spilling down her cheeks. She let Owain escort her through the bailey to the castle stairs. She walked slowly, glancing over her shoulder at Richard every few steps. He stared at her for a minute, then turned and swung into the saddle. He did not look back again.

Sirocco danced and pawed, throwing snow from his large hooves. When all the knights were mounted, Richard gave the signal and they trotted out the now open gates of Claiborne castle, disappearing into the night.

Gwen broke away from Owain and ran all the way to the master chamber, ignoring the startled looks of the servants she passed.

She burst through the door and ran to the window. Pressing her face against the glass, she watched the torches move through the valley until they faded from sight.

Gwen sank into the windowseat, sobbing anew.

God in Heaven, she was in love with Black Hawk de Claiborne.

I t was late the next day when the knights caught up to the Welsh warriors on the lower slopes of the Cambrian Mountains. They were traveling on foot, and though the cattle they'd stolen could have been driven faster, the Welsh indulgence in females cost them the race.

The village women screamed, running for the woods when their captors turned to fight. War cries hurtled through the air as the Celtic warriors drew longbows to cheeks and loosed arrows upon the knights. Once the arrows were spent, the Welshmen dropped the bows and charged with spears and battleaxes.

Even while he unsheathed his sword and prepared to charge into their midst, Richard didn't fail to admire the indomitable spirit of the Welsh. They never hesitated to attack armored knights, despite their own lack of armor.

The warriors wore leather jerkins sewn with iron scales and carried shields made of toughened goatskin. They should be no match for well-equipped knights, but often they were.

This time was no exception. Most of the Englishmen were still trying to shake the aftereffects of too much ale, and the Welsh seized on the weakness.

The fighting wore on for a quarterhour. The icy air hung heavy with the shouts and grunts of men, the weeping of women, and the wailing of cattle.

Richard was bone-weary, but he closed off that part of his mind and drew from an inner well of strength and resolve that had never failed him.

He didn't know how many men fell before his blade. He never did. He just fought until no more came, then turned and surveyed the battle scene.

Riderless horses joined the cattle. The snow ran crimson with the blood of the slain. Most of the bodies were Welsh, and for that he was thankful.

The Welshmen who still fought suddenly realized they weren't going to win and turned for the forest. The knights managed to cut off the escape route for all but a handful.

The destriers' sides heaved, their breath clouding the air with steam. Some of the knights slipped from their horses and collected the weapons from the bodies of the fallen Welshmen. Knives, broadswords, spears, and precious longbows.

Richard wiped the edge of his sword on his mantle and resheathed it. It would do no good to pursue the escapees through that tangle of trees. Let them carry their tale of defeat back to the clans.

The knights fanned out. Some gathered the cattle while others sifted through the bodies for those of their fallen comrades.

The village women huddled together at the edge of the trees, weeping. Richard shook his head in disgust, rage bubbling in his soul. Young, old, it did not matter, the Welsh had taken them all.

Couldn't they see their time was up, their way of life obsolete? King Edward offered them better. He offered them law and order and a place in a larger society. Why couldn't they just take it and end this bloody feuding for good?

Richard already knew the answer, though he didn't like it. The Welsh were proud, stubborn, independent. Their laws and customs had served them well for centuries and they weren't going to change willingly.

And he would continue to drag them, kicking and screaming and fighting, into the new realm. For their own good, and for England's.

He rode over to Andrew. "How many did we lose?"

The captain wiped a bloody hand across his face. "Four, milord. But we killed ten of 'em, and captured twelve."

Richard felt the exhaustion creeping over his body. "Let's make camp here. 'Tis almost night and we'll not get far, even if we leave now."

"Aye, milord," Andrew replied.

One of the Welshmen jerked away from the knight who was tying him and hurried toward Richard.

With a quick nod, Richard assured his knight to let the man approach.

The warrior spat on Richard's boot, his face twisting into a sneer. "*Gwalchddu!*"

Richard's gaze trailed down his leg. "Wipe it off," he said, his voice deceptively mild. His mood was already black and he was damn near ready to hang the lot of them.

The man glared at him. Frost hung on the ends of his long beard. He bared yellow teeth in a grimace. "*Na.*"

"You have a choice, my friend. Wipe it off and mayhap you will stand a chance in the king's court of justice. Otherwise, I will hang you now."

The man threw his head back and laughed. "The king's justice! Since when has there been justice for a Welshman in an English court? God rot King Edward and his justice!"

Richard lashed out with his foot and cracked the man across the jaw. He fell back in the snow, then lifted himself up and rubbed his face.

"Watch how you speak of your king!" Richard glanced at the knight who awaited his orders. "Bring him."

The man nodded and grabbed the Welshman, jerking him to his feet. The warrior yanked his arm away, then thrust out his hands to be tied.

Too quick, he grabbed the dagger from the knight's belt and hurled himself at Richard. Sirocco reared as the man latched on. The extra weight acted like an anchor, pulling Richard to earth.

His breath left him in a whoosh as he landed on his back with the Welshman on top. He fumbled blindly for his dagger, even while he struggled to breathe.

The Welshman snarled and brought the knife high. Blood dripped from the blade and Richard vaguely wondered where it had come from.

"Prepare to die, *Gwalchddu!*"

The knife descended, aiming at Richard's unprotected face. He blocked the man's arm, but the savage was too determined and Richard's grip started to waver.

And then the Welshman went limp, his eyes glazing. The knife dropped harmlessly beside Richard's head, and he uttered a silent prayer of thanks.

"Christ, milord, are ye all right?"

Andrew. The dead man was yanked off him then, and Richard looked up at his captain's worried face. "Aye," he said. He tried to sit up. "I feel dizzy…"

Andrew pushed him back down. "Don't move, milord. The bastard must have held the knife between ye when ye fell. The impact drove it through yer hauberk. Ye've been hit."

"Jesú…"

Richard closed his eyes. His last conscious thought was of Gwen and all the things he'd never had the chance to say.

"Pining for your lover?"

Gwen turned from the window as Anne came in and took a seat beside the fire.

Anne smiled sympathetically. "Poor, sweet thing. I knew a young girl like you would not be able to resist Richard. I did try to warn you, if you will remember."

"'Tis none of your business, Lady Ashford."

"Oh do call me Anne." She waved a hand, smiling sweetly. "I fancied myself in love with him once, too. 'Twas a very long time ago, before I learned what he was truly like."

Gwen didn't want to hear any more, but she had to. "What do you mean?"

Anne's look was bitter, unguarded. She gave a quick laugh, but it wasn't humorous. "Do you think you are the only one to ever sit beside him in the hall and have him whisper naughty things in your ear? Aye, he used to be that attentive with me, feeding me, teasing me, and then taking me to bed and making love all night long. You are not the first, and neither was I!"

Gwen felt a stabbing pain in her heart. "He did?"

Anne snorted. "Of course he did! 'Tis what I am trying to tell you, little innocent. He does not care for you. He only plays with you until he tires of you, then he will seek another to take your place."

Gwen desperately wanted to deny it but she could not. She'd told him she loved him and he'd said nothing. What if he didn't love her? What if she spent her life adoring a man who felt nothing for her?

It wouldn't be the first time she loved without being loved in return. Guilt swept over her then. She'd failed her father and let herself fall in love with the enemy.

She pressed her thumbs against her eyelids. How on earth could she love them both?

"Why are you telling me this?" she asked quietly. "You do not like me, nor I you."

Anne shrugged. "Nay, I do not like you. But I like Richard even less. He would have married me if not for you. But he was just greedy enough to want to marry a princess, and quite willing to toss me aside to do it."

Gwen shivered. Aye, he wanted a princess to give him access to a throne. She shot to her feet.

Once inside the passage, her steps quickened until she was running, though she knew not where. She ran until her lungs hurt, then kept on running until she flung open a door and emerged on the battlements.

An icy wind greeted her, roaring over the stone, isolating her from the sounds of the rest of the world. She raced to the edge and peered into the valley, hoping beyond hope she would see horses and riders cresting over a hill or emerging from the woods.

All she saw was a sea of white, as empty and bleak as she felt inside at this moment.

To the west, Snowdon's peak rose above the other mountains, taunting her. It seemed to stare down at her, stern, disapproving. It said: you are Welsh, he is English; you are young and naive, he is hard and jaded; you seek love, he seeks vengeance.

God, what a fool she was! How could she have fallen in love with a man who wanted nothing more than to see her father dead?

When Richard's eyes opened, he recoiled from the sight that greeted him. "Andrew!" he yelled.

"Here, milord."

Richard focused on his captain. Thank God! If Andrew was truly here then he wasn't dead yet. He peered at the thing that had startled him and realized it was an old woman.

Hundreds of deep-set wrinkles creased a brown, weather worn face. A beaked nose dominated that visage, though it was the eyes that drew the most attention. Watery-blue from age, they still crackled with a sharpness that belied the many winters they had witnessed.

"Such a handsome boy," the old crone said, pinching his cheek with more familiarity than he liked. "Don't worry yerself, yer gonna live. Didn't hit nothing vital. Just the shock of the impact and loss of blood made ye pass out."

"Who is she?" Richard demanded.

The woman cackled. She stood and ambled away, mumbling about men and impatience. Grinning, Andrew knelt beside him.

"'Tis the village healer. We brought you to yer tent and stripped off yer hauberk and she looked at yer wound. She bandaged it fer ye, though she says she don't have her herbs and can't give ye anything for pain. If ye lays quiet, it should stop bleeding."

Richard tried to shift, and winced. "Jesú, how deep is it?"

"Half a blade."

"No wonder it hurts like bloody hell." He laughed, though that hurt too. "Now why couldn't the woman have the decency to carry her herbs when her village was attacked?"

Andrew's eyes sparkled. "Mayhap she will next time."

"Have you taken care of everything?"

"Aye."

Richard yawned. Jesú, he was damn tired. "I'm going to sleep then. And whatever you do, keep that woman away from me. She about scared the piss out of me when I woke."

Andrew's grin broadened as he leaned down. "I think she likes ye, milord. Mayhap she'd make a nice bedwarmer. I could ask her fer ye…"

Richard scowled. "I'll stick your head on a pike if you do."

Andrew straightened, laughing. "Come on, good mistress," he called. "The earl no longer needs ye."

Richard heard the rustling of the tent flap, then Andrew started whistling. The sound faded before he fell asleep.

When next he awoke, he was alone. His side throbbed. Grunting, he crawled to the opening and peered out. The sky was lightening to the east, indicating that dawn was not far off.

Men already stirred from their beds, making ready for the journey home. Richard pushed to his feet and staggered from the tent.

It was colder than he remembered. He still clutched his blanket and he wrapped it tighter around him, then started off through the camp.

"How soon do we leave, Andrew?"

The captain spun around from where he was saddling Sirocco. "Jesú, milord! Ye nearly scared me to death. What are ye doin' up? Yer gonna start bleedin' again if ye ain't careful."

Richard clenched his teeth and forced his spine to remain straight. "Nay, it feels much better," he lied.

Andrew eyed him doubtfully. "Half an hour, no more. Can ye ride?"

"Do I have a choice?"

"Nay, I suppose not."

The knights broke camp quickly, gathering the cattle and taking the women up with them. The prisoners were bound and forced to walk behind the destriers.

It was several hours later when they rode into Chedwell. The village men greeted the return of wives, sisters, mothers, and daughters with great enthusiasm. The cattle received slightly less attention.

Outside the village, lumps of fresh earth blemished the snow with the graves of the dead, a gruesome reminder of the perils of the Marches. Richard couldn't tear his gaze from the ugly gashes.

"Milord?"

With great effort, he met Andrew's eyes. "Aye?"

"I think we should go straight to Claiborne. Ye doesn't look like ye should ride all the way to Shrewsbury."

Richard was suddenly very conscious of the throbbing in his side. Every step Sirocco took jarred him even more. The sooner he was off the horse, the better.

He nodded. "Aye, whatever you say, Andrew."

The captain frowned before relaying the order to the company.

Richard stripped his gauntlet and pressed his hand against his side. It was tender, and much warmer than the rest of him.

For a long time, he held his hand there, warming it. When he finally drew it away, he raised it to a level with his eyes.

Drops of pure crimson dripped from his fingers to fall onto Sirocco's neck.

28

G wen stood in the frigid bailey, waiting for the knights to ride through the gates. It was three days since Richard had ridden out after the Welshmen. Three agonizing days.

Now that he was returning, she was both relieved and terrified. Over and over she replayed those moments when she'd bared her soul to him, and his reaction afterward.

Had he only been playing games with her like Anne said?

What about the cave, and his swearing he'd had no other women since marrying her? Were those lies, calculations to win her heart, another step on his path to revenge?

Oh God, just when she thought she knew him, this happened and she was no longer certain!

Her heart hammered as the knights rode through the inner gates. Her gaze fastened on Richard, and a wave of relief swept over her, so strong it left her weak-kneed.

He slumped a little in the saddle, but that was to be expected after the long hours he'd spent riding through the unforgiving March.

Four horses were riderless, nothing but limp bundles lying across their saddles. Men on foot brought up the rear of the procession.

Gwen offered a silent prayer for the dead mens' souls. She knew Richard didn't take the deaths of his men lightly and she yearned to soothe him.

It was then her mind finally registered what her eyes had sought to deny. Black Hawk de Claiborne had captives. Welsh captives.

A sick feeling began in the pit of her stomach and spread outward. They were tethered to the destriers like dogs, their faces bruised and swollen, their clothes torn and bloodied.

Gwen bit her lip so hard she could feel the blood welling. Her inner voice began to chant: Richard was a warrior, he did what his king ordered, he was not cruel, he was not the evil *Gwalchddu* of legend…

God help her, she was no longer certain! When he'd caught the men who had attacked them at Llanwell cave, he'd taken them to Shrewsbury because they were English. But he brought the Welshmen here. Why, if not to do the things he was reputed for?

She walked toward Richard in a daze. He drew rein when he saw her. "Gwen," he said, so softly she barely heard.

"My lord," she replied, fighting her tears. She did not want to believe such terrible things about him!

He drew off his gauntlet and wiped his hand across his brow. Turning in the saddle, he said, "Put the prisoners in the west tower, Andrew."

Gwen gasped. *The tower.* Every man, woman, and child in Wales knew that few Welshmen lived to tell of the horrors of Claiborne castle.

Those who did never spoke about the tower.

But the bards told tales. Black Hawk and his men tortured prisoners— ripped off their fingernails, stabbed them in places that did not kill immediately, crushed their bones—until only raw shells of men went to the gallows if they made it that far.

'Twas only a tale! How could the hands that touched her so tenderly, hands that evoked such a sweet response in her body, be capable of such cruel acts?

She fixed her gaze on those hands and shivered. One was naked and beautiful, the other mailclad and anonymous. That one, the one encased in metal, she did not know. That one could do anything and she would believe it possible.

"Is something the matter?"

Gwen's eyes locked with his. The silver depths were different somehow. Sort of glazed, far away. The look he gave her was oddly frightening.

"N-nay," she said.

He dismounted, rather clumsily she thought, and handed his reins to a groom.

He took her by the arm and headed for the forebuilding. Once they were in the stairwell, he pulled her into his arms. She ducked away before he could kiss her, afraid she would lose herself in his embrace.

"I missed you," he said softly, enticingly.

Gwen drew in a shuddering breath. All she could think of was the pleasure his words gave her, not the fact he had prisoners nor what he might do to them. He reached for her again and this time she did not protest.

She was the worst kind of traitor. All she wanted was this man's touch, even at the expense of her own soul. Her breath broke on a sob and she buried her face against his chest.

"What is it, *cariad*?"

The Welsh endearment on his lips was her undoing. She pushed away, still fisting his surcoat. "Please," she whispered, "please do not torture them."

He stared at her for a long moment. "Torture?" Disbelief lit his features briefly, then his jaw hardened and he wrenched her hands free. "My God, you don't even know those men! You have no idea what they did, and yet all you can worry about is whether *I* will torture them."

Gwen bowed her head. The tears slipped silently down her cheeks. She grasped a girdle chain and toyed with it, not really seeing it, but needing something to occupy her hands. "You are *Gwalchddu*," she said quietly in way of defense. She'd not meant it as an accusation, but it was too late to recall it when he took it as such.

"Aye, there is that, is there not? Black Hawk, evil lord of legend, cruel, inhuman." He laughed bitterly, his hand clutching the railing so hard his knuckle was white. His eyes were bright, glittering. "Why did I ever think you were different? Why—?"

Gwen watched in numb horror as he sank heavily onto the stairs. He shook his head, his body swaying before he pitched forward at her feet.

Gwen screamed.

Richard was stretched out on the big bed in the master chamber, his torso bared to reveal a raw, ugly wound. His eyes remained closed and his skin glistened with sweat. Gwen touched him with a shaky hand. Incredible heat scorched her, and her vision shimmered.

She scrubbed her eyes and peered at the wound. Beneath the caked blood his skin was an angry red. She'd seen battle wounds before and she knew it was infected, but her mind couldn't seem to think of a course of action.

It had taken four knights to carry him up to the lord's chamber. He was a big man at any time, but when armored he was much heavier than usual.

"Alys," she whispered. "What can we do, Alys?"

She barely felt the hand on her shoulder. "It needs to be cleaned and stitched. If the fever does not break soon, he will have to be bled."

Gwen nodded.

"He should be bled now."

She looked at the man who stood on the other side of Owain. She'd not even realized the castle surgeon was here.

"Nay!" she hissed. The thought of anyone slicing into Richard was too much to bear. "We will wait!"

The surgeon frowned. "Milady, 'tis not sound. Bloodletting is always the prescribed treatment for fever. The humors are out of balance and we must right them again."

Gwen drew herself up with all the haughtiness of a princess. Once, Rhys had described a boar hunt to her. He'd told her how the boar was pierced, but managed to escape. The hunters pursued the animal, following the trail of blood it left. When they caught up, it had been lying in a pool of its own blood, too weak to fight any longer.

If losing its lifeforce weakened a boar, what would it do to a man?

"I said no! You may leave. I will send for you if I have need of you."

"Milady," he said curtly, giving her a short bow.

Alys brought a basin of water and knelt beside the bed. She dipped a cloth in it and wrung it out.

Gwen took it. "Nay, I will do it."

She washed the wound, then accepted the needle and thread Alys handed her.

"Are you sure, Gwen?"

"Aye," she replied, not looking up. She had to take care of him. It might be unreasonable, but she had this fear that if anyone else tended him, he would die.

Gwen drew in a shaky breath and inserted the needle. She knew how to do this. She'd sewn men up before, but she'd never known doing it to Richard would make her feel each stitch as though it was her own body she pierced.

When it was done, she wiped away any remaining blood and started to remove the rest of his clothes. She never noticed that Owain helped.

Gwen refused to leave his side, though Owain and Alys both offered to stay with him while she slept. But sleep was impossible.

The fever raged. She covered him and he tossed the blankets off again and again. Sweat trickled down his brow, and she mopped his forehead with a cool cloth. She swept his damp hair aside with trembling fingers, weeping at the heat he gave off.

He remained still for so long that when he began to mutter and thrash, she grew frightened. "Owain, Alys! Help me hold him down before he breaks the stitches!"

She held his shoulders while Owain straddled his midsection and Alys his legs. Richard was strong, much stronger than she'd ever imagined, and it took everything they had to keep him still. She looked up at Owain, hoping to seek some sort of solace in his usually unflappable presence.

Tears slid down the old Welshman's weathered cheeks. His lips moved, his voice barely a whisper. If she'd not been looking at him, she'd have never known he was speaking, never heard the things he said.

"How many times have I told you, boy? You're gonna get yourself killed one of these days! 'Twas a long time ago. Your king knows your worth. You don't have to keep trying to prove it! I promised Catrin I would look after you..."

Gwen's heart skipped a beat. Who was Catrin?

They held him for a long time, only easing their grip when his struggles weakened. His mutterings were largely unintelligible. Occasionally he said her name, or Elizabeth's. But he never mentioned Catrin, whoever she was.

Finally, he grew quiet, and Gwen pressed her cheek to his brow. He was still fevered and her heart sank. Mayhap she should let the surgeon bleed him after all.

Alys retired to her pallet. Owain insisted on making his own resting place near the bed. Gwen slipped beneath the blankets, fully clothed, and curled up next to Richard. She stroked her fingers rhythmically up and down his chest.

In a very little while, she would send for the surgeon.

Gwen knew despair stronger than any she'd ever imagined in her life. What if he never opened those striking eyes of his? What if she never got to touch him and taste him and feel him ever, ever again?

What if she never got to tell him she was sorry?

"Do not leave me, Richard. I have been lonely all my life until you. Do not make me go back," she whispered fiercely.

How would she survive without him? How would the world look without the magnificence and power and vibrancy of the man called Black Hawk?

Empty.

Bleak.

Monotonous.

Gwen buried her face against his throat and cried.

29

G wen dreamed. She dreamed of a cave and a man who eased her back on the cool ground and worshipped her body with his. It was summer and the scent of wild roses drifted in on a soft breeze, penetrating the depths of the glittering cave.

Her gown slipped away and her flesh burned beneath his seeking mouth. Ah God, she wanted to touch him too! Her hands roamed over him, her mouth savoring every inch of delicious skin. She kissed the scar on his side and he shuddered.

"I love you," he whispered, and her heart swelled to bursting. Life had never been so perfect.

Next, she was standing in the middle of a long room. Her father stood at one end, Richard at the other. King Edward sat on a throne in front of her. He lifted his hand.

"Choose," he said.

Horror gripped her with icy tentacles. "I-I cannot!"

"One of them will die."

She fell to her knees. "Please, Majesty…"

"If you do not choose, they will both die."

She looked at Richard, then at her father. But her father was not alone. Einion and Rhys stood with him.

Edward merely shrugged. "Choose," he commanded. "Him, or them."

The Welshmen kept multiplying. Richard remained alone. Gwen ran toward Richard, then stopped. She turned and ran toward her father and

Wales, then stopped. She started to shake, and tears streamed down her face.

She could not choose.

She screamed.

And sat bolt upright in bed. Owain hovered over her, his face pale. "Is he…?"

Gwen touched Richard's brow. Owain frowned when she started to laugh. "Nay, he is cooler now. Oh Owain, he is cooler!"

A smile spread over Owain's haggard face. "He is too stubborn to die over something so minor. 'Twould have to be a sword thrust to the heart, not a dagger wound to the side."

Gwen ran her hands over Richard's body, reassuring herself the fever had indeed broken. If anything, he was sweating more than before, but it was a different kind of sweat. Cooler, as though the fever was pouring itself out of his body now that its course was run.

Owain returned to his pallet.

Gwen stroked Richard's jaw. The images of the dream still haunted her, and she shivered.

Choose.

She pressed closer to him. It was only a dream. They didn't *always* have meaning.

When Richard opened his eyes, he was surprised to realize it was daylight and he was still in bed. He started to get up, but the dull ache in his side forced him back down.

He stared up at the canopy, and remembered.

Gwen didn't trust him, thought him capable of horrible things. He eased up and looked around. She wasn't even here.

Despite the ache, he swung his legs off the bed and sat up. Someone had stitched him. It wasn't Sir Henry's handiwork. The stitches were too small and neat.

He stood and went searching for his tunic. A gasp in the doorway brought his head around.

His heart quickened a little, and it angered him. He'd sworn his fidelity on bended knee, shared things with her that he'd never shared with anyone. Despite all that, she believed the tales she'd been raised on in her father's hall. "What are you doing here?" he demanded more harshly than he intended.

"You must get back in bed, my lord. You'll rip the stitches," she said, coming to him, her hands twisting the edges of her gown.

Richard closed his eyes. Roses, goddamn roses! He wanted to pull her against him and bury his face in her hair. "Don't you have some sewing to do? Or some menus to plan?"

"Nay," Gwen said quietly.

Her hand settled on his arm, and he thought he might come undone. He stiffened, and she snatched her hand back.

Tears shimmered in her golden-green eyes. "Please get back in bed, Richard. I will bring you something to eat."

"I have things to do, Gwen." His inner demon refused to be silenced. "After all, there are prisoners to torture."

Just for an instant, her eyes widened. She quickly recovered, but he didn't miss the fact she'd actually believed it, if only for a second.

Overwhelmed by bitterness, Richard turned his back. He knew it was a stupid thing to say. He found his tunic and struggled to get into it. When he felt her hands on him, he stopped.

"Let me help you," she said.

He stood very still while she dressed him. Every second was more unbearable than the last. All he wanted was to hold her. Just when he thought he would crack, she stepped away.

"Please be careful, Richard. I don't want you ripping those stitches. I don't think I could do as good a job the second time around."

His hand strayed to his side. "You did this?"

"Aye."

"Thank you for tending me," he said softly.

"'Tis a wife's duty, my lord," she replied, equally as soft.

Richard stiffened. "Duty. Of course. No other reason needed." Had he only imagined what happened in the bailey on the night he'd ridden out? Certes, it was possible, considering what had occurred since.

He was almost to the door when she called to him. "I feared for you," she said tearfully.

"Why?" he demanded. "Why, when you think me so terrible? Wouldn't it be easier if I had never come back?"

"Nay! How can you say that?" she cried, running to him and cupping his face between her hands. She pulled his head down and pressed her lips to his. He didn't want to, but he responded, kissing her with a desperation that frightened him.

"God, I'm sorry, Richard. I did not mean to doubt you. I know you are not capable of the things said of you. 'Twas stupid of me."

Something within him twisted and snapped. He grasped her wrists and pulled her hands away. He couldn't bear to have her say such things, then look at him like he was the devil himself when she found out his true nature. He wouldn't wait for her to learn just exactly what he was capable of.

"Nay, Gwen, I *am* capable of great cruelty."

Her eyes widened. He pulled her tighter against him, wanting to feel her soft curves molded to his body. Her lips parted. All his muscles locked in an effort to keep from kissing her again.

"Do you want to know how much?" he demanded. "Do you want to know what kind of man I am?"

"I—"

"I've never told you about Elizabeth, though I daresay you've heard of her." Her mouth closed and she nodded mutely. "I abandoned her, Gwen. I left her to have our babe alone, though she begged me not to go. I knew she was frightened and I left anyway."

Her eyes filled with tears. "I am sorry. You must have loved her very much."

Richard threw his head back. "Don't you understand? I loved her not at all! 'Tis my fault she died. 'Tis my punishment for not caring enough."

"Nay," she whispered, shaking her head.

"Yes, Gwen, yes! I am everything you thought I was, and worse, much worse."

She searched his face, then swallowed. "You did what your king commanded. You cannot be blamed for going when he called you."

He let her go and walked away. He sank onto the edge of the bed and pushed his hands through his hair. His bitter laughter broke the silence. "Is that what you think? Edward cannot be kept from Eleanor's side when she gives birth. He would not have prevented me from doing the same, especially since Kenilworth is only a few days ride from Claiborne. Nay, wife, 'twas my own cold-heartedness that kept me away."

Gwen couldn't speak. He watched her expectantly. She whirled around and went to the window. Her heart was throbbing madly in denial. It wasn't supposed to be like this!

There were so many things she wanted to say, but a lifetime of guarding her emotions was a hard habit to break. No one had ever had the kind of power to hurt her that Richard had. She didn't think she could bear telling him she loved him again and not have him say it in return.

She heard him get up. Every instinct she had told her to go to him, to tell him what she felt. But her body remained motionless, frozen in place, while her mind raced, searching for ways to avoid exposing herself to the pain of rejection.

She prayed he would come to her, wrap his arms around her, tell her everything would be all right again. But his footsteps didn't advance. They retreated.

Richard leaned against the wall of the passage. He put his hand to his side and winced. It was nothing compared to the pain he felt inside.

What had he done? Why had he told her about Elizabeth?

After a moment, he shoved away and strode to the hall. If Gwen had ever thought she loved him, he'd certainly killed it now.

And it was best that way. He cared too much for her. It had to stop before she abandoned him to face it alone.

"Jesú, Richard, you should not be up yet," Owain scolded, bringing him up short. The Welshman's expression grew wary. "What has happened?"

"Nothing, *Ewythr*. Nothing at all," Richard said smoothly, though his throat ached.

Owain's eyes darted around the room. "What is the matter with you?" he hissed.

Richard was not in a cautious mood. The only person within earshot was one of the knights in Anne's household and it was highly improbable he understood Welsh. "Leave me be, old man."

Owain's face reddened. "I don't know what is going on between you and your wife, but there is one thing I do know."

"And what is that, pray tell?" Richard asked, more out of obligation than interest.

"You are a bloody, arrogant fool."

Richard walked away. He didn't need this right now. But Owain followed. "Why don't you just tell her how you feel?"

Richard stopped and turned around. "How would you know what I feel?"

Owain stuck a finger in Richard's chest. "Because I've been with you since you were a babe! Just tell her you love her and get it over with."

"I do not love her. I cannot," he growled.

Owain snorted. "Stupid whelp! How many chances do you think you get, boy? Take it while you got it."

"You overstep your bounds, *Ewythr*."

Owain's grey eyes glittered. "Not nearly enough, *Nai*, not nearly enough."

Richard started to walk away.

"And one other thing," Owain called. "I'm going with you to London."

Richard stopped, incredulous. "You vowed you would never go there! Why now?"

Owain flushed. "Because I want to, that's why! And don't think to try and stop me either."

"I wouldn't dream of it," Richard said dryly.

Owain gave him a curt nod. "I must see to my duties, my lord."

"Of course."

Richard's hand strayed to his sword and he suddenly remembered he had forgotten to put it on. Jesú, what was his life coming to?

In just a few days the household was packed and on the way to London. The earl of Dunsmore took servants enough for a large house. Wagons of supplies rolled along half full, though they would be overflowing on the return journey with items only obtainable in a great port city like London.

Gwen patted her mare's neck absently. Her eyes sought Richard. He rode ahead with his knights, laughing and talking about whatever it was men discussed at times like this. She worried over him, but he seemed fine. If his wound pained him, he didn't show it.

She'd not been alone with him in a fortnight. The inns were too crowded to obtain a private room. Richard could have commandeered an entire inn, being a high-ranking nobleman, but he had not done so. Gwen was thankful he didn't kick people from their lodgings even if it did mean she'd had to share with Anne.

Gwen cast a glance at Alys. She'd begun to notice the woman seemed preoccupied, especially when Owain was around. It was hard to miss the way the two stared at each other.

Gwen hid a smile behind her hand. At least Alys's love life seemed in order. Hopefully hers would be too, once she and Richard were finally alone and could talk.

She hoped he would talk. She'd wanted to approach him more than once, but the timing was never right. There were always servants or knights or someone else hanging about. It didn't seem appropriate to try to discuss their lives while riding horses.

A short time later, they emerged from the forest road. Gwen's jaw dropped. "Jesú," she breathed. In the distance, London stretched across the landscape like a huge spider, tentacles gripping the hills with the firm tenacity of a creature that would not be moved.

"Is it what you expected?" Richard asked.

Gwen started. She'd not realized he'd dropped back beside her. "It's huge!"

He smiled, and her heart lurched. It was far too long since he'd smiled at her. "Aye, and full of every privilege and decadence you can imagine. Thirty thousand people live in London year-round. 'Tis crowded and dirty in many places. There are whole streets named after the tradesmen who line them: Chandler, Tailor, Wine, Cloth, Milk, Honey—it goes on forever."

"Elinor told me that people actually live on London Bridge. Is it true?"

Richard nodded. "Aye, 'tis true. London Bridge is packed with houses and shops. 'Tis easier to solve the problems of water supply and sewage when one lives over a river."

Gwen was much too excited by the sprawling city to catch the humor in his reply. She'd heard her father talk of London and she'd been unable to believe the things he'd said. It was impossible to imagine thousands of people living in a place, and yet it was true.

She turned to say something to Richard, but the words died on her lips. His expression was so intense, so hot, that a thrill coursed down her spine. There was no mistaking he wanted her.

"I want to make love to you," he said softly. "For hours—nay, days. *Days*, Gwen..."

"Weeks," she whispered, her heart soaring.

"Years," he countered, his eyes traveling over her face, down the thick folds of her velvet cloak, then back up again. "I have missed you."

"I ache for you," she said.

His eyes darkened. "Soon, wench. Very soon..."

She shivered. Talking could wait.

They did not enter the city of London, crossing instead over the Tyburn Brook to Thorney Isle and the burough of Westminster.

The snow had been cleared to the side and the horses' hooves clicked on the cobblestones. People in bright cloaks hurried past, barely noticing the arrival of yet another nobleman and his household though none hesitated to get out of the way once they looked up and saw the crimson and black livery coming their way.

Gwen gazed at her surroundings with wide eyes. Nothing Elinor or her father had ever said prepared her for this. The houses and shops were packed together tightly, stone and timber buildings rising three and four stories above the street. The dirtiness Richard spoke of was not at all apparent here.

As they rode farther into the burough, the houses became larger—sprawling stone buildings surrounded by walls that enclosed vast courtyards and grand gardens. Houses of the nobility.

Westminster Palace rose above the Thames in the distance. They rode toward it, then turned onto a street that Richard said was called the Strand.

Anne Ashford's party didn't turn with them, continuing toward the palace instead. Gwen breathed a sigh of relief. She'd hoped the woman wouldn't try to insinuate herself at Dunsmore House, but she'd fully expected it.

Dunsmore House was one of the grander residences, or palaces as they were sometimes called. Set against the flowing Thames, its white walls and intricate gardens were enhanced by the great sheets of costly glass adorning the windows. It took great wealth to indulge in such an extravagance. Gwen swallowed. She'd had no idea Richard was so wealthy. Why did a baron with the power and status he carried risk his life riding the borders?

Servants in the Dunsmore livery hurried to greet them. Richard swung down off Sirocco and came to help Gwen. Gripping her hand firmly, he turned to Owain, who was still wide-eyed from the ride through the city.

"The steward here is Sir Charles. Find him and see to the unloading. Do not disturb me unless it's important."

Owain's gaze trailed to their linked hands. A broad smile creased his face, and he bowed. "As you command, my lord."

Gwen didn't mind that Richard pulled her through the house before she got a good look at the marble columns, the spacious hall with its gilded walls, the floor-to-ceiling windows that bathed the rooms in light. She didn't care because she was as singularly minded as he at the moment.

She could see it later. Everything could wait until later. Everything but the wild heat that begged for release.

He sent her up the stairs in front of him. When she was halfway up, she turned and put her arms around his neck. Even standing on the stair below, he was taller than she.

Hungrily, they fused their mouths together. Gwen clung to him, pressed against him until she felt his hard manhood like a pillar between them.

He cupped her breasts and she whimpered. God, it was so long since they'd made love that she was extra sensitive.

Nearly mindless with need, Gwen sank backwards onto the stairs. Richard came down on top of her. Her hands slipped beneath his tunic and he shuddered as she caressed bare skin.

"Gwen, ah Christ, Gwen..." His lips moved down her throat, licking, kissing, rediscovering. "We must get upstairs before I take you here and now," he said thickly.

"I care not," she breathed.

"We must, *cariad.*"

He picked her up and started to carry her to the master chamber. "The stitches!" she cried. "You will hurt yourself!"

Richard laughed. "Jesú, wench, you are too light to injure me. I strain it more when I pull myself into the saddle than I do when holding you."

He set her down and kicked the door closed. Gwen threaded her fingers through his hair and pulled his head down. His lips on hers were firm and strong and devouring.

His fingers worked her laces until he could push her surcoat and chemise open. Then he bent to seize a nipple. Gwen cried out.

His arm wrapped around her waist and pulled her close while he suckled her breasts with heartstopping precision. Gwen kneaded his shoulders like a kitten.

He groaned when she cupped his manhood in both hands. Somehow, they found their way to the bed. Richard pressed her onto the mattress, shoving her skirts up while she worked to free his chausses.

"I want to be inside you, Gwen. I want to feel you hot and tight and clinging. I want to hear you cry my name while I'm thrusting into you," he said huskily. "I've wanted it for weeks."

"Yes, Richard, yes. I want it too…"

Someone rapped on the door. They ignored it. It came again, louder. Richard swore. "Go away!"

"Milord? Milord?"

"Later!"

Gwen almost had him free. Another minute and they would be joined. She kissed him. His tongue plunged into her mouth with the same dark rhythm his body would soon imitate.

"Milord! A message from the king, milord!"

Richard's head snapped up.

"No!" Gwen cried, trying to pull him back down. "Can't it wait?"

"Nay." He went to the door and opened it a crack. Gwen sat up. She couldn't hear what was said, but she knew as soon as he closed it he was leaving.

He walked back to the bed, straightening his clothes. Gwen tugged her skirts in place. "Please stay," she said.

He shook his head. "I cannot."

"We need to talk, Richard."

His expression softened. "Aye, I know. When I return, I promise." He snatched his mantle off the floor. "Why don't you take a hot bath and get some rest? We'll have all night for talking… and other things."

He winked before he slipped out the door.

Richard strode through the corridors of Westminster, anxious to get this meeting over with and return to Gwen.

His body still throbbed with the memory of his arousal. He'd been so hard he thought he might explode the instant she touched him.

He'd missed her. At first he was able to ignore it, thinking it would pass soon enough. But instead of going away it had only gotten worse.

She was a fever in his blood. He needed her. For weeks he'd fantasized about the kinds of things he wanted to do to her body.

He refused to believe it was anything beyond a physical connection. She was just so beautiful and passionate that he desired her above all others.

He would not deny himself any longer.

When he reached the king's solar, a youth stepped inside to announce him. The boy returned and held the door open, bowing as he swept past.

"Richard! Jesú, but you are prompt," Edward said, rising and clapping his friend on the back. "Fetch some wine. Gascon, I think," he said to a servant.

At Edward's bidding, Richard sank into an ornately carved and cushioned chair. The room was richly appointed with velvet hangings and sendal tapestries. The golden-lion banner draped across one wall. The ceiling was green, spangled in gold, and over the fireplace the wall was wainscoted and painted with scenes of the strange animals in the royal menagerie.

Richard knew, because he knew Edward, that the room had not changed since the days of Henry III, Edward's father. Henry had loved magnificence and opulence whereas his son barely took heed of it at all. Edward was a soldier at heart. His energies would more likely be directed at strengthening a keep's defenses than decorating its chambers.

"So where's the little wife?" Edward asked. "Leave her at home so you could play?"

Richard grinned. Ned was always thinking with his prick. "Nay, she's at Dunsmore House."

"Ah. Pregnant yet?"

"Not that I'm aware of."

"Jesú, I thought you'd have planted your seed deep by now."

Richard shrugged. "She is Llywelyn's daughter. Mayhap it takes longer than with other women. 'Tis not from lack of trying, I can assure you."

Edward laughed, his eyes twinkling. "I knew you'd not have a problem. That lass could get a rise out of a corpse, I'll warrant."

Richard shifted uncomfortably, remembering the rise she'd given him not too long ago. He changed the subject before he got it again. "Has the queen given birth yet?"

"Aye," Edward said, his eyes lighting. "'Tis another daughter, but she's beautiful. The next one will be a son."

Richard smiled. Ned needed an heir. The last one had died years ago, but the king never failed to rejoice over the birth of a daughter. England didn't much worry over it either. She still had Edmund and his sons if it ever came down to it.

But Edward was young yet, barely in his forties, and he had the cool confidence of a man who knew he'd give England her next king eventually.

The servant returned and poured wine into two golden goblets. When he took his leave, Edward fingered the rim of his cup and said, "The pope wants me to lead another crusade."

Richard's heart dropped to his feet. "When?"

"Sometime next year."

Richard took a drink, let it bathe his suddenly dry throat. The last crusade had taken four years.

His palms slipped on the goblet and he gripped it tighter. Ned could not require him to go. All he had to do was pay the scutage and send the knights he owed the crown. That would be enough.

His free hand strayed to his sword. He *had* to go with his king! Honor demanded it. He had sworn to always support Ned's causes, no matter what, no matter where. It was his duty.

Richard tossed back the wine and reached for the flagon to pour another.

"We'll have to call a council to discuss it, of course. Perhaps in the spring. What do you think?"

"Aye," Richard said.

Edward's face lit with excitement. "'Twill be like old times, eh Richard?"

The king continued to speak but Richard did not hear. He downed a third goblet of wine, then poured another. Why did life suddenly seem meaningless?

30

Anne, too, was partaking of wine at that moment. Except hers spilled across the hard abdomen of her lover before she could lick it all up. Dafydd groaned when she painted the tip of his penis and started to lick. Anne giggled as she drew him in her mouth.

When she'd drained him dry, he pulled her up and suckled a breast lazily. Anne arched her back.

"Did Dunsmore suspect anything?" he asked.

"Nay, he did not know 'twas your men mingled with mine."

Dafydd reached for the wine. "And how fares my niece with the mighty Black Hawk?"

Anne pouted. She didn't want to think of that flame-haired witch right now. "She loves him, though he does not return it."

That was satisfying, at least. Anne toyed with the hair on Dafydd's chest.

"'Tis fitting that fate deal her the same lot in life as her mother. Eurwen loved my brother to distraction, but he was too caught up in his precious Wales. If Eurwen had listened to me—" He took a deep swallow of blood-red wine.

"You were in love with her."

Dafydd's face was stony. He finished off the wine and set the cup aside. "Aye," he said, staring straight ahead. "Llywelyn has always beaten me in everything. Love was not an exception."

"Nay, Dafydd, you have beaten him in one thing." Anne smiled. "You have sons! You have seven children. He has but one."

"Aye, and one on the way. This one could be the boy he's been wait-ing for."

Anne traced a circle around his nipple. "Accidents do happen."

"Yes," he said carefully, "yes, they do, dearest Anne."

Anne's hand slipped to his groin. "We haven't much time left. The king will seek me as soon as the castle is abed."

Dafydd rolled her on her back. "We mustn't allow the king to bed you before we are quite certain everything is in working order."

Anne could not agree more.

Gwen luxuriated in a hot bath scented with rose oil, then slipped into a silk chemise and velvet robe. She had a quiet supper of roasted fowl and winter cabbage, followed by baked apples and honeyed wine.

It was several hours since Richard had gone and she was beginning to get annoyed. She'd saved her explorations for the house until tomorrow, thinking Richard would be back soon. Every minute that passed only in-creased her annoyance.

She stood and began to pace. The master chamber wasn't as large as the one at Claiborne, but it was luxurious nonetheless. The bed was big and canopied, its wooden posters carved with intricate designs of birds and an-imals. The hangings were crimson velvet, embroidered with a spread-winged hawk. They were pulled back to reveal sheets and pillows of linen and silk, and coverlets of fox and rabbit.

The ceiling was painted with a forest mural and a fierce hawk, and Gwen marveled at the delicacy of the work. Two narrow windows looked out over the Thames. She'd stared out them until nightfall obscured the view. It was nothing less than amazing.

Even in winter, boat traffic slogged up and down the mighty river that was England's trade link with the rest of Europe. As far as she could see, the waterfront was lined with buildings both large and small.

London was intimidating to someone born and raised in the pastoral splendor of Wales.

Sighing, she sank into a velvet-cushioned chair. Mayhap Richard had found an elegant lady he preferred over her. Certes, she could not compare with the painted and pampered ladies of the royal court.

She curled into the chair and laid her head on her arm. If he didn't come soon, she was going to bed and to hell with him.

She had no idea what time it was when she was awakened by loud voices. She stood quickly, massaging the crick in her neck. The door swung open and two men came in, supporting Richard between them.

"Is he hurt?" Gwen asked, hurrying to his side. She recoiled when the strong smell of wine hit her head-on. Fear was immediately replaced by anger.

He raised his head slowly. "Gwen," he slurred.

"Put him on the bed," Gwen said crisply.

"Aye, milady," the two men said in unison.

Richard refused to lie down, gripping the bedpost instead. The men gave up and left him standing.

"Where the hell have you been?" she demanded, knowing it was ridiculous to ask when he was not in any condition to give her a decent answer.

He blinked. "Wessminsser."

Gwen rolled her eyes, then went to him and started to remove his garments. His free hand entwined in her hair and he pulled her up to kiss him. She pushed him away.

"Lemme make love t'you," he said.

Gwen laughed ruefully. "I doubt you could, my lord."

He blinked, then lay his head against the post. Gwen got his mantle and tunic off, then started to remove his chausses. He twirled one of her curls around his finger.

"I love you…" he said, soft and slurred.

Gwen straightened, her heart skipping a beat. She searched his face, hoping for some spark of lucidity. There was none.

He was drunk. He had no idea what he was saying. He tormented her with the one thing she desired above all else when tomorrow he would have forgotten he'd ever said it.

Gwen slapped him.

His eyes widened. Perversely, he grinned. "Never do what I think."

"You are insufferable," she whispered.

"Aye."

She finished undressing him, then unwrapped his hand from the bedpost and led him to the side of the bed. He fell on it and she pulled the covers over him.

She pushed her hair over her shoulders, then raised her hand in front of her face. It was shaking, just like the rest of her.

It was the incessant pounding that woke him. His head felt like a battering ram.

Richard turned over and tried to go back to sleep. It didn't work. Finally, he sat up and looked around. It took several minutes to realize where he was and several more to focus on the still form of a woman at the window.

"Gwen?"

She started, then turned to look at him. He couldn't tell from this distance, but she looked like she'd been crying. "I did not expect you to awaken for quite some time," she said, sniffling.

Richard raked his hands through his hair. "I wish I hadn't. Jesú, what the hell happened?"

She laughed, but it didn't sound happy. "Oh I knew you would not remember." She wrapped her arms around her body. "'Tis a good thing I am accustomed to disappointments."

But unfortunately he did remember the one thing he wanted to forget. He had no idea how he'd gotten back last night, but he could never forget the crusade. His heart constricted.

The morning light was dull with sleet and snow, but where it touched Gwen, it shone like sunshine. Her glorious hair was like a river of flame and molten gold, the lushness of her form outlined by the velvet robe she wore. Richard could picture every delicious curve in perfect detail.

Oh God, how could he leave her? How, when he'd only just discovered he loved her?

Despite the ache in his head, he went to her. She refused to face him and he slipped his arms around her, pulling her against him.

Nuzzling her hair aside, his lips sought the sweet curve of her neck. "I'm sorry we did not get to talk last night. I know it was important to you."

"Aye," she said softly.

Richard knew they should probably talk now, but he couldn't stop his hands from sliding up to mold her breasts. He felt her quiver and he was encouraged. Lord God how he needed her!

One hand slipped inside her robe and down to cup her feminine mound. His tongue made light circles around her ear. Her breathing quickened.

His shaft filled and he pulled her harder against him until she was aware of his arousal. "God, I want you. Make love with me, Gwen."

His finger slipped into her cleft. She moaned her pleasure as he began to stroke her.

"That's right," he whispered. "Surrender to me."

She turned in his arms and he bent to kiss her. How had he ever thought that all he felt for this woman was desire?

She was soft and warm and he crushed her to him until she protested it was too much. He eased his grip just enough to let her breathe.

He didn't want to let go. Not ever.

He needed her so much he thought he might die of it. She was Llywelyn's daughter. She was the woman he loved.

He undid the fastenings of her robe and let it slide to the floor. Next came her chemise. He swallowed hard. He'd seen her body dozens of times, but this was the first time he saw it with the full knowledge he loved her.

"Extraordinary," he murmured, tracing the soft curve of a breast until it peaked in his fingers.

"Richard—"

Her eyes were red-rimmed, her expression serious. Richard felt a stab of pain that he had caused her grief. For one horrific moment, he wondered if last night he'd lost control of his tongue and told her of the crusade. "What, *cariad*?"

"Do you remem—?" She sighed and shook her head. "'Tis nothing."

Richard kissed her. He wanted to make her happy, wanted to see her beautiful smile, hear her beautiful laughter. He wanted all those things before he told her of the crusade. He had to tell her, of course.

Eventually.

Her hands curled into his shoulders when he sucked a nipple into his mouth and tugged gently. For once his own lust wasn't uncontrollable, and that surprised him. Her pleasure seemed more important somehow.

"Do you want me, Gwen?" he whispered huskily.

"Aye," she breathed.

He joined her on the bed, his hard dark length pressing against her soft white body. He explored her with his hands and his mouth, finding new secrets, while she gasped and moaned and clutched at him.

He didn't enter her. Instead, he brought her to climax, over and over, with his mouth and his fingers. His shaft throbbed, full and heavy, the pulse reaching all the way to his ears. When she tried to touch him, he refused to let her.

Richard knew when she reached the point she was so sated she couldn't take anymore. Her eyes were heavy with sensuality and sleep and her body was limp. He kissed his way up her belly, her breasts, her neck, finally seeking her mouth.

She kissed him back, sighing. Her hand trailed along his arm and into his hair. "What about you?"

"Sleep, Gwen. I will be here when you wake."

"Promise?" she asked, covering a yawn.

"Aye."

She smiled and his throat ached. He wouldn't always be there when she woke, and the thought was killing him.

She turned on her side and was asleep instantly. Richard curved his body around hers, more than content to hold her.

Gwen was shocked to discover the entire day had passed while she slept. Richard was still beside her, exactly as he had promised. He didn't wake when she slipped from his arms and stole to the window.

Lights dotted the waterfront, reflecting off the river like candles beneath the surface. Gwen turned, stretching. There was a tray of food on the table, a washbasin with cool water, and a crackling fire that was only recently built up.

Gwen washed, then picked at the boiled beef and peas. There was also cheese and bread, wine, and something sweet for dessert.

Her gaze stole to Richard. She blushed when she thought of all the things he'd done to her. And he'd done it without a thought for himself. How could she have fallen asleep on him like that?

She picked up the tray and carried it to the bed. First, she would take care of his real hunger and then she would relieve his sexual appetite. A shiver of anticipation slid down her spine.

He stirred when she sat in the middle of the mattress and called softly to him.

"What is that?" he asked sleepily.

"Alys brought dinner."

"That woman is priceless," he said, pushing to a sitting position.

"Aye, but she has help. She and Owain conspire together."

"How do you know this, my sweet?"

"Have you not noticed the way they moon over each other?"

Richard frowned. "Nay. Jesú, 'tis why the old devil insisted on coming to London!"

Gwen laughed then. "Mayhap they are in love."

Richard's expression was pained for a second. Gwen chided herself for even bringing up the subject of love. He clearly didn't like the notion.

She offered him a piece of beef from her fingers. He took it with his lips, his eyes intense as he caught her gaze and held it. He began to feed her. They ate in silence, their only contact the whisper of fingers across the sensitive flesh of their mouths.

Gwen felt the heat flood her body as they stared at each other. It was so erotic, touching him so briefly, wanting him more with each caress. She remembered in heartstopping detail all the things his beautiful mouth had done to her that morning. Her heart quickened along with her breathing. Her fingers lingered on his lips, and he sucked one into his mouth.

Instant, blinding heat rocked through her, centering on the bud of her femininity. Gwen gasped as the tingling exploded outward.

Richard's eyes widened. He set the tray aside and pounced on her. "It happened, didn't it?"

"Yes," she said. "I wanted you so much…"

"Jesú," he breathed, stretching on top of her and centering his hard shaft against her cleft. He began to slide back and forth, heightening the sensations, prolonging them.

"Do not make me wait any longer, Richard," she whispered. "I need you. Now."

She slipped her robe open and he spread it away from her body. He continued to slide over her, hot skin against hot skin.

She wrapped her legs high around his back. He slipped downward, then pushed into her so slowly she wanted to scream. He retreated, slowly, deliberately. Gwen moaned.

Again he slid into her with exruciating patience. He repeated the rhythm half a dozen times until Gwen was nearly mindless.

She stared at his mouth. God how she wanted to taste his mouth! "Kiss me, Richard. Make love to me. I want you. I need you… I love you!"

His tongue plunged between her lips at the same time his body drove into hers. Gwen was swept up in instant rapture.

Their lovemaking was intense, explosive, cataclysmic. Gwen arched into him, opened, took him as deep as she could, then deeper still.

She wrapped her hand around the back of his head, anchored his mouth to hers. Her tongue mated with his, their mouths sliding together like hot, wet velvet.

It went on and on and on. Finally, he grasped her buttocks and lifted her, driving into her with the ferocity of his climax. She tore her mouth from his and cried her own release as the liquid tremors started deep within.

After a few moments he rolled off her and lay with an arm across his forehead, breathing heavily, his body glistening.

Gwen felt the air waft over her, cooling her hot skin. She raised herself on her elbows and gazed at her mound of curls. Even they were damp! After all this time, it was still amazing to think of being joined with a man, this man, so intimately.

His hand threaded in her hair, cupping the back of her head. He pulled her down to kiss him then pressed her onto her back, coming up on his elbow beside her.

His fingers traced her face, her neck, her breasts. "You were made for me, Gwen. I've never known a feeling so perfect, so right, as when I'm with you."

Gwen smoothed a stray curl off his forehead. Her heart beat erratically. She thought she knew what he was trying to say. She dared not hope it was true, yet she couldn't stop herself from saying, "Tell me, Richard."

"I love you." He kissed her when her mouth dropped open. At first, she lay limp, unbelieving. Mayhap she was still asleep and merely dreaming. But the reality of his big, hard body, his unmistakable male scent, his beloved lips on hers, told her she wasn't asleep. Her arms slipped around him, stroked his hair, his neck, his back. The kiss was sweet, long, tender.

"I've never said that to anyone," he whispered against her lips. "Never wanted to, until you."

She felt tears pooling in her eyes. It was ridiculous to cry when she was so happy. "I did not think you meant it," she said. "You were drunk and—"

"I told you last night?"

She nodded.

"Ah, Christ's bones, you should not have had to hear it like that. 'Twas not the way I wanted to tell you."

Gwen laughed suddenly. "I love you, Richard. As long as you love me, I care not how you told me."

"Aye, I've fought it for so long, but I cannot deny it any longer. I love you."

"Was it because of my father you denied it?"

"Nay, 'twas because of mine." His hand trailed to her breast. She shuddered when he began to toy with her sensitive nipple. "He loved my mother so much that he was never the same after she died. I vowed to never care that much for a woman lest I be destroyed as he was."

"What happened with the king?" she asked softly, knowing instinctively that whatever it was had caused him to admit his feelings.

"Nothing that need concern you, my love. 'Tis men's business," he said, dipping his head to swirl his tongue around her aroused nipple.

"You seek to distract me," she said. His teeth closed gently over the hardened tip. "Mmm, my lord, you are insatiable."

"Aye, I cannot get enough of you."

"Please tell me what happened last night."

He moved to the other breast. "'Tis unimportant, sweet. Now cease your questions before I take you over my knee."

Gwen knew she could not sway him without the danger of rousing his temper. She decided to give in to his lovemaking instead. "Yes, Richard, please take me over your knee," she said huskily.

"Christ but you excite me," he swore. "I can think of something much more fun than spanking you though."

She squeaked when he flipped her on her stomach and tore off her robe, giggling when he bit her bottom cheeks. Her giggles soon changed to moans as his mouth paid homage to the ripe curves, licking, kissing, biting.

When he finally turned her over and would have slid into her, Gwen pushed him back and straddled him. He groaned as she slid her mouth down his chest, his abdomen.

Before he could stop her, she claimed her prize. "Tell me you love me," she commanded, then slid her tongue down his hard length.

"God yes, I love you, you brazen little temptress."

Gwen rewarded him by taking him in her mouth. He bucked and swelled against her tongue until she knew she had to feel him inside her or die. She replaced her mouth with her feminine heat.

He cupped her breasts, then lifted until he could suckle them.

"Richard," she gasped. "God, I love the things you do to me."

"I've only just begun to do things to you, *cariad*. You will have to spend the entire day in bed again just to recover."

Gwen's laugh was husky. "As long as you stay with me, I shall not mind."

He grasped her buttocks and turned her over without losing the intimate contact between them. Then he proceeded to show her just exactly what he intended to do all night.

31

'Twas Christmas Eve and the music and dancing inside the Palace of Westminster were in full swing. The Yule log had been lit and would be kept burning through Twelfth Night.

Never had Gwen seen a hall so huge. It was well over two-hundred-feet long and the ceiling soared so far above her head, it made her dizzy to look up for too long.

The room was bedecked with holly and mistletoe and boughs of evergreen, so much that it would have smelled like a forest if not for the stench of hot tallow.

Men and women laughed and talked, clustering in small groups, while others danced and sang, their bright clothes muted by the rising smoke that made the room murky and dense. Gwen remembered hearing how the king entertained thousands in this hall, throwing great feasts that lasted for days on end. Well she could believe it.

The highest lords and ladies of the realm were turned out in all their finery, partaking in the grand feasting and entertainment the king and queen provided. There would be jousting tournaments and shepherd's plays, mummers and minstrels, Welsh bards and colorful jugglers to enliven the banqueting.

Gwen had chosen a gown of crimson velvet with a gold chemise, and a jeweled girdle with emeralds, sapphires, and rubies that winked and danced in the torchlight. The sheer golden wimple she wore did little to hide her curls. She'd not braided them and they cascaded down her back in a mass of muted fire.

She glanced at Richard, and her heart swelled. He was so handsome in his crimson surcoat with the black hawk emblazoned on the front. His sword glittered at his side, reminding all who gazed upon him that here was a man of power and magnetism, a man not to be taken lightly.

King Edward approached them, smiling. "Gwenllian, my dear, you look ravishing," he said, lifting her hand to his lips.

Gwen dipped into a curtsy. "Thank you, Majesty."

Edward raised her, his eyes lingering until Richard cleared his throat. The king released her, grinning.

"Now I see why you've not been back in three days. Certes, I'd not let her out of bed either if she were mine."

Richard squeezed her hand. "My wife was overtired from the journey, Ned. I did not wish to ignore her."

Gwen was amazed at how smoothly the lie passed his lips. Actually, Edward had it right the first time. They'd not been out of bed too often in the last three days.

Richard had given her the grand tour of Dunsmore House with its elegant gothic arches, gilded artwork, and vast windows. He'd taken her up on the walls and shown her the Archbishop of Canterbury's Lambeth Palace as well as Westminster Palace and several of the highest-ranking earls' residences, which were all within close range.

They'd also walked in the garden, though it was mostly covered in snow, except where the kitchen staff tended a plot for winter herbs and vegetables.

There was an arched trellis grown over with ivy, and hedges that stretched their limbs skyward. Gwen had thrown a snowball at Richard, then ran when he chased her. He'd caught her beneath the arch and they'd fallen to the cold ground, laughing, oblivious to the snow.

"God, how I love you," he'd said before kissing her nearly senseless. As was inevitable whenever they touched, they'd soon ended up in the bedchamber.

Richard squeezed her hand again, and she knew he was remembering the same things.

The Earl of Gloucester came over, bearing a cup of wine for the king. "Ah, Dunsmore, I didn't expect you to bring your wife to court. Surely that cuts down on your fun somewhat," he said, his voice softly slurred from too much wine. "Must be tiring, plowing the same field night after night, no matter how pretty."

Gwen stiffened. Richard took a step forward. Gilbert ducked behind the king.

Richard's eyes flashed with hot fury. "You were never one for eloquent speech, Gilbert. Your lack of common sense is only exceeded by your lack of wit."

Gilbert peeked around the king, his brow knit in confusion while he considered the insult. Gwen stifled a laugh.

"You'd best leave while you can still walk," Edward murmured over his shoulder. "If you'd said that about my wife, I'd have killed you on the spot."

Richard turned to her, his features still clouded with anger. She smiled to reassure him. "You are my valient knight," she said in Welsh.

His look softened. "Keep staring at me like that, wench, and I will drag you to the nearest alcove and have my way with you," he replied in the same language.

Edward coughed politely. "Richard, I wish to discuss the cr—"

"Majesty," Richard interrupted, switching back to French. "Allow me to present my wife to the queen."

He deposited her on the dais with Eleanor and her ladies, then left to rejoin Edward. Gwen watched him walk away, apprehension knotting her stomach. Richard was hiding something, and the possibilities frightened her.

Despite having very little sleep, Gwen was up at dawn, heaving into the chamber pot. She attributed it to the variety of food she'd sampled at Westminster.

She wiped a shaking hand across her mouth, then poured a cup of water. When she felt somewhat better, she got back in bed and curled up next to Richard.

She could not be sick today. Richard had promised to show her London with all its exotic sights and its amazing bridge with houses.

After they awoke, and he'd washed and dressed, he left her to finish dressing on her own, and she again felt the pull of the chamber pot.

"You should not go riding, Gwenllian," Alys admonished. "I will send a message to Lord de Claiborne."

"Nay," Gwen cried, straightening. "'Tis over now. I feel much better."

Alys's chin thrust outward. "Nevertheless, you should remain in bed."

"Alys, I want to see London. If you tell him I've been sick, he will never take me!"

Alys glared at her for a long moment, then deflated. "Very well, my lady. But I don't like it!"

Gwen descended the stairs quickly, pulling on her gloves as she crossed through the spacious ground floor and out into the courtyard. Five knights sat their horses patiently. Richard leaned against the wall. He straightened as she approached.

"I'm sorry I took so long. I couldn't find anything suitable to wear," she lied.

He laughed. "Do not let Alys hear you say that, sweet. She'll be sewing new gowns in a trice." His eyes swept over her azure surcoat and matching cloak. He reached behind her and pulled the hood up, kissing her forehead. "I have a present for you, my love."

She followed his gaze to the grooms who led their horses from the stables. "Oh!"

"Do you like her?"

"'Tis the most beautiful horse I've ever seen!"

"Aye, she's an Arab." He took her hand and led her to the mare's side. The delicate looking animal swiveled her ears toward them and Gwen reached out to pet her. Her coat was like finest silk, even in winter.

Richard ran a hand over the horse. "She's much stronger than she looks. Arabs are hardy, despite their fine bones and delicate lines. They're usually hot-blooded, but I picked this one for her gentle nature, as well as her breeding."

He pulled a lock of molten hair from under Gwen's hood and en-twined it with the mare's mane. "'Tis the same color," he said, gazing at her before saying softly, "She and Sirocco will have beautiful babies."

"She must have cost a fortune," Gwen murmured.

"A small price to pay for your happiness."

Gwen bestowed a smile on him. "You are my happiness."

He held out his arms and she went into them. "And you are mine," he said before setting her on the mare's back.

Gwen gathered the reins in her left hand, smoothing the mare's neck with her right. "What is her name?" she asked as Richard swung onto Sirocco.

He reined in the stallion. "She doesn't have a name yet. 'Tis up to you to give her one."

Gwen stared at the flaming coat of the animal beneath her. "*Saffrwn*," she said finally.

"Saffron?"

"Aye. She is the color of it and she is also rare and costly like it. 'Tis perfect."

"Sirocco and Saffron," he said, smiling. "I like it."

London was even more amazing in person than it was from a window. They rode into town through Ludgate, first passing through the criminal neighborhood of the lower Fleet River. Gwen was appalled at the smell. Richard explained that people emptied their cesspits upriver and it was carried downsteam to empty into the Thames.

Once inside the bustle of London proper, Gwen was awestruck at the sheer numbers of people. They came in all sizes and descriptions, some hurrying through the streets, others stopping to talk and pass the time away.

The houses and shops were of wattle and daub, framed in timber, and instead of glass, had wooden shutters over the windows. Smoke rose from holes in the thatched roofs, clogging the air with the scent of burning wood.

Richard first took her to the market at Cheapside. A variety of vendors hawked their wares—cloth, wine, linen, fish, candles, leather. There were also vendors serving meat pies and ale and Christmas cakes. Mummers paraded through the streets, and troops of jugglers and musicians entertained on every corner.

It was afternoon by the time they finally reached London Bridge, and Gwen was weary. She could barely summon any excitement for the wondrous bridge with the tall houses.

She covered her mouth in sudden horror. Over the gate, severed heads were displayed on pikes, some only skulls, others in different stages of rot and being picked at by ravens.

"Are you ill?" Richard asked.

"Nay," Gwen said. She took a deep breath.

He glanced up and swore. "Forgive me, Gwen. I forgot about those damned things. I should have warned you."

She swallowed the bile in her throat. "Why are they there?"

"London doesn't tolerate traitors. Their heads on pikes are reminders to all not to follow in their footsteps."

Gwen forced a smile. "Please tell me more about the bridge. What is that city on the other side? 'Tis not still London, is it?"

"No, 'tis Southwark. This road leads to Canterbury and the Kent ports. Southwark is full of inns and... other things for the comfort of travelers."

"Other things?"

"Aye."

"Such as?"

"Jesú!" He actually looked uncomfortable for a minute, then he waved a hand casually. "Brothels, bathhouses."

"Oh," Gwen replied, not really interested.

"Are you sure you aren't ill?"

She turned to look at him. He was frowning, but she barely noticed. In the distance, the golden-lion banner snapped in the breeze over a white castle. "I am rather tired," she admitted. "Could we go back now?"

"Aye," he said, turning to follow her gaze. "'Tis the Tower."

"Ah, the Tower. My grandfather died there, you know. I never knew him, but my father says he fell to his death trying to escape. Little chance a Welshman had in a place such as this."

Richard sighed. "You see why Wales must learn to adapt to England's ways? This won't go away, Gwen. Your father and his chieftains can make war indefinitely and England will remain. Wales must adapt or die."

Gwen bristled. "The Welsh have survived for centuries, my lord. We have outlasted the Romans and the Saxons! We can outlast England."

"Even with the whole of Wales at his back, which your father has never had, he could not defeat England. I don't mean to hurt you, *cariad*, but 'tis the truth."

Gwen bit her lip. Dear God, after seeing London, she feared Richard was right, but she couldn't admit it. She turned away before she made a fool of herself and cried. "I want to go home," she said.

"Very well," he replied softly.

They turned their horses and rode back the way they'd come. Gwen's spirit sank. She'd been so excited to see the city, the grand and glorious things these English had built, but now she knew how impossible it was for Wales to ever triumph against such a formidable foe. Forget prophecy, forget determination—England was the stronger, the more powerful. England would win in the end, just like Richard said.

32

D afydd ap Gruffydd strolled confidently to his audience with the king. He'd waited two weeks for this meeting. He was irritated Edward had put him off for so long, but it was the Christmas season, and all of England had come to a grinding halt to enjoy the feasting and merrymaking.

He entered the king's solar and frowned. It was never a good sign when Black Hawk de Claiborne was around. Gilbert de Clare, Earl of Gloucester, and Henry de Lacy, Earl of Lincoln, were also in the room, as well as the king's brother, Edmund of Lancaster.

"Come, Dafydd, drink with us," Edward called out.

Dafydd accepted a goblet and took a seat beside Gloucester. He avoided the hawk-like gaze of the Earl of Dunsmore, and raised his cup in salute to the king. He would deal with Dunsmore soon enough.

"What did you wish to speak to me about, Dafydd?"

Dafydd darted his gaze around the room. "I was hoping to speak to you in private, Sire."

Edward swept his hand toward his earls. "We are in private, Dafydd. 'Tis only my closest advisors."

Dafydd gritted his teeth. He didn't bother to point out that two of the men present were the most powerful of the Marcher earls. His complaint involved lands in the Marches. "Of course, Majesty," he deferred, bowing his head. "I am certain Your Majesty could not know of these things, but the lands you so graciously have given me are being harassed."

Edward looked scandalized. He leaned forward in his chair. "How is that, Lord Dafydd?"

Dafydd knew he had emphasized the English title deliberately. It did not bode well.

"Your Justiciar of Chester, Reginald de Grey, has accused me of harboring outlaws. To that end my woods have been cut and I have been called to defend my possession of lands that are within Wales."

"Are you?"

"What?"

"Harboring outlaws?"

Dafydd gripped the goblet. He darted a look at Dunsmore. This was Black Hawk's doing, he was certain of it. Richard de Claiborne took perverse delight in thwarting his desires.

"Nay, Majesty. I am a loyal vassal. Why would I endanger my holdings so?"

"I believe you, Dafydd, do not worry. I must ask these questions though, to satisfy the concerns of my advisors."

"Of course, Majesty," Dafydd acquiesced. He toyed with his cup. "My castles have also been called into question."

"Did you obtain permission to build them?"

"I applied for writs, if that is what you mean."

"Well there can be no problem then," Edward said, leaning back in his chair.

Dafydd ran a finger around the rim of his goblet. "But what of my woods and my Welsh lands?"

"You have nothing to fear, Lord Dafydd. Just appear in court with the proof of possession and the justiciar will harass you no more."

Dafydd took a quick swallow of wine. The damn stuff was nowhere near as satisfying as a draught of Welsh mead. He checked his rising temper. The lands in question lay inside Wales. They were all he had left of the birthright denied him by his brother. He would not give them up or defend his claim in an arbitrary English court. "Majesty, by the Treaty of Aberconwy, that can only be determined by Welsh law."

"Yes, but I believe those lands connect to the ones I seized in the rebellion. Therefore, since they touch lands that are technically English, you may be called to appear in an English court."

Dafydd seethed. There was no way he was going to win this power play. "Aye, Majesty," he said, bowing his head.

Despite everything he'd done to help Edward achieve his victory, it still came down to one thing—Dafydd was not English and could never be, no matter how many titles or privileges Edward heaped upon him to hide it.

The Twelve days of Christmas were a time of merriment and cheer, a time when common men and nobles alike celebrated from sunup to sunup. The Palace of Westminster was no exception, hosting the grandest celebrations of all.

Great banquets were set up daily and kept plenished until the last revelers fell into a drunken sleep. Ale and wine flowed freely, along with mead and spiced hippocras. People danced and sang and played games until the early morning when they staggered home to rest for a few hours before starting all over again.

Tonight was Twelfth Night, the last night of the celebrations. Soon, the earl of Dunsmore's household would return to the March.

Alys laid out the cream-velvet dress that was her favorite creation. Gwen fingered the silver and gold embroidery, the white ermine trim, the string of pearls sewn into the neckline.

"Sweet Mary, 'tis beautiful!"

"There's a matching mantle and slippers, too, my lady," Alys said proudly.

"Whatever would I do without you, Alys?"

The old woman blushed and began helping Gwen into the gown. She finished lacing it, then fitted a gold and silver girdle around Gwen's waist.

Gwen smoothed the soft cloth over her belly. "I don't remember this being so tight when you fitted me."

Alys touched Gwen's cheek. "Have you thought how long 'tis been since you last had your flux?"

Gwen's hand splayed over her abdomen. "Since before..." Dear God, since before her wedding two months ago! "I am with child," she whispered.

Alys beamed, her eyes shining. "Aye, I thought you might be."

Gwen stood immobile for a long time. "Where is Richard?"

"I believe he is with Sir Charles and Owain. Shall I get him for you?"

Excitement bubbled in Gwen's soul. She wanted to tell him right away, but it was almost time to leave for the palace. "Nay."

She would wait until they returned home tonight. They would make love as usual, and when they were curled up together afterwards, she would tell the man she loved that she carried his child. It would be perfect.

When she joined Richard in the courtyard, his appreciative stare sent ribbons of heat spiraling through her. She slipped her gloved hand into his, and he drew her close.

"You look just like a fairy princess I saw once," he murmured.

"Where did you see this fairy, my lord?" she asked with a coy smile.

"In a cave of lights. 'Twas in a Welsh mountain, where sights such as that are not uncommon. A sight to behold, she was. All fire and beauty, so much that I was instantly taken with her."

"And what did you do with this fairy, my lord?"

"I impaled her on my sword," he said very seriously.

Gwen laughed. "You are so wicked! Did she like it, pray tell?"

He grinned. "She didn't complain, as I recall."

Gwen sidled up to him. "Mayhap you will demonstrate for me later," she said, her voice a husky whisper.

"Jesú, but you are a tease, wench."

She slanted him a look. "Am I exciting you?"

"Unbearably."

"Then let us skip the festivities and create our own," she said.

He swung her into his arms and set her on Saffron. "Edward is expecting us, love. The sooner we leave, the sooner we can return."

Gwen sighed her disappointment and resigned herself to a long evening. Keeping her secret turned out to be more difficult than she'd imagined.

The ride to the palace wasn't long, but she found herself staring at her husband's handsome profile, aching to tell him her news.

Fortunately, King Edward separated them as soon as they arrived, waving Richard over to where he stood with the earls of Lincoln, Warwick, Oxford, Gloucester, and Pembroke.

Gwen joined Queen Eleanor's group of ladies on the dais. Catherine de Lacy patted the seat beside her, and Gwen sat down.

"Marriage agrees with you, Gwenllian," Eleanor said.

"Thank you, Majesty." The news was bursting inside her, but she couldn't tell these ladies before she told Richard.

"You positively glow. Doesn't she glow, Margaret?"

"Indeed she does!" Margaret de Valence exclaimed. The other ladies nodded vigorously. Gwen murmured her thanks demurely.

Of course she glowed! She was in love with the most handsome man in all the world, and the proof of that love grew within her even now.

How she ached for an end to this evening so she could have Richard to herself!

But time had a funny way of dragging when you wanted it to go the fastest. The conversation on the dais was varied, ranging from babies to servants to sewing to cosmetics to war. The wives of Edward's most powerful barons were not empty-headed. Oft times, the responsibility of running the castle fell on their shoulders when their husbands were gone, and they were well versed in a variety of endeavors.

Queen Eleanor waved a hand toward where her husband clustered with his barons. "Edward is going to drive me mad with all this talk of a crusade," she said, picking at the golden lions on her surcoat. "I do not wish to make another journey to the Holy Land."

"You could always stay here with the rest of us, Majesty," Margaret offered.

Eleanor laughed, the sound like that of a small bird chirping. "Nay, I could not live without my Edward for so long. The last crusade took four years and I was with him every step of the way. When he goes, I go."

Gwen felt a sharp prickle begin at the back of her neck. It crept down her spine, growing and spreading in time with her suspicions. Richard had gone on the last crusade with King Edward. She remembered him telling her of a place called the Sahara, a place with fiery desert sands and a wind named Sirocco.

Almost frantically, her eyes sought him out. He wasn't hard to find. His dark head towered over the other barons, but even had that not been the case, he would have been unmistakable. How could any man ever compare to the splendor of Richard de Claiborne?

She watched him, unable to tear her gaze away for fear he would disappear if she couldn't see him. She *knew*—dear God, she knew!

Richard was leaving. She didn't have to ask him. The same fierce loyalty that drove him to risk his life in the borders would send him halfway across the world to fight and mayhap die for his king.

Unconsciously, Gwen clutched her stomach. What of their child, their son? Aye, she knew it was a son. She did not know how, but she knew it nonetheless. Would he grow up without a father, take his father's place long before he should?

Gwen drew in a shaky breath. It was a fact of life that men went to war. Her father had. Rhys had. But the thought of Richard in such danger terrified her to the depths of her soul.

She'd been so frantic for him when he'd left to stop the raid. If she admitted it, she'd been frantic the day she'd seen him leap onto Sirocco and charge the attackers at the cave. How would she live, fearing for him with every breath, missing him with every fiber of her being?

The smoke was choking her. Her blood pounded in her temples as the music and laughter swelled in her ears. She had to get out of the hall, had to be alone for a little while. Quietly, she rose and slipped away from the queen and her ladies.

Gwen wandered the passages and rooms of Westminster Palace. She knew not where she was or where she was going. All she wanted was to forget.

She opened a door and stumbled out into a quiet courtyard. Though the air was cold she never noticed. Angrily, she swiped at the tears trickling down her cheeks. Never had she cried so much until she married Richard!

She giggled almost hysterically. Mayhap she would not cry so much when he was gone. She sank down on a stone bench. Nay, mayhap she would never stop until he returned.

Gwen thought she understood what Richard's aversion to falling in love had been. Well she could imagine his father's grief at losing his wife. Richard had said he never wanted to care that much for a woman. Did that mean he didn't love her as much as he might? Was that why he could manage to leave her when she could not bear the thought of living without him?

She didn't know how long she sat before she felt the hand on her shoulder. She jumped, half expecting to see Richard. "Dafydd!"

He smiled. "One and the same," he replied, sitting down beside her. "What are you doing out here, Gwenllian?"

"Nothing. The hall just seemed stifling so I decided to go for a walk. What brings you out here, Lord Dafydd?"

He sighed. "Will you not call me *ewythr?*"

"Uncle?" Gwen said increduously. "I think not!"

Dafydd shrugged. "I'm not as bad as all that, Gwenllian. My brother and I just happen to disagree on the best way to run Wales."

"Is that why you tried to murder him?" Gwen couldn't keep the contempt from her voice.

"'Twas a mistake. I'd give anything to change it. And it was not just I. The prince of Powys wanted his death much more than I did."

"Gruffydd ap Gwenwynwyn," she spat. "He would have placed you on the throne merely to serve his own ends."

"Well, we did not succeed, and 'twas almost ten years ago it all began. I've had time to regret that youthful mistake."

Gwen glowered. She was too upset about her own life to worry about Dafydd's. It made her bolder than she would have dared ever dream. "Tell me about my mother. Why did she leave? Or did he send her away, as you claim?"

"He did send her away, Gwen. Not directly, but he did it all the same."

"Why?"

Dafydd hesitated. "Because he believed her unfaithful. Eurwen could not bear it, and she left."

Gwen's breath shortened. "Unfaithful?"

He nodded. "Llywelyn has never had much luck at siring children. When you came along, well…"

Gwen leaned heavily against the bench, stunned into silence. Dear God, all these years. That was why she could never gain her father's affection, why he'd bargained her future so easily. He did not believe her his child. It made so much sense now.

"He never denounced me," she whispered.

Dafydd shrugged. "He had no proof."

Gwen stared into the darkness. Her father could have denied her if he wanted, proof or not. He was the Prince of Wales for God's sake. Whether she was truly his or not, he'd raised her as his own, given her a title. If nothing else, she owed him for that much.

Gwen was too lost to hear the approaching footsteps, or to realize Dafydd had risen and was staring at the intruder in silent challenge.

"'Tis a pleasure as always, Prince Dafydd. Or would that be Lord Dafydd? I can never remember which side it is you are on."

Gwen's gaze snapped to Richard. Her heart turned over at the sight of him. She wanted to lose herself in his arms even while she wanted to slap his beloved face for not telling her about the crusade.

Dafydd smiled lazily. "One day, Dunsmore, I'm going to delight in seeing you beaten."

"I hope you intend on living a long time," Richard said, baring his teeth in a poor imitation of a smile.

"Oh I do," Dafydd replied, sauntering off toward the palace.

Gwen felt a chill wash over her. It did not surprise her they were enemies, but something in Dafydd's tone set her on edge. Too confident, too certain of himself.

But she couldn't think of that right now. All she could think of was the man towering over her. He pulled her up and drew her against him.

"Jesú, you are freezing. Why did you come out here?" he demanded.

Gwen clung to him, let his warmth flow over her. She closed her eyes. Emotion rolled through her in waves as she fisted his surcoat in both hands, pressed against him, breathed in his unique scent.

She told herself she should not behave so. She told herself she should be railing at him. Screaming, slapping, kicking, clawing. She held him tighter.

"Come," he said, pulling her toward the door.

When they were inside, he strode down the passage, then swept her into a shadowed alcove. Her teeth began to chatter.

Richard swore, then started rubbing her arms vigorously. He caught a servant hustling past and ordered him to take them to a private room with a fire.

The man bowed jerkily. "M-milord, I would have to find the chamber-lain, and—"

"Take us to a room now, my friend, or you will find yourself without a very precious part of your anatomy," Richard threatened in a quiet voice. "I care not who you have to insult to do it. Blame the earl of Dunsmore when any ask you."

"Aye, milord. This way, milord," he replied.

He led them to a richly appointed room with a roaring fire, then bowed profusely when Richard gave him gold coin for his trouble. Richard barred the door while Gwen went to stand beside the fire.

She stared at the odd-looking rug spread before the hearth. 'Twas a beast with hideous fangs, long dark hair around the head, and a smooth tawny hide.

"'Tis a lion," Richard said behind her.

"A lion," she repeated. She'd had no idea 'twas what a lion truly looked like. All she'd ever seen was the lion device on the King's coat of arms. Certes, that did not look like this.

"Why did you leave the hall without telling me?"

Gwen faced him, studied his features as they hardened with anger.

"Christ, I've been searching for you half the damn night! And what the hell were you doing with Dafydd ap Gruffydd?"

Gwen started to laugh. She couldn't stop, even when his face seemed carved from stone. He grabbed her arms and shook her softly. Gwen hiccoughed the last of her giggles, then fell into silence, staring up at him, knowing all the hurt she felt inside was written on her face.

"When were you going to tell me?"

His expression crumbled. He turned away and raked his hands through his hair, then sat heavily in a chair, his legs sprawled out in front of him. His gaze lifted to hers. "Soon," he said.

"When do you leave?"

"I do not know yet. Six months, a year." He shrugged, his finger tracing the edge of the table. "There will be a meeting in the spring to determine."

Six months! God, if he left then, she would bear his son without him. For some reason it frightened her, and she knew what Elizabeth must have felt. Her pulse quickened.

"Can you not stay?"

His jaw hardened. "Nay."

The silence stretched between them until he shot out of the chair and pulled her to her knees on the lion rug. He cupped her face between his hands, feathered kisses along her forehead, her jawbone, the slim column of her throat. "As God is my witness, I do not want to leave you, but I must."

"I am pregnant," Gwen blurted.

He leaned back on his heels. Gwen bit her trembling lip. This was not the way it was supposed to happen. She'd said it in a desperate hope he wouldn't leave her if he knew, even while she realized it was futile.

"You are certain?" he asked, his eyes wide.

Gwen nodded. "I've not had my courses since we were married."

He was kissing her suddenly, crushing her to him. He lifted her against his heart, then laid her back on the rug, leaning over her, endlessly kissing her. "I love you," he murmured in Welsh, over and over, as his lips trailed down her neck. She could feel the beat of his heart, fast and strong, mingling with hers.

Just for now, just this once, she wanted to forget the inevitable and join with him as they were meant to do in this glorious moment they shared. She would think of the Crusade, of her father, later.

There was no need for foreplay. They both knew that only when they were joined deeply would they be able to forget, at least for a while. Gwen arched her hips up to receive him, glorying in the powerful feel of him moving within her.

Their mating wasn't uncontrolled for once. Long minutes passed while Richard lay completely still, concentrating all his lovemaking on her mouth. In those moments, she could feel him deep within her, their hearts beating as one.

Gwen didn't even care when she felt the hot trickle of tears running across her temples. Richard brushed them aside, whispering love words that only made them fall faster.

"Oh Richard, 'tis not close enough," she said. "It can never be close enough."

"I know, my love, I know."

Gwen had no doubt he understood. No matter how closely they were joined, it was never close enough.

When it was over and he cradled her against him, Gwen clutched him tight, never wanting to let go.

Tonight, she'd lost a father. Soon, she would lose a husband.

33

Time was moving too fast. Richard leaned against the wall and stared at the valley below. He'd taken up Gwen's habit of coming to the castle walls whenever he was troubled. It was soothing in a way to stand so high and fool yourself into believing you were alone in the world.

They'd been home for a fortnight now, and Gwen was lovelier each day, her middle gently swelling with his child.

Richard loved to look at her, at the miracle of her body. When she was clothed, it was barely noticeable because she was still so small. But when she lay in their bed, naked before his eyes, the proof was there. Sometimes when she slept, he would pull back the covers and just look at her, stamping every moment on his memory. God only knew how long it would have to last him.

Another month and he would have to leave for the king's council in Wessex. He rubbed his forehead absently. It was all happening much too soon.

Already, he'd noticed she was withdrawing from him. It was nothing specific, nothing he could definitely place his finger on, but he sensed it all the same. It was as though she held a part of herself back, as though she refused to share her innermost self.

Richard sucked in a breath. God, he'd never thought, never dreamed he could feel so deeply for a woman. He was indeed his father's son. And she was the daughter of his father's murderer.

He shoved that thought away, again picturing her, and a shattering pain tore through him. What if she didn't survive childbirth? God forgive him, but he'd already killed one woman with his child. He could not bear to lose this one.

He refused to even think of leaving her while she was still pregnant, though the possibility existed.

His hand strayed to his sword hilt, a physical defense against a phantom threat. Going on crusade was something he had to do, something he could endure knowing he would see her again. But if she died, would he be like his father? Delusional, drunken, shattered?

"Richard?"

He spun around at the sound of her voice. God, she was beautiful! Her russet tresses were barely contained by the golden circlet she wore. Her skin, always the color of purest ivory, was rosy with the cold. And her scent…

Roses. It stole to him, borne on the chill wind. He breathed deeply. A rose in winter. She was the color of them, too, dressed in a crimson sendal surcoat and undertunic. Even her cloak was crimson.

Richard felt his loins responding, tightening, filling. She turned him into a slavering beast when she was near.

"Yes, my love?"

She smiled tentatively, and moved closer. Her delicate hands, gloved in soft velvet, splayed across his chest. Her lovely face turned up to his, and he found himself drowning in eyes the color of springtime.

Absently, he traced her lower lip with his thumb. What had he ever done to deserve the love of this woman?

"I have been thinking," she began, "since you will not stay behind when the king goes, why don't you take me with you?"

Richard closed his eyes. "Gwen…" They'd had this conversation too many times to count, though this was a new twist. Always before, she'd begged him to stay. "I cannot take you, *cariad*."

"Why not? Queen Eleanor is going."

He opened his eyes to look at her. "If I took you, you would hate me before 'twas over. The Holy Land is nothing but dust and heat so scorching it chokes the breath from you. The journey is long and miserable, cooped up on boats, sailing without seeing land for weeks at a time."

"But if I were with you—"

Richard shook his head vehemently. "'Tis too dangerous. If, God forbid, we were defeated, do you know what those heathens would do to you? One look at you my precious wife and they'd hustle you off to a harem to service some fat, balding sheik for the rest of your days."

She stared up at him, her lip trembling. Then her face clouded with anger. The change was so swift that Richard was not prepared when she flung away from him.

She whirled around in a blaze of brilliant color, spitting like a wildcat. "Fine! Go without me! You do not care what happens to me. You are willing to leave me, just like you did Eliz—"

"Silence!" he said, his voice cracking like a whip in the wintry air. She stopped, her teeth firmly seizing her lower lip. Richard clenched his fists at his side, fighting to contain his sudden rage. "I suggest if you do not wish to move us beyond what is forgivable, you will say no more."

She stood there, staring at him, her pretty breasts rising and falling. Richard thought himself a madman. Angry though he was, the thought of loosing her nipples from her gown and suckling them into arousal made him harder than the stone ramparts he was standing on.

He almost hated himself for the weakness.

He took a step toward her, not quite sure what he was going to do at this moment. She held up her hand to stop him. "I wish I'd never met you," she said, her voice edged with anguish. "The pain is too much. I hate you, even while I love you."

She backed away until she was certain he wasn't going to move, then turned and fled. Richard slumped against the unyielding stone, suddenly weary. Jesú, she was right. No wound received in battle had ever hurt this much.

Alys tsked as Gwen stabbed her needle through the embroidery.

"I didn't want to sew anyway," Gwen said, tossing the needlework aside and leaping to her feet. She paced, twisting her hands together unconsciously. Alys watched her for a minute, then shook her head and bent over her work.

Gwen felt she would burst at any moment. She was trying—God how she was trying!—to live each day with Richard as though it was their last. But the strain was wearing on her because she knew one day it *would* be their last.

She pushed him away, she pulled him to her. She loved him, she hated him.

He would not stay. He would not take her. He was determined she would have no say in the matter. Wasn't her life and her happiness at stake too? But he was a man. And bloody men always thought they knew what was best!

She stopped at the window and looked toward Snowdon. She'd not told him what Dafydd had said about her father. She'd not told anyone, not even Alys who might have known something more. Gwen couldn't bear to speak it aloud for fear it would make it true.

Her father had never denounced her and she would never denounce him. But one day she would ask him if he really believed she was not his, if that was the reason he'd never loved her like she wanted. He owed her an answer and she would accept nothing less than the truth, no matter how it hurt.

She didn't see Richard for the rest of the afternoon. When the dinner bell rang, she descended to the hall and joined him on the dais. They ate in silence while laughter floated around them, teasing and tormenting.

When the meal was over, Gwen excused herself and returned to the master chamber. She sat for a while, working on the embroidery she'd tossed aside earlier, then gave up and prepared for bed.

Lying on her side, she stroked the sheets where Richard would lay. What was happening to her? She didn't like the person she was becoming around him. Even though she knew it was wrong, she couldn't stop herself from arguing with him, from pushing him, from trying to make him as miserable as she was.

If she kept it up, he would be pleased to leave her.

She drew her hand across the sheet and settled it on her belly. Caressing the soft curve, she talked to her baby. Ridiculous it might be, but she did it nonetheless, only stopping when she heard the door open and shut.

She closed her eyes and pretended sleep when Richard came to bed. She waited, hoping he would draw her in his arms, knowing he would not.

His breathing didn't deepen, and she knew he lay awake as she did. She wanted to touch him, to breach the widening chasm between them, but it was too difficult.

"Richard?"

He sighed. "Aye?"

"You will not be faithful, will you?" she asked in a small voice.

He was silent for a long moment. Gwen cursed herself for saying it when in truth she didn't want to hear the answer. But it had been at the back of her mind for so long that she needed to get it out.

Quietly, he said, "When the need overtakes me, 'twill be your face I see, your voice I hear, your body I touch."

Gwen choked back bitter laughter. "Oh, 'tis so comforting." Why had she asked? Why? Men could not be faithful, even where there was love. She'd already known that, but she'd insisted on making him say it. Stupid, stupid, stupid!

Her voice quavered with anger and regret. "And what about me? What about my needs? Will you mind terribly if I take a lover in your absence?"

She knew she was goading him and she hated herself for doing it, but she was on a path of no return. She wanted him to feel what she was feeling.

Lightning fast he was on top of her, his hard body pressing into her soft curves, her face imprisoned between his hands. In the shadows cast by the flickering fire, she could see the outline of his features, hard, angry, breathtaking. Oddly, a rush of exhilaration roared through her veins.

"Christ almighty, Gwen! You want my fidelity? Will that ease your mind? Will you finally cease this madness?"

Gwen opened her mouth, but he rushed on before she could speak.

"By God, you have it then! On my honor, I swear to you I will bed no other. Should I be gone for one year or ten, it matters not. I will have none but you, ever."

His mouth claimed hers in a savage kiss. He was not gentle, nor did she want him to be. She needed to feel his passion for her, wanted to know he needed her desperately, so she could keep on living for another day.

"You are mine. *Mine!*" he said against her lips. "Do you need me to prove it to you? Do you need to know I hunger only for you?"

"Yes," she breathed, "*yes.*"

With a groan, he slid his hands down her sides, over her quivering thighs, and hooked them behind her knees.

Gwen whimpered softly when he brought her knees up to her chest. And then she felt him.

His voice was husky with need. "Then you had better hang on, my love. I am about to prove it to you in terms you will never forget."

A scream of delicious excitement built in her throat. He entered her in one hard thrust, drinking her cries into his mouth as his body began the pounding rhythm that would bring them both to shattering bliss before it was over.

It was late evening when Dafydd rode into the bailey of his castle on the Welsh coast, near Chester. He'd just spent a very lovely sennight at Ashford Hall, fucking the mistress of the manor.

Anne was a delightful bed partner. There was nothing she would not try. For the life of him, he couldn't figure why Dunsmore gave her up. Certes, little Gwenllian could not be that interesting.

But Anne's need to have a man between her legs was her undoing. She was quite easy to manipulate as long as she thought she might achieve some measure of power.

As long as she did what Dafydd asked, when he asked it, he cared not what he had to promise her. And right now he wanted her back inside Claiborne castle with a couple of his men in tow. If his guess was right,

Richard de Claiborne was not at all what he seemed, and Dafydd needed details.

He swung down off his destrier and tossed his reins to a waiting groom. A woman garbed in green ran to him and flung her arms around his neck. "I missed you so much, Dafydd!"

Dafydd laughed, then kissed his wife soundly. "I missed you, too, Lisbeth. How are the little ones?"

"Anxious to see their papa," she said, stepping back. She still gripped his hand and Dafydd smiled. Lisbeth was slender and pretty and she loved him with devotion. She'd given him two sons and one daughter in the five years they'd been married. And he still had four other children by his Welsh mistresses.

If there was one comfort he had, it was in knowing Llywelyn envied him for his ability to sire children. But even that wasn't entirely true anymore, now that Llywelyn's wife was expecting.

Dafydd put his arm around his wife and they walked into the hall. He stopped, his arm dropping to his side, and stared.

"Oh, Dafydd, I forgot to tell you he was waiting—"

"'Tis all right, my dear," he said.

Hywel ap Madog stood. "Prince Dafydd."

Dafydd met the other man's keen stare for some moments. Without turning, he said, "Lisbeth, send food and drink to the solar. Hywel and I will talk in there."

He heard Lisbeth swallow as she mumbled, "Aye, Dafydd," and he knew she'd not missed the significance of the greeting any more than he had. *Prince.*

The two men entered the solar. Dafydd gestured for the lord of northern Clwyd to take a seat. Hywel sank his squat bulk into a chair and Dafydd sat across from him, pulling off his gloves and tossing them on the table.

"How did the meeting with the king go?" Hywel asked.

Dafydd clenched his jaw. "As expected. He'll not rein in his justiciars or police his bailiffs and sheriffs. In short, 'tis business as usual for England, and Wales had better get used to it. And Llywelyn?"

Hywel leaned forward. "He's ready to strike, but not until the king is gone."

"And the other chieftains?"

"They are behind him." Hywel's eyes glittered suddenly. "But there are those of us who prefer not to wait. Edward may never leave, and each day sees the erosion of our lives and our culture. We cannot let him get away with it any longer."

"*Cura'r haearn tra fo'n boeth*, eh?" Dafydd said, arching an eyebrow. Strike the iron while it is hot.

Hywel nodded. "Aye."

"Are you telling me they will stand behind me?"

"Yes." It was said without hesitation.

Dafydd threw back his head and laughed. "Why should I risk it?" He swept his hand outward, encompassing the room. "Look around you, Hywel. His Majesty favors me. I have land and money and royal favors."

Hywel shot to his feet, surprisingly quick for a gnarled old warlord. He came around the table and glared down at Dafydd.

"Nay, Dafydd, you are a Welshman through and through! What's more, you are a prince of our people. You cannot sit idly by while Edward crushes Wales beneath his bootheels. 'Twas because you love Wales that you fell out with your brother. You do not agree with the way he did things, the way he defied traditions and claimed all!"

Dafydd gritted his teeth. "Aye, and look where it has gotten me."

Hywel's voice softened. "There are those who have always sympathized with you, Dafydd." He put a battle-hardened hand on Dafydd's shoulder. "*Gorau Cymro, Cymro oddi cartref.*"

"The best Welshman is the exiled," Dafydd whispered, gripping the edge of the table. God almighty! All he'd wanted in the early days was his rightful share and his equal place beside his brother. And now he had a chance to lead, another chance to lay claim to his birthright.

Edward would never change. His laws would choke the very life from Wales if something weren't done soon. Even though he'd promised to respect the Welsh and their customs, every passing day proved he did not.

Llywelyn would wait until there was nothing left to salvage. In his younger days, he'd dared to claim Wales as his own, dared to challenge feckless King Henry III, dared to contract to marry the daughter of a traitor.

Now, he wanted to sit back, wait, and play things safe. Age was creeping up on Llywelyn and making him lazy. This could be the chance Dafydd had been waiting for.

"Very well, Hywel. We shall call a meeting. I want to see who is offering me support before I decide."

Hywel ap Madog smiled and patted him on the shoulder. "Aye, Prince Dafydd."

"No!"

Richard bolted upright, wakened out of a dead sleep. His first thought was to reach for his sword, but as he became more coherent, he realized Gwen was beside him and they were alone.

"What is it, Gwen?"

"No," she said, softer, crying. He reached for her, enfolded her in his arms as he sank back against the pillows. She curled into his chest, shaking.

"Tell me, *cariad*. Let me help." Her soft crying continued and he stroked her back rhythmically. He very much feared she'd been dreaming about him leaving, and he didn't really know how to help her.

He'd demanded too much of her, made love to her until their bodies were drained of all emotion. It had been difficult on them both: the outpouring of feelings too strong to be governed, the entwining of souls too intense to be drawn out.

"Richard… I have to go home," she whispered.

"We are home," he said carefully.

"No," she said, her voice turning desperate. "Snowdon. I must go to Snowdon."

A chill washed down Richard's spine. "Snowdon? Why?"

She pushed away from him. "I *have* to go! Elinor... 'tis Elinor." Her voice broke on a sob. Richard pulled her against him, at a loss for what to say to calm her.

"What about Elinor, sweet?"

"I saw... I saw her dying."

Richard sighed. "'Tis only a bad dream. I will send a messenger if you like. We'll make sure she is all right."

She grasped his shoulders suddenly, her fingers digging into his flesh. "Richard, I beg you, you must let me go!"

"'Tis only a dream, Gwen. All will be well," he said, bewildered by her vehemence.

"You do not understand," she whispered. "They come true sometimes."

"It means nothing, sweet," he soothed.

"Yes, yes it does! You do not understand!"

Her voice rose hysterically. Richard was seized by a fear she'd hurt herself and the child she carried. Her father's court was more than twenty leagues away, through the mountains. It would be madness to try and go there in winter.

She clung to him, shaking, her tears bathing the flesh over his heart. He rested his chin on top of her head, his fingers dancing up and down her spine. Her anguish twisted inside him as though it were his own. Right now he would give her anything 'twas in his power to give.

"Hush, *cariad*. I will take you to your father's court, I promise."

Aye, he would take her to Llywelyn's court, straight into the wolf's lair...

34

The last days of February blustered their way through the mountain passes. The raw wind ate through fur-lined cloaks and woolen garments. Richard glanced at Gwen huddling on Saffron. For the thousandth time, he regretted promising to bring her here.

It was folly and he was a fool.

He had truly not considered the magnitude of the undertaking when he'd held her close—small and shaking and certain only he could make the world right again—and blindly agreed to do whatever she wanted.

Even worse than the journey, what sort of a welcome awaited Black Hawk de Claiborne in the hall of the Prince of Wales? The knights he had with him wouldn't be enough if Llywelyn decided to break the treaty of friendship.

They were awaiting the return of the messenger Richard had sent ahead for permission to proceed. He might have lost his wits where Gwen was concerned, but he'd be damned if he would surprise Llywelyn by showing up unannounced.

Christ, he should have refused! But she was so certain, and so adamant, that he knew if they hadn't come and something happened to Elinor, she would never forgive him.

Sirocco snorted and tossed his head. Snow and ice crunched beneath the stallion's hooves as Richard rode forward to meet the approaching messenger.

"Milord, they said to come at once. Princess Elinor is in childbed." He lowered his voice, though Gwen was too far away to hear. "She's having a difficult time, milord."

Richard let out a slow breath, then turned and rode back to Gwen. It must have shown on his face because all she said was, "Tell me."

"She is alive, Gwen."

Her eyes grew distant, as though she were seeing something, then focused on him once more. "She is not well."

Richard shook his head. "Nay."

She kicked Saffron forward, and Richard signaled his men to follow.

Once they reached the castle, the greeting they received was subdued. Gwen was off Saffron before Richard could help her. Without waiting for him, she raced up the steps and into her father's stronghold.

Alys scrambled after her, huffing and muttering.

Richard's gaze wandered the structure with the trained eye of a warrior. Andrew rode up beside him. "Ye see the way they're looking at us, milord?"

Richard nodded briefly. There was no mistaking the open hostility with which the Welshmen eyed Black Hawk and his men. "I'm sure Llywelyn is prepared for anything. Pray God he doesn't decide to exact a bit of retribution while we are here."

"What do ye want us to do?"

"We cannot sit on our horses and wait for a fight. Let us avail ourselves of the hospitality of the Prince of Wales. Tell the men to keep their weapons sheathed and their tongues silent. I'll listen for any signs of trouble. I doubt these men realize the enemy speaks Welsh," he said, grinning wryly.

Andrew returned the grin. "Aye, milord, I'd wager ye are correct about that."

Richard dismounted, thankful he'd worn chainmail, and allowed a bowing servant to lead him into the hall.

"Gwen," Elinor rasped, "how did you get here?"

Gwen stared in horror at the pale woman, so tiny, in the big bed before her. She sank down and took Elinor's hand.

"Elinor, you knew I'd not stay away," she said, choking back the lump in her throat. Elinor's hand burned with fever.

"'Twas a girl this time, Gwen." She turned her head to look at her husband. "The next one will be a son."

Llywelyn wiped her brow with a moist cloth. "Aye, dearest, the next one will be a boy." His hand shook as he pulled the cloth away.

"Where is your husband?" Elinor asked.

"He is with me," Gwen replied, her throat closing with unshed tears. A girl. Neither by word or deed did her father show a shred of disappointment though she knew he must hurt inside, so desperately did he want a son.

"Ah. I've thought of you often. Is he good to you?" Elinor's eyes clouded over slightly, her face creasing in a frown.

"Yes, he is good to me," Gwen said, glancing at her father. "I love him very much. And he loves me."

Elinor smiled. "I told you 'twould work out."

"Yes, you were right as usual, dearest Elinor." Elinor squeezed her hand. Gwen's heart sank at the weakness of the grip. "Oh Elinor, when you are better, I will come visit you more often, and you must come visit me. Our children can play together, and we will make soap and perfume like we used to do."

"Aye, I would like that." She pulled Gwen's hand to her cheek. "You are pregnant?"

"Yes. 'Tis due the end of August," she said, refusing even to think of whether Richard would still be with her. She glanced at her father, found him watching her for once, his expression intense.

"Oh, 'tis so lovely! I will come and stay with you, Gwen." She turned to Llywelyn. "May I go, my darling?"

"Of course you may," he whispered, smiling. "Of course."

They sat in silence until Elinor was asleep. Gwen's heart was heavy as she slipped into the adjoining solar.

"Gwen!"

"Rhys!" All her pent up emotion bubbled forth when she saw the beloved face of her friend. She ran to him, flinging herself into his arms. He sank onto a bench recessed in the wall and cradled her against his chest, rocking back and forth.

"I saw it, Rhys. I saw it," she said, tears spilling free at last as she clutched his tunic. "She is going to die."

"Shh, Gwen. Don't cry," Rhys said.

But Gwen only cried harder, all the wretchedness of the world seeming to hang on her shoulders. Soon, Elinor would be lost to her, along with Richard and her father. Rhys held her tight and let her cry, murmuring to her softly.

Richard rose from the trestle table and motioned for a page. The black hawk of Dunsmore rippled on his surcoat, and he threw his mantle back to reveal his sword, lest any forget he carried it.

The boy came to him nervously. Andrew and the other men sat in silence, drinking mead and grimacing over the sweet taste. English ale was a damn sight better.

The entire hall fell silent while Richard inquired as to the whereabouts of his wife. He spoke in French, unwilling to let them know he understood Welsh. The boy, schooled in languages as a royal page should be, understood perfectly and motioned Richard to follow.

Richard heard the murmurs as he walked through the hall. As long as the hostility was only verbal he could deal with it, but at the first sign of treachery, he and his men were ready to fight.

They climbed a flight of stairs and the boy pointed him toward a door. It wasn't completely closed and Richard pushed it open. Time froze. He stood, silent, unmoving, his heart a dead weight in his chest.

Gwen was in the arms of Rhys ap Gawain. Richard's hand strayed to his sword. His very first thoughts were black, hateful. It was all he could do not to unsheath the vicious weapon.

They were oblivious to his presence and he turned to walk away, afraid he might lose his sanity.

"Richard!"

He halted, her musical voice like a dagger to his heart. She disentangled herself from Rhys's arms and ran to him. Tears streamed down her face and she wrapped her arms around him, holding him tight.

Rhys watched, his eyes locking with Richard's, his face anguished.

"She is dying," Gwen whispered.

Richard held Rhys's gaze, his arms slowly closing around his wife. She was *his*. How could he ever imagine it otherwise? After a moment, he lowered his head and buried his face in the fragrant cloud of her hair.

"I'm so sorry, Gwen," he said. Driven by a need he didn't understand, he pressed kisses against her throat, her jaw, her cheek. He tasted the warm salt of her tears, ached to make them his own. "I'm so sorry, my angel."

"Hold me, Richard. Do not let go. Please do not let go."

Richard slipped one arm behind her knees and lifted her. She hugged him tight and he bent to press his cheek to hers.

Rhys stood rigid, his face carefully devoid of emotion. He brushed past them. Without turning, he said, "I'll show you where to take her."

Elinor, Princess of Wales, cousin to King Edward I, slipped into a deep sleep and did not awaken. She died three days later of childbed fever.

When the physician delivered the news to the group gathered in the solar, Llywelyn pushed to his feet, then shoved his way into his wife's sickroom, calling her name. Richard caught Gwen when she tried to follow.

"Let me go," she hissed, struggling.

Richard wrapped his arms around her and held her tight. She slumped against him and started to cry. Alys dabbed at her own eyes with a scrap of silk, and Rhys stood and walked to the window to stare into the bleakness beyond.

Llywelyn emerged sometime later, the only evidence of his grief in the red rimming his eyes. Richard let Gwen go. She went to her father and hugged him.

He hugged her back, then pushed her away and wiped a tear from her cheek. "Don't cry, Gwen. Elinor would not have wanted you to cry," he said, his voice raw. "Have you seen your sister? She's beautiful, like her mother."

"Father— "

Llywelyn laid his finger against her lips. "Nay, lass." He looked up then, acknowledged Richard for the first time since they'd arrived. "Dunsmore."

"Prince Llywelyn." Strangely, face to face with his enemy, Richard could only summon pity. Where was the vengeance, the hatred, that had burned in his breast for so long?

Llywelyn rubbed Gwen's arm. "Did I tell you your sister's name, lass?"

Gwen shook her head. "Nay, Father."

His answering smile was sad, infinitely far away.

"Gwenllian. Elinor insisted on naming her Gwenllian." He squeezed her shoulder, then strode from the room.

She turned, caught Richard's gaze. His heart clenched at the way she looked at him, like he was her sole source of strength in the entire world. He swept her into his arms and carried her to their chamber.

With his foot, he dragged a chair over to the fire, and sank down on it. Gwen curled in his lap, clutching his surcoat in her fists.

She began to talk, telling him of Elinor and their friendship. He laid his cheek against her hair and listened, knowing she needed him to say nothing.

The light outside the windows faded and died, and still she talked. Eventually, her voice trailed off and he thought she was asleep. His hand strayed to her stomach, and her hand closed over his. "Are you afraid I will leave you, like Elinor left my father?"

"Nay," he lied. "You are too stubborn for that." He kissed her forehead. "You will stay just so you can vex me with your sharp little tongue."

In truth, he was more frightened than he'd ever been in his life.

She yawned. "I will not go, Richard. I will not leave you."

How could she promise that which she could not control?

"I know, my love."

Even when she fell asleep, Richard didn't move. He stared into the glowing embers of the fire and thought of the man who had killed his father. Where he'd once felt burning vengeance, he now felt nothing. Jesú, was he destined to always fail his father?

But what could he do that would be worse than the hell Llywelyn was now living? Aye, Richard recognized the pain on Llywelyn's face, the same pain William de Claiborne had gone through when his beloved Catrin died.

Losing the woman he loved was punishment enough for whatever sins Llywelyn may have committed in the past. Though the prince may have taken Richard's father, he had also given him Gwen.

Fear snaked through Richard, hard and cold. She promised not to leave him. She promised. How could he do any less for her?

Life was too short, too precious, to risk a moment of it. He would never live without her. He would never leave her.

He stood and carried her to the bed. She murmured something as he untied her laces. Carefully, he undressed her and tucked her beneath the covers. Her eyelids fluttered open and she entwined her arms around his neck, pulling him close.

He captured her lips in a soft kiss, his arms slipping beneath her to mold her body to his. "I cannot live without you, Gwen. I will take you across the sea, across mountains and deserts, through dust and heat and snow and ice, though you may hate me for it eventually."

She smiled a sleepy, sad smile. "I knew you would not leave me."

Richard lowered her to the mattress. Her arms slipped from his neck and her eyes drifted closed. He undressed and climbed in beside her, tucking her into the curve of his body.

No, he would not leave her. Now he prayed she would not leave him.

For the next few days, the Great Hall of the Prince of Wales was silent, mourning the death of one too young, too kind, too beautiful to die.

Gwen found her strength in Richard. Knowing he was there gave her the courage to deal with Elinor's death, and with her father's depression.

She directed the servants as Elinor would have wished, kept the hall running smoothly, and selected one of Elinor's ladies to take over the task when she was gone.

She was busy going over the meal plan with the cook when Richard found her. He waited patiently until she sent the man on his way.

"What is it, Richard?" she asked, slipping into his embrace, uncaring they stood in the hall.

"We must return to Claiborne, sweet. 'Tis nearing time for the council."

"Oh," she said quietly, staring at his chest.

He raised her chin with a finger. "It cannot be helped, Gwen. I've waited as long as I could. Now that the funeral is over, we must leave." He smiled softly. "Besides, I think Alys pines for Owain."

Gwen swallowed the lump that had risen in her throat. "Aye, you are right. We must go home. 'Tis just that I worry about him…"

"I know, love. But he needs time alone, I think. There is nothing more you can do."

Gwen nodded. "When?"

"In the morning," he said, kissing her on the forehead.

He left her to finish the tasks she'd begun, but she sank onto a bench instead. She'd wanted to ask her father about Dafydd's claim, but there would be no time now. It was too soon to think of such things.

She noticed a group of her father's warriors staring at her. She didn't realize Rhys was with them until he stood and made his way toward her. He clutched a silver goblet in his hand, and when he sank onto the bench beside her, some of the mead sloshed over the rim and ran down his arm.

"How could you do it, Gwen?"

"Do what?" she asked, meeting his blood-shot stare.

"Do you know what they say about you?" he demanded, gesturing toward the men, spilling more mead down the side of his cup. "They say you are an Englishman's whore, Black Hawk's whore."

Gwen stiffened. "I am his wife."

"Aye, but you enjoy lying with him. You enjoy letting him touch you. You lick his bootheels like a bitch in heat."

"You have had too much mead, Rhys," Gwen said coolly, rising.

Rhys grabbed her wrist and pulled her back down. Gwen tried to twist free, but his grip only tightened. "You love the bloody bastard, don't you?"

Gwen glared at him. "Yes."

Rhys's grip loosened and she snatched her hand away. "Jesú, Gwen. How could you? You said you hated him. What happened?"

Gwen rubbed her wrist and sighed. "He is not what you think, Rhys. I did not plan to love him, but I do."

Rhys laughed. "He isn't what I think, eh? Do you plan to tell me he doesn't kill Welshmen? That he has never gone to war against us? That he does not enforce the king's laws—laws designed to punish us for being Welsh?"

"Nay," she said quietly, her eyes downcast.

"And you still love him, despite all that?"

"Aye."

Rhys shoved himself to his feet. "Then you *are* a traitor, just like everyone says."

35

The last of the snow melted away, leaving meadows of rippling green-gold silk. Thrushes chittered in the trees, too busy to notice the bright clusters of fragrant lilies blooming all around.

The journey to Devizes castle in Wessex was not unpleasant. Once in a while, Richard let Sirocco have his head and the stallion raced with the joy of a colt. Springtime was not just pleasurable to humans.

Richard had put off leaving Claiborne as long as possible, giving himself less than a week to make the one-hundred-and-fifty mile trip.

He worried about Gwen, though she swore she was fine. She was four months pregnant now, and he was more in love with her every day. She was often melancholy since they'd returned from Snowdon. He didn't ask her about it, though it hurt him to see her sad. She hadn't spoken of Elinor since the day she'd sat in his lap and told him everything about her friend. He didn't think she even realized some of the things she'd told him.

She'd shared everything with Elinor: the dreams she'd had of him, the first time he'd kissed her, the fear of being his wife. It brought a smile to his lips to know she'd thought of him as much as he'd thought of her.

His party arrived at Devizes on the Friday before Palm Sunday. He wasn't pleased to learn they still had to await the arrival of a handful of barons. By the time the middle of the following week rolled around, his anger was full-blown.

He and Edward took wine in a bright, spacious solar with the shutters thrown wide to let in the spring air.

Edward sat in the window seat and gazed outside. The breeze ruffled his hair, fluttering the golden strands between sunlight and shadow. He leaned back against the stone. The breeze whipped higher, just for a moment, as though protesting the temporary loss of Christendom's greatest warrior-king.

He turned to Richard, who sat in full sunlight with his booted feet propped on the table, brooding.

"Gloucester says the Welsh in the south have been unusually quiet all winter long. What of the north?"

Richard stirred. The warm sunshine could put a man to sleep in no time. He lifted his goblet and took a swallow of sweet wine. He stared at the crimson liquid, thinking of a woman garbed in exactly that color.

"Richard?"

"Nay, nothing in the north. Not since the raid before I left for London."

"What think you it means?"

Richard shrugged. "Mayhap they are finally accepting the new order. Or mayhap they mourn their prince's loss."

Edward sighed. "Aye. My poor little cousin. Her life was not what it should have been."

Richard studied the swirl of liquid in his goblet. "I was there, Ned. Llywelyn was devastated."

"You were there when she died? Jesú, how?"

"Gwen. She had a feeling something would happen. She insisted I take her."

Edward chuckled. "Black Hawk de Claiborne is not catering to a woman's whims, is he?"

Richard laughed. "Aye, I've gone soft."

"Yes, well, being in love will do that to a man. How does she fare with the pregnancy?"

"She is well." Richard closed his eyes, reveling in the warmth of the sun's golden rays. He'd not told Edward he was in love. Was it that obvious? "Mayhap a bit spoiled. You would not believe the things she has me do."

Edward laughed. "Oh yes I would, my friend. The king of England is like any other man when it comes to a pregnant wife. She has no respect for my royal dignity, I can assure you."

"I am bringing her with me, Ned," Richard said softly.

"Aye, well Eleanor will enjoy her company," he replied.

They sat for a while longer, each lost in his own thoughts. Richard put the empty cup on the table and leaned his head back. He must have dozed because the sound of approaching hoofbeats didn't register until he heard voices raised in alarm.

He was on his feet instantly, as was Edward. Richard started for the door, but Edward motioned him back.

"Nay, Richard. The king does not go to the news, the news comes to the king."

He smiled wryly, and Richard thought of the impatient prince he used to know. Too many years had passed since the prince became a king; a king who understood the necessity of allowing men their moments of glory.

They didn't have long to wait. The earls of Gloucester and Pembroke, along with Roger de Mortimer, the lord of Wigmore, burst into the room with a mud-caked man in front of them.

"Majesty," the man gulped, sinking to his knees. "The Welsh are in rebellion."

Gloucester, Pembroke, and de Mortimer began talking at once. Edward cut them off with a glare. His blue eyes glittered. "What?" he said, his voice dangerously low.

The man took a deep breath. "They've taken Hawarden castle. They've torched the town and put several of Your Majesty's men to death, including the justiciar."

Apprehension tingled down Richard's spine. Hawarden was on the northern coast, near Chester, not twenty miles from Claiborne.

Edward was on the edge of a Plantagenet tantrum. His face was mottled, his jaw working furiously. "Christ almighty! When did it happen?"

"Three days past, Majesty."

"Llywelyn has lost his mind," Richard said, half to himself.

The messenger's gaze flew to him. "Nay, milord. 'Twas not Lly-welyn."

"Who?" Edward demanded.

The man swallowed. "Dafydd ap Gruffydd."

Edward exploded. "Goddamn fucking whoreson! I gave that bastard everything, everything!"

"Dafydd?" Richard asked. "You are sure?"

The man nodded. "Aye, milord. 'Tis Dafydd and he has the backing of a sizable army."

"What word of Llywelyn?"

"None, milord. He's not been seen with Dafydd."

Edward paced back and forth, lightning quick. "Goddamn Welsh bastards! I'm through with them, through!" He whirled to face Richard. "I want them stopped, Richard. I want Dafydd's head on a pike, and I want those bloody Welsh put in their place once and for all."

Richard let the cold reality of duty wash over him, cleansing his soul. God would forgive him, though Gwen might not. "The first thing we should do is demand Llywelyn honor his vow of fealty. He must come to the field on the side of England and his liege lord."

Edward nodded. "Aye, 'twill split Wales in twain." He turned to Roger de Mortimer. "Get me a scribe and a messenger."

"What of the crusade, Majesty?" de Mortimer asked.

"To hell with the bloody crusade," Edward snapped. "'Tis war with Wales, man!"

Gwen plucked a rose, careful to avoid the sharp thorns. She lifted it to her nose and inhaled the sweet scent of springtime. She picked up her skirts and kept walking along the water's edge.

The day was bright and beautiful. She hadn't been able to stay within the walls of Claiborne for one more minute. Richard had been gone for almost a month and she missed him terribly. Mayhap a walk in the open would take her mind off him for a while.

Her escort sat at the top of the hill, talking. Gwen didn't have to guess what they discussed.

The whole castle was alive with talk of the Welsh uprising. She was sick of hearing about it. Dafydd was a rebel, nothing more. The Welsh followed her father. Dafydd's attempt at glory would fail because he wouldn't have the support to keep going for very long.

The sun was high overhead, bathing the verdant meadow in life-giving warmth. The river roared past, swollen with the melting snows from the mountains beyond. The air chorused with birdsong.

Vaguely, she heard hoofbeats. She spared a glance for her escort and saw they waved at the riders. She couldn't see who approached, nor did she care. Messengers were always coming and going these days.

Alys came from farther down the bank, her basket brimming over with flowers and herbs. Gwen smiled. Alys was happier than she'd ever seen her. She and Owain still tried to pretend there was nothing between them, but Gwen knew better. How could she not recognize the signs? She knew what it meant to love a man so much it hurt.

At least Alys loved a Welshman.

Gwen was accustomed to the small stab of pain in her heart by now. Rhys's accusation still hurt, but no doubt it was the truth. Maybe one day he would understand.

Gwen sank into a fragrant patch of clover. Alys sat beside her. "'Tis a lovely day, my lady. It makes the heart light to be alive on such a day."

"Aye," Gwen said, lying back against the hill and closing her eyes. "I wish it were always like this."

"Mmm, well I think I will walk a bit further down," Alys said, rising.

"Very well, Alys. I'm feeling too lazy to move right now," Gwen said. She heard Alys shuffle off, singing, and she stretched her arms above her head, arching her back against the soft clover.

She started to yawn, shock stilling her but a moment as a male mouth captured hers. Her eyes flew open at the same instant her knee drove into his groin and her fist connected with his jaw.

"Richard!"

He sat back and rubbed the side of his face. "Thank God for chain-mail," he said. "You might never know marital bliss again otherwise."

Gwen threw her arms around his neck and tumbled him backwards on the hillside. "Oh Richard, I am sorry," she said, planting quick kisses on his jaw. "You should not have frightened me like that."

He rolled her onto her back. "Kiss me, Princess," he whispered huskily.

Gwen pulled his head down, fusing her mouth to his. Her tongue slipped between his lips, engaging him in a love play that left them both breathless.

"I have missed you, Richard."

"Mmm, you seek to make me forget I am angry with you, my angel."

"Angry? But I would not have hit you if you hadn't snuck up on me."

"'Tis not what I am talking about. You should not be out here. 'Tis too dangerous with Dafydd so close by."

Gwen laughed. "Dafydd is harmless. He will not last for long. The Welsh will not follow a traitor."

His face clouded for an instant, then he reached above her head and picked up the forgotten rose. He smelled it, then trailed the soft petals from her temple to her lips.

"I should like to make love to you on a bed of rose petals," Richard said. "I would rub the petals over your soft skin and then—"

"Sweet heaven, if you do not take me home now, I will scream!"

Richard laughed. "You have a way of making a man feel very much like a man, my love." He stood and pulled her up with him. "I believe being pregnant has made you lustier."

Gwen stamped her foot. "Oh you are an insensitive beast, Richard de Claiborne! You provoke my desire apurpose, then tease me with your prattling."

"Prattling?" Richard exclaimed with mock indignance. Gwen started marching toward her horse, but he grabbed her and swung her high. She braced her hands on his shoulders, giggling down in his face as her hair fell forward to curtain them. "I will show you prattling, wench," he growled.

Richard buried his face in the hollow between her breasts, pressing hot kisses through the silk fabric. She threw her head back and laughed. He slid her down his body, kissing her throat, her chin, her lips, the tip of her nose, her forehead.

God how he wanted to take her right here beneath the brilliant turquoise sky!

They rode back to the castle, and she slipped away to their chamber while he saw to his men and the readying of the garrison. The royal host, some twelve-thousand men strong, was gathering in Worcester. Soon, they would march to Chester.

And tomorrow Richard rode north to take command of the men amassing at Rhuddlan.

But this day was for other things.

When he finally managed to get away, Gwen awaited him, dressed only in her chemise. She came to him and began to remove his armor. He helped her, unwilling to allow her to strain herself.

His arousal bulged against the cloth of his undergarments and she shot him a smug smile. "Who is the lusty one now, my lord?" she teased softly.

"You are a wicked wench."

She only laughed. When he was naked, he tried to pull her in his arms, but she evaded him. "Nay, I must bathe you first."

"'Tis some new Welsh torture device, is it not?" he grumbled as he sank into the steaming water.

She unstoppered a bottle and dribbled golden oil across the surface. The scent of roses drifted to him on curls of steam.

"Jesú, now you seek to make me smell like a pampered whore!"

Her only answer was a saucy smile.

He tried to remain unaffected as her hands moved over him, but his lust only grew until he thought he would die of it. He sucked in his breath when her hand brushed over his hard shaft.

That was the end of all pretense of patience. She gasped when he stood, then ran when he followed, naked and dripping.

"Richard! You are wet!" she cried, scrambling onto the middle of the bed.

"Aye, and so shall you be," he said, crawling after her on all fours. She huddled against the headboard, trying not to laugh. When he got too close, she kicked at him playfully. He caught her ankles and pulled her beneath him.

"You are a vicious, teasing wench," he said, burying his lips against her throat.

"You are soaking me!"

"Certes, I hope so," he whispered hotly. "It makes the whole business much more pleasant when things slide together."

"You are insufferable."

"Aye."

"Incorrigible."

"Aye."

"Insatiable."

"Aye." His hand found the edge of her chemise. She grabbed at him when he tried to lift it away.

"Nay," she said in a rush. "I am fat and you will not wish to look at me."

"I want to see you," he said firmly.

Her lip trembled as he pulled the garment up and off. "You are beautiful," he whispered, dropping down to press fervent kisses to the mound of her belly. "Beautiful."

He retrieved the rosebud from where he'd left it on his tunic, then returned to tickle her with it while his lips followed the trail he made.

When he slipped it between her legs and rubbed it over the swollen petals of her womanhood, Gwen's breath caught on a moan of pure pleasure. Never had she experienced anything so erotic.

"Let us see which tastes sweeter," he murmured, "you or the rose."

Gwen cried out as his tongue slid within her folds. Her fingers clutched his dark head until he turned her and lifted her astride him.

"Oh, sweet merciful God," he groaned, his eyes closing as they began to move together.

Much later, when they lay entwined in the sheets and each other, and the late-day sunshine streamed in the windows and cut a swath across the bed, Gwen pressed her lips to his throat and said, "I am so glad you are home."

She felt him stiffen and she pulled back to gaze at him. "You are going to fight Dafydd," she stated. She knew even before he answered.

He sighed. "Aye, Gwen."

"When?"

He tucked a stray lock of hair behind her ear. "I must leave on the morrow."

She forced a smile, but her heart fell in her breast. "It should not take long for you to beat him then. He cannot have half the men they say he does."

"Gwen..." He drew in a deep breath. "Ah Christ, I wish I didn't have to tell you this, but I would rather you hear it from me."

"What?"

He raked a hand through his tousled hair. "Your father is a vassal of the king of England. When he swore his oath of fealty, he agreed to uphold the king's writ, the king's law, and to come to the field in defense of the king if necessary."

"Yes, I know that, but—"

"Dafydd does indeed have a large army, Gwen. I know not how, but he has the support of several of your father's chieftains. Edward has demanded your father obey his oath and come to the field for England—"

"Nay! 'Twill be Welsh against Welsh! He will not do it!"

"Yes, well, he is trying to remain neutral, but he cannot for much longer. Everywhere, the Welsh rise in sympathy. They've torched the king's castles, stormed towns and killed English citizens. 'Tis war, Gwen. 'Tis not merely a rebellion, 'tis war."

Gwen pressed her palms to her eyes, willing herself not to cry.

War.

Goddamn Dafydd to hell! She knew her father, knew his pride. He would not fight for England. He would hold out if he could, but if forced he would come to war on the side of Wales. That was the one thing the bloody English never could understand. Welshmen were fiercely loyal and fiercely patriotic. And so were Welshwomen.

"And if he does not obey?"

"Then 'tis war against him as well."

She dropped her hands to her lap. "You would fight my father?"

"Yes, *cariad*, I would fight your father," he said softly. "'Tis my duty."

He didn't stop her when she left the bed and shrugged into her robe. She settled into the windowseat and stared at the green valley dotted with sheep.

Richard and her father. They would meet on the field of battle. She knew it with a certainty.

She heard Richard get out of bed and walk to the table to pour wine. She glanced at him, and found she couldn't look away. He stood in a beam of sunshine, fully naked, his bronze form so hard and magnificent that her breath caught. He was a beautiful, beautiful man.

She pictured him in a cave of glittering lights with the sweet perfume of roses all around. And then a man with golden hair said, "*Choose*."

"Gwen?"

She jerked. "Aye?" she said, her heart thudding.

He came to her and sank on one knee. "I know 'tis hard for you. I would spare you if I could, but you have a right to know," he said, stroking her cheek.

"Yes, thank you for telling me, Richard."

"We only have tonight. I do not wish it spoiled by any more talk of war."

She threaded her fingers through his and kissed his palm. "Nay, no more talk of war."

They didn't emerge from their chamber at all that night. Alys brought the evening meal up, and they fed each other bits of meat and fruit, then made love by moonlight in the windowseat.

When it was over, Richard carried her to bed and she fell asleep in his arms, not even caring that the only light was provided by the moon. As long as Richard held her close, she was safe from the darkness.

She was awakened by the sounds of chinking metal when the sky was just beginning to pinken. She sat up and saw Richard slipping into his hauberk.

"You were not going to leave without saying goodbye, were you?"

Richard spun around. Jesú, he'd hoped to spare her the pain of departure. He'd intended to be long gone before she awakened. "We said goodbye last night, *cariad*. Or have you forgotten?" he teased, suddenly wishing he could love her one more time.

On her knees, she came to the end of the bed, clutching the coverlet in front of her. "Nay, 'twas not enough. Kiss me again, Richard. Make it last."

Richard gave in to the temptation, though he told himself he should not. He pulled her soft body against him. She moaned when his tongue met hers. He kissed her, and kissed her, and kissed her, until she was breathless and clinging to him.

Then he stepped back enough to let the coverlet fall and reveal her naked body.

He kissed the valley between her breasts, then the soft swell of their child. Her fingers threaded in his hair.

"I know not how long I will be gone, Gwen." He captured her lips once again. "But I promise you I will return when 'tis time for the babe."

"I love you, Richard. God keep you safe," she whispered.

He tore himself away. Before he lost his will to leave, he forced his feet to keep moving until he was out of the room and down the stairs.

Owain stopped him as he was crossing the hall. "Be careful, boy."

Richard clasped the older man's shoulder. "Take care of her for me."

"I will indeed, milord."

Fifty knights and men-at-arms waited in the bailey. Destriers pawed the ground, eager to be off. Richard swung onto Sirocco and surveyed the castle. A garrison stayed behind to defend it if the Welsh attacked. Though Claiborne was designed to be impregnable, he prayed they would not have to find out.

He turned to find Andrew staring at him. "What?" he grumbled, though he had a good idea.

Andrew smiled. "Why I was just thinking how pretty ye smell, milord. Certes, the enemy will appreciate how clean ye are."

"Perhaps I should leave you behind, Sir Andrew."

Andrew laughed. "And disappoint my new squire?"

Richard sighed. Tristan of Ashford looked every bit of his nine years as he eagerly awaited the advent of the journey. "Mayhap that is all the more reason."

"The boy will be fine, milord. You were riding the patrols at his age."

Richard nodded in resignation. Yes, he'd ridden the patrols at the age of seven. Seen his first battle when he was eight. Killed a man when he was ten.

He'd been killing ever since.

As they started forward, Richard turned around in the saddle. He couldn't shake a sense of loss, and he knew it must be because he'd only just returned and had to leave her again so soon.

He sought the master chamber. She stood there, watching. Their eyes met across the distance and she blew him a kiss. He touched his hand to his lips before turning and riding out the gates of Claiborne.

Her scent would haunt him all the way to Rhuddlan and beyond.

36

Gwen meandered through the castle gardens. Roses and violets perfumed the air while bees and butterflies flitted between them.

She stroked her middle lovingly. The action made Richard seem not so far away. Part of him was here, inside her, and she cherished it.

Though he'd been gone over a fortnight, the memory of their last evening together was as real as if it had happened only yesterday. She caught a rose in her hand and bent to bury her nose in its scent. Her cheeks heated. Lord, she would never look at a rose the same again!

"Milady!"

"Over here, Owain," she called. Her heart skipped a beat at the look on his face. She straightened and took a halting step forward. "What is it? 'Tis not Richard? He is not—?"

"Nay!" Owain hurried to her side and wrapped a strong arm around her shoulders. "Nay, milady! Jesú, I am sorry for frightening you."

She clutched his arm, weak with relief. "'Tis all right, Owain. Mayhap I worry too much."

He led her to a bench and helped her sit. "Richard would have my hide for scaring you."

"Nay, I am well." She flashed him a bright smile to prove it. She truly was well as long as Richard was alive somewhere. "What is it you wanted of me?"

His face hardened. He spat at his feet. "That whore, Anne Ashford, begs admittance. Says she fears for her household's safety with the Welsh ravaging the countryside. She desires our protection."

Gwen laughed. "Oh Owain, you are a treasure! Let the woman in. She is one of Richard's tenants, after all. Probably 'tis safer inside Claiborne."

Owain gaped. "But-but, she is a-a…"

"You may say it, Owain. She was Richard's mistress." Gwen shrugged. "It no longer matters to me."

He swallowed, his eyes wide. "As you say, milady. I will tell the guards to let them in."

Gwen watched him go. It truly didn't matter that Anne was once Richard's lover. Anne may have known the pleasure of his body, for which Gwen seriously disliked her, but she could have never known the depth of feeling Gwen experienced with him.

As much as Gwen would have liked to have been his first and only lover, she would settle for being his first and only love.

It didn't take Anne long to seek her out, as Gwen knew it would not. She waited patiently on the bench, arranging the folds of her gown. She was still small enough that she could hide her pregnancy when seated.

"Lady de Claiborne, how lovely to see you again," Anne said, sashaying toward her. "'Tis most kind of you to allow my household refuge."

"'Tis the duty of the Countess of Dunsmore to see to her husband's tenants' welfare in his absence. You are well come to Claiborne castle, Lady Ashford."

Anne smiled lamely, her gaze flickering over Gwen's body. "Oh 'tis such a pity! I would have surely thought you would be pregnant by now. But perhaps you are your father's daughter in more ways than one. Mayhap Richard will not mind too much. He can always get a bastard on one of his mistresses, I suppose. You will learn to live with it."

Gwen rose slowly. "I do not think that will be necessary, Lady Ashford."

Anne's eyes widened briefly as the fabric settled over Gwen's belly, then hardened to icy blue specks. "I see I was mistaken. You must be delighted," she said smoothly.

Gwen smiled. "Aye, we both are."

She brushed past Anne and headed for the castle. She waited until she was almost to the door before her laughter rang through the garden.

The days of spring were quickly turning to summer. Gwen tried to keep busy so she wouldn't worry about Richard too much. She was in the hall, overseeing the task of replacing the rushes, when Sir Edgar approached. A man dressed in peasant's rags trailed behind him, stooping, his limp so pronounced it was almost too painful to watch.

"Milady, this man begs an audience. I would have turned him away, but he claims he has news of Lord de Claiborne and will give it to no one but you." The knight shot the man a scathing glance, his look clearly begging Gwen to allow him to toss the peasant out.

Gwen stared at the stranger, her heart quickening. "You have news of my husband?"

The man raised his head and winked.

She stifled a gasp. "Thank you, Sir Edgar, I will hear what this man has to say. You have done well in bringing him to me."

Edgar bowed. "Aye, milady," he mumbled, his gaze raking over the peasant doubtfully.

The man limped into the solar behind her and shut the door. He straightened and threw back his hood. "Hello, Lady de Claiborne," he said, grinning.

"Rhys ap Gawain, are you mad?"

Rhys's eyes traveled the length of her body, pausing over her middle, before returning to her face. "Jesú, Gwen, you look lovely."

"What are you doing here? You do not really have news of Richard, do you?"

His expression fell a little. "Nay, I do not. Are you truly so eager to hear of him?"

"What do you want, Rhys?" Gwen asked, her hand settling over her stomach protectively.

Rhys sighed. "You are mad at me and I do not blame you. I am sorry for the things I said before. It was not your fault you had to marry him."

Gwen shook her head. "But, Rhys, I still lo—"

"Nay," he said, coming to her and putting his fingers over her lips. "Do not say it. I cannot bear to hear it."

Gwen dropped her eyes to his chest. He pulled her against him suddenly and rested his cheek on top of her head.

She stiffened and started to push away. But his embrace was nothing more than friendly, nothing more than the simple affection that still existed between childhood companions. She relaxed and let him hold her, slipping her arms loosely around his waist.

"I have come to tell you your father is going to war."

She didn't have to ask which side of the war. "I dreamed it," she whispered. "Last night, I dreamed it."

"What did you see?"

"I saw…" She swallowed. "I saw his face. His eyes were closed and he wore a crown of ivy. But then I realized it was only his head—on a pike, Rhys!—and it was displayed over the Tower of London's walls. People came to stare and to laugh. They pointed and said, *there is Llywelyn, ruler of all of Britain.*"

"St. Dafydd's bones," he breathed.

"Don't you see, Rhys? He must not fight! You must tell him not to fight!"

Rhys let her go and sank heavily into a chair. "'Tis too late. The chieftains gather at Dolwyddelan. I just returned from the north, where Dafydd is fighting. Soon, we will strike in the south. 'Tis too late to turn back."

"Nay!" Gwen cried. "I am going with you! I will tell him. He will listen to me!"

Rhys shot to his feet. "You are pregnant!"

"I must warn him, Rhys. You cannot deny me that," Gwen said, glaring at him. If she didn't try her best to dissuade her father, then she truly was a traitor. Deep down, she did not expect he would really listen. But there were things as yet unsaid between them, truths she needed to know. If he went to war and something happened to him, she might never know.

Richard would understand. She would return soon and when he came home for the babe, she would tell him what she had done. He would understand it was something she'd had to do.

Rhys scowled.

"Please, Rhys," she said. "'Tis important to me."

He heaved a sigh. "Very well, I will take you with me, though I do not like it a bit."

It wasn't hard getting out of the castle, though it should have been. Despite Richard's orders to the contrary, Gwen still ventured from the protective walls on occasion.

This day, she left Alys behind and took her escort for a ride in the open. She wandered aimlessly through the meadows until the knights relaxed their guard.

"Sir Edgar?"

"Aye, milady?"

"I find I must relieve myself," she said, blushing enough to make it believable. "Would you and the men wait here while I slip into the woods for a moment?"

His eyes darted over the valley. "Mayhap we should return to the castle, milady."

"Oh nay, I cannot wait that long! 'Twill only take a moment." She flashed him a smile.

He cleared his throat. "As you wish, milady."

Once beneath the protective cover of the forest, she urged Saffron into a trot. A pang of guilt stabbed through her, but she ignored it. She'd left a note where Alys could find it.

When she reached Rhys and his men, they were mounted and waiting. Twenty men garbed in traditional Welsh scarlet-wool, with bare legs and leather jerkins, carrying spears and longbows. It was a vastly different picture than chainmail and shields and steam-blowing chargers.

"We must hurry," she said. "We only have a few minutes until they know I've gone."

But Welshmen were more at home in the woods than armored knights. They lost their pursuers easily, slipping higher and higher into the waiting mountains.

By the time they arrived at Dolwyddelan a few days later, the gathering of chieftains and warriors had swelled to numbers unheard of in all Llywelyn's years of leading the Welsh. For once, the entire country seemed united in the quest against England.

When Gwen finally got in to see him, his jaw dropped. "What are you doing here?"

"You look well, Father," she said.

"Lass, what are you doing here?" he demanded, his amber eyes flashing as they flickered over her middle.

She laid her hand on his arm. "I had a dream."

"You should not be on your feet," he said softly. He ushered her to a chair, then took the one across from it. "Now tell me of this dream."

When she finished, he smiled sadly. "Ah, Gwenllian, it matters not. Sometimes I think 'twould be easier to leave this life altogether. I will see this through to the end this time. If that is indeed the end, so be it."

"'Tis the curse."

He shook his head. "There is no curse. 'Tis a bard's tale. Your mother was a sweet, beautiful lass who would hurt no one. No matter how much they hurt her," he added almost absently.

"Are you my father?" she blurted, unable to hold the question back any longer.

His eyes widened, then he passed a hand over his face. "Yes," he said after a long moment. Gwen didn't say anything and he raised his head to look at her. "Were you expecting a different answer?"

"Aye. 'Twould explain so much if you'd said no."

"I've never had much luck at siring children. I was a fool to believe the things suggested to me of your mother. Since Elinor died, I've thought of many things I would have changed if I could. I've lost two women I loved in my life. I've let duty come before things I never knew were important until they were gone.

"I should have never doubted Eurwen. I've paid for it for years. If I pushed you away, lass, 'twas my own guilt that caused it and no fault of your own."

Gwen brushed aside the tears trickling down her cheeks. She clenched her hands in her lap to keep them from shaking. "I wanted to hate you for giving me as a hostage. I wanted to hate you for giving me to Black Hawk de Claiborne. But I never could." She laughed bitterly. "Christ, I wanted you to tell me I was not your daughter so I could finally hate you for all you did to me!"

"You have every right to feel that way, though I do not wish you to."

Gwen dabbed her eyes with her sleeve. "'Tis funny, but I never even realized it until this moment. I *wanted* to hate you, but you have taken that from me too."

"I am sorry, Gwen," he said softly.

"Did you even know the things I did for you? How much I wanted your attention?"

"Nay," he whispered, his expression both pained and distant.

"The first time you ever took me anywhere with you, I was so proud. And then, then—do you remember what happened then?" she asked, her anger building. She didn't give him a chance to reply. "You gave me as a hostage, then sent Einion to tell me why! I was devastated, and when I saw you again, you didn't even apologize.

"And then you gave me to *Gwalchddu*. But when you defied the king and applied to the pope to stop the marriage, I was certain you cared for me. But it was not for me, was it? It was nothing more than a power play!"

He rubbed his forehead absently. "I have wronged you, lass, and I'm sorry. I wish I could recall all the years I lost with you, but I cannot."

Gwen gazed at him, and felt her anger fading. He looked like an old man. It surprised her, though it should not. He was fifty-four, the years beginning to weigh heavily on him. He looked more tired, mayhap thinner, than when she had seen him last.

The fight leached out of her. "Well, Father, you managed to do one thing right, though I did not believe it at the time."

"Dunsmore?"

"Aye. I love him. He has more than filled the empty space in my life and my heart."

"You cannot know how much that pleases me. 'Tis true I tried to keep you from marrying him for selfish reasons—the alliance with Scotland, Arwystli—but I did worry for your safety with him." A sudden smile creased his weatherworn face. "I should have known you'd charm the savage beast. 'Tis what your mother did to me."

Gwen's tone became earnest. "You should not fight, Father. Sit it out on Snowdon. Let the English subdue Dafydd."

Llywelyn shook his head. "Nay, lass. 'Tis gone far beyond that now. Edward strangles us with his laws, starves us with his empty promises." He steepled his fingers. "I was hunting recently. We shot a stag, then chased it through the woods, following the trail of blood. It crossed the Teifi tributary and we pursued. 'Twas a Welsh stag, shot on Welsh land after all. Do you know that Edward's officials heard the cry of the hunting horn and came after us since we'd crossed into English territory? They seized the stag as their own, took the hounds, and imprisoned half my retinue. I had to pay handsomely to get my men back, though I never got the stag or the hounds."

"'Tis unfair!"

"Aye. And that is the way Edward deals with us, Gwen. Unfairly. We will allow it no longer."

He stood and helped her up, then hugged her to him in a surprisingly strong embrace. It took her a full minute to respond. As she'd wanted to do all her life, she wrapped her arms around him, and felt the answering pressure of his around her.

"You are my true daughter, Gwenllian. Never doubt it." He kissed her on the forehead. "You must return to your husband before this war gets ugly."

Gwen searched his face. This could well be the last battle of his life, the last of Wales' life. In that instant, she made her decision. "I am not leaving."

"You must, Gwen. I am at war with England. Dunsmore will not understand your presence here."

Gwen pushed away from him. "Nevertheless, I am staying."

Her heart thudded painfully, despite her brave words. Richard might not understand. He might never forgive her. She was risking everything.

But she was Welsh above all else. She could not abandon her father, her countrymen, on the eve of a war that meant life or death for Wales.

Richard had his duty. She had hers. God help them both.

37

News of Prince Llywelyn's alliance with Dafydd spread the length and breadth of Wales in a matter of days. Everywhere, the Welsh rose in great numbers. They attacked English castles, setting fires that left nothing but smoking ruins in their wake. They besieged towns and killed hated Englishmen who had previously suppressed them.

Never before had the Welsh been so determined. They pushed through the Marches, from Chester in the north to the Bristol Channel in the south. They fought across South Wales, from Chepstow castle at the mouth of the Wye to Pembroke castle on the west coast.

In the north, Dafydd attacked both Flint and Rhuddlan castles with a vengeance. Neither fell to him, though many others went up in flames.

Richard held Rhuddlan with one hundred men, confident the king would reach them long before Dafydd could manage to starve them out.

He thought of Gwen often. He worried about her, but he reasoned that if Dafydd were here, he could not be besieging Claiborne. If any stray bands of Welshmen attacked the castle, they would be repelled easily enough.

When Edward arrived with the army in mid-July, Dafydd fled to the hills to regroup. Richard and Edward sat in the same solar they had once shared with Dafydd and discussed how to proceed.

The king's strategy was simple. He would secure the coast, then build mighty fortresses to hold it. Ringing Gwynedd with English castles would assure future dominion over the volatile principality.

Eight-thousand-foot soldiers and four-thousand-mounted knights made the trek from Worcester. Of that number, nearly a thousand were crossbowmen. The experimental longbowmen numbered half that.

Fifteen-hundred-woodsmen also accompanied the army, hacking a mile-wide path through the dense forests to build roads. Edward's aim was to make Wales easy to access for English merchants and settlers.

He stood at the window and gazed out over the sprawling army encamped outside Rhuddlan's walls. "I've sent the earl of Surrey into the Vale of Clwyd to secure the territory south of Snowdonia. Forty ships from London and the Cinque Ports are on their way to Anglesey. We'll block the Menai Strait, same as before. If this campaign continues into winter, Llywelyn will find himself without a harvest."

"Who is in command of the vessels?" Richard asked.

"Luke de Tany."

"The old seneschal of Gascony? Jesú, Ned, he is an impatient man. Are you certain he is suited for this game of hide-and-seek?"

Edward waved a hand. "Aye, he will be fine. He knows he is to secure the Strait, then await my orders."

"Any word from Llywelyn?"

"Nay, though the archbishop of Canterbury has threatened him with excommunication if he does not yield." Edward clasped his hands behind his back. "I think Llywelyn means to see it through this time, Richard. Victory or annihilation."

Richard thought of Llywelyn's stricken face when he'd been told of his wife's death. "Aye," he said softly. "I think you are right, Ned. Mayhap he feels he has nothing left to lose."

Within a few days, the army moved west, toward Conway and the Menai Strait. The garrisons at Rhuddlan and Flint were secured and Richard joined the king.

They received word of Llywelyn's sorties in the south and west. He stormed Aberystwyth and took Llanbadarn castle, then cut across the center of Wales to Montgomery, taking towns and besting English forces led by the Marcher earls.

Dafydd swooped down out of the mountains to engage Edward's army, then disappeared back into the gullies and ravines the Welsh knew best.

As the middle of August approached, Richard prepared to return to Claiborne. Since Dafydd insisted on playing cat and mouse, and Llywelyn had not yet realized the threat Edward's triple offensive placed on Gwynedd, there was no need for Richard to stay.

He took twenty men and set out for Claiborne. Within three days, they were in the valley of the Dee without encountering any resistance along the way.

When Richard rode into the bailey of his castle, he sensed something was wrong. The guards looked at him with wary eyes. The servants scurried in the other direction.

Owain came to greet him, his face drained of all color. The dark circles under his eyes told of many sleepless nights.

Richard's heart stopped beating in that instant. "Gwen?"

"Richard, she—"

He shoved past Owain, not stopping when the Welshman called to him. He raced through the hall and up the steps, then flung the chamber door wide. He stopped in the center of the room, spinning around.

"Where is she?" he demanded when Owain appeared in the doorway, red-faced. "What have you done with her?"

"She is gone, Richard. We searched but we did not find—"

"Searched?" Richard braced his arm on the table for support. Dear God, he'd thought her dead, but if they'd searched, that meant she was alive. Then the significance of Owain's words hit him.

"Searched?" he repeated in a roar. "What the bloody hell do you mean, *searched*?"

"She disappeared one day. We thought she'd been captured, but—"

"When?"

Owain swallowed. "Two and a half months."

Richard gripped his sword so hard he could feel the imprint of the carved hilt cutting into his flesh. The pain was a welcome respite from the hot rage threatening to consume him. "You had better have a damn good reason for not sending for me, old man, or I swear I will kill you where you stand."

"Goddammit, kill me then! 'Twould be a relief after the hell I've been through these months past. Besides, she wasn't abducted, she left. She wrote Alys a note, though we didn't find it for a couple of days."

"Get me the note," was all Richard could manage.

Owain left, then returned with Alys. The two didn't speak, or look at each other, though Richard hardly cared what had happened between them.

Alys held out the scrap of parchment, and Richard snatched it. It was written in Welsh. The writing was sloppy, as if scribbled at the last minute.

Alys,

I have gone to my father. Do not worry, Rhys is with me.
I will see you soon.

Gwenllian

"What does this mean, she will see you soon?" Richard demanded.

Alys started to cry. "I know not, my lord, truly. I have already told Owain. I know not."

Owain's jaw tightened. "I sent a messenger. You never came."

"I never got it," Richard said numbly. "Rhuddlan was besieged."

Gwen was with Rhys ap Gawain. Rhys, whose face had so clearly told Richard the feelings he still harbored for Gwen. Feelings mayhap she returned.

The black rage that had consumed him so briefly when he'd found her in Rhys's arms returned in full force, eating at him until he thought he would explode.

"Out," he snapped. The two of them stared at him, sympathy written on their faces. It was more than he could take. *"Out, goddammit, before I kill you both!"*

Alys scurried away first, wiping her eyes on her sleeve. Owain backed out, pulling the door shut behind him. "She will return, Richard. She loves—"

Richard picked up the chair and threw it at the door. It crashed against the wood, splintering into three large pieces.

He sent the table crashing with a booted foot to the edge. The other chair followed the first. Lying Welsh bitch! She promised she would never leave. It was a lie. Everything was a lie!

He stood in the middle of the room, his chest heaving. Gwen was gone. She'd chosen her father and Rhys over him. She had sworn she would never doubt him again and she had lied. Had she been planning her betrayal the entire time they'd been making love on that last night they shared?

His gaze settled on the bed and a sharp pain ripped through his heart. He went to it slowly, his eyes never straying from it as he relived every moment, every word, every caress, every kiss.

Oh God, how could she abandon him?

His foot hit something and he looked down to see he'd kicked one of Gwen's trunks. He opened it, and the scent of roses drifted to him. He sank to his knees and lifted one of the gowns. A rosepetal fluttered to the floor, brilliant crimson against dark wood.

Settling against the bed, he brought his knees to his chest and buried his face in the dress. For the first time in twenty-odd years, the frightened little boy won the battle, and the brutal Earl of Dunsmore wept soundlessly.

Night had fallen and the torches flickered with the summer breeze drifting through the open shutters of the castle. Anne smoothed her chemise over her curves before she entered the room.

At first she did not see him in the darkened chamber. Then her gaze landed on the figure slumped at the end of the bed. His head rested on a trunk, and women's clothes were strewn around him.

"Richard." She stood over him, waiting. "Richard..."

His head lolled back. "Gwen?"

Anne gritted her teeth. "Yes, darling. I am here."

He held up his hand and she took it. He pulled her across his lap, his hands entwining in her hair, his face buried against her throat. His voice was husky, breathless. "I knew you could not leave me. I knew it was a mistake. I cannot live without you, Gwen. I cannot…"

He stiffened. Anne cried out when he shoved her away. She landed on the floor with a thud. Then she laughed. "You never used to push me away. Nay, you used to bury that big weapon of yours deep inside—"

"Shut up, bitch," he growled. "I should snap your neck for that trick." He shot to his feet.

Anne felt a surge of triumph. Oh, this was much better than she'd imagined. Richard de Claiborne actually cared for a woman, actually hurt because she'd left him. "What is the matter, my lord?" she teased. "Have you never been jilted before?"

He jerked her up, then thrust her toward the door. "You are stretching my patience, Anne. And I have precious little of it left."

Anne clutched the door and glared at him. "She left you, like you left me. 'Tis the least you deserve."

He let go of her arm and surprisingly his voice softened. "I never desired anything more from you than sex, Anne. I am sorry if you expected more from me."

"*I* wouldn't have left you if you'd married me," she said bitterly. "I hope she never comes back!"

His eyes glittered in the torchlight leaking in from the passage. "It is not her choice to make."

He shoved her through the door and shut it. Anne stood there for a moment, angry and undecided.

It is not her choice to make.

Laughing, she clapped her hands together. Oh God, it was entirely too good to be true. Richard was going after his wife. In the middle of a war, he was riding into the heart of Wales.

Dawn had barely begun its ascent into the sky when Richard vaulted onto Sirocco and clattered through the gates. Owain stood in the bailey, but Richard didn't acknowledge him.

Ten knights accompanied their lord. Where he was going, more than that would only call attention to their presence.

Llywelyn was far south, but Richard didn't believe Gwen would be with him in her condition. Nay, she would be at Dolwyddelan, or high on Snowdon in Llywelyn's summer fast.

All through the night, he'd wanted to hate her. He'd told himself he hated her even while his heart felt as if it were splitting in two.

Actually, he owed Anne for showing him the folly of that line of reasoning. When he'd awakened and thought she was Gwen, the relief and love that flooded through him was blinding. He'd been willing to forgive her anything just to hold her again.

It was then he knew he would go after her. Gwen was his wife and he had no intentions of giving her up. He would lock her in her room if he had to. He would have her guarded every hour of the day. She would never leave him again.

Her lack of faith hurt. Her willingness to leave him and take their child hurt. He would never trust her, and he would never let her go.

They rode hard throughout the day, steadily climbing upwards. Wales was wild and beautiful, with its steep hills and plunging gullies, its mixture of green meadows and gray rocks, its oaks and conifers and standing stones.

Richard signaled a halt when they came to a ravine with sheer walls rising thirty feet on either side. They'd encountered no trouble so far, but Dafydd was too close for carelessness.

"Ye want to send a scout through first?" Andrew asked.

"Aye."

Andrew nodded and motioned to one of the knights.

Richard listened for any unusual sounds, but the only things he heard were birds and the wind in the treetops.

When the knight reached the other end of the narrow valley, he signaled. Richard urged Sirocco in first and the rest of the knights followed.

They were little more than halfway through when Welsh warcries shattered the air. Richard unsheathed his sword and charged. Men dropped into the ravine from overhead while others rushed in from both ends, closing the knights in and making escape impossible.

The clashing of steel and the whining of arrows echoed through the air. Richard dropped two Welshmen instantly. Four more replaced them, coming at him faster than he could swing his sword.

He heard the shouts of his men through the roaring in his ears. Screams of death came from both quarters. Sirocco reared and struck, but six men grabbed for his head and wrestled him down.

Richard spurred the stallion. Sirocco leapt forward, dragging the Welshmen who still held him. They were almost clear when Richard was knocked to the ground.

A man sat over him, grinning. Richard twisted beneath him, but the man didn't move. It was then he realized his arms and legs were pinned down.

The Welshman took out a knife and pressed it to Richard's neck. "*Gwalchddu*, I presume? 'Twill be an honor to carve your heart from your chest."

Just as the man raised the knife, he went sprawling across the grass.

Another man stood over him, his face mottled with fury. "Alive, you idiot! Dafydd wants Dunsmore alive!"

38

Dafydd's army was encamped high in the mountains and the trip up took several hours. Richard sat on Sirocco, his hands tied behind his back. His body ached from the fighting and the hard fall to the ground.

He eyed his sword, strapped to another man's side, with longing. They'd stripped him of it, along with his dagger, and he watched the polished metal gleaming in the sunshine with impotent anger.

Andrew rode beside him, silent and withdrawn. Behind them came the three other knights who had survived the ambush. All were nursing the aches and pains of the superior Welsh assault.

When they rode into camp and halted, the Welshman who had saved Richard's life jerked him off Sirocco and shoved him toward a large tent, speaking in broken French.

Dafydd stood when they entered. He was dressed in the short tunic and leather jerkin of his people, his auburn hair grown long and curly, his green eyes glittering with unrestained glee.

The man poked Richard in the ribs with a spear. "Kneel," he said.

Dafydd laughed. "'Tis no need for that, Steffan. And 'tis no need to strain your tongue by speaking French."

"But—"

"Black Hawk de Claiborne speaks Welsh just fine, don't you, *Gwalchddu?*"

Richard did not care to deny it. He fixed Dafydd with a look of contempt. "Do you think to ransom me back to the king? Be advised he might not be willing to pay much. Earls are hardly worth going in debt over."

Dafydd tilted his head to the side and scratched his beard. "Ransom? Now that is a possibility I had not considered. Actually, I thought killing you might be more to my pleasure."

Richard met his stare evenly. "That attack was planned. Who told you where to find me?"

A female voice, speaking in French, came from the entrance of the tent. "Dafydd, darling, do you have him?"

Richard spun around. Anne ducked in and flipped her hood from her golden head. "Oh, you do!"

She giggled, coming to him and smoothing her hands over his chest. Her touch made his flesh crawl. "Greetings, my love," she whispered.

Richard ground his teeth, his fury raging within him like a tempest. "You are nothing more than a whore, Anne. You have always sold your body for favors. What did Dafydd offer you? What was the price for becoming a traitor?"

Anne's face reddened. Her hand cracked across his jaw. She whirled away, laughing gaily as she went to Dafydd's side. "God, I've always wanted to do that! You are an arrogant whoreson, Richard de Claiborne. You would not make me a countess, but Dafydd is going to make me a princess."

Richard couldn't help but laugh. "A princess? I wonder what his wife will have to say about that."

Anne glared daggers at him. "When he is prince of Wales, he can do whatever he wants, including setting his wife aside."

Dafydd gave Anne a quick kiss. "That is enough of that talk, I think."

Richard switched back into Welsh. "Planning another double-cross, Dafydd?"

"Nay, but my brother is certain to make me his heir now that his wife is dead. He has no more chances, no more time." He smiled. "And neither do you, I might add."

"If you wanted me dead, why didn't you just let your men kill me in the ambush? 'Twould have been much easier, would it not? And we both

know 'tis the Welsh way. It certainly worked for Llywelyn when he wanted my father dead."

Dafydd frowned, then smiled just as suddenly. "Ah, the previous earl
of Dunsmore! I had almost forgotten." His grin broadened. "You are making this too much fun for me, Dunsmore, but it will still get you no mercy.
Llywelyn didn't kill your father. I did."

Richard's body went rigid. The tent walls closed in around him, and
he filled his lungs with stale air, letting it out again in a rush. "*You* am-
bushed my father?"

"Aye. I had nothing against him, but you on the other hand... you I
mean to see suffer."

"Why did you kill him?"

"'Twas ten years ago," Dafydd said, his brows drawing together.
"Still, it cannot hurt to tell you now. I was trying to draw Llywelyn out. He
never would strike against the English when the timing was right, you understand. King Henry was ill and Edward was in the Holy Land. 'Twould
have been perfect.

"I led some raids in Llywelyn's name, hoping to involve him enough
that he could not back out. William de Claiborne was one of the better
known Marchers, and one I felt fairly certain would rouse the clans and
embroil Llywelyn in the uprising." He shrugged. "It didn't work, and by
that time the prince of Powys wanted to remove Llywelyn from the throne,
so I got involved in that instead."

"You bloody bastard," Richard hissed, jerking against his bindings.

Dafydd came to stand in front of him, tilting his head back to look up
at him. "You are an interesting man, Dunsmore. For instance, I wonder if
your king knows you are a Welshman?"

Richard flexed his wrists until the rope cut into his flesh. "I should
have killed you long ago," he growled. "I would have, had Edward not
stayed me."

Dafydd smiled, his finger tracing the outline of the hawk on Richard's
surcoat. "What *would* Edward say if he knew his most prized warlord was
the grandson of Madoc ap Maredudd, a prince of Gwent? Old Madoc was
fairly rebellious against Henry in his day."

The spear in Richard's ribs prevented him from lunging at Dafydd, from fighting with whatever he had available. His voice was measured, low and deadly. "I do not know how you learned these things, but it will hardly do you any good since you plan on killing me. Edward will not care when I'm dead."

Dafydd jerked his head toward the opening of the tent. A man entered, shoving another man before him. Richard sucked in his breath. "Jesú... Owain."

The old Welshman's face was bloodied. His eyes were blackened and one side of his face was beginning to swell. He smiled weakly, wincing at the split in his lip. "I am sorry, *Nai*. I failed you again."

Richard turned back to his captor. "Let him go, Dafydd. Your quarrel is with me."

"Mayhap I will. I have not decided yet, nor have I decided the best way to dispatch with you. Steffan, put them with the other prisoners," Dafydd commanded. "We will talk again, Dunsmore."

"I look forward to it," Richard answered. The spear jabbed into his ribs. He ignored it, finally obeying when the tip poked through his mail shirt.

"I brought you something, Gwen."

Gwen lumbered to her feet as Rhys came into her room. She took one look at the rosy red apple and started to cry.

Rhys set the fruit on the table and hugged her. "Shh, sweet. What is the matter? You do not like apples any longer?"

Gwen wiped her eyes on her sleeve. "Nay, 'tis not that," she whispered.

Mayhap 'twas the trip south. It had taken four days to ride to Llanfair-ym-Muallt. Being pregnant had made it more tiring, though it was over a month since they'd arrived. Her father had been ambivalent about bringing her, but she'd insisted on accompanying him.

Staying on Snowdon alone would have given her too much time to think of Richard, though God only knew how it would have been possible to think of him more than she already did.

Rhys directed her to the window seat and sat beside her. "Jesú, Gwen, all you do is cry. What will that babe of yours think of such a weepy mother?" he teased, brushing her hair from her face.

Gwen laughed through the veil of tears. "I am sorry, Rhys. I do not know what has gotten into me lately."

Rhys stroked her hand. "Gwen, listen to me. I love you." He pressed a finger to her lips. "Nay, let me finish. I love you. I have never stopped. I can make you happy. I will take care of you and your baby, I swear it. Just let me try."

"Oh Rhys," she said softly. "You deserve better. I could not do that to you." She pressed her cheek to the back of his hand. "I love you, too, but not like that."

Rhys's blue eyes clouded. "You would forget him in time."

She shook her head, staring at her lap. "Nay, I never, never will."

Rhys stood and raked a hand through his golden hair. "Do you think he will forgive you for this, Gwen? Do you think when 'tis all over, he will welcome you back with open arms?"

"No," she whispered, choking back more tears. No, Richard would not forgive her for leaving. She knew that now. She'd been a fool to think otherwise.

It had been almost three months, and he'd not even tried to contact her. Certes, he knew she was gone by now. Sometimes late at night, she pretended he didn't know. Then she would imagine him coming for her, or writing and begging her to return to him. Things she knew a proud man like the earl of Dunsmore would never do.

She caressed her abdomen. She wanted this child desperately. It was already overdue by a sennight, though she tried not to worry too much. She could not lose this babe. It was all she had left of Richard, all she had left of the love of a lifetime.

She sniffled. It would be a son with black hair and celadon eyes. A son to remind her of the man she would always love.

Damn this Godforsaken war!

Rhys knelt in front of her and took both her hands in his. "I have to go north for a few days. Please think about it while I am gone."

His face was so earnest that Gwen could not tell him no. Her answer would never change so long as she loved Richard, but she nodded anyway.

Rhys kissed both her palms. "I will return soon, Gwen. And I will make you happier than you have ever dreamed. You will see, I promise."

Gwen kept the false smile pasted on her face until she was certain he was well out of earshot. Then she buried her face in her hands and gave way to the gut-wrenching sobs deep inside her.

The war was at a draw. Neither side gave much ground or gained much either. It was fast approaching the middle of September and though Edward didn't want to campaign in Wales in winter, the likelihood increased with each passing day.

The Welsh were a hardy people, capable of sustaining harsh winters in the mountains on little more than goat's milk and mutton.

But the English army was huge, unable to forage off the land and in need of a steady convoy of supplies. That was their greatest disadvantage, and one the Welsh intended to exploit.

Dafydd's army moved swiftly, striking and retreating before the English could engage them. Richard, Andrew, and Owain, and the three other knights, were kept heavily guarded.

Dafydd had finally decided to send to the king for ransom, though he assured Richard he was going to kill him anyway.

The prisoners were bound hand and foot, linked to each other by a length of rope. They sat beneath an ancient oak, silent, each man caught up in his own thoughts as the shadows of late day cast phantom images across the camp.

"I am sorry, Richard," Owain mumbled.

Richard sighed. Every day Owain apologized. Richard tried to tell him it wasn't his fault, but the old man insisted on taking the blame for everything that had happened.

"'Tis not your fault, uncle," he said wearily.

"Nay, 'tis. I should have gone after your lady myself, should have never let that whore Anne in the castle."

"Forget about it," Richard said more harshly than he intended. Owain fell silent. Richard laid his head against the tree and closed his eyes, cursing silently.

He did not want to talk about Gwen. God, all he did was think of her. She should have had the babe by now. His heart twisted every time he thought of her going though it without him.

He drove himself crazy wondering if she'd survived it. Somehow, deep down, he knew she must have. Wouldn't he know if aught had befallen her? Wouldn't part of him have died with her?

He heard someone approaching, then opened his eyes when the footsteps halted. Steffan untied him. "Dafydd wants you, Black Hawk. Mayhap he will kill you this time."

Richard didn't bother answering. Dafydd sent for him almost daily and Steffan always taunted him that maybe this was the day he would die.

Richard ducked inside the tent. It took some moments for his eyes to adjust to the dim light. Two men sat at the table, drinking mead.

"Ah, here is my honored guest," Dafydd jested, saluting Richard with his cup. "You must tell my brother of the prize I have caught," he told the other man.

Richard didn't wait for the man to reply. "What do you want, Dafydd? Have you finally decided to kill me? Or do you just wish to amuse your guest?"

Dafydd laughed. "You see that? Even as a prisoner the man is arrogant beyond belief."

The other man stood and walked toward Richard. Richard's chest tightened as the man stopped in front of him. "Rhys ap Gawain."

Rhys held Richard's gaze. Over his shoulder, he asked, "What are you going to do with him?"

"Kill him," Dafydd said simply.

Their gazes remained locked. Rhys didn't speak. It was on the tip of Richard's tongue to ask about Gwen, about his child. He clenched his jaw. He would not give Rhys the satisfaction of denying him an answer.

"She is well," Rhys murmured.

Richard nodded briefly, his only lapse of control in the deep breath he drew. He wanted to ask more and he silently willed Rhys to tell him what he wanted to know.

But Rhys merely watched, offering nothing. Finally, he turned and went back to his seat.

Dafydd spoke. "I thought you might like to know Edward has suffered a major defeat. Luke de Tany and his men tried to surprise our forces at Bangor, but they were too hasty and did not count on the rising waters of the Strait. They were overwhelmed and the blockade destroyed." Dafydd dangled his empty cup over one finger, his face cracking in a grin. "So you see, we *will* have our harvest this winter."

Richard stood very still, very silent. If Dafydd wanted a reaction, he wasn't getting one. Goddamn that impatient De Tany! He'd tried to warn Edward, but it was too late now.

It would take much too long to get more ships into the Strait. If Edward didn't get the Welsh into the open soon, the English army would find themselves entangled in a winter campaign.

"Jesú, Dunsmore, you are no fun," Dafydd said. "'Tis just as well, for I think I've decided what to do with you. Edward is willing to pay ransom, but I am not willing to accept."

His eyes gleamed as he leaned forward. "Being a Welshman yourself, you no doubt know the piercing strength of our longbow. Since I am in need of practice, I should like to use you as a target. I am a fairly good shot, but it might take me awhile to actually hit anything vital," he said, smiling apologetically. "Mayhap if you scream loud enough, I will let Rhys end it for you. He is an excellent shot."

"'Twould be a pleasure," Rhys said evenly.

"Very good. Tomorrow morning then, Dunsmore? If you are available, of course."

"Certes. I can think of nothing I would rather do," Richard replied coolly as his guard came forward.

Steffan grinned, humming a lively tune the entire way back to the other prisoners.

Llywelyn looked up as his daughter entered the room. His eyes strayed to her middle. She did not look well lately and she was more than a fortnight overdue. His insides clenched when he thought of his Elinor, beautiful and glowing, then suddenly dead.

"Einion said you are leaving again, Father."

He nodded. "Aye. Some of the local chieftains are caving in to Marcher pressure. I must re-engage them. We cannot afford to let up now that we have Edward on the run. I will return in a few days."

She smiled, but the corners of her mouth quivered. "I understand. You must keep the forces together."

Llywelyn stood and took her hand. It was so small and delicate, just like her mother's. He wondered, not for the first time, how a man with the reputation Richard de Claiborne had could manage to be so gentle with her. He would never have believed it if he hadn't seen it for himself, though he'd not been too cognizant at the time.

"Einion will be here with you, lass. He is too old for campaigning, though you must not tell him I said that."

She laughed. "Nay, I would not."

Llywelyn touched her stomach. "'Tis the next Prince of Wales," he said quietly.

"But you can still—"

"Nay, I cannot. I am too old to begin again. I'll not sire a son of my own, I know that now." He sighed, then banished it with a smile. "Hurry up and give me my grandson so I can teach him all he needs to know, the way my grandfather taught me."

"He will be here when you return. I will make sure of it."

Llywelyn kissed her on the forehead. "You have never disappointed me. Remember that always."

He grabbed his jerkin and left her in the solar.

Gwen hugged herself as a shiver of apprehension slid down her spine. Each time he rode out, she thought of her dream, and prayed it was just that—a dream.

Richard sat with his knees drawn up and his head resting on his folded arms. Night sounds spilled across the camp—men talking and laughing, women giggling and shrieking, lovers mating. Behind it all, the chorus of crickets, nightowls, and wolves rose in natural splendor, cloaking him in melancholy.

"Dunsmore."

Richard looked up. "Ah, Rhys," he said. "Come to see the chained beast?"

Rhys stooped in front of him, glancing at the other men sleeping soundly. "You did not tell them?"

"Nay, why should I? They will know soon enough, I think."

"Aye."

"What do you want of me? A clear conscience, mayhap?" Richard snapped, his patience stretched beyond endurance. "Do you wish me to give you my blessing to make *my* wife yours?"

Rhys ignored him. "I will end it before 'tis gone too far." He touched Richard's chest. "Straight through the heart. 'Twill kill you instantly."

"Don't do me any favors!"

Rhys stood. "'Tis not for you I do it. 'Tis for Gwen."

He was almost out of earshot when Richard called to him. "And will you tell her what you did for her? Will you tell her it was your arrow that so mercifully rid her of a husband, allowing you to finally have her?"

Rhys did not turn, though Richard knew he had to have heard. He sighed and leaned against the tree. Soon, it would no longer matter.

Rhys couldn't sleep. His pallet seemed unmercifully hard and cold this night. Camp noises faded and died, and still he did not slip into the peace of slumber.

It was Gwen, of course. He did not like Richard de Claiborne, could care less what happened to the man. Certes, 'twould be a blessing to be rid of him, no matter how it was done.

But there would still be Gwen, looking at him with her seagreen eyes, those innocent eyes that had trusted him for as long as he could remember.

Rhys flipped over and jerked the blanket up. Why hadn't Dafydd just killed the man before he'd arrived? Why was it thrust in his lap of a sudden?

Rhys lay a while longer, hoping if he remained still enough his relentless mind would leave him be. Finally, he threw back the cover and bolted upright.

It was no use.

There was only one thing he could do, only one way he could ever have peace. He slipped into his boots, then belted on his knife and crept from the tent.

The answer was simple: it had to end before it ever began.

39

R ichard dozed fitfully, jerking awake when some sixth sense stirred within him. His eyes snapped open and he looked around the camp. All was quiet. The fires, like the human spirit, were at their lowest in the dark hours before dawn.

He'd not meant to sleep at all. If he was going to die anyway, what did it matter if he lost a night's sleep beforehand?

He glanced at Owain, curled up and snoring soundly. The old man looked so frail though Richard knew appearances were deceiving. The youngest son of Madoc ap Maredudd was anything but weak.

Soon, Richard would wake his uncle. There were things he needed to tell him, things he hoped would make it back to Gwen somehow.

He wanted her to know he loved her, despite her final betrayal. That he had probably loved her from the first moment he'd held her in his arms. Certes, something had happened then because he'd never been able to forget her for a moment afterward.

The last few months of his life, the months spent with her, were the best he'd ever had. For the first time ever he'd known more than the cold existence of duty, drinking, and wenching. He'd had a taste of what life could be like with a woman he loved, a woman he wanted to have children with. Jesú, he would give his soul to see their babe just once before he died.

"Do not say anything," a voice whispered from behind as a knife pressed against his throat.

Richard remained completely still, hardly daring even to breathe. Eventually, the pressure eased and the knife disappeared.

"Come to finish me off so soon, Rhys?" Richard hissed. "My, you *are* merciful."

"Shut up, Dunsmore. We've no time for talking," Rhys said as he moved in front of Richard.

The dagger flashed dully in the dim light of the campfires. Richard glared at Rhys, refusing to flinch. If the Welshman were going to kill him, then he would do it without the satisfaction of hearing Richard beg for mercy.

Their gazes held while the knife hovered between them. Rhys swore softly. The blade swept down to the ropes binding Richard's wrists. The rope snapped and Richard flexed his arms to loosen the kinks. "I'll not leave them," he said, nodding toward his uncle and his men.

"Aye, well I thought you might say that," Rhys replied, handing him a dagger. They woke the other men carefully, then sawed through their bindings.

"This way," Rhys said, leading them into the trees. They slunk through the shadows, careful not to make any loud noises that would rouse the camp. Dafydd, ever confident of his army's inaccessibility in these mountains, only posted a few sentries, all of whom were either asleep or drunk.

Richard and his men followed Rhys down a hillside. At the bottom, seven horses waited. Sirocco nickered softly when Richard went to him. Richard patted him, speaking in soothing tones as he gathered the reins and swung onto the stallion.

Rhys rode up beside him. "Catch," he said, tossing Richard a sword. "I would suggest you stay with me if you want to get out of here alive."

"How do we know we can trust you?"

Rhys smiled then. "You do not, but I don't think you have much choice in the matter."

Strangely, Richard felt more at ease. As long as Rhys's dislike was out in the open, Richard knew he could trust him.

They picked their way down the mountain, stopping on occasion to listen for signs of pursuit. Thankfully, there were none. Dawn's first light was just peeking over the hilltops when they entered a long valley and broke into a gallop.

It was nearing midday when they pulled up by a stream to water the horses and rest. Richard dismounted and grabbed Rhys's tunic, yanking him off his horse and thrusting his back against a tree.

"Where the bloody hell are you taking us?" he demanded.

Rhys shoved him away. They glared at each other while the men looked on in shock. "St. Dafydd's teeth, I cannot understand why Gwen loves you! If she did not, you would look like a lady's pin cushion by now!"

Richard pushed a hand through his hair. His temper was frayed by the last few weeks of uncertainty. Like it or not, he owed Rhys his life. "Forgive me," he said simply. Then, softer, "She said that?"

Rhys stood his ground for a long moment before his posture relaxed. "Aye, she said it. Many times." His jaw hardened. "I am taking you to Llanfair-ym-Muallt. 'Tis where Gwen is. Unless you would rather rejoin your king, of course."

"Builth Wells?" Richard said increduously. "Jesú, I did not think she would be so far south." He walked a few steps away and leaned against Sirocco while the stallion quenched his thirst in the cool stream. "You have not mentioned my child yet."

Rhys looked away. "'Twas not here when I left."

"How long ago?" Richard asked, straightening.

"Little more than a sennight."

"God's blood, 'tis overdue." Fear washed over him in waves. "You are certain she is well?" he demanded.

Rhys's blue eyes flashed angrily. "I would not have left her otherwise."

Richard tensed, his hand straying to his sword hilt. He and Rhys were like two wolves, constantly circling, testing for weakness, each aching to strike the other down.

"Why did you do it, Rhys?" he asked, startling himself with the question that had bothered him through all the leagues of their flight. "Why, when you could have walked away? I would be dead and she would have never had to know how it happened."

Rhys slapped the ends of his reins against his palm and stared into the trees beyond the brook. He laughed ruefully. "Do not think it didn't cross my mind."

In the silence that followed, the stream gurgled happily and larks chirped overhead. Nature was oblivious to the pain inherent in humankind.

Finally, Rhys sighed. "She talks to the babe when she thinks no one is listening. She insists 'tis a son, by the way. All she ever tells him is how strong and handsome his father is, how brave and noble. And she cries so often…" His brow furrowed, his eyes glittering with an unnamed sorrow. "'Tis not the Gwen I grew up with. Somehow, I do not think *this* Gwen would ever be happy again without you."

"I owe you my life." Richard's throat constricted. He had never wanted to cause Gwen a moment of grief and yet he knew he had, many, many times.

"No." Rhys drew in a deep breath. "No, 'tis to Gwen you owe it. Remember that when you see her again. Do not judge her too harshly."

Richard turned away. He did not need to be reminded of Gwen's betrayal. It still hurt no matter what Rhys said, and he would deal with it in his own way.

"Dafydd will know it was you who helped me escape."

Rhys snorted derisively. "I am sworn to Prince Llywelyn. I care naught for his traitorous brother."

"*Nid o fradwr y ceir gwladwr,*" Richard said.

"Aye. A traitor will never become a patriot," Rhys echoed.

When the horses were hobbled and munching tender shoots of grass, the men took the opportunity to shed their clothes and slip into the bracing mountain stream.

The water was cool and invigorating, washing away the bitter sting of captivity. Eventually, they straggled onto the bank and dozed in the midday sunshine streaming through the canopy overhead.

Richard was too restless for sleep, despite the precious little he'd had the night before. He lay with his arms crossed behind his head, staring up at the swaying treetops.

"Somehow, I do not think Gwen knows you are half-Welsh," Rhys said, stretching out next to Richard and propping himself on an elbow.

Richard turned his head to meet Rhys's probing stare. "Do you think you are now entitled to discuss my life with me?"

For once, Rhys did not rise to the bait. He shrugged. "It matters not to me, though 'tis surprising to find out Black Hawk de Claiborne carries the blood of those he scorns."

Richard returned to studying the treetops. "I am an Englishman, Rhys. By birth, by choice. I do not scorn the Welsh. I but do what my king commands."

"King Edward will know the truth now. Dafydd will make certain of it."

Richard let his breath out forcefully. All the years he'd guarded his heritage in fear someone would brand him incapable of doing his duty were at an end. He had proved himself loyal and capable over the last ten years. Edward would not forget that, though being half-Welsh would certainly be a drawback in the king's eyes.

Time and again, Wales defied the English crown.

And Prince Madoc had been *very* rebellious in his day. It would only be natural for Edward to wonder if it was just a matter of time.

Richard pushed himself to his feet. "I will deal with it when it happens. Now, let us tarry no longer. I wish to get on with this journey."

"Holy Christ, Dunsmore, what are you doing here?" asked Edmund de Mortimer, the new lord of Wigmore since his father had been killed in battle earlier in the year. "We thought you were in the north with the king."

Richard dismounted and joined Edmund. The bailey of Builth castle swarmed with Englishmen, though according to Rhys, Llywelyn held this castle.

He glanced at Rhys. The young Welshman's expression was strained, and Richard shook off a feeling of foreboding.

"He sent me south," Richard replied smoothly. "When did you wrest this castle from Llywelyn?"

Edmund laughed. "We did not. The bastard's dead. We surprised their forces at Orewin Bridge yesterday. Never even knew we'd got Llywelyn until the bodies were being searched."

Richard stood in numb disbelief. Llywelyn dead?

Rhys leapt from his horse. "Where is he? What have you done with him?"

Edmund stabbed his thumb at Rhys. "Who is this, Dunsmore? He's Welsh, is he not?"

Richard glared at Rhys. "Aye, he is Welsh. He is one of my men."

Rhys's gaze snapped to him. Richard murmured in Welsh, "'Tis not for you I do it."

Finally, Rhys nodded imperceptibly. Richard turned back to Edmund. "Where is Llywelyn?"

"We just laid him out in the hall. I was planning on sending his head to the king."

A chill ran down Richard's spine. Good God, if Gwen was inside she must not see her father like that.

Rhys must have had the same thought because the two of them broke into a run. They clattered up the steps and into the hall, nearly tripping over each other in their haste.

But they were too late. Llywelyn's prone form was stretched on a table and his daughter bent over him, weeping. Several men stood nearby. One grabbed her arm and tried to pull her away, but she jerked out of his grasp and held on to her father. "Get away from him, you English whoreson bastards!" she screamed.

Richard grabbed two fistfuls of the man's surcoat and threw him against the wall. "Touch her again, and I will kill you," he grated from between clenched teeth.

The man's eyes went wide. He swallowed convulsively, his head jerking as he nodded. Richard shoved him away. He fell to the floor, then scrambled to his feet and hurried from the hall.

When Richard turned, Rhys was already at Gwen's side.

"Rhys," Gwen wailed. "Oh Rhys, look what they have done." Blood stained her hands as she clutched her father's lifeless body.

Rhys's eyes gleamed with unshed tears. "I am sorry, Gwen. I should have been here. I should have stopped them." His hand shook as he touched Llywelyn's jaw then slipped down to cover Gwen's hand where it clung to her father's chest.

Gwen turned to bury her face against Rhys's shoulder. "R-Richard?"

He went to her and gently pulled her up. Dear God, she was still pregnant. If he again saw the man who had handled her so roughly, he *would* kill him. "Yes, my love, I am here."

She clung to him. He couldn't stop himself from pressing kisses to her face, from tasting her tears, from learning again the texture of her hair.

She closed her eyes and buried her face against his chest. "You are safe, you are safe, you are safe…"

He stroked her hair. "Aye, I am safe." Jesú, he'd come so close to never holding her again.

Her body shook with her sobs. She pushed away and his heart turned over at the pain written on her lovely features.

"H-he is dead, Richard. They killed him, k-killed my father—"

"Well, Dunsmore," Edmund interrupted, stopping beside Richard and gesturing toward Llywelyn's body. "We have gotten us a prize fit for a king, have we not?"

Richard could have killed him as Gwen's gaze darted between them. She seized her lip between her teeth. "I do not understand," she whispered.

He silently willed her not to even consider what he knew she must.

She took in his torn and dirty surcoat, his chain mail, his sword, and a look of dawning horror crossed her face. She shook her head vigorously. "Oh nay," she moaned, "nay, tell me you did not lead them!"

Her fists tightened in his surcoat. "Tell me 'twas not you who did this, tell me 'twas not for revenge!"

He stiffened as if she'd slapped him. He knew he should answer immediately, reassure her, deny any involvement. But he couldn't force the words out. How could she believe he would do this to her?

The answer came to him, twisting his heart with familiar bitterness. Because he was *Gwalchddu*. Run though he might, he would always be Black Hawk de Claiborne.

She stepped back, bumping into Rhys, her eyes never leaving his. "Oh my God, you got your revenge!"

Speak, goddamn you! his inner voice screamed.

"You said you would, and you did!"

Rhys gripped her arm. "Nay, Gwen—"

"No, Rhys," Richard said, surprising himself with how calm he sounded when his heart was a dead weight inside him. "'Tis not necessary to explain. My wife always thinks the worst of me."

Tears flowed unchecked down her cheeks, and she clutched her belly protectively. "I will never forgive you, never!"

Rhys wrapped his arm around her shoulders. "Let me take you to your room, Gwen. You need to rest."

"No, I cannot leave him," she said, shaking him off and rushing to her father.

Those words stabbed through Richard like nothing else ever could. She could leave *him*, despite her promise, but she couldn't leave her father.

"I won't let them do anything to him," Rhys said. "Come."

She stared at him uncertainly, then allowed him to lead her away. The sound of her soft crying faded as they ascended the steps to the upper chambers, but it was still like a dagger twisting in Richard's heart.

He stood, staring down at Llywelyn in a daze. The man who had given him Gwen had also taken her away.

Edmund pulled out his sword. Richard grabbed his arm as he raised it high. "Nay. Not here. I cannot stop you from taking his head when you are elsewhere, but if you do it in this castle with his daughter—my wife—I will send your head with it."

Edmund resheathed the weapon. "Very well, my lord earl. It can wait," he said grudgingly.

Richard caught the speculative look Edmund shot him. He knew the man wondered how the very pregnant wife of the Earl of Dunsmore came to be in an enemy castle, but he did not care to explain. Edward was the only man he need answer to.

"I need to send a messenger to the king," Richard said. Dafydd would have moved by now, but Richard could still detail his strength and tactics.

Edmund motioned for a scribe. Richard dictated the message, then slumped onto a bench and stared at Llywelyn's still form.

"I hated you for so long, old man, but 'twas not even you who did it," Richard murmured. "Mayhap she is right for suspecting me. If I'd had the opportunity, I'm not certain I wouldn't have killed you had I not known the truth."

40

"Dunsmore!"

Richard's head snapped up. Rhys stood on the stairs, waving frantically. "The babe is coming!"

Richard was on his feet and up the stairs quicker than an arrow fired from a longbow. Rhys followed on his heels, stopping when they reached Gwen's chamber. Richard flung open the door and entered, oblivious to Rhys's shouting.

"Milord, you may not come in here," the midwife said, rushing toward him with her hand outstretched.

"Like bloody hell," he growled, shoving past her.

Gwen lay on the bed, her face pale and twisted in pain. She cried out suddenly, grasping handfuls of bedding in her fists.

Richard dropped beside her, clasping her hand and smoothing the hair from her face. "I am sorry," he whispered belatedly.

Her glorious eyes were glazed. "Nay, 'tis I who am sorry. Rhys told me what happened, but I should have believed in you. I cannot blame you if you no longer want me—"

She screamed and he let her squeeze his hand until the pain passed, then kissed her moist brow. "Christ almighty, Gwen, you are my life. I will never let you go."

The midwife, regaining her bravery, hovered over them, hands planted firmly on hips. "Milord, men are *not* allowed in the birthing chamber!"

"Do you wish me to go, love?" Richard asked, stroking the hair from Gwen's damp forehead.

"Nay," she whispered. "Do not leave me. I am frightened."

He turned to the midwife. "Woman, if you wish to live beyond this day, you will tend my wife now. And if you wish me gone, then I invite you to remove me yourself."

The woman blanched. "V-very well, but you must not interfere, milord," she said in a near-whisper.

"Agreed."

"'Tis not natural," she muttered under her breath. The castle women hurried in and out of the room, fetching linens and hot water.

The midwife mixed something from her bag of herbals, then retrieved a pot and returned to Gwen's side. Dipping her hand into the pot, she lifted Gwen's chemise.

"What is that for?" Richard demanded.

The woman's hand shook. "'Tis to rub on her belly to ease the pains. I-I thought you were not going to interfere, milord."

"Aye," he said curtly, clamping his teeth together.

As the hours wore on, Richard grew frantic. Gwen was soaked in sweat, her voice raw from her cries. She still gripped his hand, which was now quite numb, and he stroked her arm with slow, steady motions, trying to ease the pain in any way he could.

Her screams tore his heart in two. He begged God to spare her, certain she was going to die, certain God was going to punish him once more. He swore that if she survived, he would never make love to her again, never risk losing her just to gratify his own selfish urges.

"I... am... sorry... Richard," she panted.

"Shh, my love."

She screamed, clamping his hand so hard it hurt.

"Yes, Gwen, hold onto me. I will share it with you." God, how he wished he could take the pain away! He had done this to her, and it was only fair he feel it with her, but Nature had contrived to make the burden solely hers.

"'Tis coming now," the midwife said at last.

The scent of blood made Richard's stomach churn. He was accustomed to the sight and smell of blood, but not when it belonged to Gwen. It was everything he could do to remain upright.

With a final hoarse cry from Gwen, the babe slid forth into the midwife's waiting hands. Gwen collapsed, so small and pale in the huge bed.

Richard bent to kiss her sweat-soaked brow. He whispered endearments to her, stroked her face with a trembling hand. Her grip on him loosened and she gazed up at him, her lashes spiky with tears.

"'Tis a son. I know 'tis a son."

A lump formed in his throat. "It matters not, sweet. 'Tis ours."

The midwife returned with the babe. "You have a son, milord," she said. As was customary, she'd washed the infant, rubbed his body with salt, his palate and gums with honey, and bound him in clean linen. And now she was holding him out to his father.

Richard didn't want to touch the small bundle. He knew nothing about babes, except that they were incredibly delicate.

He'd never been comfortable around children, and he looked at this one with a mixture of awe and trepidation. He glanced at the midwife. She smiled and nodded, urging him to take his son.

He held his arms out hesitantly and she placed the tiny bundle in them. The baby's face was pinched, his eyes screwed together tightly. His little mouth worked, mimicking suckling motions.

"He has black hair," was all Richard could manage. 'Twas miraculous, this child he and Gwen had created! The red face didn't resemble either one of them that he could see, but it didn't matter. He'd thought the love he felt for Gwen was all he was capable of, but he recognized the familiar feeling stirring in his heart.

Gwen laughed weakly. "He has your hair, but he will have my eyes. Let me hold him," she finished softly.

She held out her arms and Richard gave her their son. She cradled him to her, talking to him like they were old friends. Finally she looked up. "I have already thought of a name for him, if you agree."

"What?"

She looked down at the babe, then back up at him. "William," she said simply.

Richard's heart swelled. He knew he loved her more in that moment than he ever had before. He touched a large finger to his son's tiny cheek. "Aye, William 'tis."

Gwen recovered in a few days' time. She was up and around, though she remained in her chamber and out of the way of the Englishmen who now occupied Builth castle. Their presence was a bitter reminder of her father's defeat.

She watched from the window as they made huge piles of the weapons they had seized. Her only comfort in her father's death was knowing he was with Elinor. That alone made it bearable.

The wet nurse came to take William and she gave him up reluctantly. Noblewomen did not suckle their children.

Rhys came to see her frequently, as did Owain, and she delighted in their company. This day, however, she felt strangely alone. The empty chamber seemed to crush her beneath its solemn weight, its deafening silence.

She'd tried not to think of her father's death too often, but now she could think of nothing else. They'd already taken his body north to the king and there they would cut off his head and send it to the Tower of London.

She sank onto the bed and cried. She'd not seen Richard very often since their son was born. And when she did, he was quiet, distant. How could she blame him?

Though she'd wronged him by leaving, she would do it again if faced with the same opportunity to make things right with her father.

She knew now it was her own guilt that made her doubt Richard. She was guilty for loving him, guilty for wanting him above all else. When she doubted his motives, it was really her own she was calling into question.

She heard the door open but she couldn't stop crying. Then she was drawn into strong arms and she buried her face against his surcoat, sobbing all the harder now that he was here.

"I-I had to come, Richard," she heard herself say. And then she was spilling the details of her dream, Dafydd's claim, her entire life spent trying to win her father's approval. She told him all of her disappointments, all of her childish efforts, all the hurt she'd never shared with anyone. His arms tightened around her. She tumbled on, telling him about her reconciliation with her father, their final moments together, the treasured words he'd said: *You have never disappointed me. Remember that always.*

Richard stroked her back. When she finally looked up, one tear slid down his face, and she reached up to capture it. Her open palm shaped his cheek and he rubbed against her hand, his eyes closing.

"He did not kill my father," he said softly.

Gwen felt an enormous relief flood her. She didn't know why it was so important he believe it, but it was. "I knew he could not."

"'Twas Dafydd who did it."

She hugged him tight. "I am so sorry, Richard."

"I have not been truthful with you, Gwen."

Her heart fell to her feet. Oh God, he was going to tell her he'd never really loved her, or he was married to someone else, or—oh God, she couldn't think of the possibilities.

"Owain is my uncle."

"What? But he is Welsh."

"Aye, he is. And so was his sister, my mother."

"Catrin," she said, suddenly understanding.

"Yes. How did you know?"

"I heard him say her name, though I knew not who she was. He promised her to look after you."

A slight smile curved his mouth. "Aye. He is always reminding me of that."

When he'd told her everything, she gaped at him. "Prince Madoc?" she said. He nodded. "Sweet Mary," she breathed. "Did my father know?"

"Nay, I do not think so."

Gwen laid her head against his chest and twisted the cloth of his sleeve in her fingers. "Gwilym ap Rhisiart," she said, saying her son's name in Welsh. "He will be prince of Wales."

Richard shook his head. "Nay, Gwen. Edward will never allow it. He is finished with Wales. He means to conquer her for good."

"You cannot let him take it away. 'Tis our son's birthright. You are Welsh!"

"No! I am English, Gwen. I am not a Welshman."

Gwen pushed away from him, suddenly angry he would be so vehement in his denials. "What is wrong, my lord? Are we not good enough for you? Is it truly so shameful to be Welsh?"

"Gwen—"

"No! My father spent his entire life guarding Welsh territory, Welsh heritage! You cannot allow it to slip away, not when it rightfully belongs to our son. Not when my father *wanted* it to be so."

Richard quit the bed. "I am Richard de Claiborne, Earl of Dunsmore," he said in French, smacking his chest. "I am an English Marcher lord. King Edward is my liege lord and what he commands, I do. Do not *ever* expect me to break my solemn oaths to my king."

Gwen bit her quivering lip. "Will we never understand one another, Richard?" she whispered. "Must we always allow King Edward to come between us?"

Without a word, he spun on his heel and stalked from the chamber.

Within a few weeks, they set out for Claiborne castle. The gentle rocking of Saffron's gait put William to sleep in Gwen's arms. His chubby little cheeks quivered every now and then as his jaw worked.

She smiled. He was surely the most beautiful baby that ever lived and she loved him with all her heart. She raised her eyes to his father's back.

Until two days ago, he'd been gone, commanding Marcher forces in the south. He'd not sought her out since returning. She'd lain awake at night, wanting him to come to her, wanting him to need her like she needed him, but he had not.

How could it ever be right between them again when the lines were so firmly drawn?

He would deny his own son his birthright and Gwen refused to understand how he could do it. She looked down at the sleeping babe in her arms. God how she wished her father had lived to see his grandson!

He would have made sure William inherited all that belonged to him.

Rhys's laughter drifted to her from where he and Owain rode a few paces back. Now that her father was dead, Rhys refused to fight with Dafydd and Richard had allowed him and his men to come with them.

Gwen was surprised, but pleased. She did not know all that had passed between them, but whatever it was, they seemed to have formed a grudging truce.

Claiborne was only a few leagues away when a party of knights appeared. Gwen knew they were Richard's from the hawk banner they carried and the colors they wore. Her chest tightened as Richard rode forth to meet them.

Andrew and five of the other men who had ridden from Builth Wells joined the waiting knights. Richard turned and rode back to her.

"You are leaving," she said. She should be used to it by now, but she was not.

"Aye. I must return to the king."

"How long will you be gone this time, my lord?"

He pulled his mail gauntlet off and ran his finger down her cheek, then slipped to William's, caressing him as well. "I know not. Days, weeks…"

"Months," Gwen said dully.

"Until Dafydd is stopped," he replied. He smiled then, the first she'd seen in weeks. "What is wrong, wench? Miss me already?"

Gwen nodded and a lone tear spilled down her cheek. "Aye. I do not want you to go."

His expression sobered. He sidled Sirocco closer. "Kiss me, then. Show me how much."

He bent to her and she met him, losing herself in the heat and scent of him. It was she who insisted on deepening the kiss, she who slipped her tongue into his mouth and forced him to join her. His mouth turned ravenous as his hand came up to grip the back of her head. And then he broke away, pressed his lips to her cheek, her throat, William's forehead.

"I love you," he said. "Both of you." He whirled Sirocco around to join the others, never looking back.

The knights broke into a gallop, the thundering of horses' hooves and the chinking of metal still hanging in the air long after she'd lost sight of them.

Once again, King Edward had taken him from her.

The king was lodged at Rhuddlan castle when Richard returned to him. Since Llywelyn's death, the spirit of the Welsh uprising was sinking faster than a ship full of holes and Edward was in good spirits.

"Dafydd calls himself Prince of Wales now, but the chieftains are deserting him quicker than a whore's tongue. If we can get the slippery bastard out of the mountains, 'twill be over before the new year."

It was late in the day and the two men stood on the battlements, gazing toward the Welsh mountains. The tang of salt and keening cries of gulls drifted to them from the sea at their backs.

The army sprawled across the valley below. The sounds of men and animals mingled with those of clanking metal and chopping wood as the evening tasks were carried out.

The bitter November wind ruffled Richard's hair as he turned to look at the king. "There is something I must tell you, Ned."

"Aye?"

Richard took a deep breath. "Madoc ap Maredudd was my grandfather. My mother was Welsh."

When Edward didn't say anything, Richard continued. He told Edward everything, how his mother and father met, how they defied Prince Madoc and King Henry, how eventually no one even remembered William de Claiborne's dead wife had been a Welshwoman.

"Jesú," Edward breathed. "'Tis why you speak it so well. And the beard. I always thought you kept it because it drove the ladies crazy."

Richard laughed, rubbing his face. "Nay, 'tis because it suits me. And it reminds me of what I cannot escape."

Edward ran his fingers through his blond curls, scratching his head. "Edmund de Mortimer thinks your wife guilty of treason."

Richard sucked in his breath. "The bastard," he hissed.

"Do you deny she was with Llywelyn?"

"Nay." His jaw hardened. "I accept her reasons for doing so, though I did not approve. She is back at Claiborne now and will not leave again, I assure you."

Edward braced his arms on the wall, leaning on them and gazing at the bailey below. "We will keep this to ourselves, Richard. The fewer people who know of your parentage, the better. Welsh ancestry is not uncommon in the Marchers, but none of them are married to a princess of Wales nor do they carry the blood of a Welsh prince."

"If you think it best."

"Aye, I do. I am the king of England, but even kings have limited power. The other barons might not take it so well. I would not have another revolt on my hands if it can be helped."

They stood silent for a while longer. The setting sun turned the sky bloodred before disappearing, leaving an angry welt in its wake.

Richard voiced the question he had always dreaded. "Do you doubt my ability to serve you?"

Edward straightened, astonishment crossing his face. "Nay, Richard. God's blood, I have not doubted that since the instant you pulled the Saracen off me. This changes nothing, though I wish you had entrusted me long ago." He smiled sadly. "There are few men a king can call friend. My father made the mistake of never knowing whom to trust. I trust very few. I know you will not fail me, now or ever."

"Nay, I will not fail you," Richard echoed. "Now or ever."

He turned toward Claiborne, imagining he could see it across the leagues. William would be Earl of Dunsmore one day. That would be enough. Gwen would understand eventually.

Dafydd held the English army at bay all through the winter months, despite his dwindling support. He was finally free of his brother, finally the prince of Wales, finally in control of his country and his destiny, and he intended to wrest it from England at whatever cost.

But his role as a double-traitor did not set well with his fellow countrymen now that Llywelyn was gone. Too many times, Dafydd had betrayed Welsh interests for English gold, and his countrymen began to wonder how soon it would be before he played them false again.

He retreated to Snowdon for the winter, only emerging when the spring thaw melted the frozen mountain passes. By then Edward had Gwynedd ringed with his forces, pressing Dafydd from all sides. Victory was imminent.

In late spring, two of the chieftains who had previously supported Dafydd came to parley with Edward.

"He is on the lower slopes of Cader Idris," Edneyved ap Olfyr said before going on to detail the size and strength of Dafydd's force.

Edward listened with feverish interest. When the two men were gone, he turned to Richard and the gathered Marchers. "Richard, you will lead the force that goes after Dafydd. I want him alive."

Richard took fifty knights. They made their way southwest toward the Llyn Peninsula then cut to the east toward Cader Idris. He was anticipating a good fight with Dafydd. He wanted to kill him, but Edward forbade it.

Mayhap watching him suffer a traitor's death at the hands of the executioner would be more satisfying anyway.

They camped within sight of the mountain, careful not to light any fires that would call attention to their presence. The night was beautifully clear and they were in the saddle before dawn, picking their way by starlight toward Dafydd's hideout.

When they surprised the Welshmen shortly after dawn, Richard expected more of a fight. But knowing their time was up and lacking faith in their leader, they surrendered easily enough. Edneyved ap Olfyr marched Dafydd out of his tent at spearpoint.

"I give you this gift for your king, Black Hawk de Claiborne. Tell him to remember it well."

Richard climbed off Sirocco. Dafydd spat at his feet. "We meet again, Prince Dafydd. Or would that be Lord Dafydd? I can never remember…"

"May you rot in hell, Dunsmore! I only wish I had succeeded in killing you, you half-Welsh whoreson!"

Two women ran toward them, both crying for Dafydd. Richard recognized Anne, but not the other one.

"Lisbeth," Dafydd said, his voice cracking. She ran into his arms and he hugged her tight while she sobbed.

Anne came to an abrupt halt, her unbound hair swirling around her. "Dafydd?" she whimpered.

Dafydd didn't look up. Richard felt almost sorry for Anne in that moment.

Her tear-filled eyes landed on Richard. "You," she hissed, flying at him. Richard caught her, twisting her arms behind her. She screamed at him, blamed him for all the misfortune in her life. Then she started to sob. He freed her arms and she clung to him.

He stood rigidly. Unbidden, the image of a boy came to him.

For whatever reason, Tristan loved his mother. Certes, there must be something good about her even if Richard could not see it. Reluctantly, he put an arm around her. "Stop crying, Anne. 'Twill be all right."

She sobbed all the harder. "I hate you," she choked out.

"I know," he said softly.

They set out for Rhuddlan castle later that day. Dafydd was accompanied by his wife and seven children and his mistresses, one of whom was Anne Ashford. Dafydd's Welshmen marched to Rhuddlan as well. They would be required to swear fealty to their king, and then most of them would be released. A few of the chieftains would be tried for treason along with their prince.

Edward refused to see Dafydd, ordering him tossed into the tower instead. Lisbeth and her children were given quarters with Dafydd's other children and their mothers.

Anne was granted an audience with Edward. Richard stepped back quickly when the door to the solar flew open and Anne ran out, shrieking so loud it echoed through the stone walls of the castle.

He entered, shaking his head. The musky scent of sex permeated the air, jolting Richard with the memory of how long it had been since he'd made love to Gwen.

Edward downed a goblet of ale. "Nothing like a good tumble in the middle of the day."

"I do not believe she shared your sentiment, Ned," Richard said dryly.

Edward's laughter rang through the room. "Jesú, she just told me that was the best fuck she'd ever had. Of course that was before I told her her punishment for committing treason."

"Which was?"

"I took your advice to go easy on her. I should think a life spent in a convent would be preferable to sharing the hangman's noose with Dafydd."

"Aye," Richard said. It was less than she deserved perhaps, but more than she would be able to stand. Anne was lusty and sticking her in a convent was like depriving a starving man a crust of bread.

"I am going to convene a special parliament in Shrewsbury to try Dafydd. Hanging him outright would not send the message I want to Wales. I want them to see his humiliation, his condemnation."

"When?"

"Immediately." Edward smiled then. "I think you have time to go to Claiborne first."

Richard stood. "If you do not object, I would like to go now."

"Go then," Edward said.

Richard bowed to his king before leaving the room. He ached to see Gwen and his son again. It had been months since he'd left her enroute to Claiborne. The memory of that kiss had sustained him through all the long months of the campaign. He vowed that when he saw her again, he was going to do a hell of a lot more than kiss her.

Dafydd paced the round tower room like a caged beast. Where had he gone wrong? When had he lost control? He'd had it all, and he'd let it slip from his grasp.

Questions with no answers. Once he'd been a prince, a lord, and a knight. Now he was nothing, nothing.

He raked both his hands through his hair, then sank onto the pallet against the wall and hugged his knees to his chest. It was all over now. His life was forfeit.

Edward refused even to see him, despite the fact he'd told the messenger he had information the king might be interested in. But Edward would relent eventually, once his notorious Plantagenet temper cooled.

Dafydd curled on his side and dozed, only waking when he thought he heard a key clang in the lock. The door swung open and he was on his feet instantly.

Gilbert de Clare entered, followed by Edmund de Mortimer. Gilbert spoke first. "We hear you have information about Dunsmore. What is it?"

Dafydd's gaze went from one man to the other. Red Gilbert was not a man to mince words. Edmund's countenance was stony, as if he were irritated at the Earl of Gloucester's forthrightness.

Dafydd sat at the small table in the center of the room and crossed his legs. A lazy smile cracked across his face. "Well," he drawled. "I cannot just tell you without some sort of payment, now can I?"

Gloucester looked taken aback. His face turned red and a vein stood out in his forehead. "You are not in a position to demand payment of any kind, you Welsh rubbish!"

Dafydd refused to be cowed. What more did he have to lose? "Nevertheless, I have something you want. You will pay for it."

Gloucester took a step forward, his fists clenching. Edmund put a hand on his arm and said something too low for Dafydd to hear.

Gloucester nodded. Edmund joined Dafydd at the table. "You are a traitor to the Crown, Dafydd. If you expect us to work a miracle with the king, you are asking too much. He will not release you."

Dafydd studied his knee. "Very well," he said at last, lifting his chin proudly, defiantly. "I wish to see my wife and children again. I also wish them kept safe from Edward's wrath. 'Tis my burden, not theirs. I want him to know they are not to blame."

Edmund turned to Gloucester. A look passed between them and Red Gilbert nodded curtly.

"You have our word, Dafydd," Edmund said. "We will plead your wife's case to the king."

Dafydd sighed heavily. *May God grant him this one last boon.* "Then I will tell you what I know about the Earl of Dunsmore."

41

The first days of June were splendid. The sun commanded the sky, standing bright and pure in a sea of blue. Woolly clouds sailed across the horizon, their shapes fantastical and ordinary at the same time.

The castle gardens were ablaze with color: roses, violets, herbs, pears, apples, and a variety of vegetables grew in profusion. Along one wall, grapevines twisted and trailed, stretching emerald-hued leaves to the sun.

Gwen and Alys lounged on a blanket thrown across a shady patch of grass. A light repast of cold meat and fruit sat to one side, and a flagon of wine cooled in a bucket of water.

William crawled between the women, giggling and gurgling. Gwen thought her baby resembled his father more and more each day. He had downy-soft skin, wide green eyes fringed with thick lashes, and a head of unruly black ringlets.

Already big for his eight and a half months, he promised to be tall and broad, just like Richard. He was a happy baby, though mayhap a bit spoiled. He was always ready with a saucy smile, only crying when he didn't get his way.

Gwen sighed. Unfortunately, he was rarely denied. She just couldn't bring herself to refuse him when he turned those wide eyes and that smile that was so much like his father's on her. And she wasn't the only one.

Owain strode down the path toward them, clutching a ball Alys had made by sewing stout wool together and stuffing it with straw.

"I found it," he said, dropping onto the blanket beside Alys. He gave her a quick peck. "William, lookee what Uncle Owain has."

William held out his chubby little hand and said as imperiously as possible for a baby, "Geem."

Owain rolled the ball, shaking his head when William latched onto it and wouldn't let go. "Just like his father, he is. Demanding, even before he understands the meaning of the word."

Gwen laughed, though inside she ached. She'd thought it would grow duller as time passed, but it had not.

Seven months ago, Richard had kissed her and left her on the road to Claiborne. She'd had occasional messages from him, and she'd sent him dozens, but they were a poor substitute for being with him.

A mist of tears clouded her vision as she watched her son play with Owain. Richard had missed so much, so much.

The first few weeks without him had been hard. She'd kept expecting him to return at any time, but as the days wore on she'd given up.

Rhys was gone too. Shortly after their arrival, he'd gone to Lydford manor to be Richard's castellan. He visited occasionally, but the last time was over a month ago. He seemed happy enough, though sometimes he was wistful when they talked of her father.

Alys popped a piece of cold venison in her mouth and Gwen smiled to herself. The woman had been so thin when they'd returned. She'd worn herself down with worry, and it had taken a long time for her to regain her appetite. Fortunately, she had her plump figure back.

Owain was devoted to her, and she to him. Since Owain's return, the love they shared was out in the open. Owain wanted to marry Alys, but they had decided to wait for Richard. They felt it only fair he share in the happiness as well.

William crawled into Alys's lap. She hugged him, though he protested when it lasted too long. Owain picked him up and held him high above his head. William screamed with delight.

A bee buzzed past Gwen's ear. She swatted at it absently, her gaze drifting across the garden. She caught a flash of crimson and silver through the trees, but she dismissed it as fancy. She wanted Richard home so much that she was imagining armored men walking through the garden.

It could not be him, however, because they'd had no message he was returning. But then she saw him. He stopped at the end of the path and watched the little group on the blanket. Her heart began to pound until she felt too weak to move.

"Richard…" she whispered. He strode toward them, larger than life, more magnificent than ever.

Owain's face split in a grin. Alys's eyes widened as she took William from him. "You knew, you sly devil!"

Owain stood. "Aye, sweetling, I knew he was here. He wouldn't let me tell you."

"You have done well, uncle," Richard said, his eyes on Gwen. She found the strength to stand, though she could not move her feet once she'd done so.

He was handsomer than she remembered. Taller too. His broad shoulders and chest were covered in chainmail, but his coif was pushed back to reveal midnight hair. It was longer than she recalled, curling at his nape, and she ached to run her fingers through its silkiness.

He stopped in front of Alys, who had stood and was holding William. His jaw slackened as he stared at his son, and Gwen knew he was thinking what she had thought only moments ago.

The baby's eyes were wide, his head tilting back at an uncomfortable-looking angle as he stared up at his father. After studying the metal-clad giant for a long moment, he stretched out his arm and said, "Geem."

Gwen, Alys, and Owain laughed. Richard looked at Gwen, his brows drawn together, his beautiful mouth curved in a half-smile. He seemed confused and, if she dared say it, a little frightened. "What does he want?"

Gwen picked up the forgotten ball and held it out. "Give him this," she said softly.

Richard took it, his fingers brushing hers. Tendrils of fire blazed to life within her. Already, she burned for him. Oh God, how she burned for him!

He gave the ball to his son, who clutched it happily. Richard's finger caressed William's tiny cheek while the baby tried to chew his prize. He promptly dropped the ball and clamped onto the large hand in front of him.

Richard looked surprised at first. A broad smile spread across his features as William started chewing his finger. "He is perfect," he murmured.

William promptly tired of his father's finger and grabbed Alys's tunic instead. Richard touched the black curls of his son's hair, his eyes straying back to Gwen.

She heard Owain clear his throat, heard Alys mumble something about taking William in for his nap. When they were gone, she just stood, staring at her husband.

"I have missed you," she whispered, her eyes filling with tears of happiness and relief.

"Show me," he replied, his voice husky as he held out his hand. Gwen took it. Such a light contact, yet it burned through her, scorched her to the depths of her soul. With a little cry, she threw herself into his embrace, winding her arms around his neck, meeting the fierce hunger of his mouth.

He broke the kiss with a groan. "Jesú, Gwen, 'tis been so long, so long..." His hand strayed to her headcovering. He tugged gently, loosing her hair from its confinement. "'Tis plaited," he said in disbelief.

She laughed. "Aye, 'tis impossible to wear it loose with a baby around. He likes to pull it." Her fingers tangled in his nape. "Yours is longer than it used to be."

"Yes," he said, his mouth dipping to hers once again.

Gwen sighed. Dear God, it was like suddenly finding the way home again after being lost for untold ages. She was powerless to stop the tears slipping down her cheeks.

He lowered her to the blanket, then propped himself on an elbow, his finger tracing her kiss-swollen lips. "Why do you cry, Gwen?"

She wound her arms around his neck and pushed him back until she was lying full length on top of him. "Because I missed you, you wool-headed lout!" She framed his face between her hands and kissed him hungrily.

When they'd caught their breath, he said, "Careful, love. Such flattery might swell my head, make me insufferable."

"You are already that," Gwen teased.

Richard laughed. "Jesú, wench, can you not humor me a bit? Tell me how wonderful I am, how you have craved my company these months past?"

Gwen stroked his jaw, her eyes filling with fresh tears. "You cannot know how much I craved you, what I would have given to be with you again."

Richard rolled her onto her back and cupped the soft swell of a breast. "Can I not?" he asked softly.

Gwen's breath caught as his fingers brushed her nipple through the fabric.

"Are you hot for me?" he whispered, his hand sliding under her skirts. "Do you need me as much as I need you?"

Gwen whimpered when his fingers found the wet evidence of her need for him. She met his smoldering gaze, gasping as he stroked her. "Richard . . ."

"Sweet heaven, you are lucky I am armored," he said fervently. "I have never been so long without a woman in my life."

His fingers slid over her, then in and out of her body so quickly she couldn't think, much less speak. She clutched him, crying out as the tension built and shattered. He kissed her brow, her cheeks, her lips.

"I will die if I do not see you," he said, untying the laces of her gown.

She grabbed his hand. "Nay! We are outside! Anyone could come out here and see us."

"Think you there is a soul in that castle who knows not what the lord and lady do in the garden? None will disturb us, I assure you."

"You are outrageous," Gwen said, loosening her grip.

He smiled. "Keep flattering me, my love."

She wasn't really afraid anyone would see them. She was afraid he would not like what he saw. She'd regained her slender figure almost immediately, but the small scars across her midsection had not disappeared. They weren't very noticeable usually, but in this light they would be unmistakable.

She held her breath when he lifted off her chemise.

"Oh God," he said, closing his eyes.

Gwen snatched the garment from his hands, hurt and anger like a dagger to her heart. "I am sorry if I do not please you anymore, my lord."

"What?" he said distractedly.

She clutched the chemise to her, hiding her flawed body from his hot stare. When he tried to tug it away, she held tight. "Nay, I would not have you suffer to look at me again."

"I am fine now," he said. "The sight just caught me by surprise."

"You are such a beast!" Gwen cried. God, were all men so insensitive? The most infuriating part was that he had to be so brutally honest. And he wanted *her* to flatter him! She wanted to box his ears.

"Huh?"

"Turn around so I can dress."

"But I just undressed you." He grabbed the chemise and yanked it away.

Gwen tilted her chin up. "Can you stand it this time, my lord?"

He swallowed. "Aye." He met her gaze and smiled. "'Tis been many, many years since the sight of a woman threatened to make me spill myself. Not since I was an untried boy..."

"You do not find me repulsive?"

"Repulsive? Have you gone daft, woman?" he demanded.

Gwen laughed with sudden relief. "I thought you could not look at me because my scars repelled you."

"What scars?"

"These," she said, splaying her fingers across her middle.

He bent closer. "You call those scars?" He shook his head. "Leave it to a woman to exaggerate the tiniest thing."

Gwen kissed him. "You are impossible."

"And you are beautiful." He picked up the end of her braid and removed the thong. When he'd unbraided her hair, he ran his fingers through it, separating the silken strands until they fell to her hips. "Lie down."

Gwen lay back on the blanket and planted her feet against his mailclad chest. She felt deliciously wicked with the summer breeze wafting over her skin and the man she loved staring at her so hotly.

He lifted one of her legs, pressing his lips to the soft flesh of her inner calf. Gwen closed her eyes and moaned. He worked his way down, spreading her legs and lowering himself until her knees rested on his shoulders.

"Richard," she breathed, lifting her hips.

"Is this what you want, love?" He kissed her fiery thatch of curls.

"Yes, yes…"

"Then look at me. Watch me while I love you this way."

Gwen did as he commanded. It was exciting, erotic, to see his dark head between her legs.

"I have missed you," he said. "The scent of you, the taste of you…"

Gwen shuddered. The things he did to her, the way he made her quiver inside! Lord God, she would do anything for this man, anything at all.

He pleasured her with his mouth, slowly, exquisitely. She watched him, crying out "I love you!" at the height of her climax.

He straightened. "Help me out of this armor before I explode."

Gwen fumbled with the buckles and straps, frantic to release him. His fingers were no surer than hers, and it took an interminable amount of time to get him out of the hauberk and leggings.

Gwen pulled his gambeson and tunic off while he tugged at the laces to his braies. He didn't take the time to pull them off, just shoved them down and pushed her back on the blanket.

"I cannot wait any longer," he said, his gaze locking with hers as he positioned himself between her legs. Despite the urgency of his tone, he entered her slowly.

Gwen held her breath, reveling in the feel of him. He was so huge and so hard, filling her in a way she'd craved for all the months they'd been apart.

"I am afraid," he said, gritting his teeth. "'Tis been so long and I am afraid of hurting you. I want you too much to be gentle."

"I do not want gentleness," Gwen said. "I want *you*. Do not hold back, Richard."

Her words freed him. Richard thrust into her, hard, deep. He couldn't stop himself now if he wanted. "I have dreamed of you, of this moment," he said in her ear. "You did not have to make me vow to be faithful, *cariad*. I want no one but you."

"I love you," she cried.

The last of his control shredded, and he found himself driving into her so hard they sprawled off the blanket and into the grass.

When release finally came, he collapsed on her, shuddering.

She smoothed his sweat-dampened hair from his forehead, sighing contentedly. When he found the energy, he rolled onto his back and threw his arm across his brow. "You have killed me," he said.

Her warm lips nuzzled his chest, trailed down his abdomen. His manhood stirred. "Nay, you are not dead yet," she said against his skin, cupping the growing length of him. "You are very much alive, I would say."

Richard groaned. "The rest of my body disagrees."

But he had to admit being within her again was worth the effort it would take. He pulled her on top of him. "I cannot stop you from taking advantage of me," he said.

Strangely enough, his energy surged anew. When her inner muscles spasmed, he tumbled over the edge with her, shooting his seed into her with such force he knew he would not be able to move for quite some time.

But as she lay on top of him, kissing his neck, her sheath quivering around him, he hardened. She lifted her head, her eyes widening. "Again?"

Richard grinned. "Oh yes, again. I cannot get enough of you. I will *never* get enough of you."

Her legs wrapped around him and he pressed his lips to her throat, professing his undying love over and over.

When he had made love to her for a fourth time, he lay on top of her, catching his breath and glorying in the feel of her. He had to leave again in a fortnight, this time to Shrewsbury for Dafydd's trial. But he would not tell her just yet.

"I believe I will have some of that wine now, *cariad*. Do you want some?"

She mumbled something unintelligible and he lifted up to look at her. Her lashes fanned across her pale skin. Her mouth, ripe and swollen from his kisses, was soft in sleep. She turned her face to the side and he kissed her temple and cheek, then gently nibbled her earlobe.

She swatted at him. He laughed softly, then left her and went to get the wine. When he returned, he gathered her against him, his hands roaming over her body of their own accord before sleep claimed him as well.

William's laughter reached the solar before his father's footsteps. Gwen was helping Alys to embroider her wedding gown when she heard it. She looked up as Richard ducked through the doorway, a giggling child clinging to him.

"Richard! 'Tis too high up!" she cried. "You will make him sick."

William perched on Richard's shoulders, hands firmly entwined in his father's hair. Both of her men looked at her like she had lost her wits.

"'Tis not, Gwen. Besides, he loves it." Richard smiled. Gwen heaved a sigh. It didn't matter which of them it was—all either of them had to do was smile and she was as malleable as dough.

They were a handsome pair. Looking at them together, it was hard to believe Richard had been so wary of his son at first. William had taken to his father immediately, but Richard had been afraid to even hold him.

It was over a sennight since Richard had come home. After he'd made love to her in the garden that day, they'd retired to their chamber and spent time with their son. He wouldn't hold the baby when Gwen urged him and she'd finally gotten him to admit his fear.

It still brought a smile to her lips. Her big, powerful, warrior husband had been frightened of a tiny babe. No longer, though.

He walked to the windowseat and bent over, depositing William on the cushions. Alys and Gwen exchanged a look as Richard fussed over his son.

Alys covered a smile. "Sometimes 'tis harder to decide which of them is more adorable," she whispered.

Gwen nodded, biting her lip to hide her own smile.

Alys cleared her throat. "I believe I forgot to do something, my lady. If you will excuse me."

"Of course, Alys."

The old woman winked as she gathered her dress and left the room.

Gwen crossed to the windowseat. Richard sat on the floor while William crawled over the cushions. She stood beside Richard, entwining her fingers in his hair. He looked up and smiled. "Sometimes I look at him and I cannot believe we made him."

"Aye, 'tis the same for me," she said softly.

He pulled her into his lap and kissed her. William screamed. Richard broke away. "What is wrong with him?"

Gwen frowned. "He likes to be the center of attention."

"You have spoiled him."

It was true, but Gwen was indignant anyway. "And you have not?"

"I have not been home long enough!"

"Yes, well who is it who carries him on their shoulders? Or took him for a ride on Sirocco? Which I might add I did *not* approve of!"

"And who let him sleep with us when he awoke crying?" Richard demanded.

"It was only once!"

As if on cue, William started crying. Gwen stood and picked him up. He cried harder. "Now see what you have done?"

"I have not done anything!"

William stretched his arms toward his father. Gwen walked away, rocking him, soothing him with soft words. His chubby face was red, his screams growing louder.

"Give him to me," Richard said softly.

She turned and William reached for his father. She let him go. The baby quieted almost instantly, his screams turning to hiccoughs. He sniffled and buried his face against Richard's surcoat.

Gwen viewed the whole exchange with mixed emotions. On the one hand, she felt as if her son didn't need her. On the other, she was more than pleased he needed his father.

Richard sank into the windowseat and lay back, settling William on his chest. Within minutes, the baby fell asleep, his thumb in his mouth while Richard rubbed his back.

"You are right," Gwen said. "I have spoiled him. I do not know how to say him nay."

Richard took her hand and pressed it to his lips. "I am no better. I have no right to judge you when I've not been here very long."

Gwen dropped to her knees and cupped his cheek. "Nay! You have every right. He is your son, too. 'Tis not your fault you were not here."

He looked at the baby on his chest, then back to her. "I have to go to Shrewsbury, Gwen. Dafydd's trial begins soon."

Gwen's breath caught. They'd not spoken of Dafydd's capture, the Welsh defeat, her father's death, the future of Wales—nothing. She had not wanted to let it intrude on their lives yet and she sensed he did not either, so she'd not asked any questions.

"When?"

"The end of the week."

She stared at William's face, so much like his father's. "How long this time?"

"Not very long. A fortnight mayhap. No more than a month, surely."

"Oh."

He stood very carefully. William shifted, but didn't wake. "Come. Let us put him in his cradle."

Gwen followed him to their adjoining chamber. He put William down and covered him. Gwen stood beside him and they watched the child they had made together sleep.

At last, Richard pulled her into his arms. She didn't hesitate when he kissed her, and she was used to his urgency by now as he started to undress her. It was an urgency she still felt as well.

There was no room for words as they fell to the bed. To keep from waking the baby, he covered her mouth with his. Gwen couldn't get enough of him. She bucked against him, her own pleasure strangely elusive for once.

He stilled. As he began to understand, a slow smile curved his lips. "I know what you need, *cariad*," he whispered. He pulled her legs up and rested her calves against his shoulders. When he thrust into her again, he was so deep, so hard, stretching her almost to breaking.

It was exactly what she wanted. He joined his mouth to hers again, his tongue imitating his body, until she was completely mindless.

Later, when she was so sated she could hardly move, she heard him get up to check on William. He crawled back in bed beside her, and she pushed herself off her stomach to lie against his side.

"What will they do to Dafydd?"

"He will hang, more than likely."

She bit her lip, not wanting to ask the next question, but needing to all the same. "What of William?"

He stiffened. "Gwen, do not begin this nonsense about him being the Prince of Wales. 'Tis impossible."

Gwen fumed. How dare he dismiss everything Welsh as unimportant! "He *will* be prince. My father wanted it!"

Richard gripped her arms and pushed her up until they were both sitting. "Nay! He will not, Gwen! He is *my* son, he will be earl in my place."

"You are hurting me."

His grip eased, his expression softening. "You have to understand, sweet. Edward is the king of England and Wales. There will be no more princes. I am sorry, but 'tis true."

Gwen shrugged away from him. "You are Welsh. How can you allow your son's birthright to be taken from him? You and the king are friends. He would do it if you asked him. It was one of the conditions of our marriage."

"That was before your father rebelled," he said evenly. "And I am *not* Welsh. I am an Englishman, and so is our son. That is the end of this discussion."

Gwen gritted her teeth. She wanted to rail at him, but she knew he meant it when he said it was over. Stubborn swine!

She left the bed and yanked her clothes on. When she went to the cradle, William's eyes were open. He smiled when he saw her, and her heart swelled with love. She picked him up, cooing as he hugged her. She only wanted to protect him, wanted him to have all that was his.

Her anger dissipated the longer she held him. It was ironic really. She had once thought Richard coveted Wales for their unborn son, but now she was the one who was letting it come between them. And what had being prince ever brought her father?

Grief, strife, and death.

She thought of London, of the grand city with its amazing sights, of London Bridge and the heads rotting over its gates, of the Tower where her father's head now reigned supreme over the walls.

She squeezed William tighter. Nay, she did not want him to have it, not any of it. England had won and life for Wales would never be the same again. King Edward's new castles would ensure domination and his laws would ensure assimilation. It was over.

A sob escaped her, and she pressed her face to William's neck.

"*Cariad*," Richard whispered, his hands soft on her shoulders as he turned her to face him. She hadn't even heard him get up.

"You are right," she said, looking from him to William through a misty veil. "He will not be the prince of Wales, he will not follow in my father's footsteps. 'Tis over, 'tis lost . . ."

"I am sorry, Gwen. In time, you will see 'tis best this way," he said, hugging both her and William.

She smoothed her free hand over Richard's bare chest. He rested his chin on top of her head. "Shrewsbury is but a day's ride. Would you like to come with me?"

Gwen tilted her head back. "And William too?"

Richard smiled then. "Aye, William too. I do not wish to be parted from either of you."

42

Shrewsbury was thronged with visitors from all over England and Wales, and some from as far off as Scotland. Traveling merchants crowded the town square, competing with the permanent tradesmen whose shops lined the streets.

Vendors sold meat pies and ale, wine from Gascony and Normandy, Welsh sweet mead, and baked confections sweetened with honey.

Minstrels and jongleurs performed on street corners while musicians set up wherever they pleased, entertaining the crowds with their lively tunes.

Wedding or treason trial, Shrewsbury came alive much the same.

When the crier ascended the steps to the platform, the crowd jostled in to hear the verdict. Dressed in a surcoat displaying the king's coat of arms, he unrolled a parchment and read to the mesmerized gathering, his voice booming despite his small stature.

"For treachery to His Majesty King Edward, Dafydd ap Gruffydd is sentenced to be dragged by his heels to the gallows."

The crowd murmured their approval. Heads nodded and hands cupped the ears of the persons standing next to them.

The crier drew in his breath. "For the willful murder of English citizens, he is to be hanged. For shedding blood during Passion Week, he is to be cut down before he is dead and disemboweled."

Cheers burst forth in riotous harmony.

"For plotting the king's death by war, his body will be quartered, with the parts being distributed to the cities of Winchester, Northampton, Chester, and York. Lastly, his head will join that of his brother over the Tower of London."

The resulting tumult was deafening.

Gwen sat in the window seat, gazing out at the town. She couldn't hear Richard behind her, but she knew he was still there.

"'Tis ridiculous," she said softly. "I hate him, and yet I cannot like what will be done to him."

Dafydd *did* deserve everything he got. She hated him for betraying her father those many times, especially hated him for nearly taking Richard from her.

But if Dafydd hadn't told her the truth about her mother, she might never have reconciled with her father. She couldn't help but wonder if, somewhere inside her uncle, there was something left that was good. Certes, his wife thought so.

Gwen toyed with a golden girdle chain. "Did you see Lisbeth when 'twas announced?"

"I did not see her until they carried her away."

Richard was watching her intently, his expression soft and full of concern. It was one of the things she loved most about this fierce warlord. Inside him was a softness only visible to her, a softness solely for her and their son.

She turned back to the window. "Disbelief. 'Twas disbelief on her face, then horror, then overwhelming grief. I cannot help but imagine what it would be like to lose you in such a way…"

He came to her and pulled her up, holding her close. "Do not think of it any longer, *cariad*. 'Tis over. We will not stay to see the sentence carried out. I am taking you home."

She wrapped her arms around him, pressed her face to his chest. Losing him was her greatest fear. Her father was gone. Elinor was gone. Soon Dafydd would be gone too, though she could not grieve his loss. But it did remind her how easy it was to kill a man.

Richard held her for a long while, unspeaking, unmoving.

Gwen squeezed her eyes shut. Why was the sadness so heavy? Her father had been dead for nearly a year, Elinor longer than that. Old Einion had succumbed this past winter.

She still had Alys and Owain and Rhys. And most importantly, she had Richard and William.

Gwen pulled Richard's head down and kissed him with a desperation she felt to the depths of her soul.

"Make love to me," she whispered against his lips. "'Tis too much death, too much death…"

He swept her into his arms and carried her to bed.

The revelry in the hall that night was spirited, the feast enormous. Wine and ale flowed like water. The queen had joined her husband in Shrewsbury, and the royal court made the most of the victory banquet.

When Edward motioned Richard aside, he followed obediently. Gwen was busy chatting with Eleanor and Margaret de Valence so he didn't bother to tell her he was leaving.

"What is it, Ned?" he asked when they stood in the passage.

Edward's face was haggard. Richard recognized the look in his keen blue eyes. It was the look of a man whose duty weighed heavily on his shoulders.

"We will talk in my solar," he replied, turning to lead the way through the bowels of the castle.

When they entered the solar, Edward poured wine and handed it to Richard. "Sit."

As was the king's habit when agitated, he paced. Richard waited, his own apprehension growing.

Finally, Edward spun around and leaned against the table. "Jesú, Richard," he said, raking both his hands through his hair and letting out a long breath. "I have thought long about this and there is only one way I can save you."

Richard bolted upright, the forgotten goblet of wine falling to the floor. A crimson stain spread through the rushes. "Save me?"

Edward met his gaze. "Aye. Gloucester and De Mortimer. They know about you, as do the rest of the Marchers by now I would assume."

Richard gripped his sword hilt. "How?"

"Dafydd, no doubt. His parting gift to us."

While Richard tried to digest it, Edward went on. "They demand I strip you of everything and try you for treason."

"Treason? How in the hell do they come up with that?" Richard roared.

"Your wife. She was with Llywelyn at Builth castle. De Mortimer saw her, so we cannot deny it."

"She was not engaged in treason," Richard said stiffly.

"Aye, I know, but there is nothing I can do to make it seem otherwise. You must do as I tell you, Richard."

"I am listening."

"You must denounce your wife. I will send her to the convent at Sempringham where her half-sister now resides. Your son must go too. The royal house of Wales is no more, and the line will die with him. I will have no claimants to the throne ever again."

Richard sank into the chair he had abandoned, his legs unwilling to hold him a moment longer. Inside, he was screaming. Outside, a lifetime of control was strained to near breaking.

"You know not what you ask of me," he said in a daze. "I cannot do it."

"You have never disobeyed me, Richard. You are sworn to me."

"Christ Jesus, Ned, you cannot ask this of me."

Edward came to stand before him. "I know you care about the girl, but 'twill fade in time. You are young yet. I will find you an English heiress and you will have a castle full of children in a few years."

Richard leaned against his hand, covering his eyes. He could never have children with anyone but Gwen. Could never love anyone but Gwen.

Gwen and William. A raw ache rose in his throat. He would not give them up. "If I say no?"

"You cannot say no."

Richard snapped a defiant look at his king.

Edward's eyes widened. "Do not do this, Richard," he said quietly. "Do not throw ten years of loyalty and friendship away. If you defy me, I cannot say what the consequences will be. You will be arrested. I will sign the writs, though it will pain me to do so. And she will still end up in the convent."

Richard was drowning. How could he give her up? How could he live without her?

And yet if he refused, he could be hung for treason. Though dying would not pain him once she was gone, what about her? How could he protect her and make sure, even from afar, that she was well?

Without him to keep an eye on her and William, their lot in the convent might not be easy. At least if he were alive, he could make sure they were taken care of, had all the best of everything.

And mayhap eventually he could get them out.

Oh God, how could he even consider it? "And if I agreed to your plan, when would it happen?"

"She will not return to Claiborne with you. You would be free to go and I would have her and the child escorted to Sempringham."

Richard stood, his heart aching and heavy. "I need time. Give me a couple of days."

Edward nodded. "Very well. I wish there were another way."

Richard laughed bitterly. "Jesú, if you had not forced me into marriage in the first place, we would not be having this conversation. You gave her to me when I did not want her. Now you want to take her away when I want no other. 'Tis bloody ironic, is it not?"

"We are warriors first, Richard. We do what we must."

Richard focused on a distant point behind Edward's head. "Aye, we do what we must. We always have."

Gwen knew something was wrong with Richard. When they retired, he dismissed William's nurse, then stood by the cradle for a long time. Sometimes he touched the baby's brow or his silky curls.

Gwen tried to hold a conversation with him, but he wouldn't respond with more than an occasional grunt or nod of his head. She gave up and sat down to brush out her hair.

He was still standing by the cradle when she finished. Sighing, she stood and went to him, wrapping her arms around him from behind. "What is the matter, Richard?"

A tremor passed through his body and into hers. He turned and crushed her to him, burying his face in her hair.

"Do you have any idea how much I love you? What I would do to protect you and our child?" he asked in a voice raw with emotion.

Bewildered, Gwen tried to push away, tried to see his face, but he would not let her. She hugged him tight. "I know you love William and me. I know you will protect us."

He cupped her face and tilted her head back, kissing her with a hundred times more desperation than she'd kissed him earlier. His mood soon caught and she was meeting his fierce hunger with a very real hunger of her own.

His earlier lovemaking had been tender, calming her fears and soothing her hurts. This time it was like being lost at sea in a tempest. When he was braced above her, driving relentlessly into her body, she arched up to him, kissing and biting his hard chest to keep from crying out and waking William.

Richard groaned, pushing her back and pressing his lips against the column of her throat. "I could never feel this way with another woman. Never, never, never…"

Gwen ran her hands down the rippling muscles in his back. "My love… my life… my heart…"

With a strangled sound, he crushed his mouth to hers.

When she was too spent to move another muscle, Gwen lay on her side. He lay behind her, his big body curved around hers. His lips nuzzled the sensitive flesh behind her ear while his hand cupped her woman's mound.

"Mmm, Richard, I could stay like this for days and days."

"Forever," he said, his arms tightening around her.

William started to cry. Gwen stirred from her blissful lethargy.

"Nay, I will get him," Richard said.

Gwen lay back on the pillows while Richard picked up William and rocked him. She watched her husband walk back and forth, his naked body splendid in the candlelight, his powerful form such a contrast to the tiny babe he carried.

When William was asleep again, Richard bent to kiss his brow, then returned him to the cradle.

"You are wonderful," Gwen said as he walked back to the bed.

"Nay, I am not. You are blind to my faults," he said softly.

"What faults?" Gwen teased.

He gathered her in his arms and she laid her cheek against his chest. Absently, she kissed the taut muscles, stroking him with her palm.

His fingers threaded through her hair, massaging the back of her head. "I was empty before you came along, devoid of all things that were not dark and cold. I do not wish to be that way ever again. I do not want to lose you."

Gwen pushed herself up. She understood the dark demon tormenting him. The events of the day could rouse fear and uncertainty in the strongest of hearts.

"Oh Richard, I will not leave you ever again." She smiled, wanting to reassure him. "You are stuck with me."

If anything, his expression grew more serious. He pulled her down and held her tight against him.

His reactions tonight confused her and she tried to soothe him in the only way she knew how. She kissed his chest, lingering on his hot flesh. Her tongue traced his nipple.

His breath caught on a groan of pleasure. Between them, his manhood stretched and came to life like a lazy cat.

Gwen moved upward, touching her mouth to the pulse in his throat. It beat strong and fast beneath her tongue. After all this time, it still thrilled her she could arouse this man's passion. "I want another babe, Richard," she whispered. "Fill me with your child."

He rolled her over and sank between her thighs, sheathing himself within her slick heat. Their gazes locked for an instant. Gwen saw the flicker of torture in his eyes before he masked it.

But her question was lost as his mouth captured hers and his body took control of her senses.

Gwen wakened alone. She found William in the antechamber with his nurse and Alys. She'd tried to leave Alys at Claiborne with Owain, but the woman wouldn't hear of shirking her duties as maid.

Alys helped her to dress and plait her hair, then left to get food and drink. Gwen went to the window and threw the shutters wide. The day was miserable. Rain beat down on the glass, running past her face in rivulets.

She rubbed her arms. She was chilled suddenly, though not from cold.

Richard's behavior last night had been strange to say the least. Almost as if he were the one about to be dragged to the gallows instead of Dafydd. He had certainly loved her like a condemned man.

She shook herself as she heard the door open. "That was quick, Alys."

A man cleared his throat.

Gwen jumped. "M-majesty," she said, sinking to her knees. "I am sorry, I thought you were my maid."

"I have been called many things, but this is the first time I've been called a maid." Edward Plantagenet smiled. "I believe I told you once that formality was not necessary in private."

Gwen stood. "Aye, you did. I beg your pardon."

She thought he winced at that, but she was too nervous to be sure. The last time he'd had her alone, he'd kissed her.

Gwen swallowed. "Richard is not here, Majesty. I am not certain where he is, but you might find him in the hall."

"I didn't come to see Richard."

Gwen twisted her fingers into her dress.

Edward's eyes narrowed for a moment. Very softly, he said, "'Tis about Richard I wanted to speak to you."

Gwen's heart quickened. "What is wrong? Has something happened?"

Edward held up his hand. "Nay, but I need you to help me keep something from happening."

43

"Treason?" Gwen echoed.

Edward nodded. "Aye."

Gwen sank into a chair, tears pricking her eyes. Edward had not left anything out. It was all her fault.

"What do you want me to do?" she asked faintly.

"There is but one thing you can do to keep him safe."

"Anything! I will do anything!"

"You and your son must enter a convent. I will apply to the pope to annul the marriage so Richard will be free to remarry."

Gwen's heart ached so much she thought she might die of it. "I-I know not. I—"

"Jesú, woman! Richard could hang for this! Do you want that?"

Gwen shook her head. Tears spilled down her cheeks. Leave Richard. *Leave him... leave him... leave him...*

She had promised never to leave him.

"You must choose," Edward said.

Gwen's head snapped up. *Choose.*

The last time she had chosen, it ended in disaster. Her father was dead. If she chose Richard this time, would he die too?

She couldn't bear it. She would do anything to keep him safe, even if it meant never seeing him again. He might see it as betrayal, but at least he would be alive.

"You will not take my son from me?"

"No. He may stay with you until he is old enough to enter a monastery."

Gwen pressed a trembling hand to her abdomen. What if another child grew there even now? Dear Lord, she fervently prayed it was so. She wanted another baby to remind her of Richard.

"I will go if it will protect Richard," she said, her voice wavering. She could not think beyond the words she uttered, what they truly meant, what her life would be like without him. If she did, she would never find the strength to do it.

"You have made a wise choice, lady. Gather your child and come with me."

"N-now?"

"Aye. I would not delay any longer. The sooner 'tis done, the better."

Dazed, Gwen stood and walked to the antechamber, calling for Alys and the nurse. When she told Alys what was happening, she barely heard her own voice reciting the horrible words. They flowed from her as though from a stranger's mouth.

Alys's face showed shock and horror. And resignation.

"You do not have to accompany me, Alys. Owain needs you."

Alys swallowed hard. "Nay, my place is with you. I have been with you since you were born. I'll not forsake you now, especially not for a man." Her voice broke on the last and Gwen embraced her.

"Please stay, Alys. Do not come with me. Watch over Richard for me."

Alys shook her head stubbornly, though her eyes shone with tears. "Nay, I cannot leave you."

Edward led them to his own solar. "I will come for you at nightfall. Until then, you are not to leave this room. There will be a guard posted outside. Speak to him if you need anything."

Belatedly, it occured to Gwen she would not be allowed to see Richard before she left. "I wish to see my husband, Majesty," she said quietly, her eyes downcast so he couldn't see the emotion roiling within.

"Nay, I cannot allow it. I am sorry, but 'tis better this way."

The door thudded shut, the sound hollow and empty like that of a tomb closing on her forever.

Gwen hugged her baby close, sobs welling in her chest. When she could contain them no longer, she sank to the floor and cried. Alys came and took William from her. The old woman tried to calm her, but tears slid down her own cheeks faster and faster until she was sitting beside Gwen, her arm around Gwen's shoulders, sobbing too.

William looked from one woman to the other, then crawled away to explore his new surroundings.

Richard stood outside his and Gwen's chamber. He had to let her know what they faced. His hand strayed to the handle, then stilled. He leaned his head against the cool wood.

He must protect her and William at all costs. More than anything he wanted to fight. He wanted to fight his king and all the goddamn Marchers. He wanted to fight England herself!

Never had he felt more like a Welshman than he did right now. Repressed, stifled, crushed. He could almost understand the need for autonomy that drove Wales to keep fighting a superior foe.

Before he could dwell on it any longer, he grabbed the handle and swung the door open. No one was in the antechamber. When he walked into the main chamber, a chill slid down his spine.

There was no sign of Gwen. No Alys. No William. No nurse.

His gaze swept the room, bouncing back to the corner where William's cradle was supposed to be. His heart fell to his feet. It was gone. *They* were gone.

"No!"

He ran from the chamber, down the winding staircase, and into the hall. People gaped at him as he pushed through the crowded room.

Edward stood with Edmund of Lancaster and William de Valence. Richard stopped, his chest heaving, fury eating his insides. He gripped his sword, ready to draw it, knowing he would be cut down in minutes if he did.

"Where is she, Ned?"

"Calm down, Richard. She is safe," Edward said, his eyes flickering to Richard's hand resting on the swordhilt.

Richard forced himself to let go. "Where is she?"

"On her way to Sempringham."

Richard felt dizzy. "What? But I did not tell you I agreed yet."

Edward shrugged. "You didn't have to. She decided for you."

Richard stared at the king in disbelief. Bitter laughter bubbled in his chest. He scrubbed his fingers through his hair to quell the tingling of his scalp. "Once again, the wench has taken it upon herself to make a decision that affects me."

He felt strangely delirious at that moment. He grabbed a mug of ale off a serving wench's tray and downed it. "Jesú, she has left me without even saying goodbye. I might have known…"

He stared into the empty mug, not seeing anything through a misty haze.

Edward pulled him into an alcove. "I am sorry, Richard. I had to do it. You would have fought me."

Richard shook his head. "Nay, I would not. If 'twere only my life involved, aye, I would have. But I would not endanger them."

"You saved me once. I am saving you now. You will understand it one day. 'Twill take time, but you will forget her."

Richard met Edward's gaze then. The blue eyes were sad, sympathetic. "Could you forget Eleanor?"

Edward inhaled sharply, then smiled. "Point taken." He clasped Richard's shoulder. "Come, let us get roaring drunk."

Richard dropped the empty mug. "Aye… aye, 'tis nothing left to do."

But he found he couldn't get drunk after all. The ale was bitter, the wine cloying, the mead thicker than honey. He merely sat, brooding into cup after cup of alcohol before he poured it onto the rushes.

Red Gilbert stalked over, his face livid. "So, Dunsmore, you think to get out of it by shutting your Welsh whore of a wife away? Had enough of the pretty little piece, eh? Well, it will not work!"

Richard stood, very, very slowly. He didn't even bother drawing his sword, just leaped on Gilbert and wrapped his hands around the man's neck. They fell to the floor. The crowd scattered, ladies shrieking and men shouting encouragement as they made room for the two earls.

Richard overpowered Gloucester easily enough. Gloucester had grown fat and lazy over the years, and he was no match for the man who was only a few years younger than he.

Richard straddled him, his hands still on Gilbert's neck. "Do you have any idea how easy 'twould be for me to snap your neck, Gloucester?"

Gilbert's eyes widened.

At this point, Richard fully intended on doing it. But first he wanted his victim to beg for mercy.

Gilbert's hands covered Richard's, his voice barely audible as he mouthed the word, "Please."

"Please what? Please end it and put you out of your misery? Aye, Gilbert, 'twill be a pleasure," Richard growled.

"Let him up," Edward said. Richard was prepared to ignore his king until he felt the cold steel against his ribs. His eyes traveled the length of the blade. Edward held the sword firmly and Richard knew he would not hesitate to use it.

Richard let go and stood up. Gilbert climbed to his feet, choking and rubbing his throat.

"You are a savage, Black Hawk! Your Welsh ancestry shows itself!" Gilbert spat.

"Get the hell out of here!" Edward commanded him. "Get you back to Caerphilly castle before I decide to allow Dunsmore to kill you."

The earl of Gloucester stiffened his spine and walked proudly from the hall.

"And you," Edward said, turning his wrath on Richard. "Get back to Claiborne immediately. Do not leave again until I send for you."

Richard gave his king a curt half-bow, then spun on his heel and went the opposite direction as Gloucester.

Gwen's heart quickened when she saw the crimson and black standard of the earl of Dunsmore in the bailey below. She pressed against the glass, trying to see through the rain-streaked pane.

One glimpse. Please God, just one more glimpse of him.

A groom led Sirocco toward the gathered knights. In answer to her prayer, a tall dark man strode over and mounted the stallion.

Her stomach churned. She wanted to touch him, wanted to tell him she loved him one more time. She banged on the glass, though she knew he would never hear it in the noise of the courtyard.

She gave up and pressed her palms flat against the window. He turned Sirocco, then stopped and let his gaze wander over the castle. Gwen pounded the glass again, hoping, praying he would see her.

He turned away and signaled his men. They cantered through the bailey and out the gates.

"God go with you," she whispered against the cool pane.

Richard felt the ache all the way down to his soul. It was a bone-deep weariness that would never go away. He rode through the town without seeing the masses of people, without hearing the voices of hawkers and whores, without smelling the scents of unwashed bodies, baking bread, and roasting meat.

He would never be the same again. He understood well the loss his father had suffered, the reason he had doted on his son so much. Jesú, Richard did not even have his son left to love.

He caught sight of a girl with red hair and his pulse leaped. He spurred Sirocco forward. "Gwen!"

The stallion navigated the mass of bodies deftly while Richard kept his eyes on the girl in front of him. Vaguely, he heard Andrew giving orders to the men to wait.

"Gwen!"

He caught up and reached for her. She whirled around, stumbling backward. People scattered.

"M-m-milord?" she stammered, her brown eyes wide and fearful.

Disappointment stabbed through Richard. He was imagining he saw her everywhere. The castle, here in town.

"I-I didn't do anything, milord. Please do not hurt us."

It was then he saw she clutched a babe to her breast.

He reached into his belt and pulled out a gold coin, his mind no longer on the girl in front of him. "Here. Buy yourself something pretty."

She eyed the coin, hesitating. "I-I am not a whore, milord. You be a fine looking man, but I-I have a husband, and—"

"Take it, woman. I do not wish to bed you."

She snatched the coin, clamped it between her teeth, then tucked it into the baby's tunic. "Th-thank you, m-milord."

She still watched him like she expected him to grab her at any second.

Richard waved his hand. "Off with you."

She scurried away, disappearing into the crowd. Richard sat there, staring after her for a long time. How could he have thought she was Gwen? Her hair wasn't golden-red and silky; it was brassy and dull. Her figure wasn't slender and curvy; it was plump and saggy.

He raised his head and looked at the castle on top of the hill. He had married her here and lost her here. Was it any wonder he thought he saw her everywhere he looked?

He turned Sirocco and rode back to his men. But he didn't stop when he reached them. He kept going, toward Shrewsbury castle.

"Milord?" Andrew called. "Where are ye going, milord?"

"Back to the castle, Andrew."

His men fell in quietly behind him. Richard didn't care what they thought. He could not leave this place just yet.

Gwen knew the king would come. Since Richard had ridden away, there was no further need for delay. Edward swept into the room, a formidable presence in his deep blue surcoat and gold-embroidered mantle.

He was a king to inspire awe and admiration in the hearts of men. He was lean and tall, hard despite the temptations of fine food and drink. Gwen had oft heard him praised, even while he was being cursed, by her father's warriors. 'Twas no wonder Richard valued his loyalty to this man so highly.

William took one look at the king and started to cry. Gwen tried to soothe him, but he buried his face in her gown, sniffling and gulping.

Edward grinned and put a hand over his heart. "Jesú, I'd say the little lad does not like me. Must be his Welsh blood coming out," he teased.

Gwen smiled in spite of herself. What she wanted to do was weep, but she'd already cried so much that she had nothing left to give.

"Are you ready?" the king asked.

"Aye," Gwen replied, though in truth she would never be ready.

A commotion in the passage brought Edward's head around. Men shouted, followed by the unmistakable clashing of steel.

"God's teeth," Edward swore, yanking the door open.

Gwen heard him shouting, heard the answering voice.

Richard.

The battle sounds stopped. Fear closed her throat until she couldn't utter a word. Had they killed him?

The door opened again and Edward entered, followed by Richard. Her husband's face was dark with anger, his eyes gleaming wildly.

"You try my patience, Richard!" the king raged. "I should've let them carve you up."

Richard's gaze locked with hers. "You should not have lied to me, Ned. I have a right to see them again."

"I will give you a few minutes, no more." He motioned to Alys and the nurse, and the three of them slipped into the antechamber.

William held out his arms for his father. Gwen let him go. Richard held him tight and kissed him, then buried his face against the baby's neck.

She stood there, waiting, wanting him to hold her as well. But then she realized he would not. She had betrayed him, agreed to the king's plan, left him though she had promised never to do so again.

"You are angry with me," she said.

"Yes… no." He lifted his head. "I wanted to be, but I know you did it to protect me. I would have done the same to protect you and William."

Gwen went to him and laid her hand on his sleeve. "I did not want to do it, Richard. I only want to be with you. But if something happened to you, I—"

He wrapped one strong arm around her and crushed her to him. She tilted her face up and he kissed her. Gwen savored it, knowing it was the last time she would ever taste his kiss.

"I will miss you," she said. "I will think of you and I will remember all we have shared. I can bear it, knowing I had your love for a little while."

"Gwen…"

She stared at his chest, at the sight of her hands splayed across his surcoat. She would never touch him again. "Nay, let me finish. You must remarry, Richard." Her voice broke, and she stopped until she could continue. "You must have children and raise them to be good Englishmen, to serve their king as loyally as you do."

"I will always love you, Gwen. I will never love another," Richard said, his own voice near breaking.

The door opened. Edward came in, followed by Queen Eleanor. Richard felt raw panic welling up inside him.

"I am sorry, but your time is up," Edward said.

Eleanor rushed over to Gwen. "Oh, Gwenllian, I am so sorry. I did not know until just now."

"Thank you for your concern, Majesty," Gwen replied. "You have always been kind to me, even when I was a hostage. I am grateful to you."

Eleanor squeezed her hand. Gwen reached for William. Richard held him tight, unwilling to let go. "Richard, please," she said, her eyes red-rimmed and glistening. "Do not make it harder."

Richard caught her against him and kissed her. "I love you," he said one last time, his throat tight.

He kissed William's brow, then let her take him.

Tears slipped down her cheeks as their gazes held. Then she turned and walked to the door.

Richard spun around, unable to watch her walk out of his life forever. And it would be forever. He was certain if she left now he would never see her again.

He burned inside, burned in a way he'd never known was possible. Nothing held any importance to him anymore. Without her, he *was* nothing.

"Wait," he said.

She stopped in the door. Edward turned.

Richard crossed the room until he stood before his king. "I give it all up. All of it. The title, the castles, the fiefs I hold for you. Give me my wife and child and I will leave England and never return."

Edward's jaw dropped. "I need you, Richard. Wales is unstable. And there is still Scotland and France to consider."

"Ned, if ever you valued me, if ever I have served you faithfully and loyally, you will grant me this one last thing."

"I cannot, Richard. You are valuable to me. I need you."

"Edward," the Queen said, coming over to them. "You have dozens of warlords. You must grant Richard what he asks. If not for him, you might have been taken from me. I would not have wanted to live without you any more than he wants to live without his wife. 'Tis in your power to grant it, and you must."

Edward's temper drained from him in stages. His jaw softened, his features relaxed, his stance became less threatening. "Very well, my love. I cannot deny you." He sighed heavily. "If this is what you want, Richard, then 'tis yours."

Richard closed his eyes as relief flooded him. When he opened them again, Gwen watched him, her lip trembling, her eyes wide and brimming with tears.

Eleanor grabbed her husband's hand and pulled him out the door.

"Are you certain, Richard?" Gwen asked. "Without your lands and title, you will have lost all you ever fought for, all your father left you."

William held out his arms. Richard took him and pressed his lips to his son's cheek. William clutched Richard's surcoat in his fists. "Da," he said, smiling.

Richard touched Gwen's cheek, traced it with his finger. "You are all I need. We will go to Normandy first, I think. Then I will take you to Spain and mayhap Morocco. Italy too. And the Greek Isles. I have a fancy to see if your eyes really are the color of the water around Corfu."

Her expression remained wary. "You will not mind leaving England? You will not hate me for causing you this?"

"For causing me what? For giving me love and teaching me there is more to life than honor and duty? For taking away all the blackness in my soul? For freeing me from the guilt and pain of my failures? Nay, Gwen—my life, my love—with you I have finally found what is right, finally succeeded. The rest means less than nothing to me."

"Oh, Richard." She threw her arms around him then and he kissed her fiercely, kissed her until she was clinging to him, kissed her until she pulled away to catch her breath.

"I am your husband and that is all I want to be."

He entwined his fingers with hers, kissed their son, then led her from Shrewsbury castle and into the world beyond.

EPILOGUE

May 1285
Brindisi, Italy

Gwen looked up as Richard walked down the beach. She stood in the surf with her skirts hiked to her knees, watching William as he kicked at the miniature waves.

"Papa," he said, running to his father. Richard scooped him up in a powerful arm and spun around while his son screamed with delight.

Gwen smiled, her heart filling to bursting with the love she felt for her two men. Richard came to her, William still in his arms, and bent down to kiss her.

"I've had a letter from Edward, *cariad*."

"What does he say?"

"Eleanor has given him a son. He was born in Caernarvon castle a few months ago. Edward has made him prince of Wales."

Gwen bit her lip. "Oh," she said, the old heartache resurfacing briefly. Her son should have been prince of Wales.

But it was better this way. William would never have to struggle with England as her father had.

"He wants me to come back, Gwen."

She stared up at him. "What do you want, Richard?"

He cupped her cheek. "I want you. I don't care where we are, I only want you."

He put William down and the little boy ran to where Alys and Owain sat on a blanket beneath a twisted olive tree. He handed the seashell he'd been clutching to his nine-month old sister, Katherine, and she giggled with delight.

Richard clasped Gwen's hand and pulled her down the beach with him. "Do not wait for us," he called to Owain and Alys.

Gwen knew where he was taking her. They had found a little cove, sheltered by outcroppings of volcanic rock, and shaded by gnarled olive trees and scrubby bushes.

When they reached it, he pulled her into his arms and kissed her until she was breathless. "Richard, do you think 'tis fair to leave William and Katherine with Alys and Owain?"

His hand dipped beneath the hem of her gown. "Why not?"

Gwen giggled. "You are so wicked." She gasped as he found her. Closing her eyes, she said, "Mmm, they are newlyweds compared to us. We should watch the children while they play around."

He pressed her hand to the bulge beneath his tunic. "Think you we should go back now?" he asked, his lips nuzzling the hollow of her throat.

"Mayhap in a little while," she said.

"Aye, I thought you might say that." He unlaced her gown and pulled it over her head. "You really should not hold your skirts so high the next time."

"What?" she asked, distracted by his palms on her breasts.

"When you were standing in the surf. You roused my lust with those pretty legs of yours. All I could imagine was having them wrapped around me."

He lowered her onto the pile of clothes he'd made, his hands and mouth working their magic on her quivering flesh.

"You are turning brown, my love," he said huskily.

"'Tis because you are always undressing me outside. If I am not covered, my skin will darken like yours."

"Jesú, I thought you would never ask," he said, covering her with his body.

He brought her to ecstasy again and again, then they lay entwined while the hot Mediterranean sun filtered through the trees and caressed their bodies.

"Do you want to go back to England? Back to Claiborne?" she asked finally. At the last, Edward had allowed Richard to keep all that was his. The king figured the furor would die down in a couple of years, and Richard and Gwen could return to England if they so chose.

"Nay, I have not taken you to Corfu yet," he said indignantly. "Claiborne can wait. Andrew is doing a good job as castellan."

Gwen laughed and pushed herself up. "Whatever happened to Black Hawk de Claiborne, the man who insisted on doing everything himself?"

Richard grinned. "I hear some wanton wench addled his wits so much that all he wants to do is make love to her."

Gwen snatched a handful of sand and threw it at him, then sprinted for the water. She splashed into the blue-green Adriatic, screaming when she turned and saw Richard close behind.

He dove after her, catching her ankles and pulling her backwards. "You cannot escape me, love. I must exact a penance for your mischief."

Gwen wriggled in his arms, wet flesh sliding sensuously against wet flesh. "You will think of something, I am certain," she purred.

"Aye… give me a few moments to devise the right sort of torture," he said, his lips dipping to her bare shoulder.

"I will give you a lifetime, my love," Gwen replied, closing her eyes and tilting her head back as he exacted his revenge.

D ear Reader:

Thank you so much for reading my book, THE DARK KNIGHT'S CAPTIVE BRIDE. This is indeed my first book, though in truth it was written twenty-plus years ago. I've since gone on to have a career as a romance author under another name. This book was and is a labor of love. I loved Gwen and Richard passionately, and I've published their story exactly as it was when I finished revising it in the 1990s, which was long before I ever sold a book to a publisher. I've not changed a thing from the original story.

I spent months researching this book. I read lots of history books, and studied the reign of King Edward I quite extensively at the time. I took liberties for story reasons, which some of you who are well versed in history may discover. Any mistakes are mine alone. The list of books I used is, unfortunately, lost. You see, publishing was quite different back in 1995 when I first submitted this story. You sent off a book and then waited months or years to hear back from a publisher. In fact, I still haven't heard from one of the publishers I sent the book to. I'm going to take their non-response as a no at this point. *grin*

But you sent the book off and you waited. And if they wanted to publish your story, they sent you a contract and a check and one day you got to see your book in stores. And if they didn't want to publish you, you put the book in a drawer and chalked it up to experience. No one would ever read it and that was the end of that.

So when I didn't sell Richard and Gwen's story to a publisher, I put it away and thought it would stay in the drawer forever. I got rid of the research books and moved on to other things. But then digital publishing came along and I started to think maybe I should publish this story myself. Why not?

Why not, indeed. So many of you have loved this book and written to tell me how much you do. I am so thankful. Natasha Wild has been compared to Judith McNaught and Shannon Drake, among others, and that makes my heart glad. I worked hard on this story. I gave it everything I had. I learned how to tell a story with this book, and I took those lessons with me.

I've decided not to connect Natasha Wild and my other name for a couple of reasons. One, I wanted this book to stand on its own with no help from me. And two, the style is so different from what I write now that I didn't want to confuse my readers.

Will there be more Natasha Wild books? I hope so. I didn't know she'd find so many fans, or that anyone would want more books like this one. So, I sincerely hope to write more stories about medieval knights and the ladies who love them.

Maybe the publishers got it wrong and I got it right after all.

Blessings,
    Natasha

ABOUT THE AUTHOR

Natasha Wild is a Southern girl with a love for all things medieval. When she's not dreaming about knights and castles, she's watching cute cat videos and planning how to talk her husband into getting another cat (they have two already). Natasha loves cats, dogs, horses and hot men. She'd happily collect them all except for the aforementioned Mr. Wild, who has put his foot down about how many of each she can have. (His answer on the hot men, for the record, is one - him. And really, one man is enough to keep a girl busy for life, right?) *The Dark Knight's Captive Bride* is Natasha's debut novel. She hopes you enjoy it.

Made in the USA
Monee, IL
05 July 2021